EIGHT DOGS, OR *HAKKENDEN*

EIGHT DOGS, OR
HAKKENDEN

Part One—An Ill-Considered Jest

Chapters I through XIV of
Nansō Satomi hakkenden
by Kyokutei Bakin

Translated by

GLYNNE WALLEY

CORNELL EAST ASIA SERIES
AN IMPRINT OF
CORNELL UNIVERSITY PRESS
Ithaca and London

Number 203 in the Cornell East Asia Series

First published 2021 by Cornell University Press

Library of Congress Cataloging-in-Publication Data

Names: Takizawa, Bakin, 1767–1848, author. | Walley, Glynne, translator.
Title: Eight dogs, or "Hakkenden". Part I : an ill-considered jest, chapters I through XIV of Nansō Satomi hakkenden / by Kyokutei Bakin ; translated with annotations by Glynne Walley.
Other titles: Nansō Satomi hakkenden. Chapter 1–14. English | Hakkenden. Chapter 1–14
Description: Ithaca [New York] : Cornell University Press, 2021. | Series: Cornell East Asia series; number 203 | Includes bibliographical references.
Identifiers: LCCN 2020051022 (print) | LCCN 2020051023 (ebook) | ISBN 9781501755170 (hardcover) | ISBN 9781501758935 (paperback) | ISBN 9781501755187 (epub) | ISBN 9781501755194 (pdf)
Subjects: LCSH: Takizawa, Bakin, 1767–1848. Nansō Satomi hakkenden.
Classification: LCC PL798.4 .A2 2021 (print) | LCC PL798.4 (ebook) | DDC 895.63/34—dc23
LC record available at https://lccn.loc.gov/2020051022
LC ebook record available at https://lccn.loc.gov/2020051023

Contents

ILLUSTRATIONS

Inaugural Volume

Volume II

Acknowledgments

It strikes me that almost everybody I've studied Japanese literature with over the years has been a translator. I can remember discussing translation issues in classrooms with Van Gessel, Marvin Marcus, Rebecca Copeland, Ed Cranston, Royall Tyler, Jay Rubin, and Adam Kern in particular. Even more than any specific advice (all of it valuable), what I got from them was an assurance that translation is *worth doing*. Whether or not I am doing this translation well is up to the reader, but it still feels worth doing.

Since 2009, I've been lucky enough to teach at a university where translation is valued and celebrated. My colleagues in both East Asian Languages and Literatures and the Oregon Center for Translation Studies at the University of Oregon have my gratitude for making that true. Assistance and encouragement have also come from a number of other places at UO; I would particularly like to thank Knight Library's Kevin and Kumiko McDowell, Lauren Goss, Julia Simic, and Randy Sullivan for their help with the cover.

I am indebted to my editor at Cornell East Asia Series, Mai Shaikhanuar-Cota, for her enthusiasm for and patience with this project; to the CEAS editorial board for their openness to it; to the press's anonymous readers for their careful and generous comments; to Daniel Joseph for his sympathetic and meticulous copy editing; and to Alexis Siemon for her heroic work in getting the manuscript into production. Publication was supported by the William F. Sibley Memorial Subvention Award for Japanese Translation and by a University of Oregon Presidential Fellowship for Humanistic Study, for both of which I am profoundly grateful.

I've shown parts of this translation to quite a few people over the years, and many of them have given me helpful feedback. They include my mentors, classmates, colleagues at UO, colleagues elsewhere, students in at least five different classes, fellow guests at one memorable dinner party, and Facebook friends. I would like to mention all of them by name, but the list would be too long, so I hope they will accept this heartfelt collective thank you.

Two, however, must be singled out. One is my wife, Akiko, whose faith in this idea at times seems even greater than my own. She has always been willing to discuss with me any strange, striking, or curious passage, and to listen when I can't resist reading something aloud. I am grateful for her love and support.

The other is my father, to whom I would like to dedicate this volume. I wish he could have seen it.

Translator's Introduction

About *Hakkenden*

Kyokutei Bakin's *Hakkenden* is one of the monuments of Japanese literature. A multigenerational samurai saga that plays out across the landscape of eastern Japan in the late medieval period, it combines aspects of what readers today will recognize as the historical romance and the fantasy novel, and what readers at the time would have recognized as Japanese contemporary popular fiction and Chinese vernacular stories. It was one of the most popular and influential books of the nineteenth century, inspiring everyone from playwrights to print designers to pornographers, from moralists to popular rights activists to literary modernizers. It can be seen both as the culmination of the long tradition of premodern Japanese narrative and as the jumping-off point for the modern Japanese novel. Its fantastic story and characters have been reborn again and again in modern and contemporary film, television, fiction, and comics. It is, by any measure, a classic.

Hakkenden poses difficulties for a modern reader, however. Serialized over a period of twenty-eight years, it is one of the longest sustained narratives in the world. It was written in a (heavily modified) classical grammar and syntax, only a few decades before that language was rendered antiquated by Japan's modernization. And it was written for an audience that expected its fiction to be studded with allusions to and borrowings from the entire canons of poetry and prose of both Japan and China. All of these factors—its scale, its linguistic remoteness, and its intertextual complexity—make it a daunting read, to say the least.

Eight Dogs, or "Hakkenden": Part One—An Ill-Considered Jest is the first volume of what is intended to be a complete translation of *Hakkenden*, heretofore known in English only through brief excerpts. The translation attempts to make the book's language and allusions intelligible to readers of English while respecting the richness, not to mention the idiosyncrasies, of the original. The first part of this introduction will address some aspects of the work and its author that the reader may find helpful in appreciating *Hakkenden*.

However, much of the information in this section is extracted from my monograph (*Good Dogs: Edification, Entertainment & Kyokutei Bakin's* Nansō Satomi hakkenden), and has therefore been kept to a bare minimum here on the assumption that readers interested in more can find it there.[1] Later sections of this introduction will discuss in some detail a topic that I did not address there but which matters when contemplating a translation: the style in which *Hakkenden* is written. This will lead into a description of my approach to rendering Bakin in English.

But the reader should also know that Bakin is one of Japan's greatest storytellers, and *Hakkenden* one of its greatest stories. It can be enjoyed with little or no background: just skip to the first page and dive right in.

A Shaggy Dog Story

The first installment of *Hakkenden* was published at the end of 1814 (Bunka 11). It comprised ten chapters distributed among five Books,[2] and in an authorial aside at the end of the tenth chapter, Bakin confesses that he has not told as much of his story in those ten chapters as he had intended to:

> It was my intention, in this section, to tell all about the origin of the Eight Dog Warriors, of how they came to be . . . but the story became much longer than I had expected it to, and the pages of this Book filled up without my having concluded this section. The number of Books is set, and there is a limit to the number of pages each can have within it. I am told that when I exceed these limits in a given installment, it poses inconveniences for the vendors; it is a hard thing to ignore booksellers'

---

1. Glynne Walley, *Good Dogs: Edification, Entertainment & Kyokutei Bakin's "Nansō Satomi hakkenden"* (Ithaca, NY: Cornell East Asia Series, 2017).

2. *Hakkenden* boasts a complex internal organizational scheme, and it grows more complex as the work progresses. Chapters (*kai*) are the most basic unit. Chapters are grouped into *maki* (translated Book, and capitalized to distinguish them from other usages of the word "book"), which are in turn grouped into *shū* (translated Volume). Chapters in *Hakkenden* are numbered sequentially from the beginning of the novel to the end. The numbering of Books, though, begins again with each new Volume. Volumes are numbered sequentially to the end of the novel, but once he enters Volume IX, Bakin decides to stay with that number to the end of the story. As a result, Volume IX is roughly as long as the first eight Volumes combined, and subdivided into various Parts and Installments (among other labels). The organizational nomenclature relates, but does not precisely correspond, to the physical presentation of the book in early editions. Books in early modern Japan were often published in multiple fascicles (separately bound volumes). In *Hakkenden*, typically each Book (that is, each *maki*) constituted a single fascicle, so that Volume I comprised five Books in five fascicles. Furthermore, early Volumes corresponded to a single installment of the work: that is, however many chapters were published on a given date were collectively designated a Volume. Later Volumes, however, were originally published in multiple installments.

wishes. Therefore I shall put what remains of my draft into a new Book, and add it without fail to next year's installment. All in all, what I am writing here is but the very beginning of this novel . . . As the years pass and the Books pile up, I expect that the whole book will be comparable to my previous opus, *The Bow-Crescent Moon*.

Bakin may be playing with his readers here (he frequently did). The Inaugural Volume ends on a cliffhanger so perfect that the reader can hardly be expected to believe it was the effect of bad planning or mere narrative verbosity. It seems more likely to have been a savvy move on the part of a canny and successful author of popular fiction.

On the other hand, as readers would soon learn, everything about *Hakkenden* had (and still has) a tendency to get out of hand. Bakin mentions *The Bow-Crescent Moon: An Outlandish Tale* (*Chinsetsu yumiharizuki*), probably his best-known work up to that point, as an indication of the scale he envisioned for *Hakkenden*, but the comparison was too modest by half. By much more than half, in fact. *The Bow-Crescent Moon* was serialized from 1807 to 1811 (Bunka 4–8), and contained sixty-eight chapters. *Hakkenden* did not arrive at its grand consummation until 1842 (Tenpō 13), and it topped out at one hundred and eighty chapters. (Since what I am presenting as *Part One—An Ill-Considered Jest* comprises fourteen chapters, it amounts to less than a tenth of the whole!) And for much of the twenty-eight years of the work's serialization, Bakin had been trying (or pretending to try) to bring it to an end. In his foreword to Part I of the Last Installment of Volume IX (which began with Chapter CXVI), he predicts that he will be finishing the Last Installment (in two more parts) the following year, and thus concluding the whole work. That was in 1836 (Tenpō 7)—he still had six years and sixty-five chapters to go.

Hakkenden is huge and unwieldy, almost comically so.[3] It is, in many ways, a shaggy dog story: a seemingly endless tale whose very length and convolutedness turn it into a joke. This is undeniable. What is also undeniable, at least

---

3. At the outset I called it "one of the longest sustained narratives in the world." This is a bold claim, and of course very difficult to substantiate, especially as I know of no word count or character count for *Hakkenden*. In terms of Japanese literature, it has over three times as many chapters as *The Tale of Genji*, and the unannotated *Shinchō Nihon koten shūsei* edition of *Hakkenden* comprises twelve volumes to the eight of the annotated *Genji* in the same series. *Hakkenden* contains more chapters than any of the great Chinese vernacular novels that Bakin considered his models. If sequences of novels, such as the Western novel cycles or *romans fleuves* of the eighteenth and nineteenth century (such as the notorious ten-volume *Artamène ou le Grand Cyrus* by Madeleine de Scudéry or the totality of Alexandre Dumas's novels about the Three Musketeers), are taken into consideration, then some of them may well surpass *Hakkenden* in length, but it should be noted that none of *Hakkenen*'s volumes are capable of standing alone. In any case, it is a very long book.

to anybody who has actually read it, is that it is one of the most entertaining works of fiction ever written. It tells a gripping story filled with gnarly narrative reversals, dizzyingly intricate subplots, and epic, multigenerational quests; it peoples that story with memorable characters, from the lowliest rustic to the gods themselves; and it does it all with some of the best writing in the language. *Hakkenden* is complicated, but it can be appreciated on a quite fundamental level: great storytelling.

This principle holds true for almost everything to do with the book, which makes it worth keeping in mind. The complexity is instructive, even enlightening, and offers its own rewards, but the book also provides basic, elemental satisfactions.

The title is perhaps the most compact illustration of this, and a good place to start. In the original, the full title is *Nansō Satomi hakkenden*, which I render as *The Lives of the Eight Dogs of the Satomi of Southern Fusa*. A long title, and each of its parts is significant. Take "Southern Fusa"—this not only locates the action (or the origin of the action) in the territory that now makes up much of Chiba Prefecture—the province of Awa and its environs—but it problematizes the traditional naming of that territory in ways that Bakin will become very particular about in Chapter II (not for the last time). Or take the "Lives" element (*den*)—this is a nod to the Serial Biographies (Ch. *liezhuan*; J. *retsuden*) section of the ur-classic of Chinese historiography, *Records of the Historian* (*Shi ji*; J. *Shiki*; first century BCE), which presents, one after another, the lives of various historical actors; it is also a nod to *The Water Margin* (*Shuihu zhuan*; J. *Suikoden*; ca. sixteenth century), the great work of Chinese vernacular fiction on which *Hakkenden* is based, which uses the same final element in its title, emphasizing its nature as a collective depiction of the "lives" of a hundred and eight outlaw heroes.

The question of the title is further complicated by the fact that a number of alternate titles occur within the work itself. The cover to the first volume calls it simply *Lives of the Eight Dogs of the Satomi* (*Satomi hakkenden*), while the endpaper to that volume (in some ways equivalent to a modern title page) calls it less simply *Lives of the Eight Dog Warriors of the Satomi of Southern Fusa* (*Nansō Satomi hakkenshiden*). While the Dog Warriors themselves barely appear in our *Part One*, the possible significance of this slight variation in emphasis should still be clear. Is this the story of eight dogs or eight "dog warriors," whatever those might be? Are these Dog Warriors dogs or humans?

The title of the work is long, complicated, subject to variation and interpretation, and unwieldy. But it can also be reduced to its punchiest elements fairly easily: *Hakkenden*, far and away the most common sobriquet for the work in Japanese. And that tells us that this is the story of eight dogs.

The Story

However, those eight dogs barely appear in *Part One*.

In its most basic outlines, *Hakkenden* is the story of the rise of the Satomi, an actual family of samurai who controlled the province of Awa from sometime in the fifteenth century until 1614 (Keichō 19), when their line petered out and their holdings were confiscated by the Tokugawa shogunate. *Hakkenden* is, in other words, a historical novel (more on which later), but it bears only the loosest relationship to documented historical fact. It is, as Bakin himself occasionally reminds us, fiction.

The story begins with Yoshizane, who first establishes Satomi rule in Awa, but most of the novel takes place during the reign of Yoshizane's son Yoshinari. The book ends with Yoshinari successfully defending Awa's sovereignty by fighting off the combined forces of several neighboring warlords and two factions within the Muromachi shogunate: the Overseers of the Kantō (the *kanrei*, a position that historians tend to translate as "shogunal deputy"), and their erstwhile rival Ashikaga Shigeuji (the historical Nariuji), a relative of the shogunal line. All of these powerful figures have their own reasons (often many!) for hating the Satomi or their retainers, and they all come together to invade Awa and crush the Satomi. They fail, however, because (quite simply) the Satomi are the good guys.

This short synopsis makes *Hakkenden* sound like a war story, and in places it is. But the book is more than half over before these sides have fully arrayed themselves against one another; instead, most of the story concerns the lead-up to the stand-off, or how all these grudges came to be. In fact, most of the story (after *Part One*) does not take place in Awa at all, nor does it directly concern Yoshinari.

Rather, the focus is on eight young men who are the spiritual descendants of Yoshizane's daughter Fuse and the family dog Yatsufusa. These are the Eight Dog Warriors of the title. They are born into eight different families (all of whose surnames include the element *inu* [dog]) scattered throughout the Kantō region, and each possesses a bead that marks him as a descendant of Fuse. Each bead bears a Chinese character denoting one of eight Confucian virtues, and each Dog Warrior identifies with his designated virtue individually and with the rest of the eight bead-brothers collectively; the beads are talismans, reminding them of their heritage and duty and occasionally affording them magical protection.

The story of *Hakkenden* mostly follows the Dog Warriors' adventures as they grow up, find each other, learn their true natures, and eventually go to Awa to serve the Satomi. The aforementioned invasion of Awa by the Overseers and their allies results largely from the fact that during their adventures, the Dog Warriors manage to make enemies of most of the political and military power-holders in the Kantō; it is only fitting, then, that it is the Dog Warriors' heroism that saves Awa. But for much of the book's great length, the war that will conclude it is not even on the horizon. For many, many years during its serialization, readers would have experienced *Hakkenden* as the intertwined stories of eight heroes who had not yet met the Satomi, who had only a vague idea of how they related to each other, and who had to navigate the various vendettas and quests connected with their birth families before they could think of going to Awa to join their spiritual kin. Before they become Satomi retainers they are wandering masterless samurai, knights errant.

The "serial biographies" label may lead a reader to expect that each Dog Warrior's story will be presented more or less discretely, but this is not the case. The story jumps from one Dog Warrior's story to another with all the authorial craftiness one could ask for. Sometimes they are alone and at other times they move in bands of two or three; sometimes this is intentional on the Dog Warriors' parts, as they team up or split up to accomplish a task, but often it is accidental, as the vicissitudes of fate separate them and bring them together again. What this means for the reader is that the book is all a single story, not a series of episodes. The frequent cliffhangers and shifts from one storyline to another mean that no installment feels self-contained, and there are few natural breaks in the story.

The biggest exception comes between Chapters XIV and XV, which is why this volume of the translation, *Part One—An Ill-Considered Jest*, ends where it does. Bakin presents the first fourteen chapters as something of a prologue to the story as a whole, telling how the Dog Warriors came to be and thus setting up the long tale of their adventures that is to follow. As such, these chapters form perhaps the only really self-contained unit in the book. But thinking of them as a prologue hardly does them justice: these chapters are some of the most exciting in the book, and Princess Fuse is one of its most memorable characters.

Meanings and Morals

Part of what makes Princess Fuse so memorable is the extravagantly strange situation in which she finds herself: given in marriage to the family dog. It sounds like the punch line to a joke (and of course it is, after a fashion), but it is presented as the stage for a morality play of operatic intensity. Fuse consents to becoming the dog's bride in order to allow her father to keep his rashly given word, and this act of filial piety sets up her own moral conflict: duty demands that she follow through on this commitment, but also that she keep herself from yielding to the dog in any physical way (and part of the weirdness of Bakin's story is how he takes a situation that would be mere folk-tale whimsy in another context and treats it with horrifying gravity). She is a teenage girl alone in the mountains with a monstrous dog who sees her as his mate: she is in danger both physical and, she feels, moral. She triumphs, of course, though her death may make her victory Pyrrhic (at best) for a modern reader. For an early modern audience, on the other hand, it likely would only have sealed her moral supremacy, and in the context of the story (beyond the first fourteen chapters) it allows her to ascend to a higher plane of being, so we must see it as a triumph. And it is this triumph that makes her so memorable.

It has also made her a favorite of fans and critics trying to understand the book and to account for both its popularity and power. Princess Fuse unites within herself the book's most important ideological regimes, Confucianism and Buddhism, but also its two overriding narrative principles: didacticism and play.

Bakin is clear that moral instruction is one of his aims in *Hakkenden*. His most common formulation for describing this is *kanzen chōaku* (encouraging virtue and chastising vice) and he saw it as perhaps the most important aspect of a satisfying story. Elsewhere I have argued that for Bakin, *kanzen chōaku* was as much a structural device (readers love it when characters get their just deserts) as a matter of message, but that hardly means that the message can be ignored.[4] Indeed, it means that the message is constantly foregrounded, as it is with Fuse's triumph. Her star turn is highly dramatic, full of action, beautifully narrated, and in all other ways satisfying to read, but it is also legible as moral teaching. She faces a dilemma and makes a righteous choice.

The flamboyantly moral nature of the dilemma is part of what makes her such a perennial favorite with readers and critics. In Fuse we can clearly see the way Bakin both combines and contrasts Confucian ethics and Buddhist transcendence. She reasons her way through her various impasses with reference to cardinal virtues as defined by the Chinese classics and imparted to her by her samurai upbringing, and she expounds on questions of duty (and not just a daughter's duty, but that of a lord of men) with perfect intellectual

---

4. See *Good Dogs*, especially Chapters Two through Four.

clarity. But at the same time, she devotes herself to reading the Lotus Sutra, and to exercising a bodhisattva-like compassion toward a companion who is a lower order of being according to Confucian teachings, but whom Buddhism deems capable of enlightenment. The fusion of these two schemas is made concrete in the eight prayer beads that she possesses, and which then pass into the possession of the Dog Warriors: Confucian virtues inscribed on Buddhist tools of worship. But it is in Fuse's own person that this fusion is worked out, the here-and-now imperatives of Confucian virtue crossing with the multi-generational, trans-incarnational implications of Buddhist karma.

All of this moral baggage threatens to weigh down not just poor Fuse, but the whole story. And indeed, the *kanzen chōaku* aspect of *Hakkenden* has had its detractors, particularly among the intellectuals of the late nineteenth century, those most keen on modernizing Japanese fiction and leaving behind Bakin's seemingly feudal morality and his supposedly clumsy application of it. But any potential reader scared off by such dismissals loses the opportunity to discover what I have alluded to above: that didacticism for Bakin was as much about structure as message. He cared as much about telling a good story as about imparting a good message. For him the two aims were thoroughly fused.

This means that readers were expected to appreciate Princess Fuse's story not only for the moral lessons it ostensibly imparts, but also for the way in which it first seems like a digression from, then unexpectedly overshadows, and finally concludes and even redeems her father's story. They were expected to enjoy how the tone of the story ranges boldly through horror, romance, exaltation, action, and even subtle (very subtle) humor. They were even expected to enjoy the frequent, not to mention ostentatious, references to Chinese classics for how they deepen and broaden the world of the story and challenge the reader's own wit and erudition.

All of this is at work in the outlandish situation in which Princess Fuse finds herself. The moral issues may be all too real, but the situation that dramatizes them is fantastic. The combination captures the imagination and provokes incredulous, delighted laughter. It may even titillate readers whose imaginations run in certain directions (as did those of many early modern readers, no doubt). It is, in short, entertaining.

Hakkenden is nothing if not entertaining.

The Author

The entertaining nature of *Hakkenden* was key not only to its success, but to its very existence. It was written by an author who depended on his writing brush for his livelihood and sold by publishers who depended on printing blocks for theirs.

Hakkenden is a product of Japan's Tokugawa period (1600–1868), when the country was ruled from the city of Edo by a shogunate headed by members of the Tokugawa family. This period is also known to literary historians as Japan's early modern period, and one reason for this is the appearance and growth of a publishing industry in Japan's major cities. While this was not exactly a mass media in the modern sense, it did lead to mass production of books, the marketing of fiction to paying customers in various regions of the country, and the appearance of the professional author, all phenomena unknown in previous eras and suggestive of popular culture as we now understand the term. Kyokutei Bakin, the author of *Hakkenden*, was a key figure in this transformation in a number of ways.[5]

The author (now sometimes known as Takizawa Bakin but more properly referred to by his two-part penname Kyokutei Bakin), was born in Edo in 1767 (Meiwa 4), in the Fukagawa residence of a family of *hatamoto* (shogunal retainers) whom Bakin's father served at a low rank. Takizawa Kurazō, as the author was called as a child, was thus born into the samurai class. It was a status he was not to retain for long, however, to his later chagrin. It is not much of an oversimplification to say that Bakin's whole adult life was a struggle to re-enter the samurai class, even as he found considerable fame and success as a writer of popular fiction.

Bakin's father died in 1775 (An'ei 4), and the loss of his stipend plunged the family into poverty. Bakin had two older brothers, and for several years the family would be dependent on whichever of the three boys happened to have a paid position at any given time. His mother died in 1785 (Tenmei 5). Bakin himself spent the rest of his youth alternately wandering around Edo and its environs, experimenting with different occupations and amusements, and living with a brother or an uncle while halfheartedly trying to make his way in some official position or other. He seems never to have had much patience with the kinds of employment he could get as a samurai; outside of service, he spent time studying subjects as diverse as *haikai* poetry and medicine, and even seems to have tried his hand at fortune telling.

The turning point in his somewhat dissolute youth came in 1790 (Kansei 2), when he decided to begin writing *gesaku* (popular fiction). In an oft-repeated

---

5. What follows is condensed from material that appears in *Good Dogs*, chapter 2. Readers interested in a more detailed discussion of Bakin's life should consult Leon Zolbrod, *Takizawa Bakin* (New York: Twayne, 1967). The best biography currently available in Japanese is Takada Mamoru's *Takizawa Bakin: Momotose nochi no chiin o matsu* (Kyoto: Minerva Shobō, 2006).

anecdote, he called on well-known author Santō Kyōden (1761–1816) with some sake and asked to be taken on as a disciple. Kyōden replied that *gesaku* writers did not take apprentices, but he encouraged Bakin, and was instrumental in getting his first work published the following year. For a little over a decade, Bakin would concentrate his writing efforts on *kibyōshi* (yellow-covers), a variety of adult-oriented illustrated fiction whose visual-verbal synergy has led them to be characterized[6] as an early form of comic book. These were Kyōden's specialty, and while Bakin was never the most scintillating of *kibyōshi* authors, he did well enough to keep himself going.

At the same time that he was establishing himself as a presence in the world of popular fiction, Bakin was leaving the samurai class behind, seemingly for good. Kyōden got him a job with the publisher Tsutaya Jūzaburō, who helped him find a wife and a steady source of income: in 1793 (Kansei 5), Bakin married Aida Hyaku and took over her family's footwear business. Thus, he became a *chōnin*, a townsman, a member of the merchant class.

He neither abandoned the Takizawa name, however, nor put much effort into the footwear business; instead, he gravitated toward intellectual pursuits. He taught calligraphy, he studied, and above all, he wrote—and in time the income from his writing became sufficient to support himself and his family. He never grew wealthy, but he made ends meet, and regardless of the quality of what he wrote, this fact alone would make him important to literary historians as one of the first authors in Japan to make his living through his writing.

Through the early years of the nineteenth century, this meant first *kibyōshi*, of which Bakin produced more than eighty, and then *gōkan* (bound volumes), the successor genre to *kibyōshi*. These too were visual-verbal in nature, but emphasized action over humor. Bakin's sense of humor is perennially underrated—many critics fail to notice the sly wit at work beneath the surface of *Hakkenden*, for example—but it is true that the more serious tone of the *gōkan* allowed him to play to his strengths. So did their length—*gōkan* were often serialized over several years, and Bakin relished the opportunity this afforded for large-scale storytelling.

His greatest achievements, however, came in the genre of *yomihon*, or "books for reading"—novels, in other words, illustrated but not nearly as profusely as *kibyōshi* or *gōkan*. Bakin began experimenting with *yomihon* in the late 1790s, and began concentrating on them in 1803–1804 (Kyōwa 3–Bunka 1). He would continue to work in both *gōkan* and *yomihon* to the end

---

6. By, for example, Adam Kern, in *Manga from the Floating World: Comicbook Culture and the Kibyōshi of Edo Japan* (Cambridge: Harvard University Asia Center, 2006).

of his life. He would also produce numerous works of non-fiction, including antiquarian miscellanies, travelogues, literary criticism, and autobiography.

As a youth, Bakin had left a dead-end position as a samurai and entered the merchant class; by the time he reached middle age he was supporting himself and a family through his passion, writing. This should have left him a happy man, but his early decision to renounce his samurai status came back to haunt him. With the death of his eldest brother Rabun in 1798 (Kansei 10), Bakin was left as the only one who could carry on the Takizawa name and lineage, and he seems to have felt it his duty to return the Takizawa to samurai status. He sought to do this not by going into service himself—he never wavered from his chosen career as a writer—but by grooming his son Sōhaku, born the year before Rabun's death, as a physician in hopes of get-ting him hired by a domain. And in 1820 (Bunsei 3), Sōhaku was in fact hired by the Matsumae clan, thus bringing the Takizawa clan back into the lower strata of the samurai class.

Sōhaku, however, was chronically ill and seldom able to work, so despite his own advancing age, Bakin was still the family's financial mainstay. In 1835 (Tenpō 6), Sōhaku died, leaving the Takizawa family once again without a claim to samurai status, and with no one to provide for Sōhaku's widow and son aside from Bakin himself. At this point, Bakin's hopes for the Takizawa family shifted from his son to his grandson, Tarō (born in 1828 [Bunsei 11]). Bakin sold most of his considerable library, using the proceeds to buy Tarō a position in a unit of musketeers.

Bakin's declining years were thus spent in somewhat straitened circum-stances, so whatever his artistic goals, he had to continue writing for finan-cial reasons. This was complicated by the fact that he began to lose his sight just before Sōhaku died. By 1841 (Tenpō 12), the year his wife died, he could no longer see well enough to write. His final work was dictated to his daughter-in-law, Sōhaku's widow Michi, to whom he had taught enough Chinese characters that she could assist him. In fact, Bakin's writing had long been something of a family business, as his son Sōhaku had helped him proofread his works. In the years of his blindness, Bakin continued to compose fiction, although at a reduced pace. After finishing *Hakkenden*, he pressed ahead with other *yomihon* and *gōkan*, some of which were left uncompleted when he died in 1848 (Kaei 1) at the age of 81.

Modern scholarship tends to characterize Bakin as a man torn between commercial necessity and artistic ambition. The former followed from his decision to leave samurai life behind and ultimately to support himself and a family with his brush: he needed to write books that would sell, and he did. The latter stemmed, it seems, from his samurai education, and the urgency he felt from middle age onward to "redeem" the Takizawa name and live up to his heritage. This required money, of course, but he also seems to have felt that it required him to make something respectable out of *gesaku*, to dignify it with both sophisticated craft and intellectual (moral) heft.

Both the commercial and the aspirational aspects of Bakin's writing are on full display in *Hakkenden*, with its combination of popular storytelling and didactic exegesis. Its carefully constructed *kanzen chōaku* underpinnings represent Bakin's attempt to connect his fiction with more elevated kinds of writing, as do his frequent allusions to Chinese (and Japanese) classics. But the commercial nature of the work is inescapable, particularly when the book's full paratexts are included—the prefaces; the colophons, with their acknowledgements of copyist and block-carver as well as illustrator; the back-of-the-book blurbs for other works by Bakin; and in particular the advertisements for Bakin's sideline in patent medicines. *Hakkenden* as a book has, like its heroes, lofty ambitions, but those ambitions are played out on thoroughly low terrain.

Genre

I have been referring to *Hakkenden* as a novel, and if we use the term "novel" loosely, simply to mean an extended piece of prose fiction, then it certainly fits. Whether *Hakkenden* fits a more rigorous interpretation of the label is open to debate, as it was produced before the "novel" as a Western literary form became known in Japan, and was therefore written to meet a different set of audience expectations, governed by a different set of conventions.

Taken on its own terms, *Hakkenden* is a *yomihon*. This term seems to have been intended to distinguish these books from *kibyōshi* and *gōkan*, in other words from works in which the story was told primarily through the illustrations. *Yomihon* were illustrated, but not nearly as copiously as *kibyōshi* and *gōkan*, and the text is not nearly as tightly integrated with the illustrations as in those genres. As a *yomihon*, then, *Hakkenden* is primarily an exercise in textual storytelling (and yet the illustrations are not only of an impressively high quality, they are often narratively significant in their own right).

Yomihon was not, however, the term Bakin used most frequently to refer to *Hakkenden* and works like it. He called them *haishi* or *haishi shōsetsu*, both terms derived from Chinese tradition and neither lending themselves to easy translation. *Shōsetsu* is the word now used in Japanese as the standard equivalent for "novel" (although *shōsetsu* can include short fiction), but originally it meant something like "little stories," and referred to legends or tales circulating among the common folk. In China during the Han dynasty (206 BCE–220 CE), officials called *haikan* (Ch. *baiguan*, petty officials) were tasked with collecting these and compiling them into *haishi* (Ch. *baishi*, petty histories) that were meant to supplement official histories. Centuries later, the term *haishi shōsetsu* (Ch. *baishi xiaoshuo*) came to be applied to vernacular fiction, i.e., fiction that was written at least partly in an approximation of the contemporary spoken language rather than the age-old classical language.[7]

By calling his novels *haishi shōsetsu*, Bakin was asking readers to see them as belonging to the same genre as Chinese vernacular classics such as *The Water Margin* and *Journey to the West* (*Xiyouji*; J. *Saiyūki*). Essentially the *yomihon* were meant to be a localization of this Chinese genre. This explains at least three important features of *Hakkenden* as a text.

First, like many *yomihon*, it is itself based on a Chinese *haishi shōsetsu*. *Hakkenden* is a very loose adaptation of *The Water Margin*, which follows the fortunes of a hundred and eight outlaws as they rampage joyously across the political landscape of China during the Song dynasty (960–1279). The protagonists begin as spirits imprisoned in a pit, and are accidentally released; embodied as outlaws, they adventure singly or in small groups before finally gathering on the impregnable Mount Liang; and as a league they must withstand the attempt of imperial forces to bring them to heel. The connections between *The Water Margin* and *Hakkenden* are too convoluted to detail here; the fact that what takes up one chapter in the original (the freeing of the spirits from the pit) takes up fourteen in the adaptation should suffice to show how devious and playful Bakin's adaptational method can be.[8]

Second, *Hakkenden* is full of allusions to Chinese texts. Given the immense prestige Chinese civilization and literary culture enjoyed in Tokugawa Japan, this is not too surprising. One will find allusions to the *Analects* of Confucius (*Lunyu*; J. *Rongo*) or the *Records of the Historian* in many popular works of Bakin's day. But in the context of a *haishi shōsetsu* these allusions take on added significance. Beyond simply bolstering the story with the authority of antiquity, they contribute to a faint but persistent double vision, as if China lurks behind Japan at every turn. This is part of the aesthetic of the *haishi shōsetsu*, to make the reader feel as if this actually *is* a Chinese vernacular novel that just happens to be written in Japanese and set in Japan.

Third, *Hakkenden* deals with history. Bakin's remarks on *haishi shōsetsu* in the very pages of *Hakkenden* itself show that he was aware of the genre's distant (Han dynasty) as well as proximal (Ming dynasty, 1368–1644) antecedents,

---

7. For a more extensive discussion of this subject, see Chapter Two of *Good Dogs*.
8. For a more thorough exploration of Bakin's adaptational method, see Chapter Three of *Good Dogs*.

both of which stress the importance of popular, unofficial accounts of events as supplements to official histories. Bakin was not a historian, and readers would not have expected *Hakkenden* to be a faithful account of the historical Satomi. But he does take care to align his fantasy with known facts, to situate his invented heroes among attested historical actors.

Bakin begins his story in 1441 (Kakitsu 1), with the Battle of Yūki. This was part of a long power struggle in eastern Japan as the power of the Kyoto-based Ashikaga shogunate waned. Ashikaga rule in the Kantō was exercised through the *kubō* (which I translate as Overlord; in the opening lines of the story Bakin refers to this position by the alternate designation of *fuku shogun* [Vice-Shogun]), stationed in Kamakura. This was an unofficial post, although the Bureau of Kamakura it oversaw was real, and the position was passed down through a branch of the Ashikaga family. The *kubō* had two deputies, the *kanrei* (which I translate as Overseer), who were nominally his assistants; these positions came to be monopolized by the Yamanouchi and Ōgigayatsu branches of the Uesugi family. In 1438 (Eikyō 10), the *kubō* Mochiuji rebelled against Kyoto, but the *kanrei* supported the shogun. Mochiuji, besieged, killed himself in 1439 (Eikyō 11); his surviving followers gathered at Yūki Castle, where they were promptly besieged by forces loyal to the shogunate and the *kanrei*.

As with allusions to earlier texts, a certain level of historicity was typical of late Tokugawa popular culture. The shogunate's censorship regime largely prevented authors from setting their works in the present day, or even in the too-recent past. Most stories were set at some point in history, hung on readymade frameworks drawn from old chronicles or tales; few authors made much attempt at historical verisimilitude, and few readers cared. To some extent, *Hakkenden* is the same. It is set in the fifteenth century, well before the introduction of firearms to Japan, but Kanamari Daisuke has no trouble procuring a musket, and no eyebrows are raised when he wields it.

In other respects, however, Bakin's appeal to history seems more earnest than that found in most popular fiction of his day. For one thing, although his story quickly leads him away from the historical Battle of Yūki into the comparatively blank slate of Awa, he still refers occasionally to events closer to the political center. Thus in Chapter IX we are informed that Mochiuji's son Nariuji (as Bakin himself acknowledges, historians prefer to read the characters of his name "Shigeuji") has come of age and taken up residence in Kamakura, and in future installments the Dog Warriors will interact with Nariuji, as well as with the *kanrei* and various members of their households. While Bakin gives his creativity free reign with some aspects of the story, he is also keen to connect it at key points with historical events, perhaps reflecting a sense that the *haishi shōsetsu* demands at least a modicum of historicity.

For another thing, despite its readiness with anachronism, *Hakkenden* does contain at least the elements of a commentary on history. It is set among samurai in the Warring States era, an age of constantly shifting alliances when a samurai could expect to be drawn into battle at any moment. To be a samurai at that time meant, in other words, to be a warrior. This must have seemed particularly true from the vantage point of Bakin's day, when to be a samurai meant to be a bureaucrat. Not only could a samurai of Bakin's generation expect a life more or less free of violence, he was also (as his education would have reminded him) afforded the privilege of developing his moral faculties, and the duty of exercising them on behalf of society's lower orders. *Hakkenden* suggests that this kind of cultivation, a proper balance between prowess with weapons and familiarity with books, was beyond the medieval warrior. We see as much in the confrontation between Yoshizane and his father Suemoto in Chapter I. For all his flaws, then, we are encouraged to see Yoshizane as the model of an early modern samurai before his time. Here and elsewhere we can see Bakin conceiving of his fifteenth-century setting as a different time with its own realities, rather than just a colorful backdrop.

About Style

Bakin is one of the great writers of the Japanese language—he commands a staggering range of registers, moods, colors, and effects, and he knows how to use all of this to keep the reader turning pages. To be sure, there are slow spots, instances of puzzling repetitiveness, and obtrusive, even maddening, digressions; but there are also passages that are the equal of anything ever written in the language for pulse-pounding excitement, heartstring-tugging pathos, or thought-provoking profundity.

Most translators would probably agree that style (as opposed to content, and as distinct from accuracy) is the hardest thing to convey in a translation, though many, myself included, would also say that the challenge of conveying style is the most tantalizing aspect of the translator's task. I translate *Hakkenden* because I love its language, and want to communicate what I love about it in English. Whether or not I have at all succeeded is, of course, up to the reader, and so it is only fair to give the reader a sense of how the language works in the original, so that she may judge for herself. What follows is, therefore, a general description of the style(s) I see Bakin using in *Hakkenden*.

In illustrating it I will be drawing examples from throughout the book, not just the first fourteen chapters.[9]

To begin with, *Hakkenden* is written in *bungo* (literary language), sometimes called Classical Japanese. That is, it is written (as previously mentioned) in what was, generally speaking, the standard premodern literary language that had already been in use for centuries by Bakin's time, and which came to be seen as such a problem by language modernizers a few decades later. *Hakkenden* uses verbs, auxiliary verbs, conjugations, and other parts of speech that were still used in writing despite generally falling out of use in the spoken language over the previous centuries. Arguably, on a grammatical level *Hakkenden* has more in common with Japanese as it was written in the twelfth century than as it was spoken in the nineteenth. Syntactically, too, it largely adheres to canons established by the twelfth or thirteenth century, featuring the mixture of Chinese-derived words and native Japanese vocabulary that historians call *wakan konkōbun*.

As we will see, Bakin's use of Chinese terms in particular departs from orthodox *wakan konkōbun* in significant ways; nevertheless, this combination of classical grammar and Sino-Japanese syntax may be thought of as the basic matrix of *Hakkenden*'s style. Of course, readers familiar with premodern Japanese prose will recognize this description as being applicable, in its broad strokes, to most if not all fiction of the early modern period. These were the parameters within which almost any writer worked; style was achieved by modulating or modifying that grammar and syntax for effect. In *Hakkenden*, this happens in complicated and interesting ways. Bakin writes in several identifiable registers over the course of this long and endlessly complex tale, never completely departing from the overall elevated tone of the classical language, but still providing the reader with a heady variety of narrative and descriptive modes.

The first one the reader encounters in the story proper is what may be thought of as Bakin's epic mode, an emulation of the style found in medieval war chronicles (*gunki monogatari*) such as *The Tale of the Heike* (*Heike monogatari*, ca. thirteenth century) or the *Chronicle of Great Peace* (*Taiheiki*, late fourteenth century). Here is how Chapter I of *Hakkenden* opens:

> In pondering the deeds of Satomi Yoshizane, Major Assistant in the Governance Ministry and Minister of the Court—who, when the might at arms of the Shogun at the Capital and the Vice-Shogun at Kamakura

---

9. Chapter numbers for *Hakkenden* are given in Roman numerals for reasons explained later in this introduction.

had become weak and grasping and thus the realm become divided into warring states, escaped hardship to the shores of the Eastern Sea, opening up the land and establishing a foundation for his descendants unto the tenth generation, Lords of Awa and Kazusa—we know that he was the firstborn of the first wife of Lord Satomi Suemoto of the Minamoto, Lesser Assistant in the Governance Ministry, eleven generations from Yoshiie, General of the Pacification Bureau and Minister of the Court, called Firstborn of the god Hachiman, in the direct line of the Genji established by Emperor Seiwa.

What the translation aims to convey here is a grandeur, a magnificent pomp, that in the original is meant to put the reader in mind of the war chronicles. The way lineages and titles are foregrounded in all their complexity, and interwoven with an uncompromisingly pithy (yet vivid) description of the political and military situation, instantly transports the reader into a different age, one of stern warriors in glorious battle. We might also think of this as the historian's mode, and in that connection, we might notice that Bakin actually personalizes this formalized overture slightly by implying a unitary narrative consciousness that is doing the pondering here. As a historian (or "petty historian") he is furnishing commentary as well as facts.

As discussed above, *Hakkenden* is set in the Warring States era, only a century or so after the battles narrated in the *Chronicle of Great Peace*. That is, the stuff of Bakin's tale is precisely the kind of action detailed in the war chronicles: soldiers and lords, and their battles and political machinations. It is only fitting, then, that on a stylistic level, he looks to those chronicles in his attempt to evoke their atmosphere.

Another aspect of the medieval war chronicle style comes in battle scenes. Just one of many examples comes from Chapter XCIII:

> The battle had not been going on for very long when another concealed company of foes suddenly leapt up near Sadamasa's rearguard. The great general who stood alone at their head: in what wise was he garbed? Dark blue was his armor's lacing, and a great-horned helmet was made fast to his head; a sword four feet three inches in length rode at his waist, and the quiver on his back held twenty-four arrows fletched black in the middle; he held by its very center a bow, heavily rattaned on its lower half and intermittently rattaned on its upper, and he sat astride a stout peach palomino fitted with a saddle decorated with saddle-jewels.
>
> His voice was sharp and resounded through the heavens and earth as he cried, "Overseer Uesugi Sadamasa, hail! I am Inuyama Dōsetsu

Tadatomo, son of the late Inuyama Dōsaku, an old Nerima retainer. I made an attempt upon you once at Shirai, but was outschemed by Ōta Suketomo: my stratagem failed, and so my obsession, nurtured over many years, has endured to this day. Receive my blade!"[10]

Time and again Bakin introduces battles like this, with close attention to the details of the warrior's arms and armor—the color of the armor's lacing, the patterning of the bow's rattan wrapping, the details of the archer's grip and the rider's saddle—and to the decorum of the individual challenge. All of this bespeaks careful study of the war chronicles.

But Bakin has other registers beside the epic. The reader frequently encounters what might be called Bakin's lyrical mode, which he slips into when describing scenes of natural beauty or high emotion. In these moments his language becomes distinctly reminiscent of the courtly and poetic *monogatari* (tales) of the Heian and medieval period. Bakin is too modern (and therefore too dependent on the *kanbun* [literary Chinese]-derived syntax that later eras had brought into Japanese) to slip into a purely Heian diction, but these passages see him gesturing toward that style by bringing in phrases and techniques drawn from *waka*, classical Japanese lyric poetry. One of the most famous passages of this type (but far from the only one) comes in Chapter XII, when Princess Fuse has gone into the mountains with Yatsufusa. Although her situation is dire, she achieves a kind of rapturous enlightenment there in the wilderness, which Bakin evokes with high lyricism:

Princess Fuse, daughter of Satomi Yoshizane, Major Assistant in the Governance Ministry, had, for the sake of her father and her country, that their people might not lose their faith in words, sacrificed herself and gone, companion to the dog Yatsufusa, along those mountain paths, and once that she like setting sun had hid herself, no more did anyone inquire after her. Between the torrent and the cliffs of clay there was a cave, and this she lined with sedge and made of it her sleeping chamber—there she passed the winters, and when spring had come, when birds at morning their companions call through eightfold mists she gazed at alpine blooms and thought of springtimes past, at home with dolls and mop-topped maidens all paired off like ducks and drakes and plucking, this fine morning—ah! how dear its

---

10. Translations from passages not contained in *Part One* are based on the text as found in Hamada Keisuke, ed., *Shinchō Nihon koten shūsei bekkan: Nansō Satomi hakkenden*, 12 volumes (Shinchōsha, 2003–2004). References will consist of a volume number (in Arabic numerals) and a page number, such as: 6:58–59.

name!—mother-and-child grass; the stone on which she sat, a diamond shape like rice-cakes on the third (but made by whom?), on summer nights was faintly warm to touch in mossy robes it could not shed, but cool against her hems the wind that through the pines like comb through tangled hair did pass, and brought the evening show'rs to wash them—then, beneath those dripping, drying tresses insects sang of autumn's coming, and the brocade bed of many colors woven by the leaves of all the trees on all the valley-sides; this blanket now so brightly dyed would fade—this temporary state the hinds knew not who cried for mates in rain that never ceased until one unknown day it turned to snow that softened, as it fell, the corners sharp of stones she used for pillows: thus she had a view for ev'ry season of the trees, the spindle-trees and podocarps, in bloom but she was wretched as she knelt, beast-like, upon her mats, refused to go outside, but only thought about the life to come, the merit of her sutra-copying and chanting. Day by day she sadly grew accustomed to her sadness, felt it not as sadness. Calls of birds and cries of beasts, who nothing knew of th'floating world, she heard as long-sought boon companions' voices: thus exalted was she in her heart and mind.

Bakin here employs seasonal words (*kigo*), associative word-links (*engo*), pivot-words (*kakekotoba*), and other devices drawn from *waka*, as well as *waka*-style allusions to Heian-era customs (some of which will be explained in the footnotes to this passage). In addition, Bakin slips into meter here, alternating phrases of seven and five syllables (a style known as *shichigochō*), so that the prose is not merely redolent of poetry, but in a sense *is* poetry.

All of this draws attention to the style here as a departure from the narrative's norm, and certainly from the epic mode of battle scenes. The language here is flowery and emotive, soft and supple, and above all very *wa*—very Japanese, that is, as opposed to the more Sinified flavor of the epic passages. A tension or dialogue between domestic and continental elements is, as we have seen, built into the genre to which *Hakkenden* belongs: readers expected a reading experience that was at once both Japanese and Chinese, and one way Bakin delivers this is by modulating his prose style. At times it sounds like one or another variety of Chinese, or Chinese-inspired, writing, and at other times, as here, it works in ways that the tradition had celebrated as distinctly "Japanese." Gender is an important theme in the novel, and the stylistic shifts have gendered overtones as well; *kanbun* or *kanbun*-influenced writing had long been defined as to some degree "masculine" vis-à-vis the more "feminine" *waka* and *monogatari* styles, and here, where Princess Fuse's true nature is in question, Bakin carefully draws his reader into a "feminine," "Japanese" space through his use of language.

Bakin's use of seven-five meter is one of the most famous aspects of his style, and justly so: the attentive reader can find passages of metrical prose that go on for several lines, even a page or two at a time, and which include not only description but action and even dialogue. The author's ability to add this level of linguistic complexity to what is already a very complicated narrative is nothing short of amazing. That said, his use of meter is also fairly unobtrusive. It is not marked in any way in the original text, and since, like iambic pentameter in English, seven-five meter is fairly close to the natural rhythms of Japanese (particularly classical Japanese), it is possible to read straight through a passage without noticing its presence. For the reader unconcerned with such things, the metrical sections are experienced merely as passages of particularly intense or lovely (and perhaps difficult to parse) description.

Bakin was of course not the only early modern writer to employ *shichigochō*. He is famous for using it in his prose, but its use characterized much theatrical writing as well, notably the *jōruri* puppet plays of Chikamatsu Monzaemon (1653–1725). Given Bakin's deep knowledge of kabuki and *jōruri*, his use of meter might be as much a nod to the theatrical tradition as to the poetic. But he has what we might consider a theatrical mode that embraces much more than just meter. Bakin was deeply indebted to kabuki, and some of his action scenes sound almost like transcribed dialogue. A good example of this comes in Chapter XLVII, when two Dog Warriors, Dōsetsu and Sōsuke, formally meet for the first time. In conversation, they realize they have met once before.

> Dōsetsu looked around doubtfully, then nodded, but though he put his sword into its sheath, not yet would he dare let down his guard. "Now that I have heard your name I am not without some recollection slight of you. 'Twas on the nineteenth of the sixth month now past, in the vicinity of Mount Marutsuka; 'twas near to midnight on that night, too," he said.
>
> Sōsuke adjusted his weight onto one knee, lifting the other, and said: "You were unaware that I had overheard you mourning over the funeral pyre of the virginal Hamaji; you took the longsword Rainmaker that you might use it to avenge your lord and sire, and as you tried to leave I grasped the butt of your scabbard and, announcing my name, I
>
> > —tried to take my longsword, but I shook you off, dealt you a ringing blow, and by the glint of my blade

—I wasted not a moment, but drew my blade as well.

—Our hard-won skills we turned on each other, each a match for
   each of the other's

—blow for blow, above and below, our blades were as bound to each
   other, until the tip of mine got through to your arm

—though it was only a scratch I sustained

—but when I sliced into your shoulder

—you surprised me by piercing my lump

—and from the wound flew a small bead that, mysteriously, came
   into my hand even while the cord of my amulet-pouch stretched
   and tangled itself around the hilt of your sword—

—I never noticed, and the cord snapped, and only later did I learn
   that within that amulet-pouch was a small bead, upon which bead
   appeared, as big as life, the character for Righteousness, the second
   in Fealty,

—while upon the bead that came from within your body could be
   seen, naturally, the character for Loyalty, the first in Fealty,

—but since I knew this not, I valued my life as worth a thousand
   in gold pieces against an enemy who was no enemy indeed, and
   using the Fire Escape technique

—you hid all trace of yourself, and I knew not where you had gone.
   Then, all unintended, we were reunited tonight

—at the grove at Tafumi, where it was you, was it not, who interfered
   with my orisons.

—Then it was you, Dōsetsu, my master, worshiping at that old tomb?

—Who was it who then came between us and pushed us apart?

—I know not.

—Nor do I.

—We may find out later.[11]

An early modern reader would likely have recognized this rapid exchange of lines as an evocation of kabuki dialogue. Dōsetsu and Sōsuke are engaging in something very like the familiar kabuki practice of *kakeai* or *warizerifu*, "call and response" or "split lines," in which actors speak in such quick alternation that they seem to be completing each other's thoughts. Bakin cleverly employs punctuation (there being no paragraph breaks in the original) and leaves out his otherwise customary "he said"/"he replied" formulations in order to suggest two actors rapidly exchanging lines.

---

11. 3:244–45.

Further underscoring the sense that Bakin is imagining this dialogue as taking place between actors onstage is the fact that the graveyard encounter they describe at the end of this passage, which took place only a few pages before, was presented as happening in total darkness, with the characters stumbling around blind to each other although in clear view of the "audience," i.e., the reader. Such a scene is common enough in kabuki that it has a name: *danmari* (a struggle in darkness). In fact we can often catch Bakin "staging" scenes as if he were a kabuki playwright planning for actors' entrances, exits, costume changes, and the like. But beyond mise-en-scène, it is Bakin's ability to bring kabuki-style dialogue to life on the page that allows *Hakkenden* to work in a theatrical mode, alongside its lyrical and epic modes.

Perhaps the polar opposite of this is Bakin's use of Chinese elements in his writing. There are several aspects to this. First is the plain fact that some sections of *Hakkenden* are written in *kanbun*. Most installments have two prefaces, one in Japanese and one in *kanbun*, and many of the frontispieces contain *kanshi*, or poems in Chinese. This is not terribly remarkable; *kanbun* was, in Bakin's day, something an educated person was expected to be able to read, and Bakin is not the only writer to decorate his fiction with passages of Chinese prose, or verses in Chinese. Nevertheless, he was notably persistent about it, so that by the end of *Hakkenden* the reader would have been confronted with quite a substantial amount of writing in Chinese (for the most part confined to the paratexts).

More interesting, however, is the fact that from time to time within the story proper Bakin also writes in a style that reads as if it were translated from Chinese. As noted, an educated person was expected to be able to read *kanbun*; this had been true for perhaps a millennium by Bakin's day, and over that period of time a system had developed by which a passage of *kanbun* was marked up with symbols that would allow the reader to rearrange the sentence into Japanese syntax. This annotation system was essentially a way for Japanese readers to hack the Chinese written language (in Rebekah Clements' memorable analogy[12]), that is, to translate it in their heads so that they could read it as Japanese. The resulting Japanese is highly formalized and stiff, a style distinctive enough that it has its own name: *kanbun kundokutai*, or "the marked-up Chinese style" (also referred to as simply *kundokutai*). Many passages in *Hakkenden* are written in this style, so that they read as if they were translated from a Chinese original, even though there was none (*The Water*

---

12. Rebekah Clements, *A Cultural History of Translation in Early Modern Japan* (Cambridge: Cambridge University Press, 2015), p. 124.

Margin notwithstanding). Sometimes the writing is so *kanbun kundoku*-esque that the reader can almost "reconstruct" it into a Chinese sentence.

This happens particularly in moments when a character starts drawing moral lessons about a recent experience. *Hakkenden* is, as we have seen, a didactic novel, and when Bakin slips into a didactic mode he often writes as if he were a Confucian moralist. So in Chapter CVI, for instance, when Satomi Yoshizane finally meets Inue Shinbei Masashi, the Dog Warrior whose cardinal virtue is *jin* (benevolence), Yoshizane muses on his place in the fraternity, and it sounds like this:

> Take the Seven Dog Warriors, for example, Dōsetsu and his fellows: how many times have I sent Terubumi to summon them to my side? But they have always refused, saying that they could not come to me until they are all eight assembled. Yet now Shinbei Masashi is here without being summoned, for the time has come. Lo, of the eight virtues—benevolence, righteousness, and the rest—all are equally essential: but benevolence is the root of them all. Yea, they are even as yonder bamboo with its joints: benevolence is, as it were, its root, and the other seven virtues are its joints. Verily, neither filiality nor fraternity, loyalty nor fidelity, nor righteousness, nor propriety, nor wisdom could in their virtue attain unto sageliness without benevolence. It is for this reason that this one of the Eight Warriors, this true and infinitely praiseworthy Benevolence, Masashi alone, should be the first to rise in the world, and that Loyalty and Filiality, Righteousness and Fidelity, Propriety, Wisdom, and Fraternity should all cleave unto his Benevolence.[13]

The language in this passage is so close to Confucian sermonizing that one could almost call it pastiche; it employs characteristically *kanbun*-esque formulations (rendered in the translation by expressions such as "lo" and "verily") in the course of a diction that is, in comparison to the fluidity of the theatrical register and the mellifluity of the poetic register, noticeably rigid and lofty.

It was almost inevitable that Bakin slip into such language when drawing, or having his characters draw, moral lessons: this was quite literally the language of ethical discourse in the period. It is more striking, then, to note that Bakin uses *kundokutai* in descriptive passages as well—sometimes his lyricism is of the *kanshi* variety, rather than the *waka*. Of this, too, there is a good example in Chapter CVI. Two of Yoshizane's retainers, escorting him

13. 7:92–93.

on a pilgrimage to a mountain temple dedicated to Princess Fuse, pause to appreciate the scenery:

> . . . the mountains exhaled clouds of glory that wreathed their prodigious peaks—the wind raised a breeze in the pine-boughs that resembled the plucking of zither-strings—mystic grasses clung to the rocks' surfaces, their colors dazzling to the eye—strange birds emerged from the hollows' depths, their voices calling to companions—the gravel was mingled black and white, too finely to be distinguished—the cataract revealed its base, but its depth could not be gauged.[14]

To the reader with even a passing familiarity with the canons of Chinese poetry or lyrical prose, this passage stands out as, again, one that could almost have been translated from Chinese. It displays the syntactic parallelism one would expect from Chinese couplets—"mystic grasses" parallels "strange birds," while "clung to the rocks' surfaces" parallels "emerged from the hollows' depths," and so on. It even hints at the meter one would expect in *kanshi*—the first "couplet," with the lines beginning "the mountains exhaled" and "the wind raised a breeze," for example, can be reconstructed in the imagination into a Chinese verse of two lines of seven characters each, with the expected caesura after the fourth character. The back-formed couplet that results in this case does not display end rhyme, but elsewhere Bakin even goes that far. The point is that this passage very much resembles what Chinese poetry sounds like when rewritten in Japanese according to *kundoku* rules—yet another arrow in Bakin's stylistic quiver.

Another aspect of Bakin's use of Chinese styles in *Hakkenden* deserves notice: his use of phrases and words drawn from vernacular Chinese fiction. The passages of *kanbun kundokutai* narration described above, the ones meant to resemble translated Chinese, relate to (more or less) orthodox *kanbun* as it would have been studied by educated people. But as we have noted, readers of *haishi shōsetsu* were led to expect a close intertextual relationship between the Japanese *yomihon* and the corpus of Chinese vernacular fiction, i.e., fiction written in unorthodox Chinese, a language that resembled (to some degree) Chinese as it was spoken and that was therefore unfamiliar to most Japanese readers. Unfamiliar but tantalizing, since *Hakkenden* was part of a growing vogue for the study of vernacular Chinese among scholars and a burgeoning enthusiasm for vernacular Chinese stories among fans. Readers of both stripes expected a vernacular Chinese experience in, it seems, everything from the novel's scale and structure to its very language. So strong was

---

14. 7:105.

this expectation that publishers often referred to *yomihon* as *kokuji shōsetsu* (novels in the domestic script), as if to reassure their readers that the book they were about to buy would be written in Japanese but would otherwise transport them to the realm of Chinese vernacular fiction.

Above I suggested that the essential stylistic parameters of *Hakkenden* were the classical grammar and Sino-Japanese syntax as standardized in the medieval period, and the registers I have been describing mostly work within those parameters. But we need to add a third element: expressions drawn specifically from Chinese vernacular fiction as it came to be known in Japan during the eighteenth and nineteenth centuries, which would not have been part of a standard *kanbun* education.

Bakin's use of vernacular Chinese is an extremely complex topic, and one difficult to discuss in English; here I will simply highlight two aspects of it. First, as Bakin tells his story he employs a number of formulaic phrases that help him begin and end chapters or switch from one storyline to another, such as "Meanwhile," and "to resume our story." We are used to such phrases in modern multi-strand narratives, but the specific phrases Bakin uses were not part of traditional fiction in Japan—Bakin adopted them from Chinese vernacular fiction. So the reader finds exotic-looking strings of Chinese characters (given domesticating glosses, rather than ones based solely on the Sino-Japanese reading of the characters) functioning as signposts in the course of the narration. We find 復説 (glossed *mata toku*) or 再説 (glossed *futatabi toku*), both of which commonly occur at the beginning of a chapter, particularly when a chapter break has interrupted a scene, and which mean something like, "we resume our story." After a narrative eddy the reader will often encounter 話省饒舌 (glossed *adashi koto wa sate okitsu*): "but enough of digressions." These and many more such phrases are straight imports from Chinese vernacular fiction, but given *kanbun kundokutai*-esque glosses; they occur so frequently and so consistently, however, that the reader soon comes to separate them mentally from the more thorough-going *kundokutai* (that is, orthodox Sinitic-style Japanese prose) discussed above. Rather than a stylistic mode that the narrative can slip into and out of for temporary emphasis, phrases like this represent a kind of universal joining of certain aspects of vernacular Chinese narrative language to Japanese for consistent, overall effect.

This joining happens at the level of individual words as well. One by-product of the *kundoku* system is the way *rubi*, or phonetic glosses, can be joined to Chinese logographs (even in non-*kanbun* contexts) in unorthodox ways to create playful or thought-provoking semantic equivalencies. Since this was a standard technique in popular fiction of Bakin's day, we will not be at all surprised to find him employing it in *Hakkenden*. And indeed, he often uses *rubi* not simply to guide the reader's voicing of difficult words or phrases (such as *adashi koto wa sate okitsu*), but to make jokes, or to explain unfamiliar words to his readers.

A subset of the latter is words that he has imported from Chinese vernacular fiction—Sinitic characters in unorthodox usages, which he then glosses with more familiar Japanese translations. An example of this occurs in Chapter LXXXIII, where Bakin writes the character 听 and glosses it *kiku* (to hear or listen), a word that is usually written with the character 聽. This is a uniquely obvious example, because he self-annotates this character usage by detailing its history in Japanese and Chinese lexicographies such as *Kun'yō jigi*, a 1759 work by Itō Tōgai, and *Seijitsū* (Ch. *Zheng zitong*), compiled in the late Ming by Zhang Zilie and published in the early Qing by Liao Wenying. Bakin's explanation reads:

> 听 IS A QING VERNACULAR TERM THAT OCCURS FREQUENTLY IN NOVELS. IT IS A VERNACULAR SIMPLIFICATION OF 聽. JIGI DOES NOT COVER IT. THIS MAY BE SEEN IN THE ANNOTATION FOR 听 IN SEIJITSŪ.

Bakin's self-annotation here draws attention to one instance of something he does throughout *Hakkenden*: nearly every page has some expression or character usage that derives from vernacular Chinese rather than the orthodox literary language, and that is glossed with a familiar Japanese equivalent.

The result, in simple terms, is that (particularly for readers who paid attention to the characters used, and not just the phonetic glosses) *Hakkenden* is written in a kind of translationese, a careful fusion of the familiar and the exotic. This was what readers of *haishi shōsetsu* expected. It was not supposed to read "naturally"—whatever that might mean in an early nineteenth-century context.

To summarize, the narrative language of *Hakkenden* is, generally speaking, classical literary grammar plus a standard Japanese-Chinese syntax, but with frequent importations of newer Chinese vocabulary drawn from vernacular fiction. This basic style then incorporates passages that reach toward various identifiable registers of written language: the sonorous, declamatory style of the medieval war chronicles, the supple, lyrical language of the Heian *monogatari* and *waka* poetry, the meter and poetry of the puppet stage, the fast-paced dialogue of the kabuki stage, the expository clarity of the *kanbun* essay, the elegant parallelism of Chinese poetry. One could no doubt identify others.

And this only touches on the language of the story itself. But as a reading experience, *Hakkenden* is more than just the narrative. Most of the many installments of the novel come with prefatory and other paratextual material, much of which is couched in yet other registers of language. As already noted, usually an installment will come with a preface in Japanese and another in *kanbun*—that is, not in Japanese written as if it were translated from Chinese, but actually written in Chinese itself. Frontispiece illustrations typically include not poetically inflected prose but actual poetry, both Japanese and Chinese, usually original. And both front and back matter include passages written in what we might call the commercial mode: advertisements for forthcoming publications or other products.

One example of this will have to suffice. Like some other popular writers, Bakin supplemented his income by selling patent medicines, which he advertised in the pages of his work. Generally, these advertisements have not been included in modern typeset editions of the work, but they form a conspicuous part of original woodblock printed editions. Since this was Bakin's own family business, we are probably safe in assuming the ad copy was written by Bakin himself. The advertisement found in the Inaugural Volume reads in part:

Having a blank page here at the front of the book, and being faced with the pressing necessity of making a living, I record here the following proclamation, commending it warmly to all you gentlemen far and wide:

Water of the Divine Lady—A Family Tradition: 100 coppers per packet. Passed down in the Author's family, this infusion is good for all ailments common to ladies, and is of especially immediate efficacy when taken just before and after birthing. Thanks to this, for five generations none of the women of our house have died young during difficult births. Its uses are explained in detail on the wrapper. It gives me great joy to report that, of late, its efficacy and superiority to all other such remedies on the market have been recognized by the many gentlemen who have sought to purchase it.

. . .

Miraculous Bolus, Exactingly Prepared: Large packet [CONTAINS OVER TWO HUNDRED PELLETS], *price 2 shu; medium packet* [CONTAINS 36 PELLETS], *price 1 monme 5 bu; small packet* [CONTAINS ELEVEN PELLETS], *price 5 bu.* [NOTE THAT I AM UNABLE TO SELL IN QUANTITIES SMALLER THAN THE 5-BU PACKET.] There are numerous Miraculous Boluses in the world, but many of them are of haphazard preparation: unless the buyer selects one whose medicinal ingredients are of the highest quality, then he may find he has bought something that is a Miraculous Bolus in name only, and not in its effects. In my preparation I follow the recipe in perfect circumspection, using the ingredients in their prescribed measure without regard to their cost. The result is a Miraculous Bolus with a hundred, nay, ten thousand times the efficacy of others with which it may be compared.

This may have precious little to do with the story of the Eight Dog Warriors (although when Inusaka Keno goes undercover as a medicine peddler in Chapter LXXXVIII, this sort of language does find its way into the narrative proper). But it has everything to do with the reading experience of *Hakkenden*, which for original readers at least would have included these obvious reminders of the work's status not only as a product to be sold, but as a means of selling yet other products. These advertisements are part of the book, and so the frank (but still flowery) salesmanship of this ad is relevant to any complete assessment of the *Hakkenden*'s style. Its full range covers everything from sober ethical reasoning to dazzling hucksterism.

That this range was a conscious choice on the author's part may seem too obvious to bear pointing out, but in fact Bakin himself felt it worth drawing his readers' attention to it. His foreword to Part II of the Last Installment of Volume IX (the chapters published in 1839) is devoted to a discussion of his stylistic aims. He invokes, as I have, Heian courtly romances, military chronicles, and Chinese vernacular fiction, but takes pains to note that his prose corresponds neatly to none of them. In particular he argues that a modicum of colloquial language is essential to any attempt at expressive, capacious prose, but dismisses the notion of completely embracing the vernacular. "As a result," he writes, "my prose is, one might say, neither elegant nor vulgar; for that matter, it is neither Japanese nor Chinese. A skewbald and unconventional thing is the product of my brush . . ."[15] He hastens to point out that readers have been wise, or unwise, enough to embrace the product of his brush with great enthusiasm.

About the Translation

In General

What should be clear from the above description is that the language of *Hakkenden* is not natural. Some readers will rightly note that language use, in speech or writing, is seldom if ever "natural," in that it is always crafted, always hybridized, always contingent. And yet most of us (whatever our

---

15. 8: 310.

native language) have been conditioned to expect that the best writing is clear, simple, and direct, with the energy if not the precise syntax of the language as it is spoken. This was not what Bakin's readers expected, nor is it what they got. They got a work written in a language that eschewed the messiness and contingency of speech in favor of a canonical literary language whose resources had been developed over centuries, modified, or modulated, by Bakin for various effects. The language of *Hakkenden* is beautiful, powerful, and expressive; it is also artificial. It is a performance.

Modern readers of translations especially tend to expect clean, accessible prose that conforms to modern ideals, even if the original being translated does not behave that way.[16] This expectation can simply reflect a preference for what one has come to appreciate as "good" writing, but it can also indicate an assumption that all "good" writing at all times and places has stood in the same relation to its audience as modern "good" writing does to its audience. That is to say, modern readers often assume that premodern readers would have experienced contemporary writing as clean, accessible, and direct, and that it is only linguistic change over time that makes premodern prose feel inaccessible to the modern reader. The corollary to this assumption is that the translation should correct this inaccessibility and restore the text to its original readability.

To repeat, this is not entirely the case with *Hakkenden*. It is true that the language of *Hakkenden* was more accessible to a nineteenth-century reader than to a twenty-first century one, inasmuch as nineteenth-century readers expected linguistic performance of the type that Bakin gave them, while modern readers do not, and inasmuch as classical grammar was then widely read while is it now relegated to classrooms. That said, there was much about *Hakkenden* that would still have been challenging or strange to a contemporary reader—the ornamentation and stylization of the language are not merely "the way people wrote back then," but calculated effects achieved by a writer who was a master of his craft.

A translation that prioritizes readability and naturalness of expression might convey the fascination of Bakin's story, but it could not convey the dazzling play of his style. I aim to convey both, and so in rendering *Hakkenden* into English I have made choices that the modern reader may find puzzling, jarring, or perhaps even unnatural. The reader certainly has the right to like

---

16. This is the phenomenon that Lawrence Venuti famously describes as the Anglophone preference for translators' "invisibility." See Venuti, *The Translator's Invisibility: A History of Translation* (London: Routledge, 1995), especially chapter 1.

or dislike these choices, and what follows is not an attempt to justify them, but merely to explain them.

The first thing that will strike the reader is that the language of the translation is somewhat stiff and archaic in some places, flowery and convoluted in others. This is an attempt to mirror those qualities as I perceive them in the original. It is probably unwise for modern writers to attempt to write in archaic language, because it does not come naturally to us. Nevertheless, that is precisely what Bakin was doing, and that is what I have attempted to do. I have, to be specific, tried to reach back to English as it was written in an age when the very qualities I find in Bakin's style were appreciated and achieved (*mutatis mutandis*) by English writers. I have found early nineteenth-century writers such as Jane Austen, Walter Scott, and Herman Melville to be useful models, and I have also learned from modern writers who themselves adopted an archaic style, such as J.R.R. Tolkien and Patrick O'Brian. I do not claim to be their equal, of course, only that I see their writing doing things that I think Bakin's writing does, and that I hope this translation can do as well.

A few specific points bear mentioning. The longest limb this translation goes out on is the decision to render Bakin's meter into English meter. That is, when Bakin's prose slips into *shichigochō*, or seven-five syllabic meter, I have tried to translate it into unrhymed iambic pentameter. Just as Bakin's meter is left unmarked for the reader to discover as she will, so is the meter in the translation. Bakin's *shichigochō* is frequently irregular, containing extra syllables when necessary or departing from strict 7–5–7–5 alternation, and my meter is full of similar metrical substitutions. Bakin's *shichigochō* passages make conspicuous use of poetic devices, as noted above, and in translating them I have reached for devices such as contractions ("ev'ry," "th'floating world") that were once common in English poetry, as well as occasionally emulating things like pivot-words that have no analog in the English tradition. Some readers may find these passages barely noticeable; others may judge them obtrusive. No doubt my renderings fall short of what Bakin achieves, but if they remind the reader of what lies behind the translation, they will have served their purpose.

On the other hand, some aspects of the original text I have modified freely. Bakin's sentences are often extremely long, and while in general I have allowed the original to pull me toward longer sentences than contemporary English generally prefers (occasionally even rendering a sentence with one of equal length), I have broken up many of his sentences where it seemed appropriate to do so. Similarly, the original has few paragraph breaks, and certainly none that respect the English convention of starting a new paragraph with each change in speaker. I have started new paragraphs for each change of speaker, however, and have otherwise broken up his paragraphs even more liberally than I have his sentences.

A Few Specific Points

Time. Expressions of time in *Hakkenden* reflect the complexity of reckoning time in premodern Japan.[17]

A day was divided into twelve *koku* or *toki*, terms conventionally translated as "hour" but roughly double the length of the modern sixty-minute hour, though the length of *koku* also varied by the season. Both daylight and darkness always lasted six *koku*, i.e., the six *koku* of day began at sunrise and ended at sunset, while the six *koku* of night began at sunset and ended at sunrise. This meant, for example, that in the summer a daytime *koku* was considerably longer than it was in winter. Although this system seems strange from a modern standpoint, it had the advantage of corresponding to the movement of the sun. For a modern person, "6:00 pm" might mean bright afternoon sunlight, twilight, or full darkness, depending on the season, but for someone living under the premodern Japanese time regime, the "hour of the cock" always meant sunset.

The hours were designated according to the twelve animals of the so-called Chinese zodiac (a sequence also applied to directions and to the calendrical cycle, among other things). Beginning with sunrise, the hours were: the hare, the dragon, the snake, the horse, the sheep, the monkey, the cock, the dog, the boar, the rat, the ox, and the tiger. These hours straddled the points to which they were geared; that is, midnight (i.e., the mathematical midpoint of the hours of darkness) fell at the midpoint of the hour of the rat.

The horary cycle was referred to in other ways, too. Hours were numbered, but unfortunately not in a way that corresponds to the modern system. The noon hour (the horse) was also referred to as "nine" or "the hour of nine" (*kokonotsu*), and the hours were counted *down* toward midnight, so that the hour of the sheep (following the horse) was "eight," and so on. But the count was restarted at midnight with "nine." There was no "hour of three," "two," or "one," but only nine through four, counting down.[18] As with the

---

17. For a fuller description of time-keeping in early modern Japan (one that in some ways challenges the conventional wisdom I summarize here), see Yulia Frumer, *Making Time: Astronomical Time Measurement in Tokugawa Japan* (Chicago: University of Chicago Press, 2018), Chapter One.

18. The origins of this system are obscure, but may have had to do with early timekeeping in Buddhist temples, which was accomplished by burning sticks of incense, meaning the timekeeper was watching time diminish rather than advance. The passing hours were marked by a bell, but three

modern system, the existence of an "hour of nine" in the morning and one in the evening could lead to confusion, so people used expressions such as "six in the morning" (*akemuttsu*) to clarify.

Furthermore, time at night could also be reckoned by an entirely different system deriving from ancient guard schedules, in which the period of darkness was divided into five equal units known as *kō* (watches). These were counted in an ascending manner, so the fifth "watch" was the one that ended at dawn.

Hours (not watches) were subdivided in several ways. Then as now people referred to "half hours" (*hankoku*), although the length of these was closer to the modern hour. People also spoke of the beginning, middle, and end of an hour (*jōkoku, chūkoku, gekoku*). But hours were also divided into four equal parts, and people referred to, for example, "the third quarter of the hour of the ox" (*ushimittsu*).

Mechanical clocks had been known in Japan since the mid-sixteenth century, and had been manufactured in Japan (to reflect the seasonal variation in the length of hours described above) since the seventeenth century. Accordingly, I considered transposing all time references into a modern idiom (e.g., twelve o'clock) for the sake of readability. Given the nature of the Eight Dog Warriors themselves, however, it seems to me that any sort of animal imagery, no matter how mundane, is potentially significant in *Hakkenden*. I therefore felt it best to foreground the animal imagery inherent in premodern expressions of time, and so retained expressions like "hour of the dog," footnoting them with an approximation of the modern equivalent.

Dates. Years in *Hakkenden* are referred to in two ways. The imperial system (still in use today as an alternative to the Western calendar) saw an emperor establish an era name when he came into power. Unlike today, the era name in premodern Japan tended to change, sometimes several times, during an emperor's reign. The count of years began anew with each new era, meaning a calendar year could contain two separate era–name numbers. For example, the Eikyō era came to an end in the second month of its thirteenth year, and the era name was changed to Kakitsu. Thus the same calendar year (1441) was both Eikyō 13 and Kakitsu 1. Era–name designations used in *Hakkenden* are carried over into the translation and footnoted with the equivalent year CE.

Strictly speaking this can result in confusion because the premodern Japanese year was lunar rather than solar, with so-called intercalary months inserted from time to time to correct the discrepancy between month and

---

strikes or fewer were reserved for calling the faithful to prayer, and so they were eliminated from the timekeeping repertoire.

season. This means that the seventeenth day of the second month of Eikyō 13, when the era name was changed, did not correspond to February 17 of 1441, but rather to March 10, 1441. No attempt has been made to provide Western-calendar equivalents for months and dates, and years are given as rough CE equivalents.

Years are also referred to by the Chinese-derived sexagenary system. This combines the twelve animals of the zodiac, referred to as "branches" (*shi*) in calendrical terms, with the five elemental "stems" (*kan*) of wood, fire, earth, metal, and water. Each year is designated by one of the animals and one of the elements, each of which moves in a cycle, so that a complete cycle of unique animal-element combinations lasted sixty years, longer than many people lived. The elemental stems were also subdivided into elder and younger (*yang* and *yin*), yielding ten stems in practice. For example, Eikyō 13 / Kakitsu 1 was designated in sexagenary terms "younger-metal / cock" or *kanoto-tori* (also read *shin'yū*). In the translation the elder / younger distinction is elided, but the elements and animals are retained, for the same reasons as they are for hours.

Months were also referred to by two systems. The first of these numbered them one through twelve, as in modern Japanese, which in translation results in "the First Month" and so forth. The second was the old Japanese system for naming months, which had seasonal or cultural associations. As with modern English speakers and month names such as January, it is at best debatable whether early modern readers were habitually cognizant of the original meanings of month names such as *kisaragi*, but I have often elected to translate their literal meaning anyway (thus "the Clothes-Layering Month"), especially when the context seems to call for an awareness of the meaning of the name of the month. Bakin often writes one designation for the month in Chinese characters and glosses it with the reading for the other, or gives both readings in gloss form. The translation tries to reflect the author's choices, and footnotes them where it is unclear what numerical month is intended.

Other calendrical terms, such as for seasons or parts of seasons, are explained in footnotes as needed.

Measures. As a rule, weights, distances, and other physical measurements have been given in their customary (non-metric) English equivalents, with figures that the author seemingly means to be neat estimates given in similar round numbers rather than ungainly exact equivalents. For example, as a unit of length, one *chō* was equivalent to about 109 meters or 119 yards, but when a distance is given as one *chō*, the translation tends to render it as "a hundred yards." A special case is the *ri*: when used as a unit of measurement in the story it is translated into equivalents in miles, but when it appears in proverbial expressions and the like it is rendered "league."

Hakkenden seldom deals in specific monetary units, but when it does, the translation uses the original in romanization (e.g., *bu, mon*) with an explanation where necessary. No attempt is made to calculate equivalents in modern currency units.

Volume numbers, etc. I have adopted Roman numerals for any numbering scheme that pertains to the original of *Hakkenden* (e.g., Volume II, Book I, Chapter XIII). This is to avoid confusion with the physical volumes into which modern editions of the text are divided (Bakin's original has nine numbered volumes, which the standard modern edition distributes among twelve volumes). Numbering of the volumes of the translation will be spelled out: thus *Part One—An Ill-Considered Jest*, which contains all of Bakin's Volume I (or, as he called it, the Inaugural Volume) and the first four chapters of Volume II, Chapters I–XIV in total.

Bakin's self-annotations. In keeping with his pose as a petty historian, Bakin occasionally annotates his own story. Some of these comments are interlinear (in the original they were printed in half-size characters, two lines to one line of normal text), while others took the form of headnotes, appearing in the upper margin of the page. Interlinear comments are presented in the translation in small capital letters, italicized, and bracketed. Headnotes are presented as unnumbered footnotes, in small capital letters, italicized.

Annotations and Sources

Annotations concentrate on identifying and, where necessary, explaining Bakin's allusions to earlier texts, or to figures of Japanese or Chinese antiquity. Brief explanations have also been added of historical figures as mentioned in the text, and of other matters that may not be clear from the translation alone. In addition to overt allusions (as when a character quotes from the *Analects* and in doing so names the text), Bakin frequently quotes or paraphrases from classics without identifying the text. When possible, these allusions have also been annotated, but no doubt I have missed many.

Bakin's narration from time to time discusses the very characters with which words are written, often as a form of divination after the fact. In Chapter IX, for example, Yoshizane analyzes the character used to write his daughter Fuse's name (chosen, of course, by Yoshizane himself) and concludes that, according to it, her union with the dog was inevitable. I have endeavored to allow these discussions to take place as fully as possible in English, rather than introducing Sino-Japanese characters and words into the text (although that would have made things clearer to readers with some knowledge of Japanese). Similarly, I have seldom used annotations to draw attention to patterns of imagery or word usage that might aid interpretation of the story, preferring to allow readers to draw such conclusions on their own.

One case does bear mentioning, however. The word used to refer to the all-important beads is *tama*, and the multiple meanings and homophones of this word allow for a truly far-reaching network of imagery that the translation could only hint at. *Tama* can mean "bead," but it can also mean more generally "ball," as a child might play with. It is also used in the story to refer to the specific kind of "ball" fired from muskets—a bullet, in other words. As with the English "ball," *tama* is also used as slang for testicle, and metaphorically for masculine fortitude. In addition, *tama* has the meaning of "jewel" or "gem" (jade in the strictest usage of the term, but also pearls or precious stones in general). Written with a completely different character (and its variants), *tama* can mean "spirit," "soul," or "ghost." All of this should suggest the great weight of symbolic meaning available to these magic beads and their owners.

There is no fully annotated text of *Hakkenden* in Japanese, but late in the course of this project, Tokuda Takeshi's annotation of the first ten chapters was published. I have relied on this extensively for my annotations, although I disagree with Tokuda in some instances. I have not cited him each time I drew on his work, so the reader should assume that Tokuda's contributions were crucial in assembling the information found in the notes for Chapters I–X.

The translation is primarily based on the text as edited by Hamada Keisuke and published as *Shinchō Nihon koten shūsei bekkan: Nansō Satomi hakkenden*, 12 volumes (Shinchōsha, 2003–2004). I also consulted Tokuda Takeshi, ed. and ann., *Nansō Satomi hakkenden zenchūshaku 1* (Bensei Shuppan, 2017), as well as various original woodblock printed editions from the collections of Waseda University and the National Diet Library and found in their online databases. For sections of the novel written in *kanbun*, I consulted Takagi Gen's online *Nansō Satomi hakkenden honbun tekisuto dēta* (https://fumikura. net/text/hakkenden.html) and the anonymous fan site *Risu no hōbukuro* (http://lovekeno.iza-yoi.net/risu_ind.htm).

Illustrations are reproduced from woodblock printed editions of the work in the collection of the National Diet Library, made available for public use through the National Diet Library Digital Collection (http://dl.ndl.go.jp/). Unless otherwise noted, all illustrations are taken from the Sanseidō (first) edition, ID #000007311500; alternate illustrations (as noted) are taken from the Bunkeidō (first reprint) edition, ID #000007311502.

EIGHT DOGS, OR *HAKKENDEN*

INAUGURAL VOLUME

The Inaugural Volume of *Hakkenden* was originally published by Sanseidō, proprietor Yamazaki Heihachi, who went on to publish the next four volumes before the work changed hands. The Inaugural Volume, later known as Volume I, was reprinted a number of times while Sanseidō owned the blocks, with several different cover designs. The earliest and the best-known of the Sanseidō covers for the first volume is this, a puppy in falling snow.

Bunkeidō, proprietor Chōjiya Heibei, took over publication with Volume VIII in 1832. Shortly thereafter the blocks for Volumes I–VII came into his possession, allowing him to reprint from them. He gave Volume I this new cover design showing several puppies frolicking in snow.

Center, in green: The Lives of the Eight Dog Warriors of the Satomi of Southern Fusa.
Right of the title: Text by Master Kyokutei [Master of the Crooked Pavilion].
Left of the title: Illustrations by Yanagawa Shigenobu.
On the red Chinese ceremonial offering vessel, bottom left: Sanseidō [publisher Yamazaki Heihachi].

Preface to the Lives of the Eight Dog Warriors

When the Satomi clan first came to prominence in Awa, they led the multitude with rightminded virtue; they put down the recalcitrant with ingenious strategy. They took over both provinces of Fusa[1] and passed them down through ten generations; they held dominion over eight lands, and thus became crowned above a hundred generals. At this time they had eight courageous retainers, each of whose surname included the character for "dog." Therefore they were called the Eight Dog Warriors. Even if their cleverness was not as that of Yu Shun's Eight Virtuous Ones,[2] so loyal were their spirits, so virtuous were they to the depths of their bowels, that they could well be spoken of in the same breath as the

---

The first preface is written in *kanbun* (with minimal glosses). For a discussion of the wording of the title, and variations thereon, see the Introduction. This seal represents a cicada, and the four characters within it read "caper in the fields in the autumn wind." It refers to the last line of the poem "Reporting to Court, I Tread Moonlight on the Luo Embankment" by Shangguan Yi (608–665). The last line in full is: "Cicadas caper in the fields in the autumn wind."

1. I.e., the provinces of Kazusa ("upper Fusa") and Shimōsa ("lower Fusa").

2. Yu Shun or Shun of Yu was a legendary early Chinese emperor. His reign is discussed in the first chapter of Sima Qian's classic Han-era history *Shi ji* (J. *Shiki*), where it is noted that he employed as advisors eight virtuous men, sons of former emperor Gaoxin.

Nan[3] clan's eight retainers. Alas, it was rare in those days for anyone to put brush to paper. Thus it is only through war chronicles that have survived in the towns, and Mister Dian's *Thoughts on Characters*,[4] that we even know their names at all, and there is no way for us to know of how they began, and how they ended.

I came to lament this; I desired to polish the scratched gem, as it were. Therefore from that time on I hunted ceaselessly through ancient records, but found no settled proof. I spent a day in such a fugue, and then began to think of sleep. As I stared with bleary eyes, I had a visitor from Southern Fusa. The course of our conversation ran to the facts surrounding the Eight Dog Warriors, and his explanation of them was not that which is handed down in the war chronicles. When I pressed him on it, he said that it was all as per the oral transmissions of the elders of his village. He then ventured to ask if I would write it down. I consented, saying I would certainly endeavor to spread his strange report. Rejoicing, my visitor withdrew. I escorted him as far as my brushwood gate, beside which lay a hound. Preoccupied, I trod on its tail; a cry of pain immediately erupted from beneath my foot. Startled, I came to my senses—it had all been a dream, as of South Branch.[5] I looked all around me and saw that there had been no guest beneath my thatched roof, no howling dog by my brushwood gate.

As I pondered my visitor's tale, however, it seemed to me that I ought not simply ignore it, dream though it was, but indeed that I should record it. Already I had forgotten the greater part of it, and nothing could be done about that: and so I have stitched my story together with incidents from Chinese antiquity that I have stealthily appropriated, as when I base the discourse on dragons delivered by the Minamoto official of the Department of Rites on the *Classic of Dragons* of Wang Danlu,[6] or the delivery of a letter to Castle

---

3. Another name for the Kusunoki clan. To assimilate them into Sinitic practice, Bakin here uses only the first character of their surname. The reference is to eight famous families of retainers of Kusunoki Masashige (1294–1336), who supported Go-Daigo's efforts to topple the Kamakura shogunate, then died resisting former ally Ashikaga Takauji's campaign to establish a new shogunate in his own right. Masashige was remembered as a figure of legendary loyalty. Their story is related in the late fourteenth-century war chronicle *Taiheiki*.

4. *Shogenji kō setsuyōshū* (1717), a dictionary compiled by Makishima Terutake (whose surname is given in an abbreviated and Sinitic fashion; see note 4).

5. A reference to the Tang-era story *Nanke Taishuo zhuan* (J. *Nanka Taishu den*) by Li Gongzuo. The story tells of a former soldier, Chun Yufen, who fell asleep beneath a tree and dreamed he had been made ruler of South Branch, and who then awoke to find that he had been dreaming beneath the tree's southern branches.

6. *Longjing* (J. *Ryūkyō*), a book of dragon-related lore by Wang Danlu found in volume 50 of the early Qing compendium *Zhaodai congshu* (J. *Shōdai sōsho*).

Long[7] by means of spirit-doves on Zhang Jiuling's flying servants.[8] I modeled Princess Fuse's betrothal to Yatsufusa on Gaoxin's giving his daughter to Panhu.[9] There are too many examples besides these to bother enumerating.

Within a few months' time I had drafted five Books' worth, which, however, only constitute the stream, hardly wide enough to float a cup on, that shall nonetheless grow into a mighty river; I have not yet created the serial biographies of our Eight Warriors. In spite of this, the booksellers wrested the pages from me by main force and delivered them to the engravers. Now that the book is on the blocks, they ask me for a title. I have only the vaguest of notions, but I dare not refuse, so I name it *The Lives of the Eight Dog Warriors.*

On the nineteenth day of the ninth month of Bunka 11 (a wood-dog year),[10] in the autumn, I wash my brush in Purple Drake Pond, below Opus Hall.[11]

Selected and Interpreted by Saritsu[12] the Old-Fashioned

---

7. As with personal names, he abbreviates the name of Takita Castle in a Sinitic fashion.

8. Poet Zhang Jiuling's childhood nickname for the pigeons by which he sent messages, as recorded in the Song-era miscellany *Kaiyuan tianbao yishi* (J. *Kaigen tenpō iji*).

9. Volume 14 of Gan Bao's Jin-era collection of supernatural tales, *Soushenji* (J. *Sōshinki*), tells how Gaoxin promised his daughter to anyone who could bring him the head of his enemy. When his dog Panhu brought the head, Gaoxin balked at fulfilling his promise, but his daughter insisted that he keep his word. The Panhu story is also related in volume 86 of the Liu Song-era history *Hou Hanshu* (J. *Go Kansho*). For further details, see Chapter IX.

10. 1814.

11. "Opus Hall" (Chosakudō) was one of Bakin's pen-names, and also his nickname for his residence.

12. Saritsu (raincoat and rainhat) was another of Bakin's pen-names. "Interpreted" also nods toward Bakin's personal name, Toku (written with a character meaning "interpret" or explain).

On Bakin's seals: The seal on the left reads, in seal script, "Seal of Kyokutei Bakin, Chosakudō." The one on the right consists of a thatched hut between the Daoist trigrams for Heaven and Earth. It refers to a couplet from a poem by Tang-era poet Du Fu: "Myself and the world: a pair of tangled tresses; / Earth and Heaven: a single thatch pavilion," from the third of the five poems headed "Late Spring: On My Newly Rented Thatched Cottage at Rangxi." Stephen Owen, trans., *The Poetry of Du Fu, Volume 5* (Boston / Berlin: De Gruyter, 2016), 81.

Those known to the world as the Eight Dog Warriors of the Satomi were as follows: Inuyama Dōsetsu [CHILDHOOD NAME: MICHIMATSU], Inuzuka Shino [CHILDHOOD NAME: SHINO], Inusaka Kōzuke [CHILDHOOD NAME: KENO], Inukai Genpachi [CHILDHOOD NAME: GENKICHI], Inukawa Sōsuke, Inue Shinbei [CHILDHOOD NAME: SHINPEI],[1] Inumura Daikaku [CHILDHOOD NAME: KAKUTARŌ], and Inuta Bungo [CHILDHOOD NAME: KOBUNGO]. Their names appear in the war chronicles,[2] but only in cursory fashion, with no details given about their places of origin, their beginnings or their endings. Is this not greatly to be regretted? I have thus fashioned this novel, patterning it after the ancient Chinese tale of Gaoxin betrothing his daughter the princess to Panhu [THIS IS THE NAME OF A DOG]. Throughout, I have speculated as to karmic causes and elucidated their effects, in order to awaken women and children from their slumbers.

In the five Books of the Inaugural Volume, I tell of the origins of the Satomi Clan in Awa. I have modeled my work on Chinese books of romance, and so it differs from the war chronicles in its particulars, although in general it is similar to them. Moreover, I have employed mad language and embellishments, intermingled with vulgar expressions and sayings, stitching them all together with oafish humor—this is after all but an amusement.

This preface is written in Japanese.

1. Inue Shinbei's childhood name is written with characters that could be read "Shinhei," "Shinpei," or (conceivably) "Shinbei." Bakin glosses them as "Shinhei," both here and when the name reappears in Chapter XXXVII, but the difference between the voiced (b) and unvoiced (h) consonant is not consistently marked in early modern orthography. Most later readers seem to assume that Bakin intended the name to be pronounced "Shinpei," so I have followed that reading here.

2. While Bakin is here referring to chronicles of the historical Satomi such as *Satomi gunki* (1631), Hamada Keisuke notes that the only source that has yet been found for the eight dog-named Satomi retainers is *Shogenjikō*. Hamada, "Kaisetsu," in *Shinchō Nihon koten shūsei bekkan: Nansō Satomi Hakkenden*, 3:551.

Chapters VIII, in which Horiuchi Kurando Sadayuki finds a puppy in the village of Inukake, through X, in which Yoshizane's daughter Princess Fuse goes into the depths of Mount To, comprise the beginning of the whole tale. However, from beginning to end nothing is missing—the whole is complete and entire. In the IInd and IIIrd Volumes will be found the serial biographies of each of the Eight. This coming spring I shall begin to put them together, and within two or three years shall have made the whole book.

Reinscribed by Saritsu the Old-Fashioned

The Lives of the Eight Dogs of the Satomi of Southern Fusa

Illustrated

Inaugural Volume

Table of Contents

This is a translation of the original table of contents. Unlike modern tables of contents, this one does not include page numbers, but is simply a list of the contents of the Volume. In any case, in the first woodblock printed edition, each Book was bound as a separate fascicle, and page numbers in each Book began again with 1, so a list of page numbers would have been unhelpful.

1. In the Table of Contents, the chapter names are written in *kanbun* (with complete pronunciation glosses to enable them to be read as Japanese). When the chapter names reappear at the beginning of each chapter, they are written out as Japanese. When written as *kanbun*, the chapter names take the form of couplets, each line having the same number of characters (though this number varies). Grammatically and syntactically, too, they suggest poetic couplets through their use of *kanshi*-style parallelism.

A list of the headings covered in the Inaugural Volume, complete in X Chapters.

FRONTISPIECES

Caption: Moonlight pounds/on a Chinese mortar/sharp like the first salt/from the sea at Naniwa/ in this crabwise world—Chosakudō.

Figure: Kanamari Hachirō Takayoshi.

Notes: The poem is in Japanese, in *waka* form, and is written in an approximation of *man'yōgana* (Chinese characters as used in the eighth-century poetic anthology *Man'yōshū*, and employed for a mixture of phonetic and semantic values). It derives from *Man'yōshū* poem #3886, which is from the point of view of a crab being eaten. A banner is draped over Takayoshi's right shoulder, extending out of the frame of his illustration into the neighboring panel where a crab stands on it. The crest on the lower end of the banner, a black bar in a circle, is that of the Satomi house.

浪中得上龍門去
不歎江河歳月深

Caption: He climbs up out of the dragon gate in the waves' midst/Without sighing at the depths of time upon the great rivers.

Figure: Satomi Yoshizane, Major Assistant of the Governance Ministry.

Notes: The "dragon gate" is a proverbial figure for a rite of passage, common in Japan and China since ancient times (see Chapter III, note 11). It is commonly thought to relate to carp swimming upstream to spawn, and imagines that a carp that climbs a particularly difficult waterfall will thereby transform into a dragon. Yoshizane is here pictured riding a giant carp, while the illustration is framed by stylized images of waves, clouds, and dragons. The poem is a *kanshi*, and is unattributed.

Caption: There is no/telling what a person/is thinking/is there any smile/that hides not a blade?—Kinugasa of the Palace Stores.

Figures:

Upper register: Horiuchi Kurando Sadayuki [*top right*]. Bokuhei [*bottom right*]. Mukuzō [*bottom left*]. Sugikura Kisonosuke Ujimoto [*top left*].

Lower register: Anzai Saburōdayu Kagetsura [*right*]. Kogorō Nobutoki of the Maro [*left*].

Notes: The poem is #1826 in *Shinsen waka rokujō* (compiled 1243), and is by Kinugasa Naifu, i.e., Kinugasa Ieyoshi (1192–1264). The four figures in the upper register are pictured as if appearing in a cloud of smoke rising from Nobutoki, or perhaps from the blade he is cleaning. The meaning of the smoke and the relationship of the scene in the upper register (which does not occur in the story) to that in the lower register is unclear. In the upper register, Bokuhei and Mukuzō are wrestling over what appears to be a sword in a brocade case. Ujimoto wears a large straw hat of the type often worn by mendicant monks. In the foreground, Nobutoki kneels in front of what may be a shattered wooden picture, which Shinoda Jun'ichi suggests may be a votive picture (*ema*). *Bakin no taimu: Satomi hakkenden no sekai* (Iwanami Shoten, 2004), 77ff.

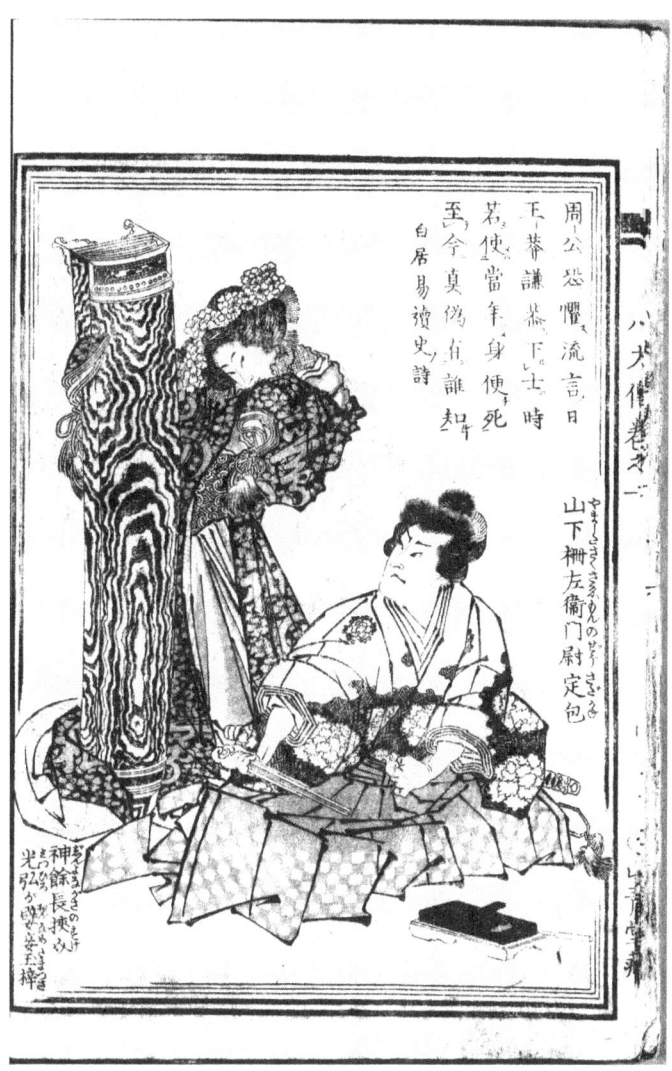

Caption: The Duke of Zhou feared the day when baseless rumors spread/Wang Mang humbled himself when going down to the mandarins/If that year had ended with them dead/Who then would there be to tell truth from falsehood?—a poem Bai Juyi composed on reading history.
Figures: Yamashita Sakuzaemon-no-jō Sadakane [*right*]. Jin'yo Nagasanosuke Mitsuhiro's concubine Tamazusa [*left*].
Notes: The lines are from the third of five poems entitled "Loose Words," by Bai Juyi (772–846). Sadakane holds a folded fan and has an inkstone and inkstick in front of him. Tamazusa is holding up a koto, propped on one end.

Caption: The stag arises/thinking what he dreamed comes true/torch-hunting mountain—Tōkōsha Rabun.

Figure: Kanamari Daisuke Takanori.

Notes: Rabun (d. 1798) was Bakin's older brother by nine years and his inspiration in haikai poetry, among other things. "Torch-hunting" was a way of hunting deer—their eyes would reflect the torch-light. The poem refers to a story in the third chapter of the Daoist classic *Liezi* (J. *Resshi*; probably dating to the Eastern Jin era), in which a woodcutter kills a deer and hides its carcass. Unable to find it later, he convinces himself it was a dream. Meanwhile, another man hears his story and finds the deer; he concludes that the woodcutter's dream had been true, but his wife convinces him that he had only dreamed the woodcutter. In the illustration, the women flanking Daisuke are unidentified; the one with her back to the viewer holds a truncheon (*jitte*).

深宮飽食
恣狳獞
臥秘眠壇
慣不驚
却被捲簾
人放出
宜男花下
吠新晴
元貢性之詩

里見義實の
愛犬八房

伏姫

Caption: Deep in the palace she feasts on beasts at will/She lies down on weavings, sleeps on felts, with no sense of wonder/One day she is loosed by the people rolling up the screens/Beneath the blossoms the mistress howls at the clear spring sky—a poem by Gong Xingzhi of the Yuan.
Figures: Princess Fuse [*right*]. Satomi Yoshizane's pet dog Yatsufusa [*left*].
Notes: The poem is titled "On the Theme of Dogs." Gong Xingzhi lived in the late Yuan and early Ming dynasties (mid-late fourteenth century). Yatsufusa holds a severed human head in his jaws. The cherry-blossom pattern on Princess Fuse's robe is echoed in the border of the illustration.

Captions:

Above margin: A picture of the Eight Dog Children as unshorn youths playing hide-and-seek.

Center right: Be peaceful and never rebel/While you are in your youth/And while in your youth/Apply yourself fully.

Center left: Summer grasses/grow thick in the garden/over any trace/of the youthful topknots/they bid be tied with them—a Japanese lyric by Lord Teika.

Figures: Inue Shinpei, Inumura Kakutarō, Inuta Kobungo, Inukawa Sōsuke, Inukai Genkichi, Inuyama Michimatsu, Inusaka Keno, Inuzuka Shino [*right side, clockwise from top right*]. The Reverend Chudai [*left*].

Notes: The poem on the right, a *kanshi*, is unattributed. That on the left is by Fujiwara no Teika (1162–1241) and is #2112 in his collection *Shūi gusō*. The first word in it, *agemaki*, referred to a

hairstyle worn by boys in ancient times, in which the hair was bound into topknots over the ears. In the caption titling this picture (and elsewhere in the story), the word is used to refer to youths before their coming of age ceremony, which for a samurai would involve shaving the pate; thus it is translated "unshorn youth." Two of the Dog Warriors (Shino and Keno) are here pictured dressed as girls, and their names also suggest this. Takada Mamoru notes that while the illustration's title says that Chudai is playing hide-and-seek (*kakureasobi*) with the children, their poses suggest instead a game of tag (*ko o toro kotoro*). *Kanpon Hakkenden no sekai* (Chikuma Gakugei Bunko, 2005), 21ff. As Shinoda notes, Chudai is depicted so as to resemble Hotei (Ch. Budai), one of the Seven Lucky Gods. *Bakin no taimu*, 262ff. The border of this illustration may be meant to suggest his sack full of auspicious objects.

A Partial List of House Remedies for Sale by Kyokutei

- Having a blank page here at the front of the book, and being faced with the pressing necessity of making a living, I record here the following proclamation, commending it warmly to all you gentlemen far and wide:

Water of the Divine Lady—A Family Tradition: 100 coppers per packet. Passed down in the Author's family, this infusion is good for all ailments common to ladies, and is of especially immediate efficacy when taken just before and after birthing. Thanks to this, for five generations none of the women of our house have died young during difficult births. Its uses are explained in detail on the wrapper. It gives me great joy to report that, of late, its efficacy and superiority to all other such remedies on the market have been recognized by the many gentlemen who have sought to purchase it.

A Cure for the Monthybugs:[1] *64 coppers per packet, 32 coppers per half packet.* Does exceeding wonders when taken by ladies who suffer pain from the monthybugs during their monthly duty. Also good for cases where discharge does not resume after birthing. Effective for all menstrual irregularities.

---

1. "Monthybugs" is a word invented by the translator to render *tsugimushi*, an obscure term seemingly derived from *tsugi* (a women's colloquial term for menses) and *mushi* (bug).

Miraculous Bolus, Exactingly Prepared: Large packet [CONTAINS OVER TWO HUN-DRED PELLETS], price 2 shu; medium packet [CONTAINS 36 PELLETS], price 1 monme 5 bu; small packet [CONTAINS ELEVEN PELLETS], price 5 bu. [NOTE THAT I AM UNABLE TO SELL IN QUANTITIES SMALLER THAN THE 5-BU PACKET.] There are numerous Miraculous Boluses in the world, but many of them are of haphazard preparation: unless the buyer selects one whose medicinal ingredients are of the highest quality, then he may find he has bought something that is a Miraculous Bolus in name only, and not in its effects. In my preparation I follow the recipe in perfect circumspection, using the ingredients in their prescribed measure without regard to their cost. The result is a Miraculous Bolus with a hundred, nay, ten thousand times the efficacy of others with which it may be compared.

Acupuncture and moxibustion treatments administered: on the 7th and 27th of each month. Heretofore they have been administered on the 23rd, but henceforth this will be moved to the 27th. From four in the morning.[2] All who desire treatment are welcome. Absolutely no tokens of appreciation accepted. This is in response to the earnest wishes of the young ones: the master of these treatments, Doctor Kosaka, will be in attendance for examinations.

The above preparations distributed and treatments administered at: Takizawa Family Medicinal Preparations, across from the Yomo miso shop, on the south side of Naka-Sakashita, in Moto Iida-machi, Edo.

Also handled by: * Kawachiya Taisuke, bookseller, just inside Karamono-chō, to the south, Shinsaibashi-suji, Osaka * Izumiya Ichibei, bookseller, in front of Shiba Shinmei, Edo

- Our signs, notices, and literature all bear the seal consisting of a grass pavilion with the Heaven and Earth trigrams. Those lacking this seal pertain to counterfeit medicines.

---

2. Mid to late morning.

The Lives of the Eight Dogs of the Satomi of Southern Fusa

Book I

Assembled by the Master of the Crooked Pavilion in the Eastern Capital

Chapter I
Suemoto dies steadfast, leaving behind a moral;
A white dragon flies southward home, threading through the clouds

In pondering the deeds of Satomi Yoshizane, Major Assistant in the Governance Ministry and Minister of the Court[1]—who, when the might at arms of the Shogun at the Capital and the Vice-Shogun at Kamakura[2] had become weak and grasping and thus the realm become divided into warring states, escaped hardship to the shores of the Eastern Sea, opening up the land and establishing a foundation for his descendants unto the tenth

---

1. These titles (*jibu no taiyu . . . ason*) are honorary, quasi-hereditary, and all but meaningless—Yoshizane never had any role at court. They are perhaps best thought of as part of Yoshizane's formal name, but I elect to translate them here, as an emphasis on their vestigial meaning as titles seems appropriate. I do not always translate such name elements. Such titles became, or were incorporated into, samurai names over time, and where it seems that is the case with a character in the story, I leave the titles untranslated; where they seem meaningful, however, I translate them, as here. Most if not all such titles have relatively conventional translations in English, though sometimes I depart from these conventions. Some examples: Major Assistant: *dayū* (sometimes translated Senior Assistant Minister); Governance Ministry: *jibu* (sometimes translated Ministry of Ceremonial); Minister of the Court: *ason* (usually left untranslated); Lesser Assistant: *shōyū* (sometimes translated Junior Assistant Minister). Henceforth most titles will not be footnoted.

2. The Shogun governed from the Muromachi district of Kyoto at this time, while Kantō affairs were overseen from Kamakura by a Vice-Shogun (*fuku shōgun*), an ad hoc position also known as the *kubō* (which I translate as Overlord).

generation, Lords of Awa and Kazusa—we know that he was the firstborn of the first wife of Lord Satomi Suemoto of the Minamoto, Lesser Assistant in the Governance Ministry, who was eleven generations from Yoshiie, General of the Pacification Bureau and Minister of the Court, called Firstborn of the god Hachiman,[3] in the direct line of the Genji established by Emperor Seiwa.

In those days the Noble Lord Mochiuji of Kamakura,[4] possessed of great ambition to stand unrivalled, heeded not the remonstrances of the Chancellor Norizane,[5] indeed ignored all his duty to his descendants, and broke out in feud with the Muromachi Shogun Lord Yoshinori,[6] which brought the armies of the Capital down to pounce swiftly upon him; Yoshinori joined forces with Norizane, now fighting and now advancing, until he had entrapped Mochiuji, along with his sons, in the Hōkoku Temple in Kamakura, where he caused Mochiuji to slit his belly. This was on the tenth day of the second month of the eleventh year of the Eikyō era of the Emperor Go-Hanazono.[7] In this way Mochiuji's eldest son Yoshinari slew himself alongside his father, his corpse to remain there in Kamakura, but the two princes—Haruō, Mochiuji's second son, and Yasuō, his third—made a hard escape through the encirclement of enemy forces, taking refuge in Shimōsa, where they were welcomed by Ujitomo of the Yūki. Ujitomo honored them as his masters, and refused to follow orders from the Capital, treating the great armies of the Overseers [KIYOKATA AND MOCHITOMO[8]] as unworthy of reckoning.

Then those warriors who felt themselves in Mochiuji's debt, led by Satomi Suemoto—who so cleaved to righteousness that he would shun not even death—all unbidden gathered running to the castle of Yūki to defend it. Surrounded though they were by a great army, not once were they taken unaware, but withstood the siege for three years, from the spring of Eikyō

---

3. Minamoto no Yoshiie (1039–1106), who was afforded the title *chinjufu shōgun* (General of the Pacification Bureau); because war is the special province of the god Hachiman, Yoshiie's prowess also earned him the nickname Hachiman-tarō (first son of Hachiman).

4. Ashikaga Mochiuji (1398–1439), overlord of Kamakura.

5. *Shikken*, a term usually translated as "regent" when it refers to the Hōjō powerholders in the Kamakura regime, but here used as another term for *kanrei* (often translated as "shogunal deputy," but which I render as overseer). Uesugi Norizane (1410–1466) held the post during the breach between Yoshinori and Mochiuji.

6. Ashikaga Yoshinori (1394–1441; r. 1429–1441).

7. 1439.

8. Uesugi Kiyokata (d. 1446) of the Yamanouchi branch of the family and Uesugi Mochitomo (1416–1467) of the Ōgigayatsu branch. As noted in the introduction, the phrases rendered in bracketed small capitals in this sentence and elsewhere are presented by Bakin as interlinear notes, as if by a commentator on a classical text.

11 to the fourth month of Kakitsu 1.[9] Then, however, there having been no reinforcements from outside, their provisions and arrows were exhausted. "There is now nowhere to flee. To our deaths, then, all!" With that, the Yūki clan, and Satomi and his followers, flung open the castle gate and gave bloody battle, sending streaming the onrushing foe, but every man was shot down, the castle finally fell, and the two princes were taken captive, to be slain at Tarui in Mino. This was what is known as the Battle of Yūki.

At that time, Suemoto's firstborn son of his first wife, the Satomi lord Yoshizane, Major Assistant in the Governance Ministry, then known as the Satomi scion Matatarō, was in age not yet twenty, but already he outstripped his forebears in martial courage and ingenious strategy, and his talent was also great in the way of learning. These three years had he been by his father's side, never flinching at the hardships of the siege, and on this day too he was at the head of the troops, charging with a mind to cut down fourteen or fifteen mounted enemies, then to grapple with a worthy foe, and finally to die by an arrow.

His father Suemoto espied him from afar and hurriedly stopped him with a word, saying, "Ho, there, Yoshizane! 'The brave warrior never forgets that he may lose his head,'[10] and so it may seem there is good reason to die today, but nothing is more disloyal to ancestors than for father and son to be shot down together. With Kyōto and Kamakura mutual enemies, I have not suffered myself to serve two masters, but now my force is depleted and my strength spent, and today the castle falls. When a father dies for the sake of integrity, what shame can there be in a son fleeing and surviving for the sake of that father? Cut your way through! Make your escape, bide your time, and then restore our house! Now go!"

Suemoto urged him on, but Yoshizane would not listen. He bowed his head until it touched his saddle, and said, "Yes, sir. But to stand aside and see my father at extremity, and then to spinelessly run away—a child of three would not be forced to do this! And I!—I was born into a house of archers, and now at nineteen I have entered into the ways of brush and sword. I know somewhat of right and wrong, good and evil, the accomplishments and failings of the ancients. All I desire is to accompany you through the darkling lands to the Yellow Springs of the dead.[11] I have no wish to provoke laughter, stain my name, and shame my ancestors by failing to die when and where I should."

---

9. 1441.

10. An aphorism of Confucius, from the second half of the third book of *Mengzi* (J. *Mōshi*; probably from the Zhou era).

11. An underground realm of the dead found in both ancient Japanese myth (as Yomi) and Chinese legend (as Huangquan; J. Kōsen, written with characters later applied to Yomi).

Brave was his answer, steady his gaze, but his father sighed again and again at his words. "You have spoken well, Yoshizane. And yet, though you would hardly disobey your father's admonition if I commanded you to shave your head and change your robes for the black ones of a monk, still you refuse to bide your time and restore our house. This is unfilial. Do you not know? Lord Ashikaga Mochiuji has not been our lord for generation upon generation. In the beginning our ancestors followed our kinsman, the Minister of the Court Nitta Yoshisada,[12] and fought with merit in the Genkō and Kenmu eras.[13] But after that, the remnants of the Nitta, loyal retainers of the Southern Court though they were, began, in Meitoku 3,[14] as the Southern Emperor made his entrance into the Capital, to feel rain seeping through the boughs of the tree beneath which they had sought shelter. Little though it corresponded with his will, my late father [SATOMI ŌINOSUKE MOTOYOSHI] responded to the invitation of the Ashikaga house in Kamakura and entered the service of Lord Mitsukane [FATHER OF MOCHIUJI]. I served Mochiuji, and now I die for the young lords, his sons. I have fulfilled my aspiration. Is it not a warrior's part simply to die, rather to reason upon the rightness of these things? Scholarship, too, is useless. Now that I have said all this, if you do not heed my words, think not of me as your father, for you are not my son!"

Thus did he reprove his son with hurried words, until Yoshizane was overcome by their rectitude. His tears unbidden wet his horse's mane, like dew they dropped onto the grass below, to drench it tip and root like son and sire, the one to leave the other on the brink of life and death's vast sea now raising up like waves its battle-cries the foe pressed on. Again did Suemoto fix his gaze on him: "You must not lose this moment." He then shot a look at his old retainers, vassals for generations, Sugikura Kisonosuke Ujimoto and Horiuchi Kurando Sadayuki, whom he had already informed of his will, and they both as one straightened themselves and said, "We shall accompany you. Let us go." No sooner had they said this than Kisonosuke tugged at Yoshizane's horse's bridle and Kurando slapped the horse's rump to make it gallop. Westward they retreated. The men-at-arms left behind mourned in their ranks, thinking how when long ago Kusunoki sent his son Masatsura back from the post-station at Sakurai, it must have been like this—here was that very same steadfastness and righteousness of spirit.[15]

---

12. 1301–1338.

13. Genkō: 1331–1334; Kenmu: 1334–1336.

14. 1392.

15. Kusunoki Masashige fought alongside Nitta Yoshisada in support of Emperor Go-Daigo against Ashikaga Takauji. Masashige perished in the Battle of Minatogawa (1336), when Go-Daigo insisted he meet Takauji's forces in an attempt to forestall being driven out of the capital. Masashige

For a time Suemoto watched after his son as he fled. Then, drawing in his reins and bringing his mount around, he said, "Ah, now is my heart at ease. Come then, let us hasten to our ends." His remaining men—they numbered less than ten—he arrayed in a crane-wings formation, and with not so much as a bow they plunged into the massive army pressing down upon them. A brave general has no weak soldiers—master and man, not one among them failed to strike down two or three mounted foemen. Their whole desire was to allow Yoshizane to make good his flight, and with nothing else in mind, they refused to allow that great host, more than their eyes could meet, to advance a single pace; climbing over the corpses of their erstwhile allies, they grappled with the enemy, exchanged thrusts with them, until not only Suemoto the general but his eight mounted followers too were each struck down amidst the moiling armies, as if laying their heads down upon the same pillow; their blood dyed the grasses along the meadow paths, their corpses scattered like counting sticks, to be buried in the dust kicked up by horses' hooves. But their fame would never corrode—theirs was a violent and valiant end, to be spoken of even unto the Capital.

At this time Satomi Yoshizane, only barely come of age, had, led by Sugikura and Horiuchi, retreated nearly a mile. Ever he was thinking, "But what has become of my father? I cannot bear not knowing," and many times did he halt his horse and look back—and now the battle cries in that direction, the shouts of the archers, became cacaphonous, and he knew that the castle had fallen. A raging fire scorched the heavens, and before he had finished crying out, he had gathered in the reins and would have ridden back, if from either side his two senior vassals had not grasped his horse's bit. They would not let him move.

"This must not be! Have you gone mad? Did you not hear His Lordship's teaching? If you were to return to that fallen castle now, you would forfeit your life. You would be as the summer moth in the ancients' poem, extinguishing his life vainly in the flame.[16] This is unbecoming to you, who have day in and day out intoned the ancients' words of wisdom that 'Lo, great

---

sent his son Masatsura away on the eve of what he knew would be a losing battle. The famous scene of their parting is found in book 16 of the late fourteenth-century war chronicle *Taiheiki*.

16. It is not clear what poem is meant here. Summer insects are used as an image of ephemerality in several *waka* (Tokuda suggests #178 in *Eikyū hyakushu* [1117], by Minamoto no Toshiyori [1055–1129]). But the distinctive phrase *natsumushi no himushi* (summer insects, fire insects) seems to come from a poem in the biography of the Emperor Nintoku in the Nara-era official history of Japan *Nihon shoki* (720); this poem, however, does not relate them to ephemerality.

faith is as no faith, great filial piety is as no piety at all.'[17] For exalted and base alike, there is but one Way of loyalty and filial piety, so how come you to be lost upon it now? Come with us."

This filial son's heart was as confused as that of the steed at which they pulled, and grief and frustration made his voice harsh: "Release me, Sadayuki! Detain me not, Ujimoto! Your remonstrances accord with my father's will, true, but were I to endure this now, I would be unworthy to be called a son. Let me go, let me go!" He brandished his riding crop, struck and stormed, but those two loyal retainers alike kept their metal-like, stone-like fists shut tight as the lid of the proverbial gemmed comb box,[18] and under the rain of blows they kept leading the horse, past Umade, past Kurakake, past Yanagisaka, the smoke growing ever more distant behind them, until at the edge of a cypress grove, safe from the flames, they were chased down by twenty riders from the Kamakura forces, flush with their victory.

These called out to them, "What a warlike appearance you present—so fleet your retreat! Scarlet-laced armor, a five-layer neckguard helmet with a sickle-blade ornament, silver mirror in the center gleaming, emblazoned with the black-bar crest—unless our eyes deceive us, one of you is a general. Turn around, you filthy lot!"

Without the least hesitation, Yoshizane rejoined, "Will you not hold your tongues, you common soldiers? We run, but not from fear of any enemy—and so nothing keeps us from turning around!" And with that, he brought round his mount, drew his sword and brandished it, and advanced.

Sugikura and Horiuchi, eager to keep their general from being struck, lined up to block their opponents' arrows, administering felling thrusts with their spears. But Yoshizane was equally eager to keep his old vassals from being struck, and he urged his horse forward; thus fought the three of them, master and men, crossing as they passed on, circling as they came back, joining into the crane-wings formation, tight together in the fish-scales formation—driving westward, drifting eastward, striking northward, and running southward, never letting their horses' hooves fall still. They were all students of the Way of War, and knew the tradition of the Three Strategies and the Law of the Eight Deployments;[19] when once the enemy

---

17. The source for this formulation has not been determined, although Tokuda (p. 31) notes that it seems related to a passage in chapter 18 of the Han-era book of rites *Liji* (J. *Raiki*): "Great fidelity is not a matter of promises."

18. *Tamakushige* (gemmed comb box) is here used as a pillow word (*makurakotoba*, a conventional poetic epithet), for the pun on *futa* (lid/two, referring to the two retainers).

19. The Three Strategies is a reference to *San lue* (J. *Sanryaku*), a Han-era Chinese military work. The Eight Deployments refers to Chinese military strategies set forth in various works.

thought they were before them, they were suddenly behind; they charged and struck, they used every secret skill, until finally the foe, numerous though they were, fell into confusion and retreated before the protean whirlwind of their blades.

Their assailants gone, Sugikura and Horiuchi remonstrated with their lord, and little by little they pressed their retreat, dropping occasional lone pursuers with long bowshots, now chasing, now being chased, through over-grown glades; some seven or eight miles onward they saw him, until finally the sun had set and the round moon of the sixteenth night had risen.

And now they were no longer pursued by enemies: master and men had wondrously escaped the tiger's maw. That night they sought lodging in a cottage, and in the morning as a parting gift they left their horses and armor with the owner—they disguised themselves, hid their faces deep beneath sedge hats, and though east and west all was enemy territory they were not without hope—they hastened along the Sagami Road, and on the third day they reached the inlet of Yatori, in Miura. From the beginning their packs had contained no provisions, and now their travel-money was gone, too; they had become, master and men, fugitives, and they were sore hungry and tired.

Yoshizane and Sugikura Kisonosuke Ujimoto sat themselves on the root of a pine and waited for Horiuchi Kurando Sadayuki, who had lagged far behind. They wished to cross to the province of Awa, but they were trapped like the proverbial fish in a wheel-rut.[20] As far as the eye could see out of the inlet stretched the deep blue sea, white gulls sleeping on the gentle billows; it was the fourth month, the time of summer haze, through which they could almost see, as they pointed, the sawtoothed ridge of Mount Nokogiri,[21] its blue-green cliffs looming ominously as if chipped out by a chisel or carved with a blade; the long, serrated coastline along which they must take their journey was enough to break their hearts, and the willows in the rainy fishing villages and the vesper bells of the distant temples were enough to kindle melancholy. They should not be in these straits, but hurry as they might to cross, not a single boat could they find.

Sugikura Kisonosuke Ujimoto beckoned to some children of the fisherfolk, who were taking in dried fish at the corner of a thatched hut, and spoke to them plainly. "You, there. I wish to ask you something. Are there no

---

20. An expression for dire straits, as a fish trapped in a puddle made by a cartwheel would have little room to swim, and no future as the water evaporates. The locus classicus is chapter 26 of the Warring States-era Daoist classic *Zhuangzi* (J. *Sōshi*).

21. *Nokogiri* means "saw." The original puns on this name, describing the mountain as looking freshly sawed.

boats, that we might cross over? We have come strangers to this cove, and are desperately hungry. If you have anything, please give it to my lord—never mind us."

Among the children was an ill-natured boy of fourteen or fifteen. His bangs hung down like a red yak's tail over a face blackened by the briny wind, and he would not brush them aside; he gave a wrenching sniffle as he stepped forward. "You speak like a fine rogue! All the boats were borrowed for the battle—we haven't even enough to go fishing in. Who would take you across? And food, in this world bitterer than the brine we boil at this bay? We have none for you. Why should we relieve the hunger of strangers, when we cannot even fill our own bellies? If your spleen is so unbearably out of joint—eat this!" And with a gloating leer he picked up a clod of earth and made as if to throw it. Ujimoto nimbly dodged, and the clod flew past him straight at the chest of Yoshizane, sitting on the pine-root. Unflappable, Yoshizane leaned his body to the left and caught the clod with his right hand.

Faced with the child's odious action, Ujimoto could not restrain himself. His eyes bulged and his voice rose as he cried, "Stupid villain! We are on a journey, that is why we begged you for a bowl of rice. And if you have none you might say so—but to throw things at us instead! Rudeness has its limits! And I shall teach them to you, if I have to split open that jaw of yours!" Enraged, Ujimoto laid his hand on the grip of his sword and made as if to dash forward and strike, but Yoshizane suddenly stopped him with a word.

"Kisonosuke, you do not act your age. The fleetest of steeds ages and lags behind the slowest; the phoenix in its extremity may be tortured by an ant. Yesterday was yesterday, today is today—have you forgotten that we have no one now to depend on? These people are unworthy of your enmity. And think on this: soil is the foundation of a country. May this be a sign that as I am about to cross over into Awa now, heaven will give unto me that country? If we see this boy as rude, then we must endure hating him, but if we take this as a good omen, then is he not a thing to be rejoiced over? How well do this day's events resemble the old story of Duke Wen of Jin at Wulu [A TOPONYM IN THE COUNTRY OF CAO]—we should bless them indeed."[22]

---

22. According to the Warring States–era historical commentary *Zuozhuan* (J. *Saden*), Zhong-er, the future Duke Wen (697–628 BCE), while traveling near Wulu in Wei (not Cao), asked a local man for food and was given a clod of dirt. Zhong-er wanted to beat the man, but his adviser convinced him to take the gesture as a sign he would soon come into possession of land. The story is found in the chapter of *Zuozhuan* dealing with Duke Xi of Lu.

Thus congratulating himself, Yoshizane raised the clod heavenward thrice and then put it away in his bosom. Ujimoto's eyes were opened, and he removed his hand from his sword-grip—letting go his anger, he gave his lord joy on his firm and certain future, while the fisherfolk children clapped their hands and scoffed.

Just then clouds billowed up over strand and hill, and the face of the sea abruptly darkened, the waters rose like dust attracted by a magnet, the wind fell on them in gusts, rain poured down thicker than the bamboo grass at Tomooka,[23] lightning flashed without pause, thunder roared as if to strike them down—the children were thrown into a tizzy, and ran each back to his own hut, locking the doors from within, to open to no knock. Yoshizane and his man were thus left without eaves to shelter under; they stood there under the beach pine, holding their sedge-hats over their heads.

The wind and rain grew fiercer, the sky alternated between darkness and light, waves surged and broke, broke and then rose again upon themselves, and in the midst of them, enwrapped in the waves and whirling, winging clouds, they saw something, though its brilliance nearly overpowered them: suddenly there appeared a white dragon, radiating light, roiling the waves, flying away southward. After a time, the rain cleared and the clouds calmed; the sun, though sinking, still lingered enough on the sea to dye brightly its waves; droplets ran along the pine boughs, to be blown clear by the wind, scattered like jewels onto the gravelly sand, into which they sank. Mountains could be seen again in the distance, their verdure deep, their peaks pale and not yet dry. But even the most astounding scenes, views impossible to tire of, may fail to distract the heart of one in distress. Ujimoto wiped the spray from Yoshizane's silks, every moment expecting Sadayuki, who had not yet joined them.

Yoshizane indicated the face of the waters and spoke. "A moment ago, when the rain was at its most violent, did you not see, Kisonosuke, between the mounting waves, a white dragon ascending to the sky from yonder rock, whirling and winging among the cloudbanks?"

At this query Kisonosuke stood straight on the tips of his toes and said, "I knew it not for a dragon, but I did glimpse a gleam as of scales on what seemed to me the thigh of some strange thing."

Yoshizane nodded. "Then thus it was. I saw only its tail and foot. O, how I resent and regret that I did not see it entire! Dragons are divine creatures,

---

23. Tomooka was a village associated in several older works (including the tenth-century glossary *Wamyōshō*) with thick stands of bamboo grass. Its exact location is unknown, although it is thought to have been in or near Nagaoka.

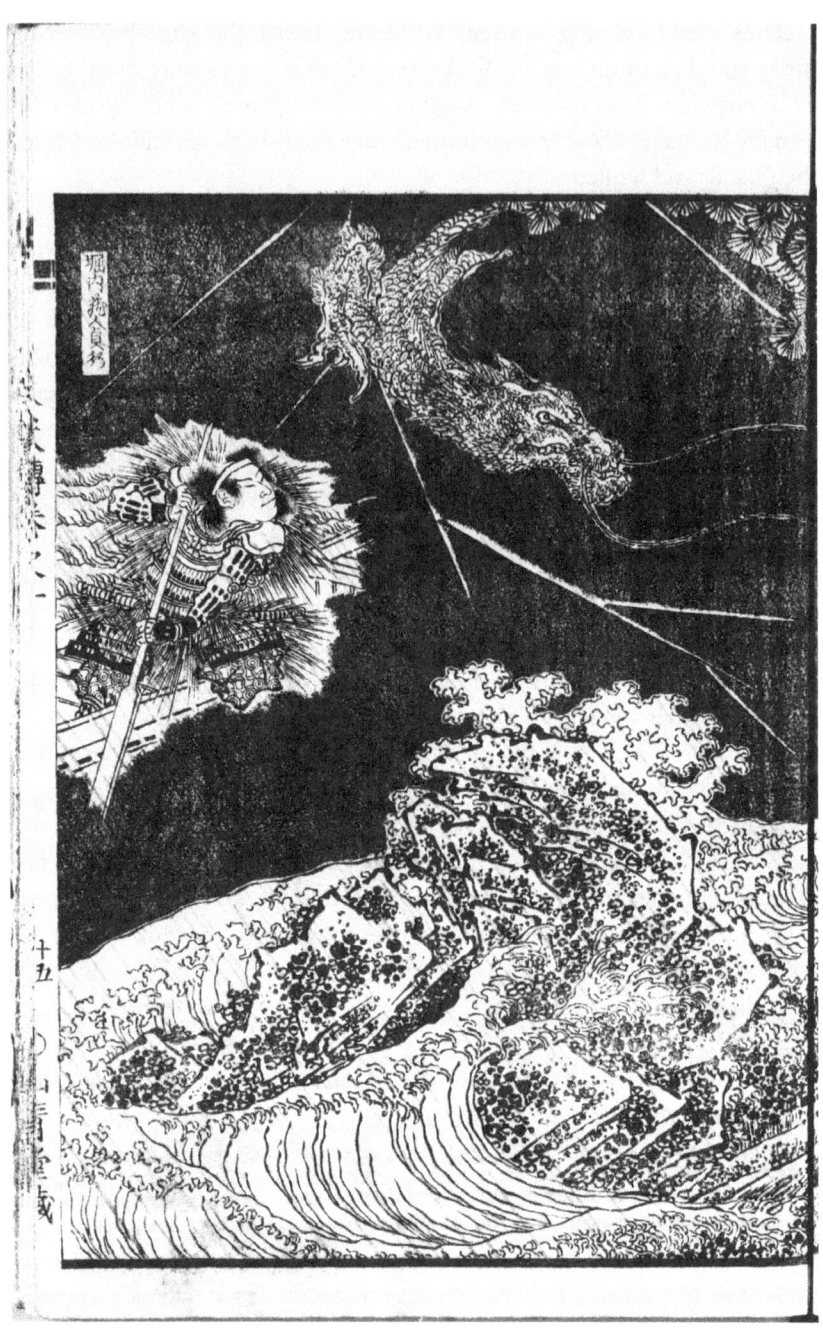

Caption: Yoshizane sees a white dragon at Miura.
Figures: Satomi Yoshizane [*far right*]. Sugikura Kisonosuke Ujimoto [*crouching by Yoshizane*]. Horiuchi Kurando Sadayuki [*far left*].

里見よし實

義実
三浦
を見る

capable by their nature of limitless transformations. The ancients spoke of dragons awaiting the first day of summer and marking the seasonal divide by bringing rain. They named such the Dragon of Division.[24] It is now the time in question. Now again, dragons are creatures of spirit, capable of appearing bright as if looming near, or dim as if receding into hidden depths. Dragons are the lords of all scaled creatures.[25] This is why, when the Duke of Zhou put in order the *Classic of Changes*,[26] he likened dragons unto holy men. Notwithstanding which, dragons have desires, making them inferior to holy men, who have none. That being so, men can keep them, or ride them, or even kill them. There are now none to whom such skills have come down, though. Now again, in Buddhist teaching there is the Dragon King Sutra.[27] In general he who prays for rain must needs intone this first. In the Lotus Sutra,[28] too, in the chapter on Devadatta, we find the story of how the eight-year-old dragon girl achieved buddhahood. One may say this is merely a case of the Buddha's expedient means, but there are those who have prayed and received signs. Therefore it is said that dragons are named Rainfashioner, or alternatively Rainmaster.

"When the dragon's form is spoken of, it is said they have horns like a deer's on heads like a horse's or camel's. Their eyes are like a demon's, while their necks are like snakes. Their bellies are like sea serpents', while their scales are like fishes'. They have claws like a falcon's on paws like a tiger's, and their ears are like oxen's. This is known as the Nine Resemblances in their Three Segments. Also, their gems are in their cheeks. They hear with their horns. At the base of their throats is a place about a foot across named the Inverse Scales: if something hits them here they are invariably angered. This is why a sovereign's anger is known as the Inverse Scales.[29] At a male dragon's cry, the wind blows up, while at a female dragon's cry the wind blows down. Their voices sound like the blowing of flutes, while their singing sounds like the clanking of iron tubs. They neither move in packs nor rest in flocks. When they come together they form a body, and when they

---

24. From the ninth chapter of *Wu zazu* (J. *Gozasso*), a Ming-era miscellany compiled by Xie Zhaozhe (1567–1624). I am particularly indebted to Tokuda's annotations of Yoshizane's discourse on dragons. For this discourse, Bakin is synthesizing information found in several Chinese texts; I will only footnote the first borrowing from each.

25. From *Longjing*. See note 7 of the *kanbun* preface to this volume.

26. The Zhou-era divination text *Yijing* (commonly known by the older romanization I Ching, J. *Ekikyō*), formerly attributed to the Duke of Zhou.

27. *Ryūōkyō*, the full title of which is *Dragon King of the Sea Sutra* (Skt. *Sāgaranāgarāja-paripṛcchā-sūtra*; Ch. *Hai longwang jing*; J. *Kairyūōkyō*).

28. *Hokekyō* (Ch. *Fahua jing*, Skt. *Saddharma Puṇḍarīka Sūtra*).

29. From chapter 23 of the Warring States–era Legalist text *Han Feizi* (J. *Kan Bishi*).

separate they form patterns. They ride the vapors and are nourished by *yin* and *yang*; at times they are bright and at times they are obscure.[30] When they make themselves large they roam the universe; when they make themselves small they can hide in a rock the size of a man's fist.[31] At the vernal equinox they ascend to the heavens, and at the autumnal equinox they enter abysses; they greet summer by rending the clouds and flourishing their scales. This is in order to enjoy the season. When winter comes they immerse themselves in mud, where they coil up in secret and do not emerge. This is in order to avoid harm.

"Dragons come in a great many varieties. There are the Flying Dragon, the Answering Dragon,[32] the Sea-Serpent Dragon, the First Dragon, the Yellow Dragon, the Green Dragon, the Red Dragon, the White Dragon, the Original Dragon,[33] and the Black Dragon. When the White Dragon exhales, the expectorate enters the ground and becomes gold; when the Purple Dragon drools, the spittle is clear like a jewel. The spongilla is dragon's seed[34]—the barbarians trade in it and use it in medicine. Those with scales are Sea-Serpent Dragons. Those with wings are Answering Dragons. Those with horns are called Horned Dragons, or Antlered Dragons. Those without horns are called Hornless Dragons, or Antlerless Dragons. The Verdant Dragon has seven houses. The Mottled Dragon is nine-hued. That which can see for a hundred leagues is named the Black-Steed Dragon; that which is self-sufficient in comfort and joy is named the Luck Dragon. That which is not thus self-sufficient is the Poor-Luck Dragon, while that which does harm is the Evil Dragon, and that which kills people is the Poison Dragon. That which suffers to give rain—this is the Raindropping Dragon, and rain that has been caused to fall by an ailing dragon is always putrid. A dragon that has not yet ascended to the heavens is what the *Classic of Changes* calls a Coiled Dragon. The Coiled Dragon is forty feet in length and greenish-black in color, with red horizontal stripes patterned like brocade. The Fire Dragon has a height of seven feet and is a rich red in color, and its flame is as that of many bonfires. Then there are the Foolish Dragon and the Lazy Dragon.

---

30. In Daoist cosmology, *yin* and *yang* (J. *in* and *yō*) are opposite and complementary forces that shape existence. *Yin* is associated with darkness, concavity, moisture, the feminine, etc., while *yang* is associated with brightness, convexity, dryness, the masculine, etc.

31. From chapter 21 of the late-Yuan or early-Ming vernacular novel *Sanguo yanyi* (J. *Sangoku engi*, commonly known in English as *The Romance of the Three Kingdoms*).

32. Discussed in the Han-era encyclopedia *Shanhai jing* (J. *Sankaikyō*), though its curious name is not explained. Likewise, the names of the First Dragon and the Original Dragon are obscure in their significance.

33. The *genryū*, unidentified.

34. From the Ming-era encyclopedia *Qianqueju leishu* (J. *Senkakukyo ruisho*), by Chen Renxi.

"The dragon is lascivious by nature, and there is nothing with which it will not couple. If it consorts with an ox it will bear a ziraph;[35] cross it with a pig and it will bear an oliphant;[36] cross it with a horse and it will bear a destrier or dragon-steed. There is also the story of the dragon that bore nine children. The first-born was called the *pulao*;[37] it likes to cry out. The dragon-heads on bells are patterned after this. The second-born was called the *qiuniu*; it likes things that make noise. It is attached as a decoration to zithers and drums. The third-born was called the *chiwu*; it likes to drink. It is painted on goblets, cups, and other drinking vessels. The fourth-born was called the *chaofeng*; it likes steep, high places. Rooftiles on halls, towers, pagodas, and pavilions are patterned after this. The fifth-born was called the *jingzi*; it likes killing. It is attached as a decoration to swords. The sixth-born was called the *fuxi*; it likes the literary. Dragon-script, stamp-handles, and the flying dragons drawn beneath the God of Literature constellation are all this. The seventh-born was called the *bian*; it likes legal proceedings. The eighth-born was called the *suanni*; that is, a lion. It likes sitting, it is said, and certain chairs and formal seats are patterned after it. The ninth-born was called the *baxia*; it likes to bear weight. The demon-faces seen on the legs of cauldrons and braziers, or on the pedestals of various things, are this. There are other children, besides. It is said that the *xianzhang* likes captivity; the *taotie* likes water; the *xiyi* likes stenches; the *manquan* likes wind and rain; the *lihu* likes colorful patterns; the *jinni* likes smoke; the *jiaotu* likes having its mouth closed; the *xiaoxie* likes to stand in high places; the *aoyu* likes fire; and the *jinwu* likes not to sleep. These are all varieties of dragon.

"Yea, great is the virtue of the dragon. In terms of the *Classic of Changes*, it is of the Way of Force. In terms of material things, it is holiness. In the multiplicity of its variations it is perhaps as with men, among whom there are both the great and wise and the base and foolish, Sons of Heaven and commoners. By authority of its virtue, the dragon causes the hundred beasts to submit themselves to it; by authority of his virtue, the Son of Heaven leads his hundred officials. For this reason the Son of Heaven has his Dragon Robes. The Son of Heaven's face is lauded as a Dragonly Countenance, and

---

35. A *qilin* (J. *kirin*). In modern Japanese (as in Ming-era China), this word has come to refer to a giraffe; it is often translated into English as "unicorn," as a magical beast that is often (but not always) depicted with one horn. "Ziraph" is an archaic spelling of "giraffe" that seems to fit the text's nod toward zoological taxonomy.

36. The unusual spelling here reflects the fact that Bakin glosses the character for elephant with both the familiar *zō* and the archaic *kisa*.

37. The names of this and the next several dragons discussed do not lend themselves to translation, as the characters have little if any relation to the descriptions attached to them.

his physical form is praised as a Dragonly Body, while when he is angered it is known as the Inverse Scales. All of these expressions refer to dragons, whose virtues are innumerable.

"Just now, a white dragon was proceeding southward. White is the color of the Genji.[38] South is Awa and Kazusa. Awa and Kazusa are the extremity of the Emperor's realm. I saw the tail of the dragon; I did not see its head. I shall rule only that land, nothing more. You saw the dragon's thigh: this means you are to be my minister, as dear to me as my own limbs. So think you not?"

As Yoshizane spoke—in such earnest, with reference to writings and ancient matters both Japanese and Chinese—Ujimoto was impressed with his perspicacity and sagacity, which extended even unto matters of his own destiny. "In this age most men born into martial houses merely pride themselves on having the courage of the common man, and rare is he who is conversant with military treatises and tactics—and yet you, at your tender age, seem to have read books unseen by men. Or, if not that, then you are truly the good general, made by heaven to be well-versed in all things. Nothing can surpass the joy I feel at my life having been spared until today, not even the resentment that I can now say I first felt at not having died at Yūki. And yet, though our future course seems so assured as the sun sets, shall that sun not also rise on us still uselessly tarrying in this cove? For, though I mean to accompany you to Awa, we have no boat. The sky may have cleared, but the night is dark, and as we wait on the road, yearning for moonlight, we shall grow only more irritated in our hearts. The sea-road is precisely what we are helpless to travel, think you not? I find it exceedingly suspicious that Horiuchi Sadayuki, lagging behind, has not yet come to us. Strangers flock to wealth, while even intimates flee from poverty. The sincerity of men is not constant—I fear he made his escape along the way," he said, brow furrowed.

Yoshizane's mouth curved into a smile. "Never fear, Kisonosuke. Did not His Eminence my father, the head of our house, choose you and him from among all his many vassals, old and young, to be my companions, because of your lofty aspirations, above those of the common run of men? I myself know Sadayuki's quality: he is not one to discard his lord and run and hide in time of danger. Let us wait here a while. The moon must rise soon." So sheaves of words untroubled did he reap from heart whose depths exceeded the ocean whence the moon of the eighteenth night emerged as bright as

---

38. As the narration establishes at the beginning of the chapter, Yoshizane is a descendant of the Genji (or Minamoto) line.

whitecaps in the inlet—even thus must shine, with gold and jewels gathered and paved, the palace of the Dragon King, they thought, master and man, as they shaded their eyes with their hands and left in spite of themselves the shade of the trees to draw closer to the waves' brink.

There they saw a swift boat, rowing its way toward them from the cape. As they gazed, wondering if it would come their way, it approached with bowshot speed, until they could hear someone aboard singing loudly an ancient song: "*She gave her word, and so/the cottage on the strand/thatched with leaves of deutzia/she visits again and again,/the Dragon-Palace Princess*" [FROM THE HOUSE COLLECTION OF NAKAMASA].[39] The boatman could hardly have understood what he sang, they thought as he rowed closer. Then the singer flung the painter onto the sand and leapt out of the boat, and they saw it was Horiuchi Sadayuki.

"How comes this to be?" Master and man with questioning faces resumed their seats beneath the trees, as Sadayuki raked together fallen pine needles and knelt.

"Since we set foot upon the Sagami road I had heard, though vaguely, of the lack of a convenient means of crossing the sea, and so I rushed ahead by a short cut and inquired at this rush hut and that for a way across, but could not produce a boat. I went here and there until finally I made for the cape, where I was able to borrow a fisherman's vessel. But then, thinking you might be hungry, I was having a meal cooked, when the thunder and rain began to rage, and I was forced to waste the day there. Thus I come late to you. As I had mentioned none of this to you before, no doubt you were growing suspicious of me."

Yoshizane barely let him finish before exclaiming in admiration, "You could hardly have told us. Neither I nor Kisonosuke had given the slightest thought to whether we might find a boat here. How indeed could we cross to Awa tonight, were it not for you, Kurando, and your matchless astuteness?"

Ujimoto rubbed his forehead and smiled, saying, "Is there, then, such a clear distinction between those of great talent and those of little? Indeed, milord Kurando, I had begun to have my doubts. You and your deep foresight had run into the treacherous shoals of my heart, and I spoke ill of you."

Sadayuki held his belly and laughed—as did Yoshizane, thinking that even thus should be the friendship of men-at-arms, as united as a warrior's

---

39. *Nakamasa kashū*, a collection of poems by Minamoto no Nakamasa, a Heian-era poet who lived from the eleventh to twelfth centuries. The poem also appears as #12915 in *Fuboku wakashō*, ca. 1310.

two swords. Yoshizane turned to Kurando Sadayuki and said, "While I was waiting for you here, unable to cross, I was vouchsafed the gift of a clod of earth. I also saw an auspicious harbinger: a white dragon. I will tell you about them both on the boat."

The boatman must have heard this, for he raised his hand to beckon them, saying, "The moon is fair, and so is the wind. Quickly, now, sirs, come aboard." The three of them, master and men, acceded to his urgings and climbed aboard the little unreinforced boat, rocking it as they did. The boatman reeled in the painter and took up his scull to row them across the foam to Awa.

Chapter II

A gallant looses an arrow and kills a white horse;
A craven usurps two districts and approaches the scarlet gate

Originally, Awa was the southern extremity of the province of Fusa. In days of yore there was no distinction made between Upper and Lower Fusa, but later it was divided, and the two halves were named Kazusa (Upper Fusa) and Shimōsa (Lower Fusa).[1] The land was wide, with many mulberry trees, and as it was well suited to the raising of silkworms, silk tassels were given as tribute to the sovereign, and the land came to be called after them.[2] Now, Fusa's southern extremity was but sparsely populated, so people from the province of Awa in the Southern Sea Circuit were moved there, so that finally this area came to be called Awa.[3]

---

1. Bakin's readers would have been familiar with the province names Kazusa and Shimōsa, as they were part of the province system codified under the Ritsuryō laws of the seventh and eighth centuries. The division of Fusa into Kazusa (or Kamitsufusa) and Shimōsa (Shimofusa, or Shimotsu-fusa) took place in the year 534, according to the chronicle *Kogo shūi* (compiled 807). Awa was formally divided from Kazusa in 718. Upper Fusa (Kazusa) was to the south of Lower Fusa (Shimōsa). Today Awa and Kazusa are contained within Chiba Prefecture, while Shimōsa is split between the prefectures of Chiba, Ibaraki, Saitama, and Tokyo. While the provincial names are now archaic, the name of the Bōsō Peninsula occupied by Chiba Prefecture combines the second characters of the names Kazusa and Awa.

2. The word *fusa* means silk tassel.

3. The Southern Sea Circuit (*Nankaidō*) was a region that encompassed the island of Shikoku and part of the Kii Peninsula; Awa was a province occupying the eastern part of Shikoku. The Awa on Shikoku is written with different characters from that on the Bōsō Peninsula.

The "water gate" or harbor mentioned in the record of the Emperor Keikō in the *Chronicles of Japan* refers to this.[4]

Awa comprised a mere four districts, called Heguri, Nagasa, Awa, and Asahina. Long ago, in the Nin'an and Jishō eras,[5] during the ascendency of the house of Taira, there were three warriors there, whose names are given in the *Mirror of the East*[6] as Maro Gorō Nobutoshi of Mikuriya, Anzai Saburō Kagemori, and Tōjō Shichirō Akinori. In the eighth month of the third year of Jishō,[7] in the autumn, the Noble Lord Yoritomo of the Minamoto was defeated in battle at Mount Ishibashi and made his way to Awa, and at this time the aforementioned warriors were the first to join his following: Anzai Saburō Kagemori served as his guide, while Nobutoshi of the Maro and Tōjō Akinori fêted him, manifesting their matchless aspirations. And so, once the Minamoto clan had consolidated their rule, those men were given the four districts of Awa to share among themselves. Their descendants for ten or more generations inherited them, not losing their home territories even as the realm passed into the hands of the Hōjō, and then began the time of the Ashikaga house.[8] Kagemori's grandson in the twelfth generation, Anzai Saburōdayū Kagetsura, was in the castle of Tateyama, in the district of Awa. Kogorōbei Nobutoki of the Maro, descendant of Nobutoshi, was in the castle of Hiratate, in the district of Asahina. And Jin'yo Nagasanosuke Mitsuhiro, descended from Akinori in the Tōjō lineage of the district of Nagasa, dwelt in the castle of Takita in the district of Heguri. All three were ancient houses, but Jin'yo joined under himself the Tōjō territories, so that he was lord of half the province of Awa, ruling the two districts of Nagasa and Heguri, having retainers and followers not a few, and even more in the way of men, horses, and equipment: nothing did he lack, so that he treated Anzai and Maro as beneath him, and insisted on calling himself the Provincial Lord.

---

4. The phrase in question (*suimon*, also glossed as *minato*) occurs in the entry for the tenth month of the fifty-third year of the reign of the Emperor Keikō (123 CE) in *Nihon shoki*, in which the emperor is described as crossing by sea into the Awa no minato from the province of Kazusa. For centuries there has been debate over whether this refers to the harbor at Tateyama or to the straits between the Miura and Bōsō peninsulas, and Bakin's phrasing here leaves the question open.

5. 1166–69 and 1177–81, respectively.

6. *Azuma kagami*, a late Kamakura-era chronicle of the Kamakura shogunate.

7. 1179.

8. Minamoto Yoritomo established a shogunate based in Kamakura after defeating the Taira in 1185. His wife Masako was a daughter of the Hōjō, a powerful family that had supported Yoritomo during his upbringing, and members of this family controlled the shogunate from the early thirteenth century to its fall in 1333. The Ashikaga family overthrew the Hōjō-controlled Kamakura shogunate in 1333, establishing their own shogunate based in the Muromachi district of Kyoto, which lasted until 1573.

At this time Mitsuhiro was lifted up in the pride of his heart, and began to indulge in sensuality and to lose himself in drink, in the thirst for which he was insatiable. Among his many concubines and consorts he particularly favored a voluptuous voluptuary named Tamazusa, and he began to consult her before deciding on matters of rewards and punishments both within and without the household; those who bribed Tamazusa were rewarded, though they be guilty, while those who failed to flatter found no employ, serviceable though they be. Thenceforth the house became disordered, as goodly retainers retreated and sycophants gained the day.

Among them there was one, a certain Yamashita Sakuzaemon Sadakane. His father was in charge of a feed depot in Aohama, dying peacefully in that position, but Sadakane was like his father in neither personality nor appearance. He was fair in complexion, with fine eyebrows, prominent nose, and red lips, and his speech was gentle to the ear. Hearing of him, Mitsuhiro summoned him and made him one of his attendants. Truly, when an audience with a woman is the channel to power, it is an aid to the sycophant. Sakuzaemon Sadakane conducted himself with humility toward those above him, while exercising his formidable cleverness in perversion upon those beneath; he was a villain seeking that which was advantageous to his glory, and he never failed to flatter and fawn on Tamazusa. That which he desired was given him, with no regard to its price, so steady was his rise, so eloquently did he please his lord. He held drinking parties, he promoted sensual pleasures, and through it all he was in secret correspondence with Tamazusa, constantly engaging in degraded behavior—but Mitsuhiro knew not a whit of it. Before long he had placed Sadakane above all his senior retainers and entrusted to him and him alone authority over all rewards and punishments, great and small, throughout the fief—it was as if Yamashita had no lord at all.

In this way those with noble qualities and aspirations were driven into retreat, unable to remonstrate with their lord, while those possessed of a drive to advance themselves willingly flattered Sadakane, cleaning the proverbial dust out of his beard for him. A cohort was formed to forestall criticism while expounding unto him profit and loss, and to revise ancient laws in order to increase the people's tribute burden and redouble their allotted duties, all without a second thought for the people's resentment. Truly was this Yamashita Sadakane an An Lushan to the Jin'yo house![9] When he reported for duty he did so riding on a white horse, while bystanders watched

---

9. An Lushan was a Tang-era military leader who rose from humble origins among border people to a position of prominence at the court of the Emperor Xuanzong, and became a particular

from averted eyes; secretly the people saddled this horse with the nickname of the Paper-Mulberry-White Man-Eater.[10] Those who happened to meet them on the road usually avoided them, hiding themselves.

Now, near Takita, in a village called Aomiko, there lived a peasant known as Bokuhei of Somaki. He was a powerful man, strong of body (as was the way of men in the Warring States era, he was skilled in combat both with weapons and without) and fierce of heart, fearless of death when facing hardship, ready to stand himself up as a gallant man, heedless of authority and solicitous of the weak. He saw the disorder of the house of Jin'yo and the great suffering of the people, and he saw that it was all the doing of Yamashita Sakuzaemon, and when he could stand it no longer he summoned in secret his friend Mukuzō of Susaki, who was every whit his match, and said, "How think you? This Paper-Mulberry-White Man-Eater has free rein to abuse the people—he causes more harm to the fields than the leaf-hopper—he slaughters innocents just like a plague-god. How are we to support our wives and children here, with him as he is? The people obey the burdensome laws because they all count their lives as precious. But what have we to fear from any law or divine wrath, in the face of this freezing and starvation and year-in, year-out fleecing? Would it not after all be much more pleasant for you and I to abandon all thought of ourselves, kill the Man-Eater, and thus relieve the multitude of their suffering?"

Mukuzō needed no convincing. He nodded: "Bravely spoken! I myself have thought along these lines—how could I not? And yet his forces are greater than those of the Lord of the Province—in all his goings-out and comings-in he is accompanied by dozens of men. Shall we raise our hand against him or let sleeping dogs lie? The hearts of men are not to be trusted—a smile may conceal a dagger—and I have kept my silence to this day, but now you all unexpectedly have revealed to me the secrets of your heart, and I find we share the same aspirations—a greater aid even than wings. However, we shall lose our lives in vain if we plan this thing in the open. I wonder if we might not best achieve our aims by waiting for a day when he has gone a-rambling in the mountains, incognito and without many companions. What think you?"

---

favorite of Xuanzong's consort Yang Guifei. In 755 he rebelled against Xuanzong and toppled the Tang dynasty, but he died two years later, and the Tang was restored in 763.

10. *Shirotae no hitokuiuma. Shirotae no* is an ancient poetic epithet often applied to such things as robes and snow-covered mountains, thought to have originally referred to white cloth made from the bark of the paper-mulberry tree (known also as tapa cloth, from the Tahitian). *Hitokuiuma* means "man-eating horse," abbreviated to "man-eater" in the translation.

Thus he whispered, to Bokuhei's unmitigated delight. "Let us make it so!" said the latter. "Then let us do this," said the other, and each lending the other his ear, they proceeded through several secret talks.

Truly did Yang Zhen caution that every secret is known by at least four.[11] Walls have ears in this world, and soon enough someone found out about the affair and reported it to Sakuzaemon. Sadakane gave no indication of being exercised by this plaint. He quickly gathered to him troops to take Bokuhei and Mukuzō into custody, but then suddenly an idea struck him, and he conceived a different plan. He wore an expression that said he suspected nothing, while increasing the numbers of his escort and refraining from going out in the morning or walking about at night, all so as to forestall this vengeance.

Meanwhile, his lord Nagasanosuke Mitsuhiro, having lost himself in long nights of lascivious indulgence, began to take ill, growing worse day after day, month after month; fine liquors and rare repasts lost their sweetness for him, he no longer found joy in risqué songs sung suggestively, and his thoughts began to run along the same lines as those of the first Qin emperor, who sought the medicine of immortality on Penglai, and of Han Wu, who sought agelessness in the skills of the adepts.[12] He pillowed his head on Tamazusa's lap and refused to emerge from behind his curtains. "The time is ripe," thought Sadakane, and so one day he spoke to his lord and master, saying, "'Tis already the beginning of summer—the new leaves in the mountain meadows are at their most charming. The pheasants are flocking to the field-paths at the hamlet of Ochiba, and the skylarks are gathering to the village of Aomugi, happy in their position and their place. Will not Your Lordship's illness only increase if you keep yourself shut up like this? Surely letting the dogs run and the falcons fly will have a recuperative effect. I will do myself the honor of accompanying you. Will you not make up your mind to do this?" Thus did he attempt to stir up his master.

Tamazusa, at his side, grew excited about this, and with both of them urging him on, Mitsuhiro at last stirred himself and spoke. "In any case I have

---

11. A reference to chapter 54 of *Hou Han shu*, the biography of statesman Yang Zhen. Yang notes that every secret is known to at least four: the teller, the listener, heaven, and earth, the implication being that no secret known to so many can stay secret for long.

12. Qin Shi Huang (259–210 BCE), first emperor of the Qin dynasty, and Han Wu (156–87 BCE), seventh emperor of the former Han dynasty, were both obsessed with attaining immortality. Qin Shi Huang once mounted an expedition to search for Mount Penglai, the island of the immortals, while Han Wu directed wizards to attempt to contoct a medicine that could grant him immortality. Both accounts are found in *Shi ji*, chapters 6 and 12 respectively.

been too idle—long has it been since I left the castle. Your remonstrances seem to me as medicine both efficacious and easy to swallow. Tomorrow we shall spend in hunting, from early morning. Let the word go out, and preparations be made."

Sadakane gestured with his fan as with a scepter, as he replied, "By Your Lordship's decree. However, in recent years the demands of public service have been exigent, and the people are weary from their allotted duties, in addition to which it is now the time for them to hoe their fields and scatter their seeds. I humbly recommend that you go out in secret. I will escort you, so all shall go according to plan. Thus shall their tillage not be disturbed, and when the inhabitants of the land learn of it later, who among them shall not call Your Lordship a benevolent ruler? This is, I submit, another technique for serving the people."

Cunningly chosen were his words, and they moved Mitsuhiro extraordinarily, so that he exclaimed, "What you say accords fully with what is right. Elders of a house should all be even as you are. I will defer to this counsel of yours." And so he forwent his usual company of beaters and followers, instead causing only eight or nine of his attendants, such as Shichirō of the Nako and Hyōnai of the Amatsu, to ready themselves to join him. The next morning, Mitsuhiro, riding a gray horse, set out in secret, leading hounds and carrying falcons.

This was all according to Yamashita Sakuzaemon Sadakane's plot. The previous day, on retiring from the castle, he had quickly summoned the Ochiba and Aomugi village headmen, and said to them, "Having been granted unexpected leave, tomorrow I am thinking of going to thus and such a place and loosing my falcon. Take it to heart." So sternly did he speak that the village headmen rushed home and hurriedly convened the farmers, cursing them into a frenzy of road-sweeping so that the broom-traces might be thoroughly visible the next day.

Bokuhei of Somaki and Mukuzō saw that their opportunity had come. "The time has come—tomorrow, without fail, we will carry out our aims," they said, rejoicing in secret. They dressed themselves as beaters, and at two o'clock in the morning they rushed out, clutching bows and arrows. They hid themselves in the tall summer grasses on a hill northeast of the hamlet of Ochiba, shielded by an ancient pine, where they waited, thinking, "Sadakane is late."

Short as men's lives are summer nights: soon the cock's cry proclaimed the dawn, and forth from Takita Castle rode Nagasanosuke Mitsuhiro, buckskin gaiters on his shins and a broad-brimmed silk-lined rush hat pulled down low over his eyes, beaters in front of him and close retainers to his right and left—eight or nine in number, Nako and Amatsu among them. Yamashita Sakuzaemon Sadakane followed a little behind, riding the white horse and leading a great number of his own troops—in case of emergency, he said. This, too, was part of his plan. He had spoken to the grooms and laid on them the charge of mingling poison in with the morning fodder. Mitsuhiro's horse went some two-thirds of a mile and then suddenly took sick. It would go no farther no matter how its rider whipped it—it bent its forelegs and abruptly lay down on the ground, sending its master sprawling face down.

Shichirō of the Nako and Amatsu Hyōnai hastened to help him up. "Bring a change of mounts for His Lordship, immediately!" they shouted, exacerbating the entourage's panic. Word was passed to the rear-guard, and Sakuzaemon Sadakane galloped up, riding-crop raised. Quickly he dismounted and addressed Mitsuhiro.

"Your Lordship was to go out hunting in secret, so we did not make preparations of that nature. If Your Lordship waits for a new mount to be brought, the time will go to waste. Here is my horse. I have had him for years, and ridden him daily: he is quite broken in, and a joy to ride. Please, take him." He immediately proffered the reins.

Mitsuhiro's expression changed at once, and he stood up, leaving behind the camp stool that he had caused to be set out for him. "Then I shall do as you suggest. You rest here, and when my replacement comes you can take it and come after. Make haste, men!" Hardly had he finished speaking when he placed a hand on the saddle and vaulted onto the horse. The morning breeze bestirred the horse's dock like ripples on the sea, like weather vanes on ships the meadow deutzia, bright'ning like the East, as through the close-spaced stands of young-leaved trees the company drew near to Ochiba.

Among them only Mitsuhiro's retainers Nako and Amatsu did not seek to shelter themselves in Yamashita's shade; they served their lord with a sincerity quite out of the ordinary. At this time they must have had an idea of something, for they instructed the beaters running before the party to abruptly change paths and "make for the village of Aomugi."

But Mitsuhiro wondered at this, and scolded them, saying, "Where are you sending the men? Today we make the hill of Ochiba our hunting ground. Slovenly sleep-sots!"

Shichirō and Hyōnai, flanking him, whispered back, "Has it not dawned on Your Lordship? Your Lordship's mount all of a sudden went down, hardly something that may be considered an auspicious sign, but that is not all: the characters for Ochiba may also be read Rakuba, which is homonymous with 'a fall from a horse.' A place to be avoided at all costs, if the name names the thing.[13] Nor is that all: the Muromachi Lord's might at arms is slackening, and armed disturbances never cease. Awa being at the southeastern extremity of the realm, it is blessedly without incident, but one cannot categorically state that there are none with ambitions to take it. It is risky enough to be out in secret like this, but if Your Lordship ignores prohibitions, disregards inauspicious signs, and takes no thought for distant dangers, then what shall be done about troubles near at hand? This is why we sought to change paths abruptly."

Thus did they with single purpose remonstrate with Mitsuhiro, but he laughed them to scorn. "You speak like women. All that lives is bound to die. What of it, if a horse goes down? And as for our hunting ground, I suppose that were it called Fall-from-a-Horse it would be worth shunning, but Ochiba means 'fallen bird,' and is a sign that we shall take much game today—is it not? Send the men there."

Speeding on his mount with stirrups' clash, he left behind Nako and Amatsu, helpless, in the summer grass so thick along the paddy-paths he raced on his orig'nal course until they came unto the hill of Ochiba, by Ochiba hamlet where were hidd'n, since late last night, Bokuhei of Somaki and Mukuzō of Susaki, who spied him from within a stand of trees.

"There is no mistaking him who rides the white horse: it is Yamashita Sakuzaemon Sadakane. Well, then." They nocked arrows to their waiting bows and drew back the strings mightily. As their target came within bowshot they let fly, one-two, as arranged, and their aim was true. The first arrow pierced Mitsuhiro's breast, and without even a cry he fell backward off the horse with a thud. "What is this?" said Hyōnai of the Amatsu in astonishment, before the second arrow pierced him straight through the throat, so that he lay down on the same pillow as his master.

Mitsuhiro's escort milled about in panic, crying "Scoundrels!" but doing nothing else—failing to ascertain whether their enemy be many or few, and not even endeavoring to strike back—so that Shichirō's eyes flashed with rage. "Gutless, you men are. Why do you hesitate? Your lord has been shot down before your very eyes! The grove may be thick, but this whole hill

---

13. The name of the hamlet of Ochiba is written with characters that mean "fallen wing," but that may also be read *rakuba*. Written with other characters, *rakuba* means "a fall from a horse." The phrase *myōsen jishō*, translated here as "the name names the thing," is a Buddhist phrase that denotes an appellation that truly describes the qualities of the thing it names.

Caption: Bokuhei and Mukuzō battle with Mitsuhiro's attendants on Ochiba Hill.
Figures: Yamashita Sadakane [*far right, background*]. Shichirō of the Nako [*right, foreground*].
Bokuhei of Somaki [*left center*]. Mukuzō of Susaki [*top left*]. Hyōnai of the Amatsu [*far left*].
Text on plinth: Commemorative Stupa.

cannot be more than a few hundred yards—let us not rest until we have searched the whole of it, even if we have to cut down every tree and mow down every blade of grass!" Cursing them, he drew his blade and approached the horse, which had left its master, cutting off a section of its mud-guard for a shield. Seeing him draw this over himself and dash up the hill inspired the others, who began to press forward, each vowing to strike down the enemy himself, though none yet knew who he might be.

Bokuhei and Mukuzō saw this and knew it would not do to let them approach, so they emerged from the shade of the grove and began loosing arrows, with the result that a dozen or so of the leading beaters were shot down in the blink of an eye. However, with this the pair exhausted all their shafts—they flung their bows a-clattering aside and drew their longswords, brandished them from heights of brav'ry where they stood and slashed about. Mitsuhiro's servants were taken aback by the vigor of their attack, and most of them melted away, leaving only seven or eight of his close retainers to gather their strength and give battle. This they did, but they were unfamiliar with this mountain slope. Some stumbled over tree stumps, some tripped and tumbled over wisteria vines, and none but received either blows or other injuries.

All this time, Shichirō of the Nako sought to weary the bandits and lure them onto level terrain by fighting a little and then falling back; Mukuzō pressed forward, and Bokuhei followed after, both thinking not to let him escape. They gave chase, and without realizing it came down off the hill. Nako whirled around and flung a rock at Mukuzō, which struck him in the forehead and wounded him so that he grew dizzy and unsteady on his feet. Nako ran up to Mukuzō from the right and sliced him from the shoulder to above the breast. Mukuzō was cut down—he fell, and then Nako straddled his back and chopped off his head. But as he went to stand, Bokuhei rushed up like a bird in flight, dragging his bloody blade, and lopped off Nako's dexter arm above the elbow. Nako reeled, and Bokuhei pushed him to the ground and stabbed him twice, thrice. Then to slake his thirst he slurped the blood that ran along his blade. But as he did so the twang of a bow rang out from beneath the trees opposite, and an unknown archer's arrow penetrated Bokuhei's thigh. He began to fall, but then braced himself on one knee: he grasped the arrow by the shaft and pulled it out. But then a war cry pierced his ears, echoed by the dozens of men-at-arms who stampeded in now to surround and capture him.

Just then Yamashita Sakuzaemon, arrows on his back and a bow at his side, rode up to a cypress on the hill and cried: "Traitorous brigands, you who have robbed the province of its ruler from generations past, and the people of a lord who was both father and mother to them—do you not recognize Yamashita Sadakane? I could have killed you with that arrow more easily than smashing an egg with a hammer, but I avoided your vital regions that I might take you alive. Men, bind him!" At his command the mass of soldiers, fluttering in the wind of his authority, bustled and jostled to be the first to the capture.

When Bokuhei heard him name himself "Sadakane," he was flabbergasted. "Then it was never the Man-Eater I felled with my arrow! Alas, my plans had sped like a bird on the wing, but now they have been crossed like a crossbill's bill. I have done harm to the Lord of the Province—I am guilty, inescapably guilty, of treason. It is Yamashita Sadakane against whom my hatred mounts—it is him I would fight." And so he pulled back to higher ground, now flattening himself in the grass, now ducking behind a tree, now appearing here, now hiding there, defending himself as he went; but his arrow wound prevented him from moving as before, and slash and shove though he might, the enemy was many. His would-be captors came on and on, and for all his efforts Bokuhei could not approach Sadakane. Perhaps he felt that this was the end for him, for he tried to slit open his belly—but a couple of men in the vanguard stayed his hands from both sides, eventually succeeding in binding him with ropes.

Sadakane wasted no time in detailing troops to search out the scoundrel's allies wherever they might be hiding, but search as they might there never were any but just those two.

Just then there came upon the scene some dozens of the castle forces, senior vassals mixed with junior, bearing a palanquin with which to greet their lord. Proclaiming to them the turn of events, Sadakane first had them stuff Mitsuhiro's corpse into the palanquin, and then he gave them Bokuhei, hands tied behind his back, and Mukuzō's head, and he followed his lord's body back to Takita Castle.

Everyone was dumbfounded—even those who were called elders of the house were so frightened of Sadakane's authority that they uttered not one phrase of reproof, but only praised him for capturing the bandit on the spot. And so Sadakane came to be even more lifted up in his pride, ordering about officers and attendants just as he did the servants. The following day, Mitsuhiro's casket was brought out and sent to the cloister at which his family had always offered incense. That very day the criminal Bokuhei of Somaki, having been lashed with switches without respite on top of a wound barely to be endured, died in prison. Sadakane ordered that his head be chopped off. Bokuhei's and Mukuzō's heads alike were then skewered on spears of green bamboo and set like owls on the branches of a chinaberry tree.[14] But this was not all: Sadakane had everyone who had ever spoken ill of him apprehended and killed at this time, saying that they were allies of Bokuhei's. Now Bokuhei's and Mukuzō's capacity for the martial arts was greater than that of other men, despite being only seashore folk, and their aspirations in attempting to strike down the brigandly retainer Sadakane, who had no use for the retainers of the house of Jin'yo, were stalwart; but they could not prevail against his bestial cunning, and unwittingly they abetted their enemy in his evil, entangling many others. Pitiful is hardly the word for it.

In this way Yamashita Sadakane had fully accomplished his aims, and to spare. One day he summoned his senior retainers and close retainers to the castle, and without exception they came. This was how the scene appeared. Sadakane wore long trousers and a raven-cap with long strings,[15] and laid his longsword down beside him as he knelt in his place at the high-seat. He was flanked by twelve powerful, handpicked men wearing cuirasses under their ceremonial dress, and he faced the crowd and said, "Our former lord has made an unlooked-for departure from this world, and he has left behind no children. We had thought of choosing from another house in a neigh-boring district one to set up as his heir, but the Anzai clan of Tateyama and the Maro clan of Hiratate have no boys, but only girls. What shall we do about this?"

As he asked this, he gazed out over the assemblage, and there was none who dared raise his countenance to Sadakane. All were as one in saying, "Your Eminence Yamashita is a man of great virtue whose meritorious ser-vice unto our former lord exceeded even that of the Hōjō clan who served as Chancellors in Kamakura. Rather than seek an heir who does not exist, will not Your Eminence assume the two districts yourself? What can any of us have against looking up to Your Eminence as our lord and devoting ourselves hereafter to loyally serving you?"

---

14. The heads of decapitated criminals or enemies were often put on display in this manner in medieval Japan. The comparison of the heads to owls perching on branches is embedded in the Sino-Japanese term for such a display, *kyōshu* (owl-head). Bakin here (and frequently hereafter) uses the simpler *kakeru* (to hang or set), but writes it with the character for owl. The term is no doubt informed by the traditional Chinese association of owls with unfilial conduct.

15. A raven-cap (*eboshi* or *ebōshi*) was so named because its blackness resembled the bird. It was worn on formal or ceremonial occasions.

Thus did they reply, flatterers to the last. Sadakane beamed at them. "I lack the virtues of which you speak, but if I fail to follow the will of this council then we shall lose that which causes the people to look up to us, and if that happens this castle cannot hope to stand long. I shall, then, assume the rulership of the two districts for the moment, with the intention of yielding it to a person who does possess those virtues. Ambition, dwell not in me." He poured his blood into a written oath, and then he held a banquet for the assembled, and gave unto them rewards, so that they all blessed him and wished that he might live ten thousand years.

Subsequently, Sadakane renamed Takita Castle, calling it Tamashita,[16] at the same time making Tamazusa his main and proper wife, installing her in the rear chambers to wait on him there; the others of Mitsuhiro's women he had assume their place at his pillow in constant rotation. He took every pleasure in his new wealth and position. He sought too to flaunt his dominion to the neighboring districts, despatching messengers to Tateyama and Hiratate to say, "The unworthy Sadakane, having been unexpectedly thrust by the people into a place of honor, and become lord of Nagasa and Heguri, has no other wish than to bind himself in goodwill to both Your Lordships. Shall he visit you? Will you do him the honor of visiting him? He leaves this up to Your Lordships' discretion." The impropriety of this left Maro and Anzai dumbfounded, and so vexed that they could hardly take counsel on it of a morning, so they sent the messenger back to say, "We will send our reply later."

Now the lord of Tateyama Castle, Anzai Saburōdayū Kagetsura, was a man of great strength and fierce heart, fond of scheming but irresolute for want of opportunity. The lord of Hiratate Castle, Kogorō Nobutoki of the Maro, was a brave general but a common, avaricious man, one to pursue his advantage in contempt of others. He wished to consult with Anzai about striking down Sadakane, so one day he set out in secret for the castle of Tateyama, leading only his closest retainers. Coming face to face with Kagetsura, he opened to him his secret thoughts concerning Sadakane, saying, "If you and I combine our strength and lead the armies of Awa and Asahina in an assault on the castle of Takita, we are assured of victory. Sadakane is vulnerable—his head is ours for the taking, and we can divide among ourselves his two districts, and will not that be pleasant?"

---

16. The characters with which this name is written mean "beneath the ball [or bead, or jewel]," the *tama* being the same as in Tamazusa's name.

Thus openly did he seek to entice him, but Kagetsura shook his head from side to side. "Both the Imperial Seat and the East of the Mountains suffer uncommonly from armed disturbances, but Awa has been without incident these many years. Its soldiers, officers and men, are uncomfortable astride their warhorses. This Yamashita is a formidable man—he must possess talent and intelligence beyond measure, considering how he made his lord's territories his own, without dirtying his hands. And his virtue and his righteousness we may know by the way the people thrust him into this place of honor, make him their lord and serve him wholeheartedly. 'Celestial timing is no match for geographical advantage, and geographical advantage is no match for harmony between persons.'[17] Already Sadakane has on his side timing, geography, and harmony among his people. We must take stock of ourselves, and him, and the distinctions between us; a battle now would be as between the two horns of the same bull—evenly matched—and therefore quite misgiven. If we submit to him for a time, and then lure him into this district, we might be able to attack him suddenly with soldiers lying in wait, and make him our captive. And yet, without a Fan Zeng to plot for the Han-Chu gathering at Hong Gate,[18] not only will our labors be in vain, they may bite us like a snake awakened when beating back brush, and then it will be too late for regrets. Let us bide our time. Once a change comes over Takita and the people begin to turn their backs on him, his rule will collapse with no need for an attack from us. Why should we hurry?"

Nobutoki heard Kagetsura's cautions but considered his approach circuitous, and so began to marshal his many and various arguments, whereupon one of Anzai's close retainers came busily around via the corridor, gently slid open the doors, and looked inquiringly after his master's expression. After a time, Kagetsura looked sharply at him and asked, "What is it?"

The retainer inched forward on his knees and said, "Your Lordship, a warrior calling himself Satomi Matatarō Yoshizane, whom we think to be eighteen or nineteen years of age, leading a mere two followers, has arrived. We made appropriate inquiries as to his coming here, to which he replied that he is a refugee from Yūki in Shimōsa, where his father Suemoto was struck down, and whence he came with these two longtime vassals, Sugikura and Horiuchi, retreating along the Sagami road and crossing the sea at Miura to land at Shirahama in our own country. The rest, he says, is not meet to be

---

17. From the second half of the second chapter of *Mengzi*.

18. A reference to an episode that took place in 206 BCE during the Han-Chu wars, when Liu Bang of Han and Xiang Yu of Chu met for a banquet at Hongmen. Xiang Yu's advisor Fan Zeng devised a plot to assassinate Liu Bang there. The plot failed, but the incident (recounted in chapter 7 of *Shi ji*) has become a legendary byword for cunning strategy.

communicated through others—he most earnestly begs an audience. What would Your Lordship have us do with him?"

An uneasiness ran through his flood of words. Kagetsura was unable to answer at once, saying only, "Now, this is unexpected." He cocked his head, furrowed his brow, and sat a while, immersed in thought.

End of Book I of the Lives of the Eight Dogs of the Satomi of Southern Fusa

The Lives of the Eight Dogs of the Satomi of Southern Fusa

Book II

Assembled by the Master of the Crooked Pavilion in the Eastern Capital

Chapter III
Kagetsura and Nobutoki secretly obstruct
Yoshizane;
Ujimoto and Sadayuki calamitously
submit to Tateyama

Anzai Saburōdayū Kagetsura, upon being informed by his attendant that Satomi Yoshizane, a Yūki refugee, had arrived by boat with two followers, harbored grave doubts but failed to fathom what harm this presaged; he could not answer swiftly, but instead turned to Nobutoki of the Maro and said, "You have heard that it is thus and such. What think you?"

No sooner had he spoken than Nobutoki replied, "Satomi is a Genji, known and named, but he has neither kith nor kin here. He was on the side of the irreplaceable Mochiuji and in intimate converse with Ujitomo of Yūki, but once the siege had come to last three years, with the enmity of the Capital and Kamakura upon him and no prospects of coming out of it with his life, he, on the day the castle fell, with no regard for his father who was struck down, did cravenly run and hide, now to wash up on our shores: how can we grant audience to such an unacceptable rogue? Let him be chased off at once," he said, with a flick of his finger.

Thus enjoined, Kagetsura cocked his head for a while before whispering, "Your thoughts are as my very own, and yet I think he is not quite useless to us. These men have withstood three years of siege, and are no strangers to battle. Yoshizane is still young, but he cannot have come here without hacking his way through tens of thousands of the enemy. Let us summon him and see him, and test his courage, and if he be serviceable, then shall we not have gained a general to strike a blow at Sadakane? If, on the other hand, he be not serviceable, we need not even chase him away: we can run him through where he stands, and thus ward off any future troubles in that direction. What think you of this counsel?"

Nobutoki nodded and urged him on. "Your plan is complete in every particular. I will join you in receiving him. Let preparations be made." Kagetsura quickly called to him a senior vassal and explained to him this matter and that, then hastened him to transmit the plan to a number of warriors in their prime, possessed of both martial artistry and natural strength. Nobutoki, too, summoned the complement of house-men he had brought with him and gave them to know what they should do. Then, together with his host Kagetsura, he went into the receiving room. This was how the scene appeared: Anzai's twenty retainers and the dozen or so of Maro's escort were arrayed in two ranks, decked out in imposing panoply of martial glory and gleaming might, while the strings of the bows that decorated the walls glittered like cataracts painted on a panel, and the spears and glaives that hung thereon seemed to float like mists on the mountains in spring. A curtain hung over the entrance to the corridor, and behind it some ten strong warriors in cuirasses, their silk-wound bowstrings taut, stood ready to burst forth at a word and take captive that lord and his men.

The Satomi youth Yoshizane had been waiting outside for over an hour when he was summoned to "Come this way." But before he had gone the length of one room, four warriors in their prime, garbed top and bottom in light blue hemp, appeared from behind free-standing screens and said, "Right this way—we will be Your Lordship's guides." No sooner had they spoken than they took up places before and behind Yoshizane, shortbows at the ready with arrows nocked and strings pulled taut. Sugikura and Horiuchi, following at a slight distance, saw this, and with a cry of "Ho, there," sought as one to rush forward, but as they did so a half dozen troops, dressed in black robes with short sleeves tied back with beaded cords and trouser legs hitched up, ran out from the same place with their spears thrust forward, points in a line, to walk along beside their guests in single file as an escort.

Despite all this, Yoshizane appeared not in the least perturbed, but said, as if to himself, "A stately reception indeed! For three years was I at Yūki— days there were when I stood up to the enemy's arrows; I know not how oft I ducked 'neath spear-shafts. I had heard that this place, beyond the seas, was without incident, untroubled even by wind and wave, a place where both good folk and mean enjoy peace. Not so, it seems."

His longtime vassals behind him also stood their ground. "A passage in one of the military treatises tells us that even in times of peace, one should keep past wars in mind, and even if an enemy seems weak, one should not take him lightly; even so, this is a rare banquet indeed your lord our host has prepared for a mere party of three—and with his own hands!—a stew of arrowheads and bowstring noodles. Well, we will eat with relish. Lead on." Master and men appeared to their escort eager to reach their seats, and so the mighty men lowered their bows and pulled back their spears and went inside the curtains all around.

Then Satomi Yoshizane, spying Kagetsura and Nobutoki from afar and yet showing no hint of obsequiousness, assumed the guest's seat, took his folding fan from his waist, and set it at his right hand.

"I, Satomi Matatarō Yoshizane, among the losing generals at Yūki, according to the last words of my late father, Lesser Assistant of the Governance Ministry Suemoto, did with great labor elude the surrounding enemy forces and wander until I came to be here. Accordingly, I would count myself surpassingly blessed if I might be permitted to become a resident of this peaceful land, which is not in league with the Overseers of Kamakura, much less with the Capital, and to shelter myself here, in my current vain and hopeless condition, even if it be in a rush hut of the fisherfolk. Such were my thoughts yesterday when I heard the strange talk in the towns, the stories in the streets. I deemed that I might be able to lend a hand in a righteous cause, and so I braved the tiger's wrath and begged an audience here, where to my surprise I was not shunned as a defeated general, but was vouchsafed a meeting, to answer all the hopes I dared harbor in my breast. These my companions are my late father's beloved retainers, Sugikura Kisonosuke Ujimoto and Horiuchi Kurando Sadayuki. We beg you, sirs, take notice of us."

Thus politely did he announce himself, and then calmly turned his gaze behind him so that Ujimoto and Sadayuki both, at length, bowed their heads.

Kagetsura, however, merely stared back at Yoshizane without returning his compliments, for he saw that Yoshizane was even younger than he had expected, and he scorned his visitor's youth. Nobutoki did not wait the pleasure of his host, but with bulging eyes raised his voice and said, "I am Kogorō of the Maro, and I have come here today from Hiratate on a special matter of my own, for which reason I am merely in attendance on this company. Ah, but you are a clever-tongued stripling! Our land of Awa is a small country, but being at the southeastern extremity of the land and surrounded on three sides by ocean, its borders are not encroached upon by its powerful enemies in neighboring countries, even as it marches not to the orders of

His Lordship at Muromachi, nor follows the two Overseers. Still and all it is ludicrous for you, a brat still smelling of his mother's milk and who lacks any connection with myself or Lord Anzai, to come to us with no position or place, and bearing the enmity of the Capital and Kamakura, and think to clack your beak to us about what is advantageous and what is not! To pity men when they are in decline is to look like Buddha with a charitable eye on all life, and to accept their foibles is to be like unto His limitless sea of blessing and longevity;[1] but who would keep a guilty man and summon the curses that attend him? Truly this is an unprofitable audience." So spoke he, with cursings and scoffings, scratchings of his jaw, and laughter.

Yoshizane broke out into a smile. "Is that you who speaks, Lord Maro—whose name is known to me? The houses of Maro, Anzai, and Tōjō are indeed old ones in this land. I had thought I knew of their stalwart bravery, their martial cunning, but it appears I may have been mistaken. Though it pains me to speak of him, Suemoto, who was my father, shut himself up in Yūki, which he always thought could not be held long, and for three years protected it against the great armies of the Capital and Kamakura, and when he looked upon death it was without rancor for he had devoted his entire life to all that can be summed up in the single character, 'righteousness.' I may not be up to my father's standard, but I neither flee in fear of my enemies nor run for love of my life. My late father's last words leave me no choice but to consign my life to Heaven and what it may have fated for me: I mean to wait for my time to come.

"When the Noble Lord Mochiuji of Kamakura was in his first ascendance, there were none among the warriors in Awa and Kazusa, nay, nor in all the Eight Provinces, who failed to incline their hearts unto him, to bow to him, to come out in his service; and yet when Mochiuji had perished, few indeed were they who for the young princes' sake forgot house and abandoned thought of self in order to join their might to Ujitomo's to hold Yūki against the siege. Men's hearts cleave to the powerful, and so they are unreliable: if you, Lord Maro, and you, Lord Anzai, elect to think more of the retribution of the Overseers than of your duty to the Noble Lord Mochiuji and so to refuse me admittance, then I will leave, brushing the dust of this land off my sleeves as I go. Truly the Overseers are powerful. Warriors from many provinces have attached themselves to them. I do not wonder that you fear them, but why do you so fear Yoshizane, with his mere brace of followers, that you call forth your mightiest men with weapons in hand? Why do you, in

---

1. Phrases that occur in chapter 25 of the Lotus Sutra, where they are used to describe the bodhisattva Avalokiteśvara (J. Kannon).

the midst of what you call tranquility, take such strenuous precautions, having bows and arrows hanging in this place of meeting, blades and speartips unsheathed, and so many strong men concealed behind your curtains?"

Thus rebuked, Nobutoki quickly grew red in the face, and he looked to Anzai, who, surprised, took a deep breath before speaking. "You cut us to the quick. A bow and arrow are a warrior's wings—his swords and spears are like tusks to an elephant—they protect him, and he cannot lay them aside, even when seated, even when lying down. Think you this is meant as a threat? The arming of your guides, however, and the concealment of those men—these are things I knew nothing about. You, there, why have you acted thus inappropriately? Leave us now!"

He chased the men out of the room, and caused the spears and glaives to be hidden with screens. Anzai's and Maro's retainers retreated, their spirits dampened and their preparations having but made things worse, some to the guard-house and some behind screens, and many to mop sweat from their brows.

Nobutoki was undaunted by all this. He inched forward on his knees, looked Yoshizane in the face, and said, "There would seem to be much that is well grounded in what you lay before us, but if indeed you fear no enemy, if you value not your life, if you are content to leave your fate to Heaven and await your moment, then I find it difficult to understand why you would land here and lean on the Anzai clan, who are not even rulers of an entire province, and with whom you have never had any friendship, when there are many Genji East of the Mountains and surely some among them on whom you may rely. The hungered cannot choose his food, and the pursued cannot choose his road: were you not lost in flight, fearing your enemies and clinging to life, how could you have come here, glowing with shame as you are? If it be so, confess to it, rather than seeking to adorn your pathetic failings— then might you find pity. Since I am present in this company, let me intercede for you. Confess to it—will you not confess to it?"

Sadayuki could not bear to listen as Maro repeated his urgings twice and thrice, but tugged at Ujimoto's sleeve, and together they pressed forward and replied, "Harken to your heart's tutelage when assessing a man and you may be led astray. It gives us pause to say this, but Your Eminence's presumptions apply only to the commonest of common soldiers. There are no such generals among the Genji. It is not the case that Yoshizane came to this country unintentionally, having lost his way with his enemies in pursuit and his life in danger. He was, rather, following ancient precedent. Long ago, when the Noble Lord Yoritomo of the Minamoto was defeated in battle at Mount Ishibashi and made his way to Awa, your ancestor, Lord

Caption: Kagetsura and Nobutoki threaten Yoshizane.
Figures: Anzai Kagetsura [*far right, background*]. Nobutoki of the Maro [*second from right, background*]. Satomi Yoshizane [*center right, foreground*]. Sugikura Ujimoto [*second from left, background*]. Horiuchi Sadayuki [*far left, background*].

Nobutoshi, and the Anzai forebear Lord Kagemori, together with Lord Tōjō, displayed their matchless aspirations by being the first to join his following, and so Yoritomo despatched them ahead such that when his party crossed into Kazusa, Hirotsune and Tsunetane[2] came out to meet him, helping to quickly form a great army, with which he went on to consolidate his base in Kamakura and finally to destroy the Heike. The Satomi are descended from Lord Hachiman,[3] of the same direct line of the Genji, and Yoshizane now seeks to follow this glorious precedent. Yet you have held him in bottomless contempt for it. We could not remain silent, so we have spoken, but only of things which are known to all. Forgive us if we have said too much."

So spoke the two old vassals, as one in the wisdom and courage of their words, and Nobutoki was so overcome with rage at their suasion that he could not speak. Yoshizane, seeing his expression, barked at his men: "Sadayuki, Ujimoto, you utter improprieties! What virtue have I that I should be likened unto Yoritomo? That is simply unreasonable. Braying asses!" He heartily scolded them into retreat, appeasing his hosts without apologizing.

Nobutoki folded his arms wordlessly, eyes flashing with ire. Kagetsura's shoulders shook with sardonic laughter he could contain no longer. "You talk and you talk—convinced your Buddha is holiest! Hear me now, you followers of the Satomi. Yoritomo's father Yoshitomo was Regulator[4] of fifteen provinces—had he not become an Enemy of the Court, what could even Kiyomori have done against him?[5] That is why when the time came for that nobleman to raise a righteous army, the warriors East of the Mountains remembered their old debts of honor and attached themselves to him even unbidden, notwithstanding his exile. The Satomi clan is hardly to be compared with that: from the time when its founder, Tarō Yoshishige, served the Noble Lord Yoritomo, it has never ruled more than a single village, nor

---

2. Kazusa Hirotsune, lord of Kazusa and Shimōsa, and his cousin Chiba Tsunetane, another powerful Genji supporter.

3. Minamoto no Yoshiie (see Chapter I, note 3).

4. *Setsudoshi* (Ch. *jiedushi*), a military office in Tang and Five Dynasties China that also existed in Japan during the Nara period, but not during the Kamakura period as indicated in the narrative. As Tokuda notes (p. 67), Bakin uses it as a term for a regional commander.

5. As related in the early Kamakura-era war chronicle *Heiji monogatari*, Yoshitomo broke with Cloistered Emperor Go-Shirakawa, who branded him an Enemy of the Court and sent the loyal Taira no Kiyomori against him. Kiyomori was victorious, and Yoshitomo was killed. Later (in events related in the war chronicle *Heike monogatari*, ca. thirteenth century), Yoshitomo's son Yoritomo ("that nobleman," in Kagetsura's phrase), who had been spared after the events of the Heiji Rebellion, led the Minamoto forces in a successful challenge to the Heike. The Minamoto's victory paved the way for their establishment of the shogunate in Kamakura.

commanded more than a hundred riders. Later the Satomi took the Palace's side,[6] seeking refuge here and there until they could hold out no longer and submitted themselves to Kamakura. They were confirmed in their holdings, but that did not last long; as I see you now, you are fugitives. You men—what argument can you have to make when even your lord holds his tongue? Had you reined in your aspirations and sought to serve Kagetsura, it should have redounded unto you commensurately—but you fail to appreciate your position or your place!" So thorough-going was his scornful arrogance that neither Ujimoto nor Sadayuki sought to counter his words; in this, though, they knew not their lord's mind.

Yoshizane grinned as he replied. "Lord Anzai, you speak true. And yet, men's mouths will not be shuttered. The current of rumor in each town I have passed through since coming to this country has been the same. The people censure you ceaselessly, saying that the retainers of your house have blocked up their lord's ears—that they tell you not what it would behoove you to know, nor remonstrate with you when it would behoove them to do so—in short, that they are exceedingly disloyal. Ujimoto and Sadayuki would not rub shoulders with such disloyal men, even if you should grant unto them a stipend of unlooked-for largesse, nor do they wish to serve a lord who has made himself as one who is deaf."

Kagetsura's expression changed. "For what reason am I censured? Tell me the rumors in the towns!"

Yoshizane stood his fan up on his knee and said, "Has it not yet dawned on Your Lordship? Yea, not on your head alone does it lie, but on yours, Lord Maro, as well. Long has this province been without incident because of the deep and ancient amity between the three houses of Jin'yo, Anzai, and Maro, which were as the hands and feet of the same body in the assistance they rendered one unto the others—until the favorite retainer of the Jin'yo, Yamashita Sadakane, by means of a wicked plot did bring harm to his lord, usurp his two districts, and take to calling himself the lord of the province. Yet you do not strike him down for the sake of the Jin'yo, but truckle and stand downwind, allowing yourselves to share his taint—is not the people's censure right and proper? I had thought to mention this to you, and then, had you seen fit to employ me, to work like a dog or a horse for you, but those hopes were in vain: I did not see you preparing to take the field. If such was

---

6. That is, the Satomi were supporters of the Southern Court (based in Yoshino) in the schism in the imperial family that divided the country during the Northern and Southern Courts period in the late fourteenth century. The Ashikaga shoguns (who ruled from Kyoto but also maintained the previous shogunate's power base in Kamakura) supported the Northern Court (in Kyoto), and emerged from the struggle with control of the country.

not among your counsels, then there was little point in my telling you of my niggling aspirations. You insist on judging us, my men and me, as to our staunchness or cowardice, but any warrior so unreliable as to fail to strike at Sadakane for the Jin'yo's sake lacks courage and righteousness. That is all I have to say. Let us leave."

He had barely finished speaking when he made as if to stand and depart, but Kagetsura hastily called to him to wait. "It was only reasonable for us to think as we did, since you did not tell us of your intentions. Now sit a little longer with us, if you please."

But Nobutoki, who had been pacing the room at his right hand, spoke without the slightest indecision. "You are not aware, then, Yoshizane, that my coming here today was for the very purpose of holding a council of war, but that we had thought it best to keep secret our designs. What would we be so careless as to tell you, whom we were meeting for the very first time? As for our courage or lack of same, if you would know that for yourself, then ask this blade!" And with a snarl of rage he placed a hand on the upthrust hilt of his sword. Ujimoto and Sadayuki, who had not let down their guard for a moment, were at their master's side in a heartbeat, turning their wary gazes all around them. Maro's escort saw this and shuffled quickly forward on their knees, rubbing clenched fists.

Just then their panicked host Kagetsura bustled over and clasped Nobutoki in his arms to restrain him—he brought his mouth to Nobutoki's ear and whispered some persuasion in it—then, at length, he gave a glance to his right and left, accompanied by an explanatory thrust of his jaw. His retainers and Maro's escort stood straight up and accompanied him to the next room. Through it all Yoshizane remained as if pinned in place, fanning his gaze over the scene though not contesting it, as the company blanched.

Now Anzai Kagetsura returned to the place he had previously occupied, and spoke. "What must you think, sir? It is the way of the military man to fight, even to the death, over a single word, but Maro is a buffoon. Let this not weigh upon your heart. However, he who knows time and the tide of events protects himself with forbearance. All this we have done by way of testing you, and you are indeed our man. You may have been among the generals defending Yūki, but now you have drifted into my harbor; you run to me, seeking to join my encampment, and to strike at Sadakane. Should you join me, you will no doubt find it difficult to oppose my commands. Should you distinguish yourself for your loyalty among my officers and men and display great merit on the battlefield, you shall find honor and rewards to be yours. But should you consider the prospect of serving me ignominious, from pride in your origins and over-reliance on your talents, it will show in opposition to my commands. Then I cannot use you. Perhaps you would rather destroy the brigand yourself and take Takita Castle with what force you may have. I would hardly begrudge it you, though you became lord of both districts yourself. Whether you leave or stay now depends entirely on what counsel you take. Settle the matter in your heart and give me an answer."

Thus did Kagetsura renew his manner of speech to Yoshizane, who, though he knew hardships might lay concealed therein, faltered not a mite in his response. "Now that I am become an unmoored boat, any firm shore shall be my master. I am being vouchsafed shelter and employment—what objection can I raise? I am yours to command in all things, milord."

Kagetsura nodded. "This is a beginning. But you absolutely must not disobey me. Now, it is one of the blessed customs of my house that upon launching an expedition we do celebrate our worship of the God of War, in which as an offering we present a great carp. If you lower a fishhook and bring me back such a carp, it shall be no different from if you had grappled with a worthy enemy and taken his head. Will you do this?"

Yoshizane listened as Kagetsura laid this task before him, and not a shadow of refusal crossed his face as he answered, "I will." At last he rose to leave, only for Ujimoto and Sadayuki, standing behind their lord on either side, to clutch at his sleeves and restrain him. They stepped forward as one. "We would say a word to you, Lord Anzai, concerning this blessed custom of your house of which you speak. Surely no one knows more about inclining a rod, dropping a hook, and catching a fish—all while sleeping peacefully in a boat—than a fisherman. This is not an activity for a warrior to engage in—it would not become Yoshizane. The ancients said that when a prince is shamed, his minister dies.[7] Perhaps you had better take our heads and make them your offerings."

Kagetsura hardly heard them out before fixing them with a glare and saying, "How exceedingly rude you fellows are. Or is it that your ears deceive you? Yoshizane has already given his assent to this, for he has a proper fear of our rules. You have failed to hew to your duty as his servants, and have violated my command. This is no trifling offense of which you are guilty. Take them outside and cut them down!"

Ujimoto and Sadayuki thought nothing of his violent rage, but advanced as if to argue further, whereupon Yoshizane scolded them fiercely, driving them back, and then apologized on their behalf. Kagetsura's expression calmed. "Well, then, I entrust them to your custody until I see a carp. You

---

7. Found in chapter 2, book 8 of *Guoyu* (J. *Kokugo*), a Spring and Autumn period history often attributed to Zuo Qiuming.

must catch it yourself and bring it to me, and that within three days. Should you squander the time, you shall be seen for a rogue and worse. Take this to heart."

Yoshizane acquiesced, deferring to each of Kagetsura's requirements as he stated them. Then, "Let us to our lodgings," he said, and rousted his glowering old vassals to depart. Maro Kogorō Nobutoki, who had been eavesdropping in the next room, opened the gauze-screen door and watched him leave with a sneer before going to stand beside his host.

"Lord Anzai, you are very lenient. Wherefore did you spare Satomi's followers, and send them away with him? I had my mind set on striking Yoshizane down, but you acted as his shield. You let the fish escape our net," he grumbled.

Kagetsura smiled as he said, "I, too, had from the beginning steeled myself against any eventuality—but Yoshizane is the son of a famous house, and though a mere youth he is possessed of uncommon discernment and erudition. And his followers—the way their spirits show in their countenances, I should say each is worth a thousand men. Had I raised a hand against them, it would have meant the deaths of many. A beast, when driven to extremity, will bite, and a bird will peck—how, then, could a brave general and fierce soldiers simply fold their arms and await the blade? 'Tis said the hunter kills not the bird that flies to him in refuge; had we killed this man, against whom we hold no grudge, while striking not at Sakadane, the people's censure of us would but increase, and only with great difficulty could we carry out our great purpose. Had we, on the other hand, kept Yoshizane here, it would have been like trying to adopt a wild beast: uneasy must have been our rest. A mouse pokes its head out of its hole fearing danger from all sides; I examined the problem from all sides, and dug a hole for these men. To wit, I imposed on their tolerance by requiring a food-offering for our celebrations. The province of Awa contains no carp: they do not live here, perhaps due to our air, or our soil. Those three do not know this, and so when they return empty-handed, having wasted their days in standing by pools or rummaging through rapids, we shall cut them down, according to our regulations. Thus when I kill them it will be because their guilt demands it, and none can call it a private act on my part. Indeed, how could I spare them?"

His face shone with pride as he explained his plan, which could hardly have been more to Nobutoki's liking. The latter clapped his hands together and blurted out words of praise. "Well-plotted, and most wondrous! Indeed, if we had rashly run him off, Yoshizane might have made for Takita to follow Sadakane—we would have been giving a tiger wings! And yet you would have regretted employing him here—you would have been lending him a room only to find him ruining the main house. Retaining him in order to kill him later—nothing could be better than this plan. O, how prodigious, how wondrous!"

At that moment Yoshizane was making with quickened pace for his inn at Shirahama, but as the road was very long, the day was dark ere he reached it. Shirahama is within the district of Asahina in Awa. It seems to be a very old hamlet, as its name appears in the *Compendium of Japanese Names for Things*.[8] It is said to be adjacent to the village of Takiguchi. Nowadays it is part of the stretch of shore known collectively as the Seven Inlets, where may be found old traces of the Satomi clan, including temples connected to them. The so-called Seven Inlets of Awa are: Kawashimo, Iwame, Oto, Shioura, Hara, Otonohama, and Shiramatsu.

Enough of trivial matters. At dawn Yoshizane returned to Shirahama, and without even a wink of sleep he began to prepare himself to go fishing. Uji-moto and Sadayuki were not pleased. "Has it not dawned on Your Lordship? Nobutoki's is the proverbial boldness of the common man,[9] while Kagetsura is exceedingly perverse—he despises ability, is jealous of talent. What will it gain you to scrounge up a carp for such unreliable men, who see you only as an enemy? We beg Your Lordship, avoid their poisonous evil—leave now for Kazusa."

Thus did they remonstrate with him in unison, but Yoshizane shook his head. "No, you men are mistaken. By nature, Maro and Anzai are on inti-mate terms with their own advantage, and have little to do with righteous-ness. Their deeds bely their words. They fear Sadakane, but that is all—they have no stomach for striking at Takita. I am not ignorant of all this. If, how-ever, I leave here now and go to Kazusa and it proves no different there, where then should I go, since Shimōsa is enemy territory? When the prince gains the tide of the times, he enjoys it; when he loses the tide of the times, he still enjoys it. Lu Shang, whom the world calls Grand Duke Wang, was unknown to the world until he was nearly seventy years of age. He was fish-ing on the banks of the Wei when King Wen found him, and then he earned great merit by destroying King Zhou.[10] He was enfeoffed in Qi, and it passed down to his descendants through dozens of generations. Thus it was even for

---

8. *Wamyōshō* (see Chapter I, note 24).

9. A reference to a line in *Mengzi* (second half of chapter 1). He who has the boldness of the common man is fit to face a single opponent, but not to do great works.

10. Recounted in chapter 32 of *Shiji*. Lu Shang is better known as Jiang Ziya (Grand Duke Wang, or "Grand Duke Hopeful," was another of his titles, as was Duke Tai or "Great Duke"). As Yoshizane relates, Lu Shang was recruited by Wen of Zhou during the reign of King Zhou, decadent last ruler

one such as Grand Duke Wang. I have lost both time and tide—why should I abhor a little fishing? Moreover, the carp is an auspicious fish. It is handed down that when a carp climbs the cascade at the Dragon Gate in Annan, it is transformed into a dragon.[11] I saw a dragon's tail at Miura. Now I come to Shirahama and am told to catch a carp. Are these not reliable harbingers? If I take anything, I will bring it to Kagetsura and watch, for a while, what he does. Let us go once it is light."

As he urged them on, Ujimoto and Sadayuki were moved to admiration by his lofty arguments. They sought out fishhooks, rigged poles, and hung compartmented baskets from their waists, and then the three of them, master and men, set out in search of a pool whose name they did not know, while the ravens of the forest left their boughs for the gently brightening firmament.

---

of the Shang dynasty. Later, Lu Shang helped Wen's son Wu overthrow the Shang, and King Wu's Zhou dynasty succeeded them in ruling China. Lu Shang was given the rule of the territory of Qi.

11. The early Song-era encyclopedia *Taiping guangji* (J. *Taihei kōki*) includes this information, taken from the no longer extant *Sanqin ji* (J. *Sanshinki*). The Dragon's Gate was a set of rapids in the Yellow River where it passed through the mountains of Hedong, said to have been made by legendary ancient ruler Yu (Da Yu, or Yu the Great).

Chapter IV
In Kominato, Yoshizane gathers the righteous;
In a bamboo thicket, Takayoshi seeks his revenge

Thus did Yoshizane and his men pass the day following path after path, now to a pond, now to a river, visiting pools and standing by rapids. At night they returned not to their inn at Shirahama, but went on even into the district of Nagasa, and there they fished the river Shirahashi until, all too soon, the third day came. It vexed them bitterly that this day should be their last, and that while they caught no end of fish, no carp, not even one tiny crucian, ever hung from their hook. In the age of the gods almighty, the August Deity Hikohohodemi himself visited the palace of the Dragon King of the Sea in search of a lost fishhook, while the Urashima boy "fished for bonito / fished for bream / caught none for se'en days / and so came not home," a precedent descending in a line of cruelly tangled fortune to these three.[1] Each looked at the others to find them looking at him, and they sighed as one.

---

1. The story of Hikohohodemi is related in the second book of *Nihon shoki*. The fishhook actually belonged to Hikohohodemi's brother, who demanded it back. Hikohohodemi then went to the seaside and grieved aloud, whereupon an old man appeared and directed him to the Dragon King's palace, where he recovered the hook from a bream and married the Dragon King's daughter, living undersea for three years. The quotation about the Urashima boy comes from a poem (#1740) in *Man'yōshū*. In the original, however, the boy's fishing is successful enough that he gets carried away and ultimately meets the Dragon King's daughter, marrying her and going to live under the sea for three years.

Just then a man came toward them from further down the river, singing at the top of his voice. Yoshizane and his men turned to see a rather filthy-looking beggar. O, what a sight did he present: his loose, tangled hair looked like silvergrass growing on a moor scorched last spring;[2] his dragging skirts resembled sea-pine thrown up onto the shore in the autumn.[3] Boils and sores covered him, even his hands and face, so that he seemed to have no human skin at all—worse it was than the shell of a ripe lychee, or the flesh of a ruptured pomegranate, or the back of a great old toad. Indeed, his life was such as to be despaired of—scorned by the world, hated by men, yet unable to die. To see him was to abhor him, but he seemed unbothered by it, to listen to how he banged on his round-bottomed bowl and sang in his throaty voice:

I see my village
I see my village
White sails running
On a fair-blowing breeze
The boats that come
To Awa port
No wave can smash
No tide can rot
So pull, men, pull
And I'll pull, too

He sang it again and again as he came up to the spot on the riverbank where Yoshizane and his men stood, where he stopped to watch them with great interest as they fished. Master and men covered their noses at the stench of the bloody pus that streamed from his sores; they wished to themselves that he might go away quickly, but instead he stood there a long while. Then he came even closer. He peered under the brims of their sedge-hats, each in turn, and said, "No, I simply cannot understand the way Your Worships fish. You throw back the crucians, the shrimp, and everything else that swallows your hooks—what is it Your Worships would catch?"

So insistent was his query that Ujimoto was forced to turn his head and answer him. "Carp is what we want. None of these other fish will do. We release them all, for we would not take life wantonly."

---

2. The image of silvergrass on a scorched field (*suguro no susuki*) comes from a poem (I:45) in *Go shūi wakashū* by Jōen that runs *Awazuno no suguro no susuki tsunogumeba fuyu tachinazumu koma zo ibayuru* (On Awazu Moor/scorched, the silvergrass/hornlike sprouts/winter has come, and/this braying steed will not go).

3. "Sea-pine" is a direct translation of the characters for *miru*, the Japanese common name for the seaweed known colloquially in English as "dead man's fingers" (*Codium fragile*).

No sooner had he heard this than the beggar began to laugh so hard he had to hug his belly. "Looking for carp here, Your Worships? You might as well be looking for foxes on Sado Isle or horses on the Great Island of Izu—no labor could be more wasted! Has nobody told Your Worships? Carp do not live in the province of Awa, nor yet in Kai. It may be due to the air of this place, or the soil, or it may be, as one explanation has it, that that fish will not live in a province of fewer than ten districts, for it is the crown of the water-creatures. For Your Worships to be seeking that which does not exist—such indeed is a wanton taking of life." He laughed them to scorn, clapping his hands and cackling loudly.

Yoshizane allowed his pole to drop from his hand. "Truly a big fish lives not in a small pond, nor does the phoenix visit a songbird's grove. What am I that I find the world thus straitened, that I must stand hunched beneath the lofty heavens, that I must step softly on the earth's sturdy surface, and that I may not be accepted even by the lord of a single district of Awa? I was a fool to pin my hopes on a carp's destiny, and to take it for an ensample of a dragon. The heart of that man who, knowing there were never any carp in this country, ordered me to catch one nonetheless, is a muddy stream, and yet in it I see now the reflection of some deep cunning. His venomous plot would have worked upon me, had I not met this beggar. Ah, the peril I was in!" Again and again he cried out in anguish.

The beggar sought to comfort him. "Your Worship must not let yourself be so downhearted. There are no carp in Michinoku, either, and it has fifty-four districts—in which case can it really be that the carp's generation in a province depends upon that province's size? Then it is no more than specious rationalizing—is it not?—to say that there are no carp here because the province comprises fewer than ten districts. As the Sage said, even in a hamlet of ten houses there may be men of loyalty and good faith.[4] The Satomi scion, for example, is a man of Kamitsuke,[5] but before he could know that province he has drifted here, where he has no house, as it were, in which to shelter himself."

Master and men exchanged glances upon hearing this, and then fixed their stares on the beggar's countenance. Yoshizane, who had sighed at each new utterance of the beggar's, spoke. "We must not judge a man by his appearance. Your discourse is not that of a beggar. Are you of the ilk

---

4. From chapter 5 of *Lunyu* (J. *Rongo*), traditionally known as the Analects of Confucius.

5. Or Kōzuke, site of the village of Satomi, the clan's original holding.

Captions:
Foreground, bottom right: Fishing on the Shirahashi River, Yoshizane meets a righteous warrior.
Background, top left: Kanamari Takayoshi gathers the villagers at night.
Figures: Satomi Yoshizane [*right, foreground*]. Horiuchi Sadayuki [*center, foreground*]. Sugikura Ujimoto [*left, foreground*]. Kanamari Hachirō [*left, background*].

青堂梓

of Jie Yu, the madman of Chu,[6] or of that avatar whose filth the Empress Kōmyō scraped away?[7] Did you know me all along, then? I would ask your name."

He spoke warily, but the beggar smiled at him. "This place is too frequented by passersby—come with me," he said, and led the way. Yoshizane and his men, still suspicious, hastened to put away their poles, and then followed him to a secluded spot at the foot of a hill near the village of Komatsubara. There the beggar took off the mat he had worn as a cape, brushed the dirt from it, and spread it out beneath the trees for Yoshizane to sit on. Ujimoto and Sadayuki plucked summer weeds enough to cushion themselves as they knelt on either side of their master.

Then the beggar fell back in reverence and touched his forehead to the ground. "No doubt you find me dubious, Your Lordship, as I have not yet been granted the pleasure of an audience with you. I am a retainer of Jin'yo Nagasanosuke Mitsuhiro: I am Kanamari Hachirō Takayoshi, or what remains of him. The Kanamari are of the Jin'yo lineage and proper warriors, but served the main house as retainers for we are descended from a secondary wife. For all that, though, we sat first among the senior retainers. But I lost my father and mother early, and because I was not yet twenty it was thought that I was not equal to the position, and so my stipend was reduced to a pittance and I was used as a mere attendant.

"Thus it was that my lord's behavior deteriorated—he took pleasure in the flesh, ravaged himself with drink, and foundered in the charms of his concubine Tamazusa—he would not leave the inner chambers, but bestowed favor on the sycophant Sadakane, placing rewards and punishments under his charge, and thenceforth the house fell into severe disorder—the gods grew angry and the people resentful. The precariousness of the situation was like stacking eggs,[8] but the senior vassals refused to remonstrate with him for the sake of their stipends, though they knew full well his shortcomings, while the people feared to petition. Our lord broke his own laws, and there was no way to make him know it: I myself on a number of occasions risked discountenancing him by remonstrating with him even unto

---

6. A reference to a passage in the eighteenth chapter of the Analects, in which a madman approaches Confucius and speaks a riddle to him, then flees before Confucius can question him.

7. According to book 6 of the late twelfth-century collection of Buddhist stories *Hōbutsushū*, this eighth-century empress, a devout Buddhist, once ministered to a leper who turned out to be an avatar of the buddha Akshobhya (J. Ashuku).

8. A reference to section 50 of the Heian-era poetry-tale collection *Ise monogatari*, where the difficulty of loving someone who does not return that love is compared to that of stacking a hundred eggs.

quarreling, but to no avail. Bi Gan had his liver skewered on a swordpoint,[9] and Wu Zixu had his eyeballs hung on the Eastern Gate;[10] one might as well die as remonstrate repeatedly and be ignored, I thought, and yet as I pondered it seemed that for a retainer to speak of his lord's shortcomings was itself no trifling crime. When a great hall is about to fall, how can a single post hope to support it?[11]

"Having made up my mind that there was nothing for it but to remove myself, I spoke of my aspirations to two colleagues of mine, Shichirō of the Nako and Hyōnai of the Amatsu, and then, with the light heart of one with neither wife nor child, I absconded, fading into the night. I made for Kazusa, crossed into Shimōsa, traveled Kamitsuke and Shimotsuke—I journeyed day after day, even to the ends of Michinoku, and to make ends meet I set myself up as an instructor in whatever skills in armed and unarmed combat I happened to have picked up—I spent half a year here, a season there, passing days and months that refused to wait, until already five years had passed. The welfare of my old lord began to weigh upon my heart, and so this year I returned in secret to Kazusa, but O! it was useless: my lord's house had fallen.

"It rent my innards, it ground my bones, to hear how he had fallen to the hunting arrows of Bokuhei of Somaki and Mukuzō, and all because of Sadakane's mutinous intent. Those men, Bokuhei and Mukuzō, were private soldiers serving my family—they had grown up with us from my father's time. They had been taught the sword-fighting techniques belonging to our house, and possessed considerable gallantry of their own. They were born the children of farmers but never loved tilling and harvesting, and though I, whom they had thought to serve forever, had abandoned them so that they must live as peasants, they, suffering under burdensome laws, determined to shoot down Sadakane, their lord's enemy and their own—such was their aim, when they did their despicable deed. This much I guessed, though I can never hate those mutinous brigands enough.

"I thought to train my arrows on him myself, but although I know him by sight from of old, I have no way of getting close to him, so I emulated

---

9. According to chapter 3 of *Shi ji*, Bi Gan was an uncle and counselor of King Zhou of Yin. When he remonstrated too persistently, Zhou noted that sages were supposed to have seven chest-openings, and tested the legend by having Bi Gan slaughtered.

10. According to chapter 66 of *Shi ji*, Wu Zixu was an advisor to King Fuchai of Wu when Wu was at war with the state of Yue. Yue surrendered, but Zixu counseled against accepting the surrender. Angered, Fuchai ordered Zixu to kill himself; prior to doing so, Zixu directed that his eyes be posted at the gate so he could watch Yue invade the city.

11. A question posed in the third section of the Tang-era miscellany *Wen Zhongzi zhongshuo* (J. *Bun Chūshi chūsetsu*).

Yu Rang of Jin and disguised myself by lacquering my body;[12] day after day I roamed around Takita, keeping watch always, but never with any hint of a sign, and as there were those who began to grow suspicious, I decided to distance myself from that place for a time. I came here, where the irrepressible talk of the town was that milord Yoshizane, the Satomi youth, had fled here from the Yūki cantonment, that he had tried to rely on Maro and Anzai, but that they, despising ability and being jealous of talent, refused to take him into their service, erecting a blind of many words and behind it plotting to kill him—this incredible tale I heard, but had no connection or means that I might tell you of it, my lord.

"From the first time I heard your name I yearned for you as a babe for his dam, but I could hardly go casting about openly for your whereabouts, and so I suffered, in silence. Still I wandered hither and yon, with no aim but the thought that I should come upon you somehow, yet how could I have known it would be today, here, on Shirahashi shore, where I saw Your Worships fishing? Methought you hailed from elsewhere, and your countenances and frames marked you as no ordinary men; you appeared to be intimates, and yet your observance of decorum gave you the air of a master and his men. I surmised that this must be that lord for whom I sought, but I dared not speak to you plainly, and so I disguised my meaning as the plain song of a mean fisherman as he rows along the strand.

"How must it have sounded to Your Lordship? '*I see my village*' expressed the joy of the people at having gained the Satomi Lord for their own.[13] '*White sails running on a fair-flowing breeze*'—the white sails are the flags of the House of Minamoto, and concealed within these lines is this meaning: that, should you raise righteous soldiers here, there are among the people none who would not bend like the grass to the wind of your authority. '*The boats that come/To Awa port/No wave can smash/No tide can rot/So pull, men, pull/And I'll pull, too*' means just this: the prince—that is Your Lordship—is, as Xunzi says, a boat.[14] Your Lordship is adrift at present, and, shunned by Maro and Anzai, you will be buffeted about, but in the end you will be unscathed, for the inhabitants of this province will support you, and you will crush your

---

12. According to book 86 of *Shi ji*, Yu Rang went undercover to avenge his murdered lord. To make himself unrecognizable, he spread lacquer sap all over his body, which causes a severe skin irritation.

13. In addition, *sato miete* ("I see my village") is partially homophonous with Satomi (the characters for which literally mean "village" and "see").

14. In the ninth chapter of his eponymous Han-era book, Xunzi (J. Junshi) expounds upon the old saying that (in Watson's translation) "The ruler is the boat and the common people are the water. It is the water that bears the boat up, and the water that capsizes it." See Burton Watson, trans., *Hsün Tzu: Basic Writings* (New York: Columbia University Press, 1996), 37.

enemies in Takita, Tateyama, and Hiratate, mighty though they be. I con-gratulate you upon it—and that is why I sang thus. If, cleaving unto righ-teousness, you will now raise up your flag—if you will immediately press on to Takita, enumerate Sadakane's crimes, and attack him without delay—you will take the castle in one fell swoop. Once you have chastised that brigand into submission and taken Heguri and Nagasa, Maro and Anzai will fall with-out you striking a blow. To seize the initiative is to dominate your opponent; to delay is to come under domination. May Your Lordship take it into your mind to do this, but quickly, quickly.

"Now, about that castle: it is like this," he said, and lay before his listeners its situation and fortifications so vividly that they felt they could reach out and touch it. Ujimoto and Sadayuki felt him to be of all men the most reli-able, and pricked up their ears.

Yoshizane, however, showed no signs of willingness to follow his counsel, and replied, "What you say is beyond me. Your plan is a good one, but we cannot oppose so many with so few. Moreover, I am adrift upon the waves, masterless. On what grounds shall I seek to summon allies? We here now, master and men, are three, perhaps four—were we to attack Takita Castle we should be like katydids brandishing hatchets against a cartwheel. We can hardly hope to succeed."

Kanamari Hachirō shuffled forward on his knees. "Such words hardly bear the saying of them, Your Lordship. The farming folk of these two prov-inces have been downtrodden by that mutinous brigand, and are angry to the marrow, but being oppressed by authority and terrified of power, they have bowed down to him for a time. But that is all: it is as natural for men to cleave unto righteousness as it is for the grass and trees to turn toward the sun. Refuse not this lonely task—but once raise your flag, strike back on behalf of the Jin'yo, save the people from their degradation—and the people, like ants to nectar or an echo to its source, will come running to your side; gladly will they lay down their lives in a battle for the sake of righteousness and benevolence. There are none among them who do not wish to gnaw on Sadakane's flesh before departing this life. I, Takayoshi, may of myself count for little, but through devices I can raise great numbers of people as easily as turning over a hand. Those devices are—" and he came close and whispered them.

"Indeed," said Yoshizane, nodding faintly.

"Prodigious!" exclaimed Ujimoto and his companion, listening by Yoshi-zane's side and reappraising the beggar with thorough gazes. "'Tis a pity, Lord Kanamari, though it be all for loyalty, that your flesh be thus enveloped in boils—you hardly appear human. In this state how can you hope to gather allies to you? Even those who know you will not think it is you, though you tell them your name. How inopportune that we have no efficacious balm to quickly heal your sores. Oh, for medicine!"

He spoke as if to comfort Takayoshi, but the latter hitched up his sleeves and said, rubbing and scratching his arms, "I do not love my body as I do my late lord. If I can destroy that mutinous brigand, then I shall count my desires as fulfilled, though I am become an invalid. My appearance is changed, but that will prove not the slightest hindrance, for this army I would raise is not for myself—let it not weigh upon your minds, sirs."

Yoshizane considered for a time, and then said, "Such, I am sure, are your aspirations. However, as these are sores that can be healed, how can we do better than to heal them? Lacquer hates crab. It is said that if crab has been boiled in a house that works with lacquer, the workers find that the lacquer sap does not flow. It occurs to me that your lesions come not from internal causes, but merely from external ones—from having touched the lacquer poison—and that therefore if we administer crab to the poison, you may be cured as you stand here. Let us try it."

Takayoshi was most impressed by Yoshizane's wisdom, and could not refuse. "Crab is plentiful in this cove. By all means, let us make the attempt."

Their timing as they spoke was propitious, for some children of the fisher-folk then approached, creels perched on their heads. Sadayuki and Ujimoto hastened to detain them with a "Ho, there." They stopped, and the men inquired, "What have you there?" It was crab. "A happy coincidence!" Smiling, they bought all the children had, over thirty in all.

Yoshizane, looking on, taught Takayoshi what to do, and when Takayoshi had fully understood he took half the still-living crabs and, cracking open their shells, set about spreading their innards over his flesh. While he was doing this, Sadayuki and his colleague broke up some dead pine boughs and made a fire, striking together the flints they carried at their waists; they then roasted the remaining crabs, separated them from their shells and took off their legs, and gave them to Takayoshi. When he had ingested each and every one, the foul-smelling bloody pus dried up, the scabs fell away as he scratched them, and he was healed in every particular. Indeed, it appeared that the gods and buddhas, pitying his lonely loyalty, had shown him a miracle in the marvelous effects of this medicine.

"A prodigy!" exclaimed Ujimoto, as together with Sadayuki he examined Takayoshi from every angle. "Look there," he then said, pointing to a horse's hoofprint that had filled with water.

Takayoshi looked closely at his reflection in it, then said through tears he was powerless to prevent, "My flesh, so ravaged by lesions and scratching that no part of it was left whole, has been healed as I stand here! It is a gift from a virtuous general proficient in the ways of brush and sword! It is said that a great physician can heal a country. Of myself, I am nothing but refuse. If Your Lordship subdues the discord in this province and saves the people from their sufferings, it will truly be a feat of unsurpassed benevolence. This place is neither Maro's nor Anzai's territory—they have no recourse, though your appointed day is past. Yet we must not delay. Quickly, Your Lordship, let us go to that place of which I whispered to you before." As he repeated his urgings, he raked his fingers through his thicket of hair and then tied it back into a short topknot; for a belt he had but a rope, but into it he thrust the dirk he had carried hidden, even as he sought to thrust Yoshizane onto the path along the cove to Kominato.

And so Kanamari Hachirō Takayoshi guided the Satomi lord and his men toward Kominato. The day, though summer-long, grew quickly dark, and the twenty-day-old moon, wait though they might, rose not—only the Tanjō temple bells, which could with straining just be heard, proclaimed how late it was: the hour of the boar.[15] Now, Tanjō Temple—the Temple of the Birth, or the Holy Mountain of Lofty Illumination[16]—is located in the village of Aekawa, in Kominato. This being the place where Nichiren the Exalted was born, his disciple Nikka the Exalted founded here a retreat, naming it Tanjō Temple.[17] This sect of the Dharma has prospered these long ages, for the surrounding country-folk, both goodly and mean, thirsted for its teachings and became parishioners. This was what is vulgarly known as the Seven League Lotus of Kazusa, or the Sutra Sect of the Seven Inlets of Awa—that is, the majority of the locals were Passagers[18]—but of all the region, the district of Nagasa, being the birthplace of the Founder, was the most full of tendentious believers, not admitting, even conditionally, any other sects.

The first thing Kanamari Takayoshi did, having planned his actions beforehand, was to set fire to a stand of bamboo by the side of the Tanjō Temple in order to bring together the villagers. The night was black as leopard-flower

---

15. The hour before that of midnight.

16. The temple's full name was Kōkōsan Tanjōji, meaning "Temple of the Birth, Mountain of Lofty Illumination." The "Mountain" in its name is metaphorical, rather than a reference to an actual geographical feature in the neighborhood.

17. Nichiren (1222–1282) was a fiery Buddhist reformer whose sect, which emphasizes the importance of the Lotus Sutra, survives even today. Tanjōji was founded in 1276 by a monk now known as Nike (1258–1315), although Bakin glosses the characters of his name as "Nikka."

18. The "Seven League Lotus" (*shichiri hokke*) referred to the preponderance of Nichiren adherents in this area of Awa. The other two names were nicknames by which Nichiren's sect was known: the Sutra Sect (*kyōshū*) because of Nichiren's emphasis on the Lotus Sutra, and the Passagers (*daimokushū*) because of the sect's practice of reciting a particular passage from it.

seeds, and even with such paltry tinder, the flames leapt quickly to the heavens, stirring the birds asleep in the boughs—the priests rushed to the bell and struck it again and again. Villagers all around were startled awake, and as they pushed open the gate to peer in, they cursed, saying, "Something is amiss at our temple! Wake up! Come, all!" Villagers dragging staves, peasants carrying farm implements, fishermen, boat captains—everybody and his brother came at a run, gasping for breath, vying to be first, only to find the temple unharmed. All that had burned—though even that was to be regretted—was an unfrequented bamboo grove a few hundred yards from the temple.

The night was quiet, the air still, and the village was quite distant with no cottages nearby—by the time the people had gathered, the fire had largely died out, and the bells had fallen silent. This puzzled everyone; some undid the hand-towels they had tied around their heads and mopped the sweat from their brows, and some said, "What blackguardly mischief is this? A wildfire that spread? The ignorance! And here we are, you and I, awakened in the night, running here as if on wings—nearly a mile for the closest, and the farthest ten miles or more—with both hunger and tempers rising, and no sop for either. What shall we do about it?" while others said, "Should we not at least rejoice that it was nothing worse?" Some burst into laughter, some fell into cursing, but none of them dispersed while they could rest and catch their breaths.

Then Kanamari Takayoshi stepped forth from what was left of the scorched thicket, coughing. All eyes were on him in astonishment and confusion: "Look at that—is it man or devil?"

Takayoshi raised his hand and spoke: "Men, be not alarmed! I have been awaiting you here since evening."

Thus he sought to enlighten them, but they just exchanged glances and said, "So you are the blackguard who has deceived us all with false deeds! Strike him! Bind him!"

There was jostling and bickering as they pressed forward upon him, but he was unperturbed. He advanced and spoke. "'Tis meet you should think thus, for I have not told you the meaning of my actions—and yet, would I send up flames and gather you here without reason? I will tell you my name," he said, and when he had forced them into silence, he continued.

"The country falls into chaos, and a loyal retainer appears; the house falls onto hard times, and a filial son emerges. Thus says the Ancient. 'Tis from aspiration that I thus 'neath woven hat and rain-cloak hide myself, destroy my body, in this floating world. Although you would never think it, no doubt, I am Kanamari Hachirō Takayoshi, late of the service of the old lord of this country. In former days I remonstrated with my lord and failed, and so I made my retreat, though it went against my heart—many years have I spent in traveler's lodgings, but how could I forget what I owe my lord? And so I returned in secret to my old home, changing my name and disguising my appearance, all in order that I might smite the treasonous retainer Sadakane. I kept a watchful eye open for an opportunity, but alas, with enough men you can defeat Heaven,[19] and my enemy has ten thousand followers, and is in a three-league fortress.[20] Yu Rang lurked under a bridge, honing his blade,[21] while Tadamitsu once covered his eye with a fish-scale[22]—neither to any avail.

"However, Maro and Anzai, in Hiratate and Tateyama, are unclean in their hearts; they have not stinted to cooperate with the rebel, and so I cannot easily bring them into my confidence, despite their old association with my late lord. I was left to my rage at this lusterless world and this useless body in which I am entombed. I was at the point of slitting my belly, thinking to slough off this useless locust-shell in which I am so helpless, to die and as a spirit finally visit my wrath upon Sadakane, when the Satomi youth Lord Yoshizane, having slashed his way through attackers at Yūki, drifted ashore at Shirahama. He sought to rely on Anzai and Maro, who hated him and would not let him stay even a little while but plotted with words of thus-and-such import to kill him—but affairs have not yet reached that pass. I happened to meet him by chance on the Shirahashi riverbank, and I addressed him openly, meaning secretly to try him. I found that lord, young though he is, to be possessed of benevolence and righteousness in language and address. He is truly a goodly general with command over both brush and sword.

"It is a happiness not to me alone, but to all of you who have these many years in secret bewailed your abuse at the hands of that mutinous brigand Sadakane, that this master and his men escaped the tiger's jaws at Yūki when so many of the besieged fell or were captured—few were saved, but these came here. If you do not now quickly join this lord's following and defeat Sadakane, you are but a brigandly people, and the whole province

---

19. A phrase from chapter 66 of *Shi ji*.

20. A phrase from *Mengzi* (second part of chapter 2). The passage goes on to say that for an enemy to take such a city requires the assistance of heaven.

21. Yu Rang (see note 12) hid under a bridge to take his revenge, but was unsuccessful when his target apprehended him.

22. A reference to an incident recorded in the *Azuma kagami* (entry for 1/21/1192), in which a laborer was found to be blind in his left eye. Upon further investigation the man proved to be the Taira straggler Tadamitsu, trying to sneak into Kamakura in disguise—he had feigned blindness by covering his eye with a fish's scale.

will reap suffering because of you. If, however, you cleave unto righteousness by striking a blow for your country against this reversal, then are you a good people—you will long escape calamity, and your descendants will reap joy on your account. It was this, and no passing fancy, that forced me to raise this blaze and gather you thus to this grove: I wished to proclaim these things to you, but could not tell you individually, as the matter would have leaked out."

Once he had explained all this, the people all clapped their hands and rejoiced. "We said things we did not mean—so superbly did you dissemble yourself that even those who should have recognized you did not know you, Lord Kanamari. May it please Your Lordship to forgive us. We are as bugs, by nature lacking wisdom and talent, but who among us can forget what he owes the lord of his province? Who among us does not abhor Sadakane? We find him hateful, but have been too powerless to mount a force against him, and so we have bewailed our state, in which neither moon nor sun shines upon us. And yet we have heard of the Satomi lord, though in whose words, carried by what wind, we could not say. Inquiry into his lineage told us he was of the main line of the Minamoto house, a goodly general such as is rarely seen, and from the moment we heard this we yearned after him— we were as if standing on tiptoe, craning our necks for him, every one. We people of the soil are withering beneath a false sovereign more burdensome than any summer sun—O pity us and raise an army here, and be unto this land great happiness! No one here would stint to give his life. We beg and pray you, Lord Kanamari, tell him this."

Thus as one they answered him. Takayoshi glanced behind him. "Did Your Lordship hear that? How quickly it is settled!"

At this cue, Yoshizane came out from the shadow of the grove, leading Ujimoto and Sadayuki; together they stepped deliberately forward and faced the crowd. "I am that Satomi Yoshizane of whom you speak. I may be a bird who flew around a field of slaughter until winged by an arrow, as is the wont of him who takes up the bow, but I shall not shelter beneath an evil tree,[23] though it be the way of a world in chaos. I have no virtue for you to look upon me as your father and mother, but if a people sees fit not to discard me, shall I not cleave unto their counsels? Even the swiftest steed cannot run without his legs; even the fleetest phoenix cannot fly without his wings.

---

23. The Three Kingdoms/Jin-era poet Lu Ji's *Meng hu xing* (J. *Mōko kō*) begins: "No matter how thirsty, I would never drink at Thieves' Spring/no matter how hot, I would never shelter under an evil tree."

I am but a lonely soldier in retreat, but now have I gained the assistance of a multitude. Shall I not do this thing? And yet Takita is a formidable enemy. We would be ill advised to move against it lightly, without horses and equipage, and stores for the men. What can be done about this?"

At this question, his listeners all looked at one another, saying, "What, indeed?" None answered him for a time.

Then two or three of their number, old men who seemed to be village heads, broke from the crowd and came forward. "By your leave, sir, we have a trifle of an idea we would propose, foolish though it no doubt is. The district of Nagasa has been entrusted to Sadakane's right-hand man, the old vassal Shietage Kokuroku, who occupies the castle of Tōjō. It is not far from here. Launching your campaign with a strike against Kokuroku will immediately deliver a district into your hands, not to mention equipage and provisions. It will also give you freedom of movement when you attack Takita, will it not?"

Yoshizane was moved to exclamation by the careful proposal. He looked about him and said, "Did every man hear that? 'There are men of merit to be found among the common folk'—the proverb could have been coined for these elders. Speed is of the essence when executing cunning strategies against an enemy. Let us press forward immediately, this very night, and take him unprepared. Now, this is what I would have you do."

He made known unto Takayoshi and the others his plan, and when they had understood it, Takayoshi, Ujimoto, and Sadayuki counted the assembled villagers. There were a hundred and fifty or so. These they separated into three companies, telling them the plan. Everyone rejoiced to receive their orders, and those who had come empty-handed cut down great stalks of bamboo from the thicket and tucked them under their arms as spears. The first company consisted of some forty men, and was led by Horiuchi Sadayuki; it advanced as the vanguard, with Kanamari Takayoshi in fetters. This was according to Yoshizane's strategy. The rearguard consisted of fifty men, with Sugikura Ujimoto in command; the center, sixty men, Yoshizane led personally, and these two companies came around by circuitous paths, hastening to a place beside the main gate of the castle where they were to form a single body of men.

Meanwhile, at Tōjō, Sadakane's steward, Shietage Kokurokurō Motoyori, had already the previous evening dispatched troops to "Put out that fire at Kominato!" But the fire had already gone out when they reached that far village, and they were told that it had been but a wildfire, so they returned to the castle where they proceeded to rejoin their dreams, it being near dawn.

But then came a mob of people pounding on the castle's main doors. Startled, the men-at-arms manning the gate cried, "Who is it?"

The reply came that the head of the village of Aekawa in Kominato had, with others, apprehended a thief and brought him to the castle. The gatekeepers inquired further into the matter, and were told, "Yes, sirs, last evening when we went to put out the fire in the bamboo grove by Tanjō Temple, we took this villain. In strength, in quickness, in visage and spirit, he is not of the common run of men. Straightaway we questioned him, pointedly, about where he had come from, but he would not utter a true word and only cursed us. There was one who knew him, however, who said he was Kanamari Hachirō Takayoshi, that had served the original lord of the province. It transpired that he had disguised himself and changed his name, and had been haunting Takita for a matter of months seeking to avenge his old master. This was no mean criminal, and if we had let him escape through some error of our own the guilt of it would have been impossible for us to evade. So we marshalled a great number of men and marched him here, not waiting for daylight. Pray tell your masters this," came the petition in raised voice.

The men-at-arms manning the gate opened a window and one peered out. "Well done! I will tell them." Hardly had he spoken when he shut the window and rushed away—presumably to report to somebody or other, for after a time came the rasping of a bolt, and a small door beside the gate was pushed open, and the call came to "quickly, come inside." Takayoshi, advancing in front, pretending to be fettered, suddenly shook off his bonds and grasped the hilt of the sword belonging to the man-at-arms standing to the right of him. He drew the sword, stealing it from its owner, and in a single flash of the blade its owner's head flew from its perch and landed on the ground.

"What havoc is this?" cried the other men-at-arms—this was something quite unlooked-for. But Sadayuki pressed forward, chasing them away, and joined forces with Takayoshi and the others: together they lay about them with their blades, felling foes, and their advance was like entering a deserted village. Quickly they pressed their attack on the second gate of the castle. Meanwhile the peasants pushed open the great gate and raised a battle cry.

Yoshizane, who had joined his men to the first company and had approached to the edge of the moat, heard this and immediately cried out his commands: "The time is now! Seize the chance! Charge!" How could the multitude not take courage? Finally the voices joined in battle cry were as the bubbling up of the tide; they came on in a headlong charge, breaking down the first and second castle gates.

"Come out, Shietage, you dog's vassal! The Satomi youth Lord Yoshizane, having been pleased to sojourn in this land, has been pressed by the multitude into accepting exaltation as their lord. He means to smite the mutinous brigand Sadakane and sweep away the stain from this province, and who will stand against him in this benevolent, righteous battle? Everywhere he goes, every place he passes, he is fêted by the old and weak 'with baskets of food and pots of drink,'[24] and now as an offering on this occasion they give unto him this castle. He who regrets his past failings must now submit if he would keep his head. He who dallies will be crushed, be he fine jewel or common stone. Come out!" came the call, and Yoshizane and his men darted about unhindered, surrounding the castle-soldiers, who were all too cowed to put up a defense. The defenders doffed their helmets, discarded their bows and arrows, and prostrated themselves to beg for their lives.

Thus did Satomi Yoshizane take Tōjō Castle without bloodying his blade. He inquired after the bandit general Shietage Kokuroku, and was told, "He fled early on, we know not where."

Yoshizane's brow furrowed when he heard this. "Had he let shame harrow his soul unto repentance so that he renewed his aspirations—had he followed me from this day forward—I should not have reproached him for prior wrongs, but he woke not from his intoxication, and remains benighted. That he fled so quickly is not in itself a thing I can much mourn, but if he runs straight back to Takita and tells Sadakane, then Sadakane will connive with Anzai and Maro to press an attack here before many days have passed. I have now gained a castle, and some two or three hundred officers and men, but those who have surrendered to me make up the majority. The lord's vigor and his men's differ in degree. Should our plans not fall into place and we be faced with enemies on three sides, with what shall we meet them? Truly this is no small matter—we must avert it. Kokuroku has already fled, but he cannot have gone far. Ujimoto, Sadayuki—separate into two companies and apprehend him at once."

So commanded he, and no sooner had they answered, "Yes, my lord," than they made to leave. Just then, though, Kanamari Hachirō Takayoshi, having run off somewhere, suddenly returned at the head of a dozen or so soldiers and uttered these words to the general Yoshizane: "This day's work was well performed by all alike, but I know this castle well. So it was that I went ahead of the main body of the army and smashed the castle's third gate; I thought to search out the brigand general Shietage Kokuroku and

---

24. An image from *Mengzi* (second part of chapter 1) describing how the people of a land greet their liberator.

Caption: In the Thornvale, Takayoshi smites Kokuroku.
Figure labels: Kanamari Hachirō [*right*]. Shietage Kokuroku [*left*].

capture him alive, but I was unable to learn where he was. Then it occurred to me that there is a single escape from the castle, to the northwest. It faces a cypress-covered mountainside; to the right is thick forest, while to the left the cliff is sheer as if cut away, with below it a river wending through a ravine of depth most profound. This is the castle's ultimate fastness, and it is kept secret from others—it is named the Thornvale.

"Surmising that he might have fled this way, I rounded up some soldiers whose hearts would answer and we made our way along the precipice, clinging to vines, and came out by the escape route. We gazed ahead of us until we spied someone fleeing southeast, with seven or eight men following and his wife and children on a litter. We watched them more closely—it was Kokuroku. Once he, too, was a veteran Jin'yo vassal, and stood much higher than I did in our lord's esteem, but he had it not within him to die for the sake of loyalty and righteousness, even as he fattened himself and supported his dependents on his stipend; he played the sycophant to the mutineer so that he was established in Tōjō Castle, where he abused the people to his heart's content—but in the end he could not elude Heaven's punishment for it, and today the castle fell.

"Run he might, but how could I let him escape? 'I, Kanamari Hachirō, am here—bring yourselves back!' I called to him, and immediately began to give chase. This frightened the palanquin-bearers, who in their haste tripped and collapsed, dashing the litter to the ground—the woman and children aboard it, crying out all the while, tumbled into the abyss, where they were struck against stumps and smashed against rocks until they died, leaving no bones behind. Shietage saw his wife and children perish before his eyes, and he was powerless to save them; he stood on the brink, leaning on his spear and staring back at us, doubtless thinking how difficult it would be for him to escape. Master and men—seven of them—deployed themselves in a fish-scale formation and waited for us to come to them.

"My allies were strung out in a crane-wings formation, and with a cry we fell to the attack like birds of prey smiting songbirds or a whirlwind whipping up grit. The place was every bit as precarious as its name claimed. Brightening were the heavens but still deep in cloud, and deep was the darkness under the trees in the shadow of the peaks; it was every man for himself, whether to advance or retreat, and we could see each other's faces. The heroism of my men, ducking past each other to reach the enemy first, possessed their opponents' legs to carry them away—they held for a time and then scattered. As they ran we chased them down and captured them alive, every last one, and finally struck down the bandit general Shietage."

After he had finished his hurried speech, he brought forth the prisoners, sat them down, and presented them for Yoshizane's inspection along with Kokuroku's head. Yoshizane sighed in spite of himself. "A soldier is an instrument of misfortune.[25] When virtue declines, the military arts are propounded; when enlightenment fails, authority becomes the means of control. This is merely what cannot be avoided. I attacked this castle, fought for this land, because I would deliver the people; I take no pleasure in killing. Nor is everyone who follows Sadakane evil. No doubt eight or nine in ten of them do it out of a fear of some immediate harm, or because they reoriented their aspirations according to the tide of the times. For this reason I would not only have spared the lives of any who repented their wrongs and came to me as an ally, I would have given them employ as well, would I not? How is it that while the troops who followed Shietage were taken alive, Shietage himself had his head taken, and his wife and children dashed to pieces on the rocks in the stream? His cannot have been a case of simply allowing his aspirations to be reoriented, according to the tide of the time, to serving a rebel—he must have been vicious in a way that Heaven could not forgive. Yea, though one find oneself following evil, one must never do evil oneself. Circumspection!"

Having thus elucidated matters, he released the captives Kanamari had brought. Then he said, "There will, at a later date, be rewards of gratitude to those who have newly joined me, according to the degree of merit they displayed in the battle." So earnestly did he speak that his listeners could not hold back their tears. "O that we had followed this lord from the beginning, forfeit as our lives are," they said, their shame harrowing their souls unto repentance; they knew not where they might find a place for themselves henceforth.

Yoshizane again spake unto Takayoshi, saying, "It had made me uneasy to think that if Kokuroku escaped to Takita, Sadakane would come sweeping down on us like wildfire. Takayoshi, with your deeds today, it is as if you knew this thought I harbored in my breast. But though no soldiers from the castle have scattered in flight, news of this will be heard in every place within three days from the morrow, I doubt not. With that, Maro and Anzai will aid Sadakane out of envy. To seize the initiative is to dominate your opponent; to delay is to come under domination. If we set out this evening at twilight and run all night to Heguri, it will put a chill in the enemy's bowels, will it

---

25. A quotation from the eighth chapter of *Wei Liao zi* (J. *Utsu Ryōshi*) a Chinese Warring States–era military treatise by Wei Liao.

not? Once the advantage in the initial battle goes to our side, Maro and Anzai will blanch to hear it, and will not dare stick their heads out. Well, be that as it may, let me first issue word as to rewards."

He decreed that Kanamari Hachirō Takayoshi should be first rewarded, and granted him great estates, but Takayoshi said, "Long have I had my own thoughts on the matter," and firmly refused them.

Second, Yoshizane called forth the three old men who, at Kominato, had urged him to "take Tōjō, if it please Your Lordship." He asked their names, and they answered: Sanpei, Shijirō, Nisō. Hearing this, Yoshizane smiled and said, "Now these are happy names! Sanpei—'three flat'—is, as we should say, a portent of how we shall flatten those three formidable foes, Yamashita, Maro, and Anzai. Shiji—'four rule'—is a sign that I shall rule the four districts. Nisō—'two tassels'—means Kazusa and Shimōsa, signifying that they shall pass into my hands. Combine those three names—three fours is twelve villages, and add twice that again—and you shall be the head of thirty-six places." His listeners, having been graced with this rescript, intoned wishes that Yoshizane might live ten thousand years, and then, hearts emboldened by joy, they withdrew.

Third came Ujimoto and Sadayuki, and various others of their companions too numerous to record. Unto them were given emoluments or presentations, and each one did a formal dance of attendance upon him while singing, as if it were a popular air:

> Weighty his rewards, and light his punishments!
> The dead come back to life! The living prosper!
> The fish in the wheel-rut returns to the river!
> An evergreen under the snow!
> May our lord's age never fail
> Until pebbles turn to boulders!

After this manner did they hail him with great excitement.

Thus did Yoshizane relax the laws, caressing the people, and rectify the military regulations, encouraging the officers and men, with the result that hundreds now came unbidden to join him. The greater part of them he caused to stay and guard the castle with Sugikura Ujimoto; a mere two hundred and some mounted men did he pick to lead—with Takayoshi in the vanguard and Sadayuki in the rearguard—in the advance on Heguri. Ujimoto whispered to him in determined remonstrance: "Your forces are unconscionably few. Two or three hundred officers and troops would suffice to guard the castle—you should take more."

Yoshizane shook his head. "Nay, this castle is now my nest. If it be smashed, then whereunto shall I return? The battle goes not always to the many. If the advantage is on my side, then my two hundred mounted men will be as a thousand, or two thousand. Concern yourself not with me, but protect this castle well. Now, I have somewhat more I would say. Let us be reconciled with Maro and Anzai. We must not fight with them. Should enemy troops come to you from Takita, fight them off even unto the last ounce of your strength. But you must not go out in pursuit of them. This is a good strategy, and a safe one. Let not your vigilance fail." Having expounded these things in great earnest, Yoshizane then hastened the vanguard on its way, and finally his army departed.

As might have been foretold, when the Satomi army that night crossed the bridge that formed the boundary between the region of the inlet of Maehara and Hamaogi, it was overtaken by a couple of hundred mounted men, led by grassroots warriors and village samurai, who yearned for Yoshizane's virtue and sought after his ways: they came to submit to him, and thus his forces swelled to a thousand mounted men and this bridge was known to later ages as the Thousand-Knight Bridge. Nor is that all, for long ago when the Noble Lord Yoritomo of the Minamoto pressed his way into this land bound for Kazusa, he caused his rearguard to wait on the banks of this river; thus there came to be a shrine there called Shirahata—"White Banner"—near unto the place known as Matsusaki—"the Cape of Waiting." Yoshizane there dismounted and made an offering of two war-arrows. He spent a while in prayer, and then—although it was the middle of the night—two white doves in a flutter of wingbeats left their pine-bough perch in front of the shrine and flew off toward Heguri. All the soldiers who saw this said, "Victory shall be ours!" Not a one but was greatly emboldened by it.

End of Book II of the Lives of the Eight Dogs of
the Satomi of Southern Fusa

The Lives of the Eight Dogs of the Satomi of Southern Fusa

Book III

Assembled by the Master of the Crooked Pavilion in the Eastern Capital

Chapter V
A good general foils a plot and his soldiers learn benevolence;
A tame pigeon delivers a missive and a rebel surrenders his head

The messenger Yamashita Sakuzaemonnojō Sadakane had sent to Maro and Anzai returned to Takita. "Those two cronies did not speak openly of submission, but they were sore afraid. I make no doubt that in the not too distant future they will come personally before you, apologize for their crimes, and seek to place themselves under your command. The way of it was thus and such and so on and so forth," he said, speaking of things that were not just as though they were, embroidering events with fine detail, spouting flattery to the last.

Sadakane gave his heart even more fully over to extravagance. He made merry all day and through the night, while ignoring the resentment of his officers and men; he sought amusement among the blossoms in the inner garden, sharing a hand-cart[1] with Tamazusa, or gathered beauties in a high tower to dandle the moon—one day he drank like a cow at a pond of sake, and the

---

1. As Tokuda notes (p. 99), this image suggests transgressive familiarity, and may refer to a poem by Du Fu called *Aijiang tou* (J. *Aikō tō*) describing Yang Guifei (about whom see Chapter II, note 9).

next he gorged himself as if in a forest of flesh.[2] Since their principal was thus, his elder vassals, too, faded into lasciviousness and drunkenness; they grasped greedily and never knew satisfaction, spent furiously and never knew exhaustion. When Wang Mang controlled the realm, when Lushan toppled the Tang government,[3] the sun in the heavens seemed to shine for them alone, but rebels never live long. Many knew that Sadakane must needs fall before very long, and they kept their eyes trained on him, flicking their fingers in disgust.

In the midst of this there arose a great commotion both within and without the castle, accompanied by an extraordinary amount of cursing—"An enemy army approaches!" Sadakane was in revelry in an inner chamber, and he showed no sign of excitement upon hearing this, but said, "What could it possibly be? If it is not Anzai and Maro seeking rashly to beard the tiger, then it is no doubt brigands from the mountains trying to threaten the people into giving them things. Go and have a look at them, and then come back."

He sent a scout, who returned after a time to report, breathlessly, "The enemy are not Anzai and Maro, nor are they brigands from the mountains. I know not who they are, but they are no ordinary foe: they have over a thousand mounted men all arrayed like stalks of rice or hemp, organized by company and squad, and in the van they fly a white flag. They are resting men and horses about a mile and a half from here, but they look to be about to press on again. They are not to be scoffed at."

Sadakane heard this with knitted brows. "White is the color of the Genji's livery. I know of no one in Awa or Kazusa who uses a white banner. This may well be a scheme of the enemy's, intended to confuse us. Be that as it may, they are no doubt tired from their long march, and mean to attack at dawn. If we attack their fatigued troops with our fresh ones, how can we not be victorious? Now chase them away," he ordered, and entrusted five hundred soldiers to Iwakuma Donpei and Sabitsuka Ikunai, senior vassals and bosom friends of Sadakane's, who gladly accepted the charge. Hastily they assumed their places, riding out from the main gate at the head of their men, and proud and brave they galloped off.

Now, Iwakuma and Sabitsuka were men peerless in might, and in martial skill as well they stood far above the crowd, but they were vicious flatterers at heart: in everything, they did as Sadakane would have them do. Sadakane favored them foremost among his senior vassals as if there were no one else, and everyone bit their tongues, swallowed their resentment, and took up

---

2. Images of indulgence referring to King Zhou of Shang, who filled a pond with wine and festooned trees with roasted meat (see *Shi ji*, chapter 3).

3. Two famous usurpers. Wang Mang took power from the former Han Dynasty from 8–23 CE; for An Lushan, see Chapter II, note 9.

positions beneath Iwakuma and Sabitsuka. For this reason Sadakane relied on them daily, and on this day, too, he selected them to be generals over his forces. "I am certain that they will scatter the attackers with one kick. Indeed, there is nothing to be alarmed about," he said, merely setting men-at-arms to guard the four gates of the castle before removing himself back to the inner chambers, there to summon again his girl-servants to make merry with lascivious song and dance.

At the height of these revels there arose a commotion in the front rooms, and shouts of "'Tis no good! 'Tis no good!" Sadakane caused the pipers and strummers to cease playing and pricked up his ears. "By those voices, something is not as it should be. Boys, go and have a look." But just as the two serving boys who waited at his elbows made to stand, some fifty or sixty of the soldiers who had been sent to meet the attack came in unexpectedly by the garden gate, each bearing deep wounds in several places, and together carrying their commander Iwakuma Donpei bound to a shield. They carried him to the outer veranda, where they presented themselves, crying in unison, "Our report," and setting the injured man down with a thud before splitting into two bands to kneel and truckle.

They were the remnant of the army that had retreated, but they each bore wounds in two or three places. Tamazusa was in a tizzy, and her maidservants helped her to hide herself behind a screen. From their manner and appearance, the dumbfounded Sadakane could see that they had been defeated. "What is this?" he asked.

An old man-at-arms in the front of the ranks scratched his head. "I cannot hold my head up and say this, my lord. Our forces did not move in unison at our commander's signals. The enemy's generals were more courageous and their troopers fiercer than we had heard, and their army larger: strike and shoot though we might, it was as nothing to them. The commander at the head of their vanguard was a madman. He wore rough-laced wide-plated armor over his chain; he twirled a ten-foot spear about him, and he leaned right up against his horse's withers as, with bulging eyes, he raised a great cry:

"'Ye brigands in your bands shall not evade Heaven's punishment! Fools— to ignorantly defy the tiger's authority, while the bare blade is stretched out toward your necks! Know you not that Satomi Yoshizane, Minister of the Court, has come, and that the people of this region insist on looking upon him as their lord? He will smite the rebellious and reward the unjustly accused. As a first step he has reduced Tōjō Castle and executed Shietage Kokuroku, and now means to take Takita Castle and chastise the brigand lord Sadakane. I, Takayoshi, have been given charge of the vanguard, and am to guide him on his way. Do mine eyes deceive me, or is that Sabitsuka and

Iwakuma commanding this company of bandits? You cannot have forgotten Kanamari Hachirō, who only yesterday served together with you under our old lord, drawing his stipend from the Jin'yo just as you did. For the sake of that former lord of ours, I am following the example of solitary loyalty set by Zhang Zifang, who struck at Qin and Chu in the aid of Han.[4] I have joined myself in submission to the Satomi lord: I raised righteous soldiers for him, and we took one castle without me bloodying my sword—we have occupied two districts, and are now closing in on the bandits' lair. He who repents his wrongs and doffs his helmet to join the Satomi side shall live. He who rashly elects to defend these brigands will find it like spitting at Heaven or standing by a pool trying to strike a blow against the water: it will be a laborious, meritless task, and the guilt of it will be visited upon him. Come out and try us!'

"With that cry, he spurred on his horse and, with weapon flashing and flying unopposed, he quickly broke our first ranks and joined spears with our commander Sabitsuka. They fought with no interference from anyone. With a great cry of battle, Takayoshi twisted Ikunai's spear out of his hands and thrust his own at Ikunai's chest. Run through, Ikunai fell from his horse with a crash; some common soldiers rushed up to him and, holding him down, took his head. Sabitsuka having met his end, Iwakuma Donpei, whom you see here before you, was greatly angered, and he brandished his longsword, four and a half feet long, and galloped in a beeline for Kanamari, meaning to smite him.

"Then from the van of Satomi's army came one of his senior vassals, announcing himself as Horiuchi Kurando Sadayuki. He wore armor with dark blue lacing and a helmet with a crescent crest, rode a massive dapple-gray steed, and carried a Bizen glaive with an iris pattern on the ridge. He cried to Kanamari, 'Let me have at him,' and when Kanamari had acknowledged him, he charged forward to block Donpei's way, his horse's hooves dancing nimbly over the field. Their swordtips rang and clashed, scattering sparks, as they fought—now one had the upper hand, now the other, and as they blended into a whirlwind of blades, no watcher could tell the better from the worse; but then somehow Iwakuma's horse's withers were slashed open and it collapsed with its rider, and Sadayuki stretched out his glaive, piercing Iwakuma's helmet even unto its inner layer.

"As soon as we saw that Donpei had been smitten, we threw him over our shoulders and managed an escape. Majestic and forbidding in his splendorous armor, astride his three-year-old mount with its saddle and cloud-gem

---

4. This refers to Zhang's aid in the establishment of the Han dynasty after the demise of the the Qin emperor. Zhang's military advice and aid were instrumental in the rise of the new dynasty, but he did not assume a position of power within the new regime (see *Shi ji*, chapter 55).

crupper ornament,[5] the enemy general Satomi Yoshizane surveyed the field and gestured expansively with his tasseled baton: 'After them!' His men, as they followed his command, were as the welling up of the tide; they came on with loud shouts, and our side cowered. Not a few of our men doffed their helmets, lay down their bows, and surrendered, and then began shooting at us instead. A mere sixty or so riders remained to us, none without some manner of injury, but at length we managed to escape certain death and to flee here."

Donpei, shamefaced, tried to speak, but he had a laceration near one of his temples and his back had been trampled on by a horse; he could not raise his head. A bee in winter waiting for the sun he was, with swelling and distended wounds; the breath that passed his lips was far too weak to profit him in anything withal.

Sadakane hardly heard the soldier out. His brows knit, and he took a deep breath and said, "Satomi was among Yūki's allies. I had heard he was cut down when their castle fell, and yet he has now drifted here and raised a great army. I simply cannot understand it. If Tōjō Castle has truly fallen, and Kokuroku been struck down, then soldiers from that castle would have come here and reported it—I cannot imagine they would have failed to do so. And as for this Kanamari Takayoshi, he is a hereditary retainer of the Jin'yo, but he is also an absconding villain. Failing to find refuge, he must have crept back into this region. This must be a false plan of his, to deceive the foolish peasants, rally the wild warriors to him, and with a flood of words dampen our heroic spirits. It follows, then, that the chief commander of the attackers is not really Satomi at all. And yet these brave retainers of mine, who were as my hands and feet, are for my sake stricken—Ikunai sent untimely to his grave, and Donpei weighed down with deep wounds. One may say that it was their ordained time, but still, this is an enemy not to be trifled with. Let us then guard our four gates well—I will send a runner to Tōjō to ask how they fare there. We shall know the truth of this eventually."

The words had not left his mouth when some attendants rushed to his side and informed him that some refugees from Tōjō had arrived. Hearing this, Sadakane said, "Well, then, it was not a false report. I will hear the nature of the affair for myself, however. Bring them in through the garden gate. Quickly, now," he urged them, and they ran off with his orders.

A short time later three or four soldiers from Tōjō, followers of Kokuroku's who had through great hardship made good their escape, came staggering in through the garden gate. Imposing they were in their cuirasses and

---

5. An ornament found on ancient continental-style saddles in Japan. "Cloud-gem" is a literal translation of *uzu*; the ornament is shaped like a Buddhist *hōju* (magical jewel).

their greaves and gauntlets with extensions that looked like the hats of the ten judges of Hell; but in their fatigue they looked like starving demons, hands on their knees, dragging their feet, limping. Sadakane gathered them close to him and affixed them with a glare. "Ho there, you lot! If Tōjō was under attack, you would have done well to inform me of it before it fell—and yet here you are, coming to me all lily-livered and only after the enemy has arrived! You are as useless to me now as irises on the sixth or chrysanthemums on the tenth![6] You have failed me—I cannot see it otherwise."

With great trepidation, the four replied as one. "We would not dare think Your Lordship's anger unfounded, but the whole affair happened in the space of a single breath—there was no time to inform Your Lordship before the castle fell. The reasons were thus-and-such, so on and so forth," they said, and they told in detail of how the Kominato village heads had brought Kanamari Hachirō in fetters; how they had by scheming gotten the soldiers to open the castle gates in the middle of the night; how the great army of the enemy had seized the moment and come marching in, taking the castle in one fell swoop; how Shietage Kokuroku had led his family through the Thornvale in retreat only to be overtaken there by Kanamari Hachirō; how Shietage's wife and children had tumbled into the ravine to be dashed, skin and bones, to their deaths; how Kanamari smote Shietage. "Not for an instant did we consider not reporting this to Your Lordship, but the greater part of the soldiers of the castle surrendered and the enemy was further strengthened thereby. We made no doubt but that we should have been overtaken and struck down had we fled along the highway, so we went around by other paths, crossing the mountains, and if we have now arrived only after the enemy, and have thus invited Your Lordship's censure, we have nothing else to say in our defense." Thus did they seek to dispel his anger by apology.

Sadakane gnashed his teeth in wrath, jumped up, and said, "It all comes from Kanamari Hachirō bringing in this refugee from Yūki—this is all a plot of his! Well, then! I must ride out myself and take this damnable Kanamari—nothing else will cool this rage that burns within me. Prepare to march immediately!"

His veteran men-at-arms muttered, "'Tis pointless," and, with a glance at the remnant of the Tōjō forces, they raised up the wounded Iwakuma Donpei and all left together. Sadakane was unaware of this, however, and he continued to fulminate, until suddenly he looked about and saw there was no one left to hear him.

---

6. Irises were associated with a festival held on the fifth day of the fifth month, chrysanthemums with one held on the ninth day of the ninth month. One day later, each would be considered superfluous.

Then a thought struck him. "To go forth rashly and attack would be quite risky. Something else is called for." He nodded to himself, then summoned his senior vassals and attendants and bid them in every particular to make ready to withstand a siege. "Yoshizane's is a great army, but with no more cohesion than a conspiracy of ravens. Within ten days their supplies will be gone and they will retreat. That is when we attack. Taking their general Yoshizane then, not to mention this Kanamari, will be easier than plucking something from a sack. That being said, should Maro and Anzai unite themselves with Yoshizane and march here to join him, it would make this a much graver affair. It strikes me, upon reflection, that Kogorō of the Maro is courageous but common; we need not take him into account. It is Anzai that bothers me. I have heard that he possesses some discernment. If I tempt him with advantage, however, and arrange things in thus and such a manner so that he takes back Tōjō for me, then Yoshizane may flee for a moment, but he will have no place to return to. That will put an end to his advances, and his retreats, too: he will die at the hands of his soldiers. Let us send such a messenger now, before the enemy arrives. Whom shall I send now to carry this message for me to Tateyama and Hiratate?" he asked, and considered the matter.

In response to his words, a man named Tsumatate Togorō stepped forward. "I would undertake this charge, Your Lordship."

Sadakane was much pleased. "You know my will no less than Ikunai and Donpei did. Since you beg to go, how can I not allow it? You shall run to Tateyama and Hiratate, and this is what you shall say to Kagetsura and the other one: 'Sadakane, to preserve his late lord's heritage, has recently become ruler over two districts, but now Satomi Yoshizane, refugee from Yūki, has drifted to this land, where he has deceived the foolish commoners and gathered unto himself fighters from the countryside. Staging a sudden uprising, he has usurped Tōjō Castle and, buoyed by his success, has now come to put pressure on Takita. When a rabbit stews, a fox frets—lest the misery visited on the one be, in the near future, visited on his fellow as well.[7] Sadakane, unworthy though he may be, has inherited the Jin'yo possessions properly, with all the old friendships belonging to that house. How can you two lords not wish to come to the relief of a neighbor's soldiery, and to bear with him his burdens? March forth speedily and conquer Tōjō, then attack the enemy from behind; even if he had three faces and six arms, Yoshizane could not meet enemies on three sides. He will be unable to defend himself, and will be decimated—there can be no doubt of it. Once Yoshizane has been thus easily crushed, it will be a boon to you two lords. The single district of Heguri, with

---

7. A variation on a saying with its source in chapter 477 of the Yuan-era history *Song shi* (J. *Sōshi*).

the single castle of Takita, is sufficient for Sadakane. The district of Nagasa shall be given unto him who first conquers Tōjō.' Make this clear to them."

Togorō lifted his gaze and replied, "As you deem good, milord, so let it be done. But what use will it be to see Yoshizane destroyed if, in requesting outside help to do it, Your Lordship allows Nagasa to pass into another's hands, thereby dimishing your domains? Unless Your Lordship brings all your perspicacity to bear on this, you will come to regret it."

Thus did he, in concert with other senior vassals, protest, but Sadakane hardly heard them out before smiling and saying, "You think so too, do you? This, though, is my plan: the snipe may grasp the mussel but be taken by the fisherman.[8] Using the district of Nagasa as bait, I will have Anzai and Maro take Tōjō back for me; but once they have destroyed Satomi, Kagetsura and Nobutoki will become deluded by their desire for advantage, even unto obstinacy. Those two commanders will fight over that land, and over the course of many battles, inevitably one will be hurt though the other be struck down. I shall step into the void left thereby and take both Awa and Asahina; I shall bring all four districts within my grasp, thus bringing order to the province, all while sitting here—will not that be pleasant?" His countenance as he expounded his plan shone with confidence, and Togorō was mightily impressed. He received Sadakane's missive, clad himself in light armor, and whipped his steed, making for Tateyama.

Meanwhile, the great Satomi army surrounded Takita Castle before dawn and began their relentless attack; the fortress was sturdy, however, the stronghold of several generations of Jin'yo, and it was not to be reduced in a single morning. For three days and nights they pressed the assault, but the castle's soldiers would not come forth to fight, and the attackers began, as well they might, to be fatigued; yet they continued their assault, albeit from a distance. Then a single mounted warrior sought, like the lowering sun, to go in through the western gate of the castle. As his horse brought him nearer to the edge of the moat, Horiuchi Sadayuki fixed his gaze on him and cried out, "He must have ridden from the castle to beg assistance of Maro and Anzai—now he thinks to return. Take him alive!"

"Yes, sir!" cried several eager young warriors, and no sooner had they spoken than they galloped off in pursuit. Those within the castle saw this and pushed open the western gate of the castle, saying, "Do not let them hit Tsumatate!" Togorō rode straight in, and the bridge was hauled up after

---

8. A reference to the account of the strategies of the state of Yan in the Warring States–era treatise on strategy *Zhanguo ce* (J. *Sangoku saku*), which tells the story of a snipe and a mussel that were so engrossed in their own conflict that both were captured by a fisherman.

him—the attackers, unable to harry him in retreat, were left feeling like hunters who had let a bird slip away.

In their frustration they called for a charge that would break through in a single thrust, but Yoshizane summoned them back, saying to Sadayuki and the others, "If we give in to rage in our conduct of this affair, we shall surely regret it later. Even if we had captured that warrior and interrogated him until he gave us his information—even if we had lopped off his head—still would we ultimately fail to reduce this castle if Anzai and Maro should collude to attack us from the rear. Our best course now by far is to sew up all the approaches, ready our rearguard, attack in front, and in every respect marshal the energies of the serpent of Mount Chang,"[9] he explained, quite conscientiously. Then, "We must defend against Maro and Anzai," he said, dividing out five hundred soldiers and placing them in the rearguard under Horiuchi Sadayuki. In addition, he sent a man to Tōjō to proclaim thus and such to Sugikura Ujimoto and to bid him "be not lax in your defense of the castle," and when he had made known unto the messenger his heart, Yoshizane personally rode around the fortress together with Kanamari Takayoshi, then immediately commenced to attack it.

Meanwhile, Sadakane received word that Tsumatate Togorō had returned safely, and he quickly summoned him into his presence to ask how he had fared. Wiping away the sweat that streamed from his brow, Togorō replied, "Indeed, Your Lordship, Kagetsura and Nobutoki acceded without even taking counsel. Also, it appears that Satomi and his men first betook themselves to Anzai in Tateyama, but that in response to threats of no common nature Yoshizane fled, howling like a dog—he is a blackguard. Neither Kagetsura nor Nobutoki can fathom how he managed to raise such a great army in so few days, and as they are both vexed thereby, I make no doubt that they will attack Tōjō."

Sadakane rejoiced at Togorō's report and commended him, lading him generously. "Strengthen our defenses," he called, and settled down to wait for assistance from Tateyama and Hiratate.

In this way, the days passed and the attackers exhausted their provisions: their three days' stores were gone. Sadayuki and Takayoshi lamented this to Yoshizane, saying, "It has been some seven or eight days since we marched from camp, and Tōjō has never sent provisions. It occurs to us that while Sugikura Ujimoto is a man-at-arms of ancient merit, he is but newly in possession

---

9. As discussed by Sunzi in chapter 11 of his Spring and Autumn–era strategy manual *Bing fa* (J. *Hyōhō*), this serpent would always fight back, no matter which part of it was attacked—if its head was struck, its tail would fight, and so on.

Caption: During the attack on Takita Castle, Sadayuki et al. pursue Tsumatate Togorō.
Figures: Kanamari Hachirō [*far right*]. Satomi Yoshizane [*just left of Kanamari*]. Horiuchi Sadayuki [*bottom center*]. Tsumatate Togorō [*left, on horseback*].
Text on banner carried by Sadayuki: Hail to the Lotus Sutra, the Marvelous Law
Note: "Hail to the Lotus Sutra . . ." (*namu myōhō renge kyō*) is the mantra associated with Nichiren (see Chapter IV).

of the castle. Perhaps the people do not respond to his reminders, and thus he is unable to assemble the goods. It is now early summer—harvest-time for wheat—and behold, the grainfields ripen on the distant mountains. Shall we not order them to be reaped?"

But Yoshizane shook his head and said, "Nay—my purpose in attacking Takita was to alleviate the people's suffering. Were I now to usurp the fruits of their labor and steal their newly harvested wheat to make provisions for my soldiers, I would be no different from the tiger or the wolf who fattens himself on the flesh of men. Moreover, if the farm-folk of Nagasa fail to heed reminders and assemble provisions, it is because my virtue is insufficient, in which case I shall quickly break camp to store up virtue by mollifying the people—I shall await a better time to attack Takita. Do you not agree?"

Sadayuki cocked his head at this for a time, and then spoke. "Rare indeed is the heart so full of benevolence as to show mercy unto the people even unto blaming himself, as Your Lordship does. And yet there will be hardship if we now retreat—the castle's forces will surely come out and strike. How would it be if this evening we increased the numbers of our torches, as if to attack soon? Then after midnight we can pull back our soldiers from the rear-guard, leaving them in ambuscades thick in the forest, with Your Lordship in the van and myself guarding your retreat so that even if men from the castle are on our backs, I can keep them at bay."

Takayoshi would not hear him out. "This plan is not without its merits, but all it accomplishes is self-preservation while defending against the enemy. Foolish though I am, I propose a plan by which we deliver our strategy unto three or four hundred prime warriors, whom we shall have carry the banners of Maro and Anzai—perhaps we shall even deck them out, each man, with those lords' pennants and headgear-insignia, and at a time just after twilight they will pass by our main encampment on the northwest, as if desirous to enter the castle, and we shall gallop forth to prevent them. We shall fight each other. When those within the castle see this, they will think, 'Men-at-arms from Tateyama and Hiratate have come—we must not let them be struck down,' and they will open the gates—they will join their strength to that of their supposed relievers, and not stop until they have brought them into the castle. Then our three armies, with those soldiers at their head, shall seize the moment and enter at will, taking the castle with one fell swoop. What think Your Lordships?"

He explained his plan in great earnest, and Yoshizane heard him out carefully, then said, "Sadayuki's plan risks little, but profits me nothing; Takayoshi's plan is cunningly wrought, but exceedingly risky. It occurs to me that when the holy kings and wise generals of yore made righteous and benevolent war, they never sought to win by means of a lie. Duke Wen of Jin was counted one of the Five Hegemons and gave great aid to the house of Zhou, all without resorting to duplicitous schemes.[10] The military strategies of Masters Sun and Wu are based on the ways of duplicity.[11] This is the way of a world of warring states. Plotting is all well and good, but if I defeat the enemy with duplicity and keep his land, how am I then to instruct the people? It is for this reason that I have difficulty in following your plans, both of them. Sadakane possesses bounteous lands and is locked within well-appointed fortifications, but even if he had three years' worth of supplies, his means of defense are not out of the ordinary and so we need not call him invincible; and yet, to take his castle all at once would be to send many innocent people to their deaths. As I have said often enough before this, not everyone who follows Sadakane is evil. It pains me to think of those who, pressured by his power and cowed by his authority, have stayed besieged with him in his castle, without sharing his pleasures—to think that they will share his final sorrows, and even die there. Think not only of the brutal Xiang Yu, who buried alive eighty thousand surrendering Qin troops,[12] but also of Meng Tian of Qin,[13] or of Huo Guang of the Han.[14] Even such wise and brave commanders as they had no future, because that they killed many people. All I want is Sadakane himself—if I could only punish him, it would suffice. Nothing beyond this bears planning for." Thus did he conscientiously expound unto them, and Sadayuki and Takayoshi were so moved that neither could reply with anything but inchoate sounds.

After a time, they both sighed in spite of themselves, saying, "Your Lordship's discernment has exceeded our mean intelligence. Even among the holy kings and wise generals of yore, was there ever one greater than Your Lordship? And yet, we live in a diminished age: exceedingly numerous are they who flock to advantage, while those who cleave unto virtue are few beyond measure. The impartiality of Your Lordship's goodwill is truly deep—you even wish to aid the people under siege in an enemy castle—and yet your

---

10. See Chapter I, note 23.

11. Master Sun is Sunzi; see note 9 above. Master Wu is Wu Qi, author of the Warring States–era treatise on strategy *Wuzi* (J. *Goshi*).

12. This took place after Qin leader Zhang Han surrendered to Xiang Yu in 207 BCE. Xiang's career ended with his suicide while on the run from enemies (see *Shi ji*, chapter 7).

13. Meng Tian had a successful military career, but was forced to commit suicide in 210 BCE after the death of the first Qin emperor, whom he had served, because of his cruelty to the people (see *Shi ji*, chapter 88).

14. In 74 BCE, Huo Guang deposed the reigning emperor, claiming it was for the good of the state. He died of illness in 68 BCE, having held de facto power for six years. After his death, his descendants were exterminated by Emperor Xuan.

aims cannot both be accomplished. You refuse to take over the castle by means of deception, although our provisions have run out, and yet you will not countenance a retreat that entails deception—if we continue to pass the days in vain here, in the end our thousand-and-some allies will begin to turn their backs on us, unable to endure their privations. When that happens, who then will stand with you in upholding this great affair? The benevolence of Duke Xiang of Song,[15] Wei Sheng's faithfulness[16]—have these not long been the stuff of laughter? Exercise your discernment once more, Your Lordship, and see if it is not so."

Yoshizane grinned. "I do not grieve at the news that we are destitute of provisions. Our many ponderings have come to naught. I cast my gaze about us and behold a flock of tame pigeons feeding in a beanfield yonder, there to the southeast. Look—whence gather they? In the morning they come here from Takita Castle, and in the evening they return there. The dove is said to be the messenger of the enshrined Hachiman, the tutelary deity of the Minamoto house. This gives us some slight unexpected means toward our end—that is, praying to the god, I secretly explained my wishes to a few fine youths and sent them out with a net, and they have captured some fifty or sixty of the birds. If we write out several copies of a manifesto, tie them to the pigeons' legs, and release them, they will carry them back to the castle. The people there will wonder, and they will catch the birds and read their message. If perchance they do not capture the birds, some of the knots will work loose and drop the messages on them. All within the fortress will peruse the manifesto, and it will inspire their hearts to abandon rebellion and return to obedience—a change will occur, and the castle will fall without our attacking it. If things happen thusly, we shall be able to fulfill the desire of the people by punishing the brigand lord Sadakane, enemy of the province, and him alone. I believe that even those of the castle troops who had not a mind to follow Sadakane now protect the castle and serve our enemy because they foresee stern punishment should they come unto us; I pity them. Truly, this must seem a child's feeble plan. However, on the way here I prayed to the god of Shirahata, near Matsusaki, and received an omen in the form of a mountain dove. Here and now, I can only pray for the aid of these tame pigeons. Let us try it, leaving success up to the gods."

---

15. In a battle against Chu, Duke Xiang refused to attack at moments when his opponent was off guard, and his forces lost the battle. The incident is recorded in *Zuo zhuan*, in the section dealing with the 22nd year of Duke Xi of Lu.

16. Wei Sheng had promised to meet a woman under a bridge. The woman never came, while heavy rains caused the river to flood. Wei refused to leave, and ended up drowning. The story is told in chapter 29 of *Zhuangzi*.

Sadayuki and Takayoshi savored his words as he spake, and they answered him as one. "Exquisitely well planned, Your Lordship. To enumerate Sadakane's crimes and make them known unto those within the castle—no strategy could surpass this. Once the soldiers and citizens have examined the letter, they will be energized unto rebellion, and they will present unto you the brigand chief's head. May it please Your Lordship to quickly put this plan into effect."

Kanamari Takayoshi undertook to compose a draft, after which several officers and men who could write quickly were assembled and tasked with making several dozen copies of it. They copied it out right then and there, and when they had finished, the day was not yet dark.

Then Yoshizane and his men lit incense, poured an offering of sake, and worshiped the Shirahata shrine at remove. They tied the manifesto to the feet of the several dozen pigeons Yoshizane had earlier caused to be captured, and then released the birds—the birds, just as expected, fluttered into the air and then flew off all together back to the castle. The letters not having been tied tightly, there was not one but whose knot came loose on its own, once the pigeon bearing it had entered the castle; even more mysterious was that the messages fell unerringly to the ground beside the huts of the Heguri peasants who had been driven into the castle for military service. "What in the world might this be?" they asked each other in puzzlement. They all gathered up the letters, and hurriedly spread them open, to find written thereon:

Water never flows uphill, and good folk never support a rebellion.[17] *For them to aid Jie*[18] *and strike at Yao*[19] *would be as water moving up a slope—it is an affront to Heaven, and such a state of affairs, though it may wish to, cannot long obtain. Now behold, the brigand lord Sadakane through wicked deception toppled his lord. He has abused the people, gnawing at them like a termite. What more can be said than that he is as Wang Mang or Lushan?*[20] *We respectfully reflect that but a very few days have passed since our lord, the Minamoto Minister of the Court, came southward, and yet he has been pressed by the people to avenge their wrongs and deliver them from their sufferings. His virtue is as Cheng Tang's, his luster as Zhou Wu's.*[21] *Verily, is it*

---

17. In Bakin's text, this letter is written in *kanbun*, but with a complete Japanese gloss.

18. Jie was the last ruler of the Xia dynasty. He is remembered as a violent sovereign who paid more attention to his mistress Mo Xi than affairs of state, and who was thus violently overthrown.

19. Yao was a mythical sage-king.

20. For Wang Mang, see note 3 above. For An Lushan, see Chapter II, note 9.

21. Cheng Tang was the first ruler of the Shang dynasty, which he founded after overthrowing Jie (see note 18 above). Zhou Wu, or Wu of Zhou, founded the Zhou dynasty after defeating the last ruler of the Shang dynasty, King Zhou.

because of this that he has taken Tōjō and seeks to combine under himself two districts by destroying the brigands' nest? Ye gathered therein deserve to be shown mercy, not to lose your lives in a lair of bandits. For this reason we thus make all manifest unto you. Why would you not speedily return to obedience? Why would you not atone for your guilt with meritorious deeds? Each of you, do away with your hesitation—what cause can you have for regret? Heaven's sight is unerring; there is to be no laxity in kingship.[22] The above is respectfully made manifest by command in this

Fifth month (summer) of the first year (metal-cock) of Kakitsu[23]
humbly written by Kanamari Hachirō Takayoshi, et al.

Upon seeing this, the soldiers and people all rejoiced: "The Satomi scion is a benevolent master! He took Tōjō without bloodying his blade, and now behold how he showers mercy upon us! We had heard his name, and had even thought dearly of him, but alas, we hied ourselves into this castle, where, surrounded by ten, even twenty, layers of fortifications, we had no hope of going to him—and even if we had been able to get over the walls and across the moat and take ourselves to him, we thought he would never forgive us, and so kept still. Considering all in all, we could try corresponding secretly with the attackers, but as we passed the days watching for our chance the matter would surely be discovered, and we should be unable to go to them; we should be slaughtered instead. Rather we might make up our minds quickly to set fire to the keep, and by raising smoke provoke the attackers so that in the course of events we might burst in and kill the Man-Eater; if we bring his head as an offering for an audience, then on the one hand we shall be repaying a years-old debt of resentment, and on the other we shall be earning eightfold gratitude from the Satomi lord. Is it not so?"

And as they gathered in secret they decided this by common consent, and yet a doubt was raised: "The wiliest of Sadakane's men, Sabitsuka Ikunai, has been killed, but it is said that the other one, Iwakuma Donpei, has mostly recovered from his injuries and guards the second gate of the castle. When the reign of our former lord [JIN'YO MITSUHIRO] was at its height, Iwakuma was a groom, but he has a fierce heart and mighty thews. After Sadakane usurped the two districts, Iwakuma rose higher and higher in his favor, for he was

---

22. The first phrase echoes language in poem #236 of the ancient poetry collection *Shi jing* (J. *Shikyō*), while the second is a quotation from a poem by Bao Yu in the Odes of Tang section of *Shi jing*.

23. 1441; "metal-cock" refers to the year's designation according to the sexagenary cycle that matched one of the elements (metal, wood, etc.) with one of the animals of the zodiac (cock, rat, etc.). For a more thorough explanation, see the Introduction.

hardly less cunning than his lord in wringing the people dry. For that matter, Tsumatate Togorō, too, has from the time he was a youth with unshorn
locks been employed by Sadakane as his closest attendant. In martial skill,
talent, and art, he excels other men, and even now he never leaves his lord's
side. And they have many vassals: unless we strike down those two, even if
we break into the keep, they will obstruct us and we shall find it hard to carry
out our intent. What of this counsel?"

Thus it was whispered, and everyone answered, "Indeed," and then: "In
which case, we first strike down those two, and clip the wings of their aid—then
we shall be able to act as we wish." They sorted themselves out for the task.

The next day, Tsumatate Togorō chanced upon a copy of the manifesto.
His shock mounted as he read it, and in a frenzy he rushed to Iwakuma Donpei's headquarters at the castle's second gate. "See what is afoot! We must see
that His Lordship hears of it, we must round up the peasants, we must nip
this catastrophe in the bud, or it will be a grave matter. See here." And he took
from his breast the copy of the manifesto, opened it, and proferred it, but Donpei barely glanced at it. "I have only just now run across an identical manifesto,
which greatly amazed me. Here," he said, and produced it. They compared
the two and found them identical in every line, every word, every jot.

Togorō gasped in spite of himself. "If our assailants' spies have been
effective, and if any among our allies harbors ambitions, then this castle
cannot long be held. This is no negligible thing—come with me, now, and
let us proclaim it to His Lordship." As he spoke he began to rise, but the
other grasped at his sleeve to prevent him. "Wait, Master Tsumatate. There
is something I would have you know." Thus detaining him without reason,
Iwakuma sat Tsumatate forcibly down beside him. Constantly looking from
side to side like a pecking bird though a glance showed that no one else
was around, he brought his fan up to cover his mouth and leaned close to
Tsumatate's ear.

"Ever since obtaining this secret missive, I have been turning my attention
this way and that, and it transpires that you and I are the only ones who do
not incline toward our attackers, yearning to present unto them the castle;
indeed, it has just been whispered to me that the crowd has already taken the
decision to strike us down, you and me, that they might do the thing. When
a great structure is collapsing, how can a single post support it?[24] Would it
not be rotten to die at the hands of that rabble because we sought rashly to
uphold righteousness? By quickly making up our minds, running Sadakane
through, and surrendering to His Lordship Satomi along with the others in

---

24. See Chapter IV, note 11.

the castle, we should not only dispel the crowd's wrath and escape death, but we should secure whatever rewards we desire, and glory to be transmitted to our descendants. Now, what thoughts do you harbor in your breast?"

Togorō was nearly dumbfounded at this query. "What is this, have you gone mad? When you served the Jin'yo you merely led horses around by the bit, but my lord gave you much greater employment, entrusting great things to you even as to Mitsuhiro's senior vassals Sabitsuka and Shietage—is this not so? I, though young, am part of the personal retinue of the Provincial Lord [SADAKANE]. He has treated me with more indulgence than even he did when he was among the senior Jin'yo vassals.[25] How can I be called human if I accept such a burden of gratitude and then ignore it, rewarding it instead with enmity? To be stingy with one's life is cowardly, and to turn one's back on one's lord is treasonous. Say another word to me about this and I shall not let you leave this seat." Enraged, he rose up on one knee and grasped the hilt of his sword.

Iwakuma, unperturbed, laughed him to scorn. "Loyalty and righteousness depend on the lord in question! You speak like a braying ass. To execute Sadakane now would be to avenge our former lord. How can that be called mutiny? You cannot know the depths of Sadakane's plotting, how he worked through Bokuhei and Mukuzō, who hated him so, to strike down his lord and master—I have never spoken openly of it before. Indeed, it was a cloudy morning, a cold day in summer on the hill of Ochiba, when, rather than a bird pursued by a hawk, it was Mitsuhiro's mount, a dappled dun, that fell beneath him; Sadakane presented his own white horse to his lord and master and then withdrew, saying he would wait for a change of mounts. At length Bokuhei and Mukuzō spied that white horse from afar and thought that Sadakane had come: They waited until he came within bowshot and then bent their bows and loosed their arrows, piercing the breast of Mitsuhiro, Minister of the Court, who fell with a thud from his horse.

"The day before this, Sadakane had summoned me in secret: 'Thus and such a conspiracy is in motion. Will you be persuaded, on the morrow when the hunt departs, to administer poison to the mount of the Provincial Lord? When the affair is accomplished I shall have an important place for you. Here is your reward for the meantime,' he said, and gave me many things. I thought to myself that this must not be, but he was a senior retainer, and

25. This sentence contains echoes of a passage in section 226 of Yoshida Kenkō's miscellany *Tsurezuregusa* (1330–1332) describing the young scholar Shinano-no-zenji Yukinaga. A public error had led to courtly ridicule, but the priest Jichin took Yukinaga under his wing, with the indulgence here alluded to.

I but a servant with no strength to oppose him. Had I refused, he would have killed me. And so I hardly needed to take counsel with myself—nothing can replace a lost life—before I undertook his charge, and I brought down that horse that day.

"In this way I allowed Sadakane to take the two districts and both castles. To reward such virtue and rectitude he has given me a place behind his senior vassals and delegated unto me matters of importance, but one could hardly say I owe him a debt of gratitude. Only Shietage and Sabitsuka knew of these things, and they have gone down beneath the Springs.[26] Now there is only you. And you, Master Tsumatate—I have long guessed that you nurture a love unobtainable, that you fantasize about the Mistress, and have done every day for many months. If that is so, then consider this: how easy it will be, once you have struck down the Man-Eater, to take Tamazusa to wife in lieu of a reward. Now, do you still refuse to join me?"

The persistence of Iwakuma's argument caused Togorō's heart to leap, and he unfolded his arms and slapped his knee. "Indeed, you speak the truth. If I am to cleanse myself of the stain of having followed a mutinous brigand, I must abandon petty reasoning and magnify the greater righteousness— I must follow your counsel. Quickly, now," he said, assenting with uncommon zeal. Donpei rejoiced greatly, and they lent each other their ears, saying, "Then let us," and "Let us then," busily discoursing upon the matter.

At this time Yamashita Sadakane had not emerged from the inner chambers, as he had yet to recover from the previous day's drunkenness. Attended only by girls at either hand, and with the blinds rolled up halfway, he leaned against a pillar meant for that purpose, blowing idly on a flute in his unassuageable boredom; he thought of nothing else. Then Iwakuma Donpei came, preceded by Tsumatate Togorō, both crying, "Something has happened! Something has happened!" They threw open each sliding door they came to and left them that way, until they came to their lord's side. A few dozen troops who knew Iwakuma's mind came a little after, lightly armored and carrying weapons, and hid themselves in the next room behind sliding doors paneled waist-high with wood on which were drawn a variety of birds and flowers; through these they peered into the inner chamber.

Sadakane ceased sounding his flute as he saw Donpei and his companion approach in such an agitated state. He hardly had time to ask, "What is this?" before they raised their voices as one and said, "'A house that accumulates

26. The Yellow Springs, i.e., the land of the dead (see Chapter I, note 11).

Caption: Donpei and Togorō smite Sadakane in his chambers.
Figures: Iwakuma Donpei [*right*]. Tsumatate Togorō [*center*]. Yamashita Sadakane [*left*].

岩熊とん平

妻立戸五郎

wickedness will know calamity and to spare.'[27] The people within the castle have all risen up and brought the attackers within the gates—nothing can turn them aside—the castle will fall. We beg of you, Your Lordship, slit your belly. We will serve as your seconds." But before they had finished speaking, Togorō, standing in front, drew his blade with a flash, and, slashing, leapt upon him.

"Meddler!" cried Sadakane, receiving the blow squarely with his flute—it was sliced cleanly in two, at an angle to the grain, and the top of it sailed off to land some distance away. Togorō thus unexpectedly damaged his main blade, on top of which he cowered in his heart to think that this was his lord he was attacking; warrior though he was, he trembled as his feelings battled within him, and he could not advance.

Sadakane stared at him with eyes that rage had narrowed to slits. "So, the two of you have plotted a rebellion, and now you come to strike me down! Impudent oafs!" Even as his wrath mounted higher his body sank lower, ducking beneath Togorō's and Donpei's blades as they swung them, finding space where there seemed to be none, deflecting the blows, using the flute, gleaming sharp where it had been cut, like a spearhead on a javelin, for he had not an inch of steel on his person.

He flung the flute-bamboo like a throwing-knife, and it pierced Togorō through the upper arm—he abruptly let out a cry of pain, dropped his blade, and sat heavily down on the floor. "I have you!" shouted Sadakane, but as he rushed in to claim the abandoned sword, Donpei attacked him from behind, his sword flashing, its blade pointing downward—he dealt Sadakane a mighty blow, slicing him from the tip of his shoulder to the hollow of his back. Sadakane had no chance to take up the blade—instead he batted Donpei's sword away at the hilt, even as it descended upon him again, and then grappled with his assailant. Now he was on top, now beneath, and they struggled like that for some time, but Sadakane was severely wounded and weakened, and in the end he found himself pinned beneath his opponent's knees.

Sadakane called out again and again for someone to come to him, and Donpei fumbled at his waist, thinking to take the man's head, but his dagger, too, had fallen during the fight and lay somewhere behind him. "This is a tight spot," he muttered with fluttering heart. He forgot himself and looked behind him, to find Tsumatate Togorō lying near his right hand with the bamboo flute-end sticking out of him. "This will do splendidly," he said, and pulled it out. Sadakane was desperately trying to overturn him, but Donpei

---

27. A reference to a line that occurs at the end of book 8 of *Taiheiki*, where it is spoken regarding, among other events, the defeat of the Hōjō at Kamakura. The formulation is traceable to the Han-era *Shuoyuan* (J. *Zeien*), a collection of moralizing tales.

plunged the flute into his neck. Togorō immediately came to himself again when the bamboo was plucked from his body: he sat bolt upright, saw what had been done, and collected his dropped blade and handed it to Donpei, who used it to cut off Sadakane's head. Then he stood up.

The many men-at-arms who had been recruited by Donpei and had come with him as far as the adjoining room had been unable to predict the victor and so had not rushed to assist him, but now that they saw Sadakane struck down they hurried to break down the screen doors and raise a battle cry. All this while, the girls who had been waiting on their lord at either hand were in a tizzy of fear: They ran out by the garden gate and told of the matter to whomever they encountered, so that as the affair was drawing to a close some of Sadakane's close retainers arrived from the outer guard-house, but they were detained by the aforementioned men-at-arms; many were struck down at this time. Of course Sadakane's innumerable women were reduced to weeping and wailing. Donpei commanded that they all be rounded up, Tamazusa not excepted; his men filched all the women's gold, silver, and other treasures and fled to the main keep.

Truly Heaven punishes a man when the time is right, and never errs as to degree of severity. Sadakane had waxed strong in his cunning, doing injury to his lord and usurping his territories while laying up for himself ephemeral treasures, but before a hundred days had passed he was himself killed by a retainer. Not only that, but Iwakuma Donpei did not use a blade when taking his head, but rather—though he had not planned it—the sharpened end of a bamboo flute: Sadakane's fate resembled execution by bamboo spear. Tsumatate Togorō, for his part, was one of Sadakane's most favored; that he was struck by that same bamboo throwing-knife and lay as if dead for a time was darkling retribution, a thing greatly to be feared, for his striking at his lord, no matter how evil that lord was. Meanwhile, there is nothing to which Donpei's crimes may be compared. As a groom to the Jin'yo, he poisoned his lord's mount on Sadakane's behalf, knowing full well it was part of a rebellious conspiracy; while serving Sadakane, he aided him more and more in his evil, causing the people to suffer great torments such that the evil rewards of them came to be visited upon him, to escape which he again struck down his lord. Even if he joined the ranks of the good, could he long prosper thus? Long ago, the Emperor Guangwu of the Later Han created Zi Mi the Marquis Unrighteous.[28] Better far to end as a common man and

---

28. During the reign of Guangwu (Liu Xiu), founder of the Later Han dynasty, his former general Peng Chong rebelled. Peng's slave Zi Mi assassinated Peng in 29 CE and surrendered to Guangwu, but the Emperor judged his actions to have been wicked. He awarded him the title of Marquis, but called him the Marquis Unrighteous (see book 12 of *Hou Hanshu*).

not be counted unrighteous than to be ennobled through wickedness! The Author is perpetually reading the historical and military accounts, and each time he comes to such an entry he heaves a great sigh. Thus do I here attach a personal annotation, to point this out to the ignorant children. Accounts of Yamashita Sadakane may be found in military writings and old records. They are not very detailed, but they all agree that he was a villain who acted injuriously toward his lord of the Jin'yo. Traces of that time still remain in that land, but as I am weary I will not record them now. I will speak of them in a later Book.

Chapter VI

Yoshizane opens the granaries and stirs up two districts;
Takayoshi accepts his lord's command and executes three bandits

        The army and inhabitants of Takita pressed their attack, crowding the castle's second gate, intending to strike down Donpei and the others. They raised a battle cry, but then, unlooked-for, from within the walls a severed head was raised, impaled on a spear tip. "You who have gathered here, what will you do with us?" came a cry. "Having repented our wrongs, abandoned our rebellious ways, and transferred our aspirations to our attackers, we executed the traitorous bandit Sadakane. Shall we not together throw open the castle gates and welcome the Satomi lord? Let us not fight each other." The door was thrust open as by a gale to reveal Iwakuma Donpei and Tsumatate Togorō, resplendent in their under-armor straight-robes, attended by soldiers before and behind, and both of them seated on camp stools. They beckoned with their war fans, and the assembled soldiers and commoners gazed up in dumbfounded confusion at the head—there was no mistaking it. It was Sadakane's, become a trophy.

    "All that has happened is that Donpei and Togorō knew they could not escape, so they killed Sadakane before we could. Despicable." So ran the thinking, but fighting each other now would do no good, so the assembled had no choice but to obey Donpei and Togorō's commands and fly a flag of surrender from the watchtower; they pushed open the main gate and, with Donpei and Togorō at their head, welcomed at last their attackers.

Kanamari Hachirō of the Satomi vanguard listened to the details of the affair. Then he received Sadakane's head, while at the same time, and in accordance with military law, confiscating Donpei's and the others' weapons, even down to the daggers at their waists. He sent a report back to his commander, and Yoshizane advanced the body of his army so that he quickly came unto that place where Donpei and the rest truckled, grinding their foreheads into the gravel by way of welcome to him. The castle soldiers knelt in two ranks, and everyone hailed Yoshizane with cries of "May he live ten thousand years!" A short time later, Sadayuki arrived from the rearguard to arrange squads to go before and behind, and the general then deliberately made his entry into the castle.

He made a thorough tour, finding that the place had sunk into overweening opulence since the days of the Jin'yo: everything was grand, beautified, bejeweled, and bespoke much outlay of gold. Nor was that all, for the storehouses were filled with the grain and treasure that Sadakane had wrung from the folk and hoarded up for himself. One would think that the entrance of the Duke of Pei, the Great Progenitor, into Afang was like this,[1] or the day when the shogunate, in the person of Yoritomo, defeated Yasuhira.[2] In spite of this, Yoshizane disturbed not an iota of it, but opened up the storehouses and shared out their contents among the farmers of the two districts. Sadayuki and others remonstrated with him, saying with knitted brows, "Sadakane has been put down, but Maro and Anzai still remain, strong enemies, in Hiratate and Tateyama. Having happily captured this castle, our armies might have been alleviated of their want of provisions, but instead Your Lordship gives it all to the farmers, laying up not even a scrap in storage—I cannot see the wisdom in this."

Yoshizane heard them out and nodded. "That would seem to be reasonable, and clear enough, and yet: the people are the foundation of the state.[3] The farmers of Nagasa and Heguri have these many years suffered under evil governance; that they have now forsaken rebellion and returned to obedience is solely in order to avoid famine. Were I to now greedily refuse to impart this bounty unto those suffering folk, I should be no different from

---

1. The "Duke of Pei" is Liu Bang, the founder or Great Progenitor (Bakin gives two glosses to the same set of characters both here and with Yoritomo—see following note) of the Han dynasty. Afang Palace was the seat of his predecessor, the Qin emperor.

2. In 1189, Minamoto no Yoritomo, founder of the Kamakura shogunate, invaded the prosperous northern territory of Hiraizumi and defeated the army of Fujiwara no Yasuhira. Yasuhira's father Hidehira had sheltered Yoritomo's brother Yoshitsune from Yoritomo's wrath. After Hidehira's death, Yasuhira had Yoshitsune killed to appease Yoritomo, but to no avail: Yoritomo crushed Yasuhira.

3. This phrase comes from chapter 8 of the ancient document compendium *Shu jing* (J. *Shokyō*).

Sadakane and his men. Though our storehouses overflow with millet, if the people turn against us, with whom shall we keep our castles, and with whom shall we fight off our enemies? Lo, the people are the foundation of the state—their prosperity is my own. If virtuous governance prove not to be in vain, then provisions will come unsought to our armies when needed. What need is there for stinginess?" Thus spake he, and Sadayuki and the others had not the wherewithal to respond—nor could they hold back tears of deep feeling from coursing down their cheeks as they withdrew from his presence.

Thus it was that on the following day, Yoshizane came to the front chambers, where official business was conducted. After concluding his inspection of Sadakane's head, he called forth those who had yielded, Donpei and Togorō, and set Kanamari Hachirō to interrogate them as to the killing of their lord. They answered as one: "Sadakane was a mutinous brigand—he deposed his lord and usurped his lands. We were not able to kill him, however, and so we attached ourselves to him, but only because in secret we were waiting for time or fortune to favor us, so that when yesterday Your Lordship in your wisdom vouchsafed us your manifesto, we deserted Jie to follow Tang,[4] as it were, and as an offering, should you receive us, we brought you his head as a trophy."

Brashly did they deliver these claims, and Kanamari Hachirō laughed them to scorn. "Your speech is cunning, but your words are bald-faced lies. You cannot hide the fact that both of you from the start aided Sadakane in his evil and abused the folk of the country. This is why the soldiers and inhabitants of the castle sought to attack you; but you, when you heard that they were gathering together their companions, attacked Sadakane in order to deflect reproach from yourselves. Is this not so? I know it is, for I, Takayoshi, being commanded to inquire among the people of the castle, learned everything from them. Will you make such claims in the face of this?"

Both men were astonished, and Donpei, wide-eyed, said, "They must have been speaking of Togorō! Ever since he was a youth with unshorn locks he served Sadakane—he was his keenest blade. To make matters worse, Togorō harbored a secret desire for the beauty Tamazusa: it was only in order to carry out his clandestine affair that he joined forces with me and struck the first blow. I guessed what was in the depths of his heart, though, and to prove myself spotless I had Tamazusa captured and imprisoned. If Your Lordship will summon her, all shall become clear. I pray Your Lordship, judge by this whether we be pure or polluted, respectively."

---

4. See Chapter V, notes 18 and 21.

Hardly had he finished when Togorō shot him a glare and raised his voice. "Milord Hachirō, hear this man's words for the lies they are. How could I cut down my lord, how could I ally myself with Your Lordship, simply because I had feelings for Tamazusa? In the beginning, Donpei was a groom for the Jin'yo. At the hunt on Ochiba hill, Sadakane talked him into feeding poison to his lord's mount, and my lord Mitsuhiro was lost. As Sadakane took over the two districts, Donpei was his keenest blade, and thus the people bore him uncommon resentment, in order to escape which he struck down his second lord. Be not deceived!"

He spoke through his pain, determined to uphold his denial of Donpei's story. The two of them thus sought each to undermine the other, each to increase the other's guilt, quarreling without surcease. Hachirō cackled with laughter. "Your speech reveals what our questions could not! Your perversions are such that you could never in any life, in any world, keep your heads attached to your bodies. Sadakane may have been a rebel and a bandit, but you, Togorō, were his retainer, and when all hope of escape was cut off, you killed him—an inhuman act. Donpei harmed his lord for Sadakane's sake, and then stood in his shadow—and when matters became pressing, he struck down Sadakane, taking his treachery to its fullest extreme. My lord's heart is set upon benevolence and charity—on being father and mother to his people—but if he should forgive you your crimes, then he would lose all ability to administer rewards and punishments, and loyalty and filial piety would fall by the wayside evermore. We have already brought everything to light—we did not wait for your speeches—but we brought you here to this court of law that we might have it from your own mouths. You have already been set down as guilty. Under the codes it is difficult to see how you may be forgiven. Bind them!" he cried, and some footsoldiers rushed in to kick Donpei and Togorō to the ground, pin them, and wrap ropes around them.

The two men panicked like sheep bound for the slaughter, glaring and apologizing and importuning most persistently, until Kanamari was enraged and shouted, "The punishment decreed by Heaven for the treachery you have brought forth and that comes back to you now is for you to be torn into eighths! Quickly, now!" he urged the soldiers, and they undertook the charge, dragging the struggling criminals to the outer yard, where before long their two heads could be seen impaled on shafts of green bamboo, ready for inspection. Then Kanamari issued another order: "Bring Tamazusa in."

So Tamazusa—ah, cruel fate!—was brought, the flower of her visage cruelly blown and wilted from the heart by midnight storms; was bound with Heaven's net of no escape; was drawn with ropes like melons on trellis-cords, nervously jumping at scarecrow-clapper sounds, and though 'twas not that

Caption: Clarifying rewards and punishments, Yoshizane executes Tamazusa.
Figures: Tamazusa [*center*]. Sadakane's head [*bottom right*]. Togorō's head [*bottom center*]. Donpei's head [*bottom left*].

sparrow-colored hour, her gazing eyes were darkened[5] as they sat her on the outer porch, ashamed before Takayoshi, whom she once knew; for a time she did not raise her head. Kanamari called, "Lift your face," then inched forward on his knees and spoke.

"Tamazusa, you were the concubine of the former lord of this province—there are none who do not know of this. You grew proud in his favor and charmed him from his senses; you stretched out your hand even unto the Way of Governance,[6] and violated his loyal retainers—this is your first crime. You swathed yourself in twills and gauzes, made meals of jewels and fires of katsura wood—all in all you pursued luxury and amusement to the furthest extremity, and even this did not satisfy you, so you conducted illicit liaisons with Sadakane. This is your second crime. These things I, Takayoshi, know of myself—I had no need for others to inform me of them. Then Yamashita Sadakane's rebellious conspiracy was realized, and he usurped the two districts. From that day you became his wife, displaying neither shame nor restraint—it is karmic retribution for the evil you have done that your life was spared until the castle fell. Alive, you are to be bound with fetters of punishment; dead, you will be an unhallowed spirit. Consider these the punishments of Heaven and the State!"

After he had rebuked her with raised voice, Tamazusa finally raised her head. "It is difficult for me to accept what you say. Is it not said that women are in all things flighty as foam—that since they have no homes of their own in the Three Realms,[7] but must make theirs in men's houses, the pain or pleasure of the centuries come to them from others?[8] What is more, I was not the main wife of our former lord—when Mitsuhiro had passed away, I was left as a drifting boat, unmoored. Then Lord Yamashita, alas, turned his attentions to me, settling me in the depths of his chambers, where I had barely time to rest my head and resume my dreaming before I was thus taken captive—must this not have been fate, the result of karma from a past life?

"As for claims that while I first served our former lord I meddled in administration, or violated loyal retainers, or had aught to do with Lord Yamashita, they are but backbiting and jealousy, entirely without substance.

---

5. "Scarecrow-clappers" (naruko) were small wooden clappers strung across fields to scare crows. Here the image is suggested by the melon trellis lines in the previous phrase, and in turn suggests the comparison of dusk to the brown of a sparrow, which finally suggests the darkness of Tamazusa's eyes.

6. Despite its apparently Chinese resonance, this term (J. seidō) seems to be Japanese, and to go back only into medieval writings. Generally it refers to the conduct of state affairs, and specifically to the administering of rewards and punishments.

7. The three spheres of existence in Buddhism: desire, form, and formlessness.

8. This echoes a line from Bo Juyi's poem Taixing lu (J. Taikōro).

For example, the senior and junior Jin'yo vassals, even those with large stipends and high office, served a second master with uncommon willingness, none of them displaying a drop of shame. Take the likes of you, sir. Rashly you absconded, abandoning your lord, and then you compounded this by following Satomi and conquering Takita Castle, and was this on behalf of your former lord? Not a hare's hair of it. This one serves that one, that one follows this one, each seeking his own glory and advantage. It is thus even among males. As for females—many are they who go through the world as if it were the Tsukuma Festival, and they with pots on their heads.[9] Why, then, do you thus single out Tamazusa, to heap upon her head crimes she did not commit? Why, my lord, do you hate me so implacably? This is slander unconscionable," she finished, glowering.

Hachirō pounded the floor where he sat. "Your tongue has wagged one time too many! Your perversion is not a matter of guesswork, but has been seen by the proverbial eyes of ten, and pointed out by the proverbial fingers of ten.[10] Yet you will not admit it, but seek instead to excuse yourself by citing examples. Truly you are 'a bodhisattva outwardly but inwardly a yaksha'[11]—your countenance and your heart are at odds—you are like a poisonous stone in a brocade bag! But then, were you not such a sturdy woman, how could you have toppled the castle?[12] Do you not know? Kokuroku and Donpei—hereditary senior vassals of the Jin'yo though they were—forsook righteousness for the sake of advantage, followed rebellion and increased in evil, but in the end could not evade punishment occult, decreed out of sight of men. They have been riven in eight. I, Takayoshi, am different from them. I ate ash and covered myself with lacquer, changing my appeareance, all to aim a blow at my late lord's enemy. But alone I could not accomplish it; and so, as five fingers are better used as a fist than flicking in anger individually, I joined myself to the Satomi lord, gathered stalwart allies, and now, in annihilating Sadakane and his tribe, I have fulfilled my aspirations. And yet how can you say that what I have done brings not a hare's hair of profit to our former lord? Yours are the whinings of a woman who embraces a swine

9. In the Tsukuma festival parade, women were required to wear pots on their heads in a number equal to the number of men they had slept with.

10. A formulation from the Confucian classic *Daxue* (J. *Daigaku*), according to which whatever has been thus attested to must be taken seriously.

11. An unidentified saying dating from the Heian period. A yaksha was a kind of demon or monster in Indian belief, known in Japan through Buddhism.

12. Courtesans were often referred to as "castle topplers" (*keisei*), from the idea that a beautiful woman could be distracting enough to cause a castle to fall (from a passage in the Han-era history *Han shu* [J. *Kansho*], chapter 97, part 1).

Caption: Ujimoto displays his valor by killing Nobutoki of the Maro.
Figures: Sugikura Ujimoto [*right*]. Maro Nobutoki [*left*].

氏元うづもと　男を奮いて　麻呂まろの　信時を撃つ

枚倉氏元

and forgets the stench, but still, how can you excuse yourself while thus accusing others? Prepare yourself!"

He assailed Tamazusa with wrath and reason, and she moaned uncontrollably. "Truly, I am guilty! But Lord Satomi is a benevolent ruler. Both here and at Tōjō his rewards have been weighty and his punishments light—I even hear that he refrained from killing enemy officers and soldiers who submitted to him, but gave them employ instead. Of what reckoning is a woman, guilty though she be? I beg Your Lordship, forgive me, let me go home—it will be an unsurpassed happiness to me. Lord Hachirō: as man and woman we are of different orders, but we both once served the house of Jin'yo. For old amity's sake, I pray you, intervene for me." The face she raised, though blossoming in a smile, was as a flowering crabapple swept with rain;[13] her ebon tresses, spilling scent, were draped about her shoulders like a willow's boughs in spring, for all the world as if they beckoned men.

Yoshizane, in the high seat with many close retainers in attendance beside him, heard out this speech, taking her measure. "Tamazusa, so like a jewel, may have her flaws, but she regrets her wrongs and begs for her life to be spared. I find her pitiable, and wonder if I might pardon her," he thought. "Takayoshi, Takayoshi," he said, summoning him close, "Tamazusa's crimes are not light, but as she is a woman, sparing her should not prevent us from properly establishing rewards and punishments. It is my wish that you find a way to make it so."

Earnestly he spoke, but Kanamari Hachirō's mien changed. "As you decree, my lord, but this slattern Tamazusa is a rebel and a brigand second only to Sadakane. Not only when he chased away so many loyal retainers but even when he arranged for Mitsuhiro to lose his life, Tamazusa was hard by Sadakane's side, sharing the thoughts of his heart, plotting in secret: were it not so, the affair could not have endured a single morning. If Your Lordship fails to recognize this and pardons this brigandess, people's voices will rise in criticism of you for these signs of favoritism—they will say you, too, fancy her charms. Lady Da was killed in Chaoge,[14] while Taizhen was strangled in Makuai.[15] These were beauties who toppled kingdoms—of a different order

---

13. This image perhaps conflates two common descriptions of Yang Guifei, one that compares her to a rain-bedraggled pear blossom, and another that compares her to a flowering crabapple (or aronia). For more on Yang Guifei, see Chapter II, note 9.

14. Daji (Lady Da) was the favored consort of Dixin, last ruler of the Shang dynasty (ca. 1100 BCE). Legends circulated regarding her wickedness, some claiming that she was actually a fox spirit. Chaoge was the capital of Shang, and when King Wu of Zhou conquered the Shang, he executed Daji for her crimes.

15. Taizhen was another name of Yang Guifei. She was killed in Mawei (the second character of which is similar to the one Bakin uses).

than Tamazusa. Nevertheless, on a day when her country is thrown into chaos and her castle is broken, how can she escape the chopping-block? Does Your Lordship truly think of pardoning her?"

He remonstrated in words both solemn and proper. Yoshizane nodded often as he listened, and then raised his voice and said, "I was wrong—mistaken. Out with her now, and off with her head!"

No sooner had Tamazusa heard this than her flowery countenance flushed scarlet; she gnashed her gourd-seed-white teeth and fixed master and men with a glare, saying, "Despicable, Kanamari Hachirō, to reject your lord's command to be merciful, and slay me instead—if you do this, you yourself will ere long be but rust on a blade, and your house shall long be ruined! And Yoshizane—your deeds hardly bear speaking of! Your tongue would not rest once it had bidden mercy—overcome by Takayoshi's persuasions, making a plaything of a person's life, you are a foolish commander, not at all like what I had heard. Kill me if you will! I shall lead your descendants along the way of beasts—I shall make them dogs of the passions of this world!"

Thus she cursed them. "Suffer her to speak no more! Take her away!" Responding to Kanamari's orders, four or five footsoldiers came at her and dragged her, still madly cursing, outside, where they finally lopped off her head. When this was done, Hachirō did as he had been bidden, taking the head of the bandit lord Sadakane and that of Tamazusa, along with those of Donpei and Togorō, and hanging them below Takita Castle where they loomed like owls. Truly, as a reward for accumulated evil, it was as it should be, but after all it was an eye-opening thing, and for days spectators lined up like pickets in a fence.

Meanwhile, at dawn, a messenger from Sugikura Kisonosuke Ujimoto, one Amasaki Jūrō Terutake, arrived at a gallop from Tōjō, cracking his whip on his lathered steed; he presented the head of Kogorō Nobutoki of the Maro, taken as a trophy by Ujimoto, and spoke of a battle, giving all the details, great and small, of its form and figure. A drawing of this we include here, but as the event itself is long, we shall begin a new chapter and discuss it at the beginning of our seventh section. In addition, we shall see how Tamazusa's evil will was unable to fasten upon the good general and the righteous warrior but entwined itself about each man's child, and how through many mysterious events, suffering was finally turned into the beginning of great good fortune—but that passage is still far off. O Reader, I pray you, keep that brigand woman's hateful words in your heart, and consider them well.

End of Book III of the Lives of the Eight Dogs of the Satomi of Southern Fusa

The Lives of the Eight Dogs of the Satomi of Southern Fusa

Book IV

Assembled by the Master of the Crooked Pavilion in the Eastern Capital

Chapter VII
Kagetsura sells Nobutoki—a nefarious plot; Takayoshi quits Yoshizane—unbending righteousness

Sugikura Kisonosuke Ujimoto's messenger Amasaki Jūrō Terutake had come at a gallop from Tōjō to present Nobutoki of the Maro's head as a trophy. Yoshizane went to the edge of the riser on which he sat, beckoned the messenger close, and personally asked about the battle's form and figure.

Amasaki Jūrō replied: "It weighed on Ujimoto's heart that the army's provisions were running low, so he sought to stir the farmers up to remembrance, that they might send more; but Anzai Kagetsura and Maro Nobutoki had already been persuaded by Sadakane to block passage by land and sea, and they lay in wait for us, to seize our pack trains. As our condition rose to a high pitch of hardship, Ujimoto suffered greater pangs of regret with each passing, wasted day. Then one night Kagetsura sent word to Ujimoto in secret, by a servant named something-or-other, saying:

"'Yamashita Sadakane is a mutinous brigand. Even if he had employed Su Qin and Zhang Yi[1] to persuade me, even if they had offered me a hundred or

---

1. Warring States–era roving strategists and diplomats, influential (on opposite sides) in the struggle between the state of Qin and its six neighbors.

even a thousand reasons, I never should have thought to undertake to do his will, but that Nobutoki inveigled me into it: for his sake, I blocked the roads and caused a good general and his brave officers to suffer. A wretched thing, if I do say so myself, and regret for it gnaws at my innards, but Nobutoki simply hones his arrowheads and will not rethink his course despite what I say to him—I am like a man trying to scratch an itch through his shoes. Carefully considering the temper of this matter, it strikes me that Nobutoki is coura-geous but common: he abandons righteousness for the sake of advantage, and his greed is insatiable. Although I, Kagetsura, joined with him out of consider-ation for our ancient amity, were I not to repent my error I would be like a sane man chasing a madman—indistinguishable while both are running. In sum, my concern now is the reverse of the impulse that made me join him: I would first strike down Nobutoki, opening a way for the transport of provisions, then join my strength to Lord Satomi's and smite the bandit chief Sadakane, in order to advance the good. My failure to retain Master Satomi when he chanced to come to me, or to receive him with the propriety incumbent upon a host, was due to Nobutoki's refusal. I pray you, my lord, sally forth from the castle in sudden attack. As a warrior, Nobutoki is little but a wild boar: when he sees an enemy he advances his men as a body without a second thought. When he does, I, Kagetsura, shall attack him from the rear, wedging him in, and Nobutoki will be ours—to take him will be as easy as overturning your hand. Do not, I pray, err in this great matter through skittishness. I earnestly await your reply.'

"Ujimoto, however, thought that this might be a scheme of the ene-my's, and he did not fall in with it lightly, but sent messengers back and forth repeatedly until it sounded to him as if it was not a lie. Then he con-sulted with Anzai about an attack on Nobutoki, and on a night when fit-ful fifth-month rains made indistinguishable black and white, he led forth some two hundred mounted men—horses bitted and men gagged—until they had surrounded the stockades at Hamaogi behind which Nobutoki of the Maro was encamped. Then, when they had pressed in close upon the enemy, they raised a mighty battle-cry and burst in without a look back. Maro's men had not been looking for an enemy attack, and the whole camp rose in an uproar: they whipped their mounts without untether-ing them, they fitted arrows to unstrung bows, and everywhere were in a tangle, seeking only a means of escape—none there were who sought to stand and fight.

"Just then Nobutoki raised his voice with boldness: 'Now you men show how little you can be relied upon! The enemy is few! Shall we not round them up and strike them down? Let us not be put to flight and thereby become a laughing stock for Anzai at Maehara! Charge! Strike!' With great vehemence did he command them, and then rode straight out, laying about him with his spear, felling onrushing attackers as he met them. He was as a mad tiger raging in a flock of sheep. His officers and men were encouraged thereby, and perhaps thinking that Anzai had come from their rear to aid them, they turned on their fleeing heels and fought, shouting and yelling, so that in spite of themselves our vanguard was repulsed and driven back outside, where they could not gain footing in the muck and, slipping and tripping, were unable to pull back.

"Then Sugikura Ujimoto, eyes flashing, raised a cry: 'Are we to be driven back to the first and second stockades, that we have already destroyed? All those who know shame and value their names, follow me!' No sooner had he spoken than he seized a white banner and thrust it into his belt, and with a clatter of stirrups he urged his mount forward, twirling his glaive like a waterwheel flashing in the raven-black night. He attacked Nobutoki, who glared at him in the torchlight and called, 'You must be Ujimoto, eh? A worthy adversary. Hold your ground!' And he twisted his spear around and dealt a crashing thrust, which Ujimoto deflected like a tossed stone; they gave it their utmost, one advancing as the other withdrew, one giving way as the other came on, now one with the upper hand, now the other. With their commanders fighting thus, the armies left no soldier idle, so that there were none to ride to their leaders' aid, and Ujimoto and Nobutoki fought with no man's intervention until Nobutoki in his vexation gave a thrust. Ujimoto brushed aside his speartip with his left hand, and as Nobutoki looked up with a startled cry, Ujimoto stretched out his glaive and stabbed it into Nobutoki's helmet, pushing him backwards off his mount. Warrior though he was, Nobutoki could not endure a wound in such a vital spot, and, still clutching his spear, he tumbled from his horse with a thud. We turned our gaze toward the sound, and then flew to the spot and took his head."

Yoshizane listened, rapt, to this detailed report, then said, "Ujimoto's valor at arms that night merits reward, but he failed to plan sufficiently. Not without reason would Kagetsura have had so sudden a change of heart and attacked Nobutoki. No, 'two heroes cannot stand alongside one another.'[2] Though Nobutoki and Kagetsura banded together to attack me, he who did not emerge personally victorious would have seen a change in his fortunes. As it stands, in allowing himself to be spurred on by Anzai to strike down

---

2. A dictum from chapter 113 of *Shi ji*.

Nobutoki, Ujimoto has done something that redounds not to our advantage, but rather to Kagetsura's. And what did Anzai do?"

To this inquiry, Amasaki Jūrō replied, "Your Lordship is quite right: that night he did not loose a single arrow on our behalf, but before we knew it had retreated behind his stockades at Maehara."

Yoshizane slapped his knee with his fan. "Then Kagetsura's nefarious plot is clear. It would have been difficult to gauge the outcome of my attack on Takita, but given that Sadakane was a brigand and a rebel hated by the gods of Heaven and the deities of the land, not to mention deemed unforgivable by the people, Kagetsura must have thought that his position could not be forever secure, though he might appear to have the advantage for the moment. Once Sadakane had finally met his end and I, Yoshizane, had possessed his lands, Nobutoki could no longer be expected to provide any shelter for Anzai under his wing. Rather, his courage would impel them to hasten into a reckless war, one that Anzai feared them too weak to win; and so Anzai gave the appearance of joining himself to me, causing Ujimoto to kill Nobutoki. Kagetsura himself would step into the resulting void, reducing Hiratate and annexing the district of Asahina, and thus setting himself up as one of the bull's two horns, with me as the other. My arrows may not always hit the target, but I think my guess is on the mark."

Thus did Yoshizane speak in great detail, as if pointing out his enemy's vitals on a chart, whereupon someone rushed in with another memorial from Ujimoto. "Nobutoki having been cut down, his remaining forces dissolved into panic and fled. Ujimoto straightaway forebore the pursuit of them, but assembled his own soldiers and returned finally to Tōjō. There he found—who would have thought it?—that Kagetsura had already withdrawn from Maehara and occupied Hiratate Castle, making Maro's territory, the district of Asahina, all his own. Like a hound who labors to flush prey that the falcon then catches, Ujimoto's efforts were uncrowned with merit. If Your Lordship would turn his forces that way, Ujimoto would gladly take the vanguard and wreak slaughter at Kagetsura's lair, not to mention the district of Asahina, so as to assuage his wrath. I pray Your Lordship, let it be so." The messenger gave letters to this effect to Takayoshi and Sadayuki.

Both men, having to this point been deeply impressed by their lord's perspicacity and wisdom, repeatedly urged him to "quickly strike at Kagetsura." But Yoshizane shook his head.

"No, we must not strike at Anzai. I slew Sadakane not for my own glory and advantage, but to save the people from their sufferings. It is happiness unsurpassed for me that through the strength of the masses I am become lord of Nagasa and Heguri. Rapacious Kagetsura may be, but he is not of Sadakane's stripe. Let his basic intentions be what they may, Kagetsura lent his aspirations to me so that Kisonosuke Ujimoto might slay Nobutoki, and then adroitly he plucked the castle of Hiratate for himself. Nevertheless, to raise an army, quarrel over land, strand myself between the horns of a dilemma, kill men, and do damage to the people, all out of jealousy over that: this is what I will not do. If, in spite of having carried out his nefarious plot and taken Hiratate, Kagetsura is not sated but turns his attack on me, then in an instant it will be decided which of us is the man. Barring that, we will guard our borders, and start nothing. Take this to heart, all of you."

His earnestness opened their eyes, and neither Takayoshi nor Sadayuki spoke further; of the attendants and comrades who flanked him, including Amasaki, none failed to be moved, and as one they praised him, saying, "Could the holy wisdom of antiquity have surpassed this?" And so Yoshizane personally wrote a missive to Ujimoto, praising him and opening his eyes, and forbidding him to strike at Anzai, saying, "When you reach to take from another, forget not what is in your own hand. As the proverb says, a bird in the hand is worth two in the bush.[3] Hold fast in the castle: let nothing superfluous be done, no other action be taken." He sent Amasaki Jūrō and the others back with his commands.

As Yoshizane occupied himself with this and that, the cold summer advanced, the deutzia-rotting rains came and went, and the waterless sixth-month days of waiting for the wind—the dog days—followed them.[4] At this time Anzai Kagetsura entrusted two or three local delicacies to a senior vassal named Kabuto Toppei and dispatched him to Takita Castle, where he delivered congratulations to Yoshizane on the occasion of Sadakane's sudden demise and Yoshizane's own establishment of a base there. He offered amity, saying, "Since the day I first beheld your phoenix brow, I have held you in the highest regard and admiration, and it has always shamed me that Nobutoki should have transgressed against your seat as guest with such shocking rudeness—your resentment must have resembled that of Duke Wen of Jin when he bypassed Cao.[5] However, without that, who would have spurred you on to such great feats as you have now accomplished? Truth be told, from the beginning I considered Your Lordship no common man, although I, Kagetsura, being a man whose aspirations are not as lofty as they should be, assumed a pitiless expression in my dealings with you. It was for this reason that I proclaimed my foolish intent

---

3. In the original, the proverb is "the greedy falcon ruptures his talons" (i.e., by trying to grasp too much).

4. "Dog days" translates *doyō*, the last eighteen days of a season, but particularly summer, of which the sixth was the last month under the old calendar.

5. Prior to ascending the throne in his native Jin, Prince Zhong'er (the future Duke Wen) spent nineteen years wandering from state to state. Upon coming to the state of Cao, he was treated rudely, so he quickly moved on.

and removed Nobutoki for Your Lordship, after which I was rewarded in broad daylight. Attaching myself to such a stallion as yourself redounded mysteriously to my merit, and I captured the castle of Hiratate. Now that we have divided this province with its four districts between the two of us, would it not be a pleasant thing if we were to assist each other like the wings of a bird, never infringing upon one another, and thus transmit these lands to our children and grandchildren? I present you with three riding horses and a hundred bolts of white cloth—trifling and rusticated goods that are wholly insufficient to the meaning they are intended to convey, but accompanied by my prayer that our relations may continue unchanged forever. It would be great happiness for me if Your Lordship would accept them."

The messenger spoke courteously, and Horiuchi Sadayuki relayed his words to Yoshizane, whose expression betrayed not the shadow of a doubt. At length he bade Sadayuki and Takayoshi make Kabuto Toppei welcome, saying, "I would meet this messenger face to face. Let us not stint on our hospitality to him."

He spoke earnestly, but Sadayuki and Takayoshi were not pleased. "How can Your Lordship, with all your sagacity, allow yourself to be deceived by that old tanuki?[6] Were Kagetsura truly a man dedicated to good and devoted to virtue, he would not have plotted to kill you by sending you off in search of a carp, something that did not exist in this land. Now once again he extends to you empty felicitations, offers amity, and gives you trifles, but it is all by way of building a fence around himself, while behind it he hatches who knows what nefarious plots. How can you receive his messenger? He is unworthy of a personal audience with Your Lordship."

Thus did they privately remonstrate with him, but Yoshizane flashed a grin and said, "Even if Kagetsura's offer of amity is not backed by the actual feeling itself, what I hear and see now does not deserve my hatred. Moreover, were I to obstinately blame him for his former evils and refuse to cement relations with him, I would be simply turning my back on him. Were I to act thus, were I to quarrel with him, people would hold me to be unrighteous. And while the unrighteous may prove victorious, that is not what I, Yoshizane, desire. We must try our utmost not to doubt him."

Having thus convinced and enlightened them as he had time and again, Yoshizane personally met with the messenger. Then, when Toppei departed,

---

6. The *tanuki* is a raccoon dog (*Nyctereutes procyonoides*)—more closely related to a dog than a raccoon, which it nonetheless resembles. In Japanese folklore various supernatural powers and mischievous motives are ascribed to them. The word is variously translated "raccoon-dog," "raccoon," or even "badger," but I have elected to retain the original Japanese word, here and hereafter, partly because Bakin later introduces badgers and other similar animals into the story, carefully distinguishing them from tanuki.

Yoshizane sent Kanamari Hachirō along with him to the district of Awa to reciprocate the jade-ornament rites,[7] and to present gifts as form dictated. He swore that their relations should not be severed henceforth, which caused Kagetsura great rejoicing. He extended Takayoshi every hospitality and wrote out an oath with his own hand, which he sent to Yoshizane.

From this time forward, Anzai ruled the two districts of Awa and Asahina, while Yoshizane ruled the old Jin'yo territories, the two districts of Nagasa and Heguri; there were neither trespasses nor quarrels, and the realm was become tranquil. Sugikura Kisonosuke Ujimoto was recalled from Tōjō, and for the first time, lord and retainer knew security; superior and inferior turned their smiles on one another, and all was pleasant for all.

In this way the seventh month arrived, and the night of the star celebration.[8] That evening Yoshizane went out to the edge of the veranda, where he assembled only his most meritorious retainers—Sugikura Ujimoto, Horiuchi Sadayuki, and Kanamari Takayoshi—and conducted the tea rite [THE RITE OF TEA WAS ONE OF THE ANCIENT CUSTOMS OF THE SATOMI HOUSE, AS MENTIONED IN THE COMPENDIUM OF MATERIALS PERTAINING TO AWA AND KAZUSA[9]], after the conclusion of which he invited them to speak of what they had been through, listening to each of them.

Then he addressed these meritorious retainers, saying, "In the time since I was fortunate enough to obtain these two districts, our affairs have been as smooth as a lake untroubled by wind or wave, and yet in the relentless press of obligations, I have not offered my gratitude to the god to which I prayed. Nor have I administered rewards to my meritorious retainers—it is as if I am making a Mount Jie here.[10] Ujimoto and Sadayuki, your loyalty and faithfulness in following me through my tribulations, at my late honored father's command, hardly needs repeating; but had we not encountered Kanamari Takayoshi on the banks of the Shirahashi River, how could we have erected such meritorious accomplishments in this land? And would Sadakane have surrendered his head had the pigeons not delivered our missive? All of you have done me laudable service of the first order. Without it I should have either been beheaded according to military law as a result of

7. In ancient China, ornaments of jade were given by the ruler to his subordinates, signifying the territories they had been entrusted.

8. Commonly known as Tanabata, this observance on the seventh night of the seventh month commemorates the nearest approach of the two stars Vega and Altair (associated in legend with the sundered lovers Orihime and Hikoboshi).

9. *Bōsō shiryō*, written in 1761 (Hōreki 11) by Nakamura Kunika.

10. A reference to Jie Zitui, a legendary by-word for good service that goes unrewarded. Jie was a retainer of Duke Wen of Jin (Zhong'er; see note 5 above). The Duke rewarded other advisors, but not Jie, who then retired to Mount Mian. Later, men loyal to Jie called the Duke's attention to his oversight, and in deference to Jie the Duke renamed the mountain Mount Jie. See chapter 39 of *Shi ji*.

Anzai and Maro's scheme, or taken captive by the enemy after succumbing to weariness and hunger once our provisions had run out—only these two were possible.

"Now at last the time has brought us to this refreshing cool, this night when it is said the two stars meet, that we might recite lyrics and compose poetry, our rootless sheaves of words like dew descending onto the leaves. Lord and retainer, superior and inferior, are distinguished among the stars—men's fortunes, for good or ill, depend on it. Now, I have already sworn to Heaven to establish a holy seat for Hachiman at each of the eight corners of this castle, that I might worship thereat every autumn, and furthermore to promulgate a decree throughout my territories forbidding the killing of pigeons. In addition, I mean to detach half of the district of Nagasa and give it to Kanamari Hachirō Takayoshi, making him master of Tōjō Castle. Unto Ujimoto and Sadayuki I shall give possessions worth five thousand strings of cash. Accept this as my will." He spoke sincerely as he laid these matters before them, and then he presented Takayoshi a commendation written in his own hand.

Takayoshi thrice lifted the commendation above his head to honor it, but then gave it back, speaking as if to relinquish his seat. "Your Lordship again does me great honor in placing me before your senior retainers and hereditary aides, an honor far be it from me to refuse. But I have never had my heart set on renown and advantage. My only thoughts were for executing my late lord's mutinous retainer. Truly Your Lordship could give me no greater boon than what, in your overpowering goodness, you already have in carrying out my long-cherished aspiration."

Yoshizane smiled at this and said, "To achieve merit and then withdraw himself, without regard for fame and glory: indeed this is the aspiration of a warrior, and as such, it is as it should be. And yet, we have the example from China of Zhang Liang, who defeated Qin and Chu for the sake of his late lord and afterward finally accepted an enfeoffment from the Han, being created the Marquis of Liu. I have not the virtue of the Great Progenitor of the Han, but you do possess the solitary loyalty of Zhang Liang.[11] In addition to which, should I fail to reward those who merit it, how can I encourage them to aspire to loyalty, filial piety, self-control, righteousness? Oblige me—do my will in this."

---

11. Zhang Liang was born into a line of ministers of the Han dynasty, but the Han fell to the Qin before he could take his place in service. In helping Liu Bang destroy Qin and its shortlived successor state of Chu, Zhang was in effect serving his father's lords, the former Han dynasty. Liu Bang, upon restoring the dynasty, became known as Gaozu, or the Great Progenitor, of the Later Han.

After he had thus explained matters, Ujimoto and Sadayuki both advised Takayoshi to accept, and they picked up the commendation where it lay and handed it to him. Kanamari Hachirō had no choice but to take it from them. He opened and read it, then said, "For me to refuse this would be to blindly insist on doing my own will, as if unconscious of the principle of gratitude. And yet to accept it is to be disloyal to my late lord. But there is a way for Takayoshi to both accept and not accept this—to serve both my lord in this world and my lord in that other." No sooner had he spoken than he drew his sword with a flash—he wrapped the commendation around it and then thrust it straight into his belly.

"What is this?" The three onlookers, master and men, crowded closer; Yoshizane gingerly lifted Takayoshi's elbow and examined the wound this way and that, then spoke. "The point has gone in too deep—you cannot survive this injury. And yet if the affair ends like this, everyone will say you went mad. Endure the pain and tell me what you were thinking—empty your heart to me."

Takayoshi, hearing these words, glanced up and took a breath. "I should have slit my belly immediately upon learning of my late master's untimely death—I lived on, thinking only of striking down Sadakane—but I could not accomplish it alone. Thus do time and fate rule all. Once I chanced to make Your Lordship's acquaintance, I worked like a horse or a dog—and now to receive such a boon, rewards so much greater than my merit, makes it seem as if I had turned my late lord's unexpected, unsucceeded death to my own happiness. This is one reason I cannot prolong my life. And yet there is more. Bokuhei of Somaki and Mukuzō, who on Ochiba hill felled the lord of the province, thinking he was Sadakane, originally served my house. Their martial artistry they owed to me—'twas I who taught them the use of their swords—so although I knew naught of it, by imparting stratagems unto those too mean to deserve it, I, Takayoshi, paved the way for that great wound upon our province: the error is as my own, and I am uneasy because of it. This is the second reason I find it hard to live on. Nothing do I know of what Zhang Liang of the Han court may have felt; if it comes to that, I yearn after Tian Heng's virile aspirations, that remained so even after death.[12] My lords, I pray you will forgive my crime of impropriety in staining your mats at these revels."

---

12. Tian Heng was a general in, and then King of, the state of Qi during the rise of the later Han. Once Liu Bang (see previous note) had restored the Han dynasty, Tian Heng killed himself rather than serve a new master. Five hundred of his men followed him in suicide.

Caption: Takayoshi dies a principled death, leaving an only child behind.
Figures: Sugikura Ujimoto [*right, with fan*]. Kanamari Hachirō [*center right*]. Satomi Yoshizane [*center left*]. Issaku, a farmer [*bottom left, kneeling*]. Daisuke of Kazusa [*on Issaku's back*]. Tamazusa's angry spirit [*top left*].

With this, raising one knee, he at length sought to twist and pull the blade toward the right. "Stop him!" cried Yoshizane in a fervor, and Sadayuki and Ujimoto clung to Takayoshi's clenched fists, saying, "You hear His Lordship's command: there is absolutely no reason for you to hasten to make your bed in that darkling land."

Out of words, Yoshizane sighed again and again. Then he said, "I knew of Takayoshi's aspirations, but I never thought it would come to this. It was my rashness in informing him of his reward that spurred him on to death; this is the greatest mistake of my life. Behold, Hachirō, I have a gift for you on the occasion of your departure for the Yellow Springs. Kisonosuke, summon the old man, but quickly."

"Yes, sir," replied Ujimoto. He then went to the edge of the veranda and in a loud voice called, "Issaku of Kazusa, come forth now!"

A reply came: "Yes, sir." The voice was choked, the eyes were teary of the peasant in his sixties who, unnoticed, had been standing in the garden's depths amidst a stand of trees. Coarse-woven were his gaiters, and his hems were hitched up high; a sedge-hat held he in his right hand, while his left hand clutched that of a boy, no more than five. Bowing low, they came in through the garden gate. "Come here, come here," said Ujimoto, beckoning them forward until the peasant placed his hands on the veranda's edge and then straightened himself.

"Behold, milord Hachirō, master Takayoshi. I have come from Kazusa—'tis Issaku! This is the son my daughter Kohagi bore you. How is it that on the very day I have finally searched you out, you slit your belly? Is there nothing you can say?" His tears and bitterness he fought to hide—although the Gate of Scruples this was not,[13] it was a gathering of noble men, which made him want to present his best face.

When Takayoshi heard him name himself as Issaku, his eyes he opened wide: he stared and stared, but not a word did speak. Then Sugikura Ujimoto turned to Takayoshi and said, "Hachirō, do you see this man? When I was coming here to the manor, this ancient was standing on the roadside, and he asked my companions, 'Where is the house of the Kanamari clan?' Hearing this, I could not pass him by, so I inquired as to how he had come to be there. He told me, not neglecting to explain the babe, whom, too, I could not leave there. 'Takayoshi is not in his lodgings today. If you would find him, follow me,' I said, and led him on to our lord's place, where I first made the matter known unto Kurando, and then reported it unto His Lordship, who

---

13. The Gate of Scruples refers to Habakari no Seki, an ancient post-station in the province of Mutsu whose name made it a convenient reference in classical poetry.

spake thus: 'This is interesting! If this child is Hachirō's secret son, then we may expect great things from him in the future. I shall bring them together myself. Until then, do not let Kanamari know of it.' Therefore we caused Issaku, together with the child, to hide behind the gates in the inner garden, there to await a word from His Lordship. Who would have thought that before it could be spoken, you would kill yourself? What must this old man have been feeling as he watched you from without? It is our lord's wish that you might proclaim yourself, if only for this moment, father to this son—this is His Lordship's gift to you. What say you, Hachirō?"

As if Ujimoto's words had called him back to life, Takayoshi abruptly raised his head and said, "Of what use would it be to proclaim us father and son now that things have come to this pass? When I left Takita, having failed in my remonstrations with my lord and master, there was in the village of Seki in the district of Amaha in the province of Kazusa a peasant named Issaku—that is, this old man before you. In my father's time he had been a junior vassal of ours, and so I decided to pause in my wanderings and lodge with him a while. He had a daughter named Kohagi, and it came to pass, during my stay, that we knew each other—was it but a dream?—and though it was for but the dew's duration, yet we swore our constancy would last a thousand years.

"And as we shared a pillow time and again, she came to be of no ordinary bodily state. She told me, and I was astonished, to the bottom of my heart; truly is it said in the world that lust leads to evils unexpected, and it might have been said of me. I was a traveler with no fixed destination, and she was of a house with which I had never been intimate; we had not been formally betrothed, and for me to give us infamy as lovers was to damage the daughter of a man whose dealings with me had never been anything but sincerity itself. Her father might now forgive me, but I cannot face him. My actions were wretched, but though my regret for them might mount up a hundredfold, a thousandfold, it would be to no avail. In secret I simply advised Kohagi to abort, and having no other ideas, I wrote out a letter of apology, useless though it was, and left it behind for Issaku when I fled Seki.

"Thence I wandered hither and yon for five years, until that day this summer on which I heard tell of my late lord's untimely death, and decided to return to my home village in secret to strike at Sadakane. And although it was not inconvenient, it would seem, to my road, I sent no word to Issaku, but passed by, and to this day I never once put brush to paper to inquire after Kohagi. Thus to see now that the child was safely delivered, and has been nurtured with such evident sincerity, fills me with even greater shame." His voice came in gasps as he said this.

"How truly reasonable," said Issaku, sobbing and blowing his nose, unable to comfort Takayoshi. "Indeed, even the most stalwart warrior is only a man, and thus vulnerable to love. And for you, sir, with neither wife nor child, to while away your traveling hours with the comforts of a maid like Kohagi—while it may appear mischief, it was no such thing. I will say it outright: For that girl to host the seed of our late lord, of firm and proven lineage, makes of her one singularly blessed by fate, and her old mother and I rejoiced in our hearts that we had such a goodly prospective groom for her. You seemed to have guessed our thoughts, sir, though we pretended not to know, for you left and did not return.

"Even as we sadly searched for your whereabouts, my daughter reached her term, and gave birth to a boy child. A happy event, but one there was no time to bless, for, weighed down by cares, Kohagi did not recover, but instead set out to traverse the myriad lands between here and paradise, never to return. The se'ennight observance of her death fell on the second se'ennight of the child's life. Truly were we harried—he had to make do with a little rice in my hand, and a little milk we begged, and he drifted among the three realms on the border of life and death. I cannot properly tell of all his sufferings in my corrupted speech.

"In spite of it all, the babe was sound. I looked on him as a memento of my master and my daughter, and thought him adorable, and I clung to him; day in and day out I clutched him to my breast, and night in and night out I and my old wife would take turns sleeping beside him. If he stood, we hurried him into crawling; if he laughed, we hurried him to say something—he drew out our hearts like the cotton thread that you spin while singing a lullaby, he pulled us along like a horse by its reins, did our grandson, until we were like scarecrows in a poor paddy in need of weeding. We passed the days, all alike, and the years piled up until he was four, and then, last autumn, his grandmother took sick. I nursed her with one hand, the other bound to a bawling child. I took down the medicine pot from its out-of-reach shelf and heated it, but by the time it was fully infused the year had diffused, and on the eve of the New Year, his grandmother departed this life for the next.

"There were only three of us now: me, the infant, and a wooden doll with one arm wrenched off. We watched over her coffin as the New Year came, an unpolished gem, and the pine we had set by the gate to greet it looked like a mile marker on the darkling road; I strove to look on it with the comprehending eyes of a Zen monk, but I am a common man, not easy to enlighten. Though I am sixty-eight this year, all the travails of my lifetime together could not equal this double, treble calamity. This old man was not ashamed to weep in front of his grandson, and though the distant mountains of spring may have laughed at me, the icicles into which my tears froze melted, and the plum at our back door, an offering to the Buddha, broke out in five-petal buds just as the boy turned five, old enough to mimic me mindlessly, yawning with the first disorientation of sleep, as I chanted the Buddha's name.

"But ah, the nights are short in spring! And the season soon passed, and toward the end of the fourth month rumors of the neighboring province began to reach us in the backwoods of Kazusa—rumors of you, sir, as your battles could not be kept hidden. I was amazed at first, but then courage filled my heart, and I thought to go and seek you out. Then, however, it occurred to me how dangerous it should be for me, an old man who can hardly walk, to visit the field of battle while carrying an infant, and I changed my mind and decided to await a better time. Then I heard that all the blows had been struck, and the fighting put down, and that settled me to come here today for what has proved to be this useless, temporary meeting. My sadness as I reflect on my karmic rewards from lives gone by is as refuse; what, rather, of the boy's lifelong anguish at having grown up never knowing his parents' faces? Here, Katami—this is your daddy. Remember his face well."

He pointed, and the child straightened himself and spoke: "Father?"

That parent looked up when called to, but could do no more—his lips, as he moved them in a desire to speak, were discolored, and he appeared to be nearing his end.

Yoshizane beckoned the child close to him and, turning his gaze on both of them, said, "He does look very much like his father Hachirō. What is his name?"

Issaku, kneeling, looked up and said, "He has none, sir, not formally. But I have been used to calling him Katami, as he is a keepsake of both my late master and my daughter."[14]

"No doubt he is. I would have you leave the boy with me. His father Takayoshi came to my aid with sterling valor. This shall be made manifest in the boy's name: he shall be called Kanamari Daisuke Takanori, and carry on his father's loyalty and righteousness.[15] When he becomes a man, as a keepsake of his father, I will detach half the district of Nagasa and give it to him, making him master of Tōjō Castle. Issaku, you are related to him on his mother's side—stay you here together with Daisuke, to watch over and support him. Now, I would have the child accept, by way of reward and

---

14. The boy's nickname, Katami, is written with characters that mean "threefold much increase," but it is also homophonous with a word that means "keepsake."

15. Daisuke is written with characters that mean "great aid," and Takanori with characters that mean "filial piety" and "virtue." The character read "taka" is the same as that in the name of his father, Takayoshi.

encouragement, five hundred strings of cash. Take this with you as a memento to those darkling lands, Hachirō, and may you finally attain Buddhahood."

Heartened by these words, Takayoshi raised his blood-dyed left hand and did obeisance to his lord and master. Then at last he grasped his innards where they extruded through the hole his blade had made as he dragged it so sharply across himself, and as his final words, he said, "Second me, men, I beg of you." As he stretched out his neck, Yoshizane could bear it no longer. "You shall not suffer," he said, drawing the blade at his side and personally moving to stand behind Takayoshi. Ah, the futility! Hachirō's head fell forward.

Though he had braced himself, Issaku could not bear it, and he wept, not stinting at raising his voice. Ujimoto and Sadayuki bore the brunt of the old man's mutterings as they sought solemnly to comfort him, while the child toddled about, bitter tears streaming down his cheeks, though he understood not why; pitiable he was as he peered into the face of his father, cut off in his prime.

When Kanamari Hachirō died the stars had set, the seventh-month moon had sunk in the west, and in the inky dark a spirit-fire flared—a woman's form, like a shadow, appeared alongside Daisuke's body, obscuring him as if he had vanished. Yoshizane was the only one who saw this; the rest knew nothing of it. And so Yoshizane beckoned Ujimoto and Sadayuki close and commanded them earnestly concerning Takayoshi's obsequies and the nurturing of Daisuke, and then at length he went inside. By the loud sounds of the water clock, it was already the tenth hour, and the night was far advanced.

Author's note: This passage takes place at the beginning of the seventh month. However, the clothing in the illustration resembles that of winter. Indeed, even when one draws light silks, without color they are difficult to distinguish as such. I choose not to be finicky about such things, but leave them to the discretion of the illustrator. This sort of thing happens rather frequently. Do not, O Reader, reproach us overmuch.

Also: in this illustration Ujimoto appears, while Sadayuki is left out. They are both uncommonly important characters, but not here, so I saved Master Block-Carver the trouble.

Also: from the passage about the Battle of Yūki at the beginning of Chapter I to now has involved a mere four months—the story begins in the fourth month of the first year of Kakitsu and ends in the seventh month of that year, a period of some eighty days, were one to count them.[16] In Chapter VIII, time

---

16. 1441. In referring to four months, Bakin is (as was the custom with ages) referring to the number of calendar months in which action had taken place, not the number of thirty-day spans that had elapsed.

will pass more quickly, and we shall move forward some sixteen or seventeen years. In that interval all we shall have to speak of at length will be Princess Fuse's growth, and where there is no story to tell we shall not insist on telling it, but shall abbreviate. These things are hardly out of the ordinary—things treated in detail will necessarily appear differently than those treated in a cursory fashion—and to say it thus openly is rather like gluing a notice to a pole, but I decided to make a note of it myself for the sake of those who do not read carefully, that they might not mistake the order of things.

Chapter VIII
At the Ascetic's Grotto, an old man divines for Princess Fuse;
Near Takita, a tanuki nurtures a puppy

Those ignorant of the aspirations behind Kana-mari Hachirō Takayoshi's sudden suicide censured him, saying, "He need not have died. Affairs would have resolved themselves—it must have been his shame at having been so roundly cursed by Tamazusa that led him to refuse rewards he deserved, and so pitiably to lose his life." But it was not so. A wise man once said, If a man's desires are few he avoids a multitude of harms, and if a lady is free from jealousy she hides a multitude of defects.[1] How much more so when morality, benevolence, and righteousness are present?

Now, Yoshizane's virtue was such that he need not stand alone;[2] warriors from neighboring lands looked on him with admiration, and many sought to deepen their amity with him through bonds of matrimony. Yoshizane heard vague reports that the daughter of one of these men—Jōren, the Mariya Inititate, the lord of Shiitsu Castle in Kazusa—had a daughter called Isarago, who was both wise and comely of feature. Yoshizane took her to wife, and she bore him a daughter and a son. The elder, his daughter, was born in the second year of Kakitsu,[3] near the end of the summer—during the season of

---

1. Bakin is here juxtaposing and paraphrasing two maxims originally found in separate chapters (9 and 8, respectively) of *Wu zazu*.

2. A reference to chapter 4 of *Lunyu* ("Virtue is not solitary: it will surely have neighbors").

3. 1442.

the Three Concealments, in expression of which she was named Princess Fuse.[4] The second, his son, was born at the end of the following year, and was called Jirotarō.[5] Later he would carry on his father's work and be known as Yoshinari, Lord Protector of Awa; in his castle at Inamura his might at arms would ascend ever higher.

For her part, Princess Fuse had skin as clear as translucent jade, and at birth her hair came down to the nape of her neck—even in swaddling clothes she made onlookers think of that maiden nonpareil born from the bamboo.[6] She was lacking in none of the proverbial thirty-two aspects of beauty, and her father and mother doted on her even more than is common in the world, assigning her ladies-in-waiting in great numbers. And yet Princess Fuse was colicky night and day, so that even at the age of three she refused to speak or smile, but merely cried. Her father and mother were aggrieved in their hearts; for three years they had tried every treatment medicine could provide, and every rite and prayer that high monks and practitioners could offer, but to no sign of improvement.

Now, in the district of Awa there stood a most ancient and godly shrine, worshipped under the name of the Bright God of Susaki.[7] At the foot of the mountain behind the shrine was a great cave, and within this grotto stood a stone statue of En the Ascetic. A spring bubbled up here, the Vajra Pool,[8] and it never dried up even in drought. It is said that long ago, in the days of the

---

4. The "season of the Three Concealments" refers, most basically, to the late summer and early fall. The Chinese calendrical cycle designates days as belonging to one of the five elements (fire, water, earth, wood, metal), and further designates "elder" and "younger" of each of these days. The element of fire is ascendant in the summer, and since fire trumps metal, the metal days falling during the hottest part of the summer were said to "conceal" themselves, or retreat. Specifically, the third and fourth elder-metal days following the summer solstice, and the first elder-metal day after the beginning of fall, were known as the "Three Concealments" (*sanpuku*). Princess Fuse was born during this period, so the character for "concealment" (*fuku* or *-puku* in its Sinified reading, *fuseru* in its Japanese) was used for her name.

5. A somewhat oxymoronic name. *Jirō* (of which *jiro* is an alternate form) means "second son," while *tarō* means "first son." The sense seems to have been that while this boy was Yoshizane's second child, he was also his eldest son.

6. A reference to the legend of Princess Kaguya (Kaguyahime), as related in the early-Heian *Taketori monogatari*. Kaguyahime is found shining in a stalk of bamboo by a good-hearted bamboo-cutter, and he and his wife adopt and raise her. After fending off several suitors, she is taken home to the moon, whence, the reader learns, she had come.

7. "Bright God" translates *myōjin*, a common epithet in shrine names suggesting a particularly venerable holiness.

8. More precisely, the "single-pronged vajra" pool. A vajra is a Buddhist ritual object with two heads connected by a shaft. Often the two heads have several prongs (separating and then meeting again in a point), while a single-pronged vajra (J. *tokko* or *dokko*) has one pointed prong at either end of the shaft.

Upper register:
Caption: A stranger sees Princess Fuse and knows future hardship.
Figure: Princess Fuse.
Lower register:
Caption: In a village near Takita, a tanuki raises a puppy.
Figures: Tamazusa's angry spirit [*right, by tree*]. Horiuchi Sadayuki [*left*].

Note: The label "Tamazusa's angry spirit" applies to the column of smoke or mist arising from the tanuki and the puppy. This vapor wafts off the page to the right to trail off over the text on the other side of the page. Original readers, progressing right to left, would have first encountered the tail end of the vapor while reading, then followed it by turning the page to discover its source in the illustration.

悉くかく靈驗を顯し多くの人その像紙に造りて彼石窟に安措せし

靈應今も著明にして一たび祈願をかくるもの成就せずといふことなしとかくて

経いつゞく。大きなりども……えゝがもん母君五十子は伏姫のゐぶ願ふ

月三日彼窟へ代参其の形遺して既に三年かなるものゝうちさせ給へり

中

益ゝいるゝれども姫君へ参るゝともかくも生育のためその驗ゆゑであらん

けれど武實もとのる張いるゝみふれあら福洲崎八里見の来地なるとも

ぞんみつらら彼処みぶるのがいうぐ奇特のるゝやむと殿へ歓せるひ

なる彼処へ遺さじ世のゆゑへ軽獲して思ひとゞより多くとそ容易なるひ

今も安西か野心あるべうもあらざれれどもかるゝゆく檡兄ものゝ残そ

ざら弔一ゞ靖るゝよ変かさなるゝまゝく歎止ぐうく思召けん倶ゆれ老さぶ

男女を擇く潜ゞふ姫つ祓洲崎へ遣してひけうきさぶ祖かふ伏姫か輿子ゞ

Emperor Monmu, Lord Shōkaku of the En was banished to the Izu Islands.[9] It being a mere forty-four miles by sea from this place to the Great Isle of Izu, Shōkaku would often hie himself to Susaki, treading the waves, and there manifest his mystical attainments, so that future generations made this statue of him and installed it in the grotto. To this day, it was said, the place was so wondrously responsive to spiritual power that none who offered up prayers there saw them go unanswered.

Learning of the cave's extraordinary reputation, Princess Fuse's mother, Isarago, had sent representatives there monthly to offer up pleas on the child's behalf. For three years had she done this to no discernible avail, but still she cried to His Lordship, saying, "Is it not manifestation enough of the cave's power that the Princess's life has been preserved, that she is, despite all, growing? How can greater marvels fail to occur if she goes there in person?"

Yoshizane, for his part, could hardly refuse, nor yet could he easily allow it. "Susaki is not Satomi territory. Anzai does not appear to be harboring any particular ambitions at the moment, but nevertheless we should brook disapproval from all quarters were we to send one so tender in years to such a place. Think no more of this, I pray you," said he. Yet Isarago persisted in her entreaties, and would not be quieted. And so, selecting an old man and woman as an escort, he sent the Princess in secret to Susaki.

Thus Princess Fuse was placed in a palanquin, where she was cradled on her wetnurse's knee; she was taken past novel scenery, with singing and playing at every turn, but she showed no signs of being pleased by any of it: she cried the whole way, so that her companions found it painful to be beside her, and put on even greater haste. In this way they reached Susaki, where they lodged at the Yōrō Temple, warden temple to the Bright God's shrine, and for seven days in succession visited the Cave of the Ascetic.

The days of their vow having been thus fulfilled, the Princess's escort urged the party homeward; they left their lodgings and had carried her palanquin some two or three miles in the direction of Heguri when the Princess became terribly colicky. Her maids and wetnurse could not comfort her, so they took her out of the palanquin and set to wheedling and humoring her. Finally, cradling the Princess in their arms, the party began to hasten down the road again. But it was not to be.

---

9. Monmu reigned 697–707. En's exile occurred in 699. En no Shōkaku (also called En no Ozunu) is popularly known as En no Gyōja (En the Ascetic). His exile and peculiar powers are recounted in the ninth-century collection of Buddhist stories *Nihon ryōiki*. He was considered the founder of *shugendō*, a form of asceticism practiced by *yamabushi*, mountain priests who figure prominently in medieval story and legend.

For just then there appeared before them an old man of eighty or more, with sloping, frost-white eyebrows. He clutched a cane whose grip was carved in the shape of a dove,[10] for he was bowed at the waist like a catalpa bow,[11] and he stood in the very center of the road as if taking his rest. As theirs was ostensibly a secret journey, the Princess's escort could not chase him away. The old man did not avert his eyes, but fixed Princess Fuse with a piercing gaze and said, "This is the Satomi Princess, is it not? You seem to be on your way home from the cave. Allow an old man to perform a rite for you."

Thus addressed, the Princess's companions were amazed and flustered. They returned the venerable one's gaze, and indeed by his appearance he was no ordinary man. "It would go ill for us if we rashly refused to speak the truth," they thought, and the old vassal and the old woman faced the old man and told him everything about the affair, concealing nothing.

The old man nodded again and again. "Truly it is a spirit's curse, visiting unhappiness upon this child. It should not be difficult to dispel, but ill fortune and good are like a rope intertwined.[12] Even though one loses a child, if one is later greatly aided thereby, the tragedy is no tragedy. It is always thus in matters of gain and loss. One should neither rejoice nor grieve. Pray tell this to Yoshizane and his wife when you return home. I give the Princess this, for protection—she shall understand it someday." His face beaming with pride, from his bosom he took a string of crystal prayer beads upon which were incised the eight characters for Benevolence, Righteousness, Propriety, Wisdom, Loyalty, Fidelity, Filiality, and Fraternity. In a flash the old man had placed the beads about the Princess's neck.

The old vassal and old woman were amazed and confused, and bowed so that their foreheads touched the ground. "What spirit? What curse? Please, we beg you, tell us about it in full, and dispel or propitiate the thing for all time to come."

The old man smiled and replied, "The monstrous can never triumph over the virtuous.[13] Even if there is an evil spirit at work, the Satomi house will

---

10. In ancient China and Japan, such canes were given as presents to aged retainers. According to Tokuda (p. 155), doves were auspicious birds for the aged because they were thought not to choke when they ate.

11. Bows made of catalpa wood were anciently used for hunting, but also in shamanistic rituals such as summoning or repelling spirits. The catalpa bow was also a poetic image for graceful curvature. Here the latter meaning (describing the old man's bent waist) is primary, but the association with mystic practices is no doubt intended as well.

12. This aphorism, recurrent in *Eight Dogs*, may have originally come from chapter 113 of *Shi ji*. A close variant also appears in *Heiji monogatari*.

13. A maxim from chapter 3 of *Shi ji*.

rise to still greater heights of prosperity. What waxes must also wane. What would you have me dispel? I fear that were I to make known unto you every particular, I should risk revealing the workings of Heaven. Understand what you will, what you can, from her name: Fuse. And yet, I tell you that from this day forward this child will cry no more. Now go, quickly. I must go back soon myself."

Saying thus, he started off in the direction of Susaki, and, moving as with the speed of flight, he was gone from view. The Princess's escort stood and looked after him a while, stupefied, before it occurred to them: "That was En the Ascetic, manifesting himself unto us!" They prostrated themselves in adoration, then set out again to return to Takita.

The Princess did not fuss or cry as they made their way, but played and played as if quite pleased; indeed, from this day forward, her utterances were superior to those of a normal child of three. Those who accompanied her were both rejoiced and alarmed as they carried her back to Takita, where they spoke unto Yoshizane and Isarago of what had occurred, and showed unto them the prayer beads. This was darkling aid of such an uncommon nature that Yoshizane could not do nothing: he dispatched Kurando Sada-yuki to the Susaki shrine and the Cave of the Ascetic, where he presented sacred offerings and prayed that the Princess be preserved from harm forever after; Yoshizane also caused that Princess Fuse should wear the beads at her collar at all times.

In this way four springs came and went, and as the Princess turned seven, it came to pass not only that Heaven had given her beauty without its like in this world, comparable only to the first egg of a golden phoenix or the first fruit of a jade tree, but that she was clever and wise, too. All day long she worked at her copybooks, her attention never flagging; deep into the night she played at her music, her interest never wavering. By the age of eleven or twelve she was well versed in the reading of tomes both Japanese and Chinese, and assiduously sought to apprehend principles and reasons; her heart never went astray after foolish things; she honored her parents, had compassion for those beneath her, and at all times and in all her doings displayed dutifulness, chastity, loyalty, and kindness. Her mother doted on her, needless to say, while Yoshizane, without realizing that he did so, spoke proudly of her to others.

Now, in those days a wondrous tale was heard in the district of Nagasa, in a hamlet this side of Mount To. A dog belonging to a peasant named Azana Wazahei gave birth to a single pup. It was a male, with unrivalled sturdi-ness and strength as befitted such a rarity as a single-pup litter, and Wazahei prized it greatly—he erected a shelter of straw as a nursery for the pup and its dam by his back gate, and there he brought table scraps to the dogs morning and night.

Seven days passed in this way, and then on the seventh night, a wolf broke in through the back fence and attacked the dam, rending her with its jaws before leaving. The next morning, Wazahei saw the blood and discovered what had happened, but though he was enraged, he could do nothing about it. At least, he observed, the pup had not been eaten—indeed, it had been left mysteriously unharmed, the pitiful thing. It had not yet opened its eyes, nor had it been weaned. Having no milk to give it, Wazahei crushed some rice into a paste, doing his best to shelter the pup under the wings of his heart. Yet this could he not accomplish—Wazahei had neither wife nor child, but had always lived alone, and he spent his days out working in the fields, seldom coming back to his house. All he could do was wait with folded arms for the pup to die, and so he put it out of his mind and went into the wilds.

A day passed, then two, but strangely, the pup showed no signs whatsoever of starvation, and on the tenth day it opened its eyes, and was fatter than ever it had been. This, Wazahei thought, was no ordinary occurrence. He told others about it, and every morning and evening he made a point of peeking in on the pup. One morning he awoke and looked before it was fully light and saw a tanuki, quite old, emerge from the kennel at a run and retreat in the direction of Mount To. "Well, then, it seems that the pup is being nurtured by yon tanuki. Never have I heard of such a thing! How can it be?" gasped Wazahei in astonishment.

He decided he must see it again by way of confirmation, so he said nothing to anyone, but that evening, in the gloaming, hid himself by the back gate, there to wait for the tanuki to come. The pup was barking noisily, missing his dam. Just then something came flashing from the direction of Takita—demonfire or soulfire, Wazahei thought—and fell from the sky with a thud, suddenly disappearing in the vicinity of the kennel. Then, as he watched, the tanuki he had seen that morning bustled in at a run from the direction of Mount To, and entered the nursery, at which time the pup abruptly stopped bawling. The sounds of it sucking at a teat could be heard. Some forty or fifty days passed in this manner, until the dog had grown enough to walk around and eat on its own and the tanuki came no more. From this the place came to be called Inukake.[14] [THE COMPENDIUM OF MATERI-ALS PERTAINING TO AWA AND KAZUSA[15] SAYS THAT THERE WAS A ROAD FROM FUCHŪ IN THE

---

14. "Dog Tether" or "Dog Hang" (as explained elsewhere, *inu* means "dog," while a number of translations are possible for the element *kake*).

15. See Chapter VII, note 9.

DISTRICT OF AWA TO THE ŌYAMA TEMPLE IN THE DISTRICT OF NAGASA. THOSE WISHING TO
CLIMB MOUNT TO WOULD GO AROUND TO THE LEFT AT INUKAKE. IT ALSO SAYS THAT TO THE
WEST WAS HEGURI; THIS MUST HAVE BEEN WHERE THOSE AREAS REFERRED TO AS TAKITA,
YAMASHITA, AND THE INUKAKE REGION LAY.]

Now, at this time Sugikura Kisonosuke Ujimoto and Horiuchi Kurando Sadayuki were, by Yoshizane's dictate, alternately entrusted with the defense of Tōjō Castle, each for one year at a time. This being Sadayuki's year of rest, he turned the castle over to Ujimoto and set out to return to Takita, and as he passed through said hamlet of Inukake, he happened to hear of the tanuki. Sadayuki at first would not accept the tale, and in order to learn the truth of it he went to Wazahei's home, where he had a careful look at the dog in question and heard all about the affair from the master of the house, whose story matched in every particular the tale being told in the village. In appearance the dog was, it may be said, even as Luhan of China, or, in our own land of Japan, as Ayuki.[16]

This being such a rare occurrence, utterly without precedent, upon his return Sadayuki went to the Minister of the Court, Yoshizane, to tell him that such a thing had happened. Yoshizane pricked up his ears while Sadayuki told him everything just as he had seen it; he unconsciously inched forward on his knees.

Then Yoshizane spake, saying, "Ever since she was in swaddling clothes, Princess Fuse has been tormented unto tears. Because of this we have always kept dogs, tethering them in the inner garden, but never have we had such a singular beast as this one would seem to be, if what you say is true. Long ago in Tanba, in the village of Kuwata, a man named Mikaso had a dog named Ayuki. One day this dog killed a bageard.[17] From its belly came an 'eight-foot' curved gem[18] —so it is written in the *Chronicles of Japan*, in the chronicle of Suinin. For a tanuki, in utter contrast to this, to raise the offspring of a dog, nurturing it as if it were her own—it is beyond mysterious. Indeed, dogs are shunned by tanuki, foxes, and their ilk; and yet this one saw a pup with no dam and so far forgot their mutual antagonism as to offer him her teat and

---

16. As Tokuda notes (p. 160), the Song-era reference work *Shiwen leiju* (J. *Shibun ruishū*) mentions "A good dog Lu of Han." Bakin interprets the name as Luhan. The dog Ayuki's story is given below, as related in *Nihon shoki*.

17. The word here translated as "bageard" is *mujina*, an old term for the badger (usually known as *anaguma* in modern Japanese). It should be noted, however, that the term *mujina* was also known to refer to tanuki. In order to retain the suggestive ambiguity and archaic feel of the term I have used an old form of the English word "badger."

18. *Yasakani no magatama*. Opinions differ as to the meaning of the term "*yasakani*," which is written "eight-foot jewel" but almost certainly did not describe a gem eight feet in length. *Yasaka* may have been a place name, or it may have referred to the length of the cord on which a gem was strung.

nurture it, an action characteristic of the Way of Impartial Love.[19] Furthermore, the character for tanuki comes from the combination of two other characters: village and dog. A Satomi dog, in other words.[20] I would fain see that dog. Bring him to me."

Sadayuki took his master's words to heart, and before many days had passed he brought the dog. Yoshizane looked and saw that it was big-boned and sharp-eyed, twice as tall as the average dog, and its drooping ears and curly tail were such as to evoke love in the onlooker, and a desire to train him up as one's own. His coat was white with black intermingled, with eight spots scattered over the length and girth of his body, so that Yoshizane named him Yatsufusa,[21] tethering him in the inner garden; Yoshizane also gave a suitable emolument to Wazahei, the dog's former master.

From that time forth Yatsufusa was treated so well that people wondered if even the Ichijō emperor's dog Okinamaru—loved by persons of rank and quality, fed to utter satiation, and allowed to sleep on cushions—could have surpassed him in favor.[22] People found it jarring, but, as he was the beloved pet of their lord and master, they pampered him with all diligence. Princess Fuse loved him, too, and long would; on days when she went out onto the veranda, she would call him to her—"Yatsufusa, Yatsufusa!"—and he would come at a run, tail wagging, and not leave her side for a moment.

The springtime blossoms and autumn leaves the branches dyed with their successive hues, again, again, and many more agains, until Princess Fuse was twice eight, and of a beauty so surpassingly refined 'twas like the lingering midmonth moon casting its sixteen-night-old light on blossoms newly

---

19. A doctrine taught by the philosopher Mozi, a contemporary of Confucius.

20. The first character in "Satomi" means "village." The character for tanuki is indeed composed of that same character for "village" combined with that for "dog."

21. *Yatsu* is written with the character for "eight," while *fusa* is written with a character that can mean "bunch," and is homophonous with the character *fusa* used in Kazusa and Shimōsa (see Chapter II, note 1 for more on these names). The character read *fusa* in the dog's name is also the second character in the name of the district of Awa.

22. Okinamaro's story is told in section 7 of the eleventh-century miscellany *Makura no sōshi* (The Pillow Book) by Sei Shōnagon. The person charged with caring for the Emperor's cat finds the animal sleeping and mischievously decides to sick the dog Okinamaro on it. Obediently, Okinamaro gives chase to the cat, which flees, frightened. The Emperor punishes the dog by having it beaten. Sei describes hearing the dog's howling, and then being told it died during its beating. However, she and her fellow ladies-in-waiting later find a dog wandering around the grounds, terribly swollen from a beating. They wonder if this is Okinamaro, but it does not respond to the name. Later, however, when Sei says the dog's name, it whimpers pitifully in answer. The court concludes that Okinamaro had been trying to remain unidentified for his own safety, but in his misery revealed himself. The dog is eventually pardoned. (On this occurrence, Bakin's text glosses the dog's name Okinamaru, a plausible reading of the characters in its name; when next mentioned in Chapter IX, the name is glossed correctly as Okinamaro.)

opened, spilling scent. In the autumn of this year, in the eighth month, the grain harvest failed in the districts of Awa and Asahina, Anzai Kagetsura's territory, and Kagetsura sent his senior vassal Kabuto Toppei to Takita Castle to present the following request:

"Heaven has seen fit to bring suffering upon my lord's possessions, casting both high and low abruptly into the direst of straits. Yet we hear that this autumn has again brought a bountiful harvest to Your Excellency's lands. We beg the loan of five thousand bales of rice, which we shall repay twofold out of next year's duties. Kagetsura has passed his seventh decade and is bowed down with age, and yet he has no son, nor even a daughter. He often thinks of how he should like to adopt Your Excellency's daughter, selecting for her a husband from among his kin, and then to yield unto them his possessions. Should you graciously consent to this, his allotment of happiness will be exceedingly great."

Earnestly he spoke, and Yoshizane heard him out and then replied, "Had I many sons, 'twould be no difficult thing to let Anzai adopt one. What am I to do, though, with only one girl and one boy? And even if I did send him Princess Fuse, since he has neither wife nor child of his own, it could profit neither him nor me. This thing I cannot undertake to do. Now, a disastrous harvest is a matter of fate choosing its time, and this one has fallen not on Anzai alone, has it? I could not escape Heaven's censure if I heard of desolation in a neighbouring country and rendered no aid. I shall refuse him, then, on the matter of the girl, while the rice I will send, according to protocol." His answer was straightforward, and then he sent Toppei back.

At this time Horiuchi Sadayuki was in Tōjō Castle, and Sugikura Ujimoto had retired to his quarters, stricken with the infirmity of age; there was none to speak to Yoshizane of advantage and harm. However, among Yoshizane's attendants was Kanamari Daisuke Takanori, who had turned twenty that year. His maternal grandfather Issaku had sloughed off this mortal coil five years previously; Daisuke had personally attended at his sickbed, refusing to entrust even the most unclean of tasks to servants, and in this way he had displayed a nurturing filiality down to the depths of his soul. Nor was this all: as he grew he inherited his father Takayoshi's aspirations, becoming a youth whose loyalty and righteousness far outstripped the pack's.

Thus it was that he sought to remonstrate with his lord, saying, "Kagetsura has always kept his distance, only now, in his distress, to seek Your Lordship's daughter and to borrow grain. Is he a man to understand a debt of gratitude? If Your Lordship seizes this chance to strike, I make no doubt that you can unite the entire province of Awa in your grasp. If Your Lordship accedes to his request, it will be like giving provisions to a thief, or lending a blade to your sworn enemy. Rather let preparations be made for an expedition, my lord."

He spoke without the shadow of deference. Yoshizane would not listen, but said, "You are yet young: what do you know? Even if the man were my enemy, it is not the act of a good general or a courageous warrior to take advantage of calamity by attacking. Moreover, Anzai Kagetsura is not now my enemy. Am I to take up arms against him for no reason? There would be no honor in an army raised for such a purpose, and an army with no honor will not attract men. What useless things this man says!" Yoshizane was moved to wrath, and gave Daisuke a tongue-lashing before sending the five thousand bales of rice to Anzai.

The next year came, and now crops were ravaged in Heguri and Nagasa, Yoshizane's territory, while in Kagetsura's lands alone the ears grew eight feet tall; and yet he would not repay the rice he had formerly borrowed, so that in Takita both high and low knew privation, and hardship was not long in coming. At this time Kanamari Daisuke spoke many times in secret unto his lord and master, saying, "What profit is it to forge bonds of amity with one's neighbor if he refuses to aid one in distress, to render mutual assistance, to supply one's lack? Last autumn master Anzai borrowed much grain from us, yet now, knowing our plight, he does not repay it. Why does Your Lordship not requisition it from him? It would hardly be begging."

Yoshizane loved Daisuke as his own son, but for fear of provoking envy he was in the habit of scolding the boy severely, chiding him for insufficiently lofty aspirations. Now Daisuke had passed twenty years of age, and was so much his father's equal in both capacity and physiognomy that Yoshizane wished to see him lord of Tōjō Castle, and was preparing to make it so, when it occurred to him that, "No doubt there are those among the older of my vassals who would be jealous of his youth—if only there were a work of great merit I could cause him to perform for me, that I might raise him up by way of reward."

Such were his thoughts even now, and he nodded as he heard Daisuke out, then said, "Your argument accords with my own thoughts. I will send you as my messenger. However, you will not requisition from him the five thousand bales. Instead, say to him this." Earnestly he spoke until he had made clear his charge, and on the morrow he sent Daisuke to Anzai.

And so Kanamari Daisuke Takanori departed Takita before dawn, mounted and armed with a spear, leading an escort of some ten men. Through the night they hurried and straight on into the day, making for Kagetsura's seat at Mano. There they were received by his senior vassal Kabuto Toppei. Daisuke spoke at length, according to his lord's command, of how the grain harvest in the Satomi territories had failed and how hardship would soon be upon them, and he requested five thousand bales of rice. His manner of speech was courteous. Toppei did not give an answer, but went within, saying, "I will tell my master."

For more than half a day he did not come back. While Daisuke waited, neck extended expectantly, thinking that any moment he might appear, the day grew dark. As it did so, finally Kabuto Toppei returned. He addressed Daisuke, saying, "I reported to my master the particulars of the charge you bear from His Excellency, and this is his reply: 'I, Kagetsura, ought to receive you personally, but what am I to do? For some time now a cold has laid me low, and I am unable to get out of bed just now. Last autumn His Lordship saved us in our time of crisis; I know of no reason why we should not repay our debt of gratitude to you by emptying our granaries, even without being asked. And yet this is the year after our own year of famine, and we do not yet have sufficient for ourselves. I shall summon my senior vassals and take counsel with them, weighing the yeas and nays of the matter, and then we shall have an answer for you.' Therefore tarry a while in this land, rest your men and horses." Toppei personally invited Daisuke to an inn, where he showed him every courtesy.

In this way, without in any way meaning to, Daisuke passed five or six days there. He became annoyed, and reminded Toppei of his errand, asking, "Shall I have an answer? What of the yeas and nays of the matter?" So harshly did he take Toppei to task that Toppei feigned illness, that he should not have to meet with Daisuke again.

With things at such a pass, Daisuke abruptly began to grow suspicious. Making up his mind, he stealthily observed the state of affairs in the castle and discovered an uproar of activity—the men were in armor, the horses caparisoned, as if preparing to march at any moment. "I do not understand this," he thought in astonishment, but then calmed himself enough to reflect, "That lord and his man were merely getting me out of the way, it would seem, while they pressed forward with their craven scheme to take advantage of our calamity by attacking Takita unawares. Had I been a day later in awakening to it, I should have ended up captive to an enemy. A tight spot indeed!"

Still wondering, he opened his heart to his followers. They disguised themselves, figure and form, then master and men, alone or in pairs, slipped into the rush of activity and out of the castle, and ran toward Takita. Daisuke, once he had gone two or three miles, decided to stop and wait for his lagging companions. He cupped his hands at a spring and slaked his thirst, then seated himself against one of a row of pines and began to mop up the sweat that ran down his body in rivulets.

Caption: In a grove of pines at Mano, Toppei chases down Daisuke.
Figures: Kanamari Daisuke [*center right*]. Kabuto Toppei [*left*].

Just then Toppei appeared, leading soldiers in pursuit—he galloped straight on, standing in his stirrups and shouting, "A filthy deed, Takanori, to flee now! Your master Yoshizane is a vagabond who came to us begging! He washed up at Shirahama and deluded foolish folk until he had usurped land and made himself lord of two districts—but that was only because my lord helped by destroying Nobutoki of the Maro! And now Yoshizane, who by rights should bow to Lord Anzai, who should attach himself to Lord Anzai as a retainer and attend upon him often, so far exalts himself as to think he can requisition rice from us simply because he gave us a little once? This is the act of a mean man. Nor is that all: my lord, hearing of the beauty of Yoshizane's daughter Princess Fuse, summoned her to himself, thinking, under guise of adopting her, to make her his concubine—but Yoshizane foolishly refused to go along. In everything he has been rude. My lord has tolerated it all these years for the time was not yet right, but you and your master were fools for thinking it should always be springtime for you. Have you not heard? My lord has already taken Tōjō Castle with three thousand warhorses, and now he attacks Takita. You have no place to which you may return! If you value your life, surrender to me now!"

On and on he boasted, but Daisuke would not hear him out. "You are a braying ass with a company of rats! I heard all this when I was very young! Your lord Kagetsura forsook righteousness when he attacked Nobutoki of the Maro—he annexed Maro's lands and even then did not count it sufficient. Nevertheless, my lord did not brandish the executioner's axe, but did as your lord begged him to and forged bonds of amity with his neighbor—which your lord did not, as he might have, consider unparalleled good fortune. He rather worked all his cunning upon us, first begging much rice from us, then forsaking his promises and refusing now to return it. But though you spy on our deficiencies and take advantage of our misfortunes, though you attack us with great armies, the gods of heaven and earth will not enlist in an unrighteous cause! You shall be yourselves defeated and taken, as if in mirror image of your intentions for us. I, Takanori, am to return in vain, having failed to carry out my master's commission—the least I can do is to rip off your head and carry it back with me to present to my lord! Hold your ground, now!" With that, Daisuke, jaw set, brandishing his spear and flanked by his followers, plunged into the midst of the gathered foemen, laying about him without let or hindrance.

And so Kanamari Daisuke and his mere seven or eight followers, having resigned themselves to a desperate struggle, fought bloodily for an hour or more, ignoring wounds by arrow and blade, trading blow for blow, advancing and retreating, until some thirty of the enemy's mounted men had been cut down, their corpses strewn across the road, while all seven of Daisuke's allies had lost their lives and he was left alone—but even then he did not give way by even so much as a single pace, but continually sought to engage with Toppei himself. Around and around he ran, disappearing and reappearing unaccountably, but the enemy was too numerous to take in at a glance, and, separated from his quarry by men and horses, Daisuke could not hope to run him down.

Truly did the Sage say that the prince may be tricked, but never fooled.[23] Yoshizane was a leader of overarching goodness, who sheltered his people within the benevolence of his heart and built his relations with his neighbors on a basis of righteousness and good faith. Kagetsura was a schemer of unbounded wickedness. The one can be tricked by the other with what seems right. Moreover, for a prince to suspect what seems right would be to lose that which allows him to be called a man. Even if Yoshizane had possessed the talent of a Zichan, was it not proper, rather, that he should have been taken in by this fraud?[24]

End of Book IV of the Lives of the Eight Dogs of the Satomi of Southern Fusa

---

23. From chapter 6 of *Lunyu*.

24. Zichan was a minister of the state of Zheng during the Spring and Autumn period, famed for his adroit diplomacy. In the second part of chapter 5 of *Mengzi*, the following anecdote is told of him: Zichan was given a live fish as a present, and delivered it to the keeper of his pond with instructions to free the fish in the pond. The official ate the fish, then lied and told Zichan that the fish had swum free. Zichan believed him, thus (the text says) illustrating Confucius's statement (quoted above) that the princely man may after all be tricked. The implication is that Zichan could not be truly fooled in a weighty matter, even if he could be hoodwinked in a minor one such as this, and that, as Bakin suggests of Yoshizane, a certain amount of guilelessness may reflect well on a person.

The Lives of the Eight Dogs of the Satomi of Southern Fusa

Book V

Assembled by the Master of the Crooked Pavilion in the Eastern Capital

Chapter IX
Kagetsura breaks his oath and lays siege to two castles;
Yatsufusa believes a jest and offers up a head

Thus it was that Anzai Kagetsura did by deception detain Yoshizane's emissary Kanamari Daisuke, and, dividing his army, send a great press of men by surprise against the two Satomi castles. Kagetsura personally led one company, some two thousand mounted men, against Takita Castle, which he surrounded so as to block all four of its gates and then assaulted both by day and by night without pause. He made Kabuto Toppei commander of the other company, a thousand mounted men, and caused them to surround Tōjō Castle, in which Horiuchi Sadayuki had shut himself. His goal, as he mounted his attack, was to, come what may, "crush both castles with one blow!" His armies' appearance was as of rice and hemp in a wind-driven melée; their vigor that of bamboo snapping apart when split at one end.

Now, at this time both Satomi castles were suffering a dearth of provisions, while the folk of the land were so weary from the pestilences of a famine year that their only response to repeated reminders of their duty was silence. But in spite of this, Yoshizane did not lack for courageous officers and fierce soldiers who, for the sake of the debt of righteousness they owed, would count their own lives as but little and the enemy as naught. They struggled sternly to defend themselves. But guest and host, attacker and attacked, were not alike in energy. Provisions soon ran out, and there came a time when Yoshizane's forces had not eaten for seven days. When they could no longer endure it, officers and men alike stole over the ramparts by night to rifle enemy corpses felled by arrows for the provisions they carried at their waists—some barely staved off hunger in this way, while others killed horses, or even fed upon the flesh of dead men. This gave Yoshizane great cause for lamentation, and he summoned Sugikura Kisonosuke Ujimoto and all the rest of his officers and men, and spoke to them, saying:

"Kagetsura is a two-faced warrior: in his base deception he has violated our alliance and transgressed against righteousness. But this is hardly worth mentioning now. Nor is he, for all that, an enemy to be feared. He leads the men of two districts in attack upon my two castles, but I, too, have the men of two districts, ready to meet his. We are as evenly matched as a bull's horns—even were we not fully assured of victory, we should be able to fight him to a draw. Yet so lacking am I in virtue that our harvest has failed; within, our granaries are empty, while without stands a great enemy army. We are at the limits of our strength without even having been tested. Even if I had a hundred of Fan Kuai,[1] how could they strike down our enemy in the face of starvation? I cannot bear that all the officers and men in this castle should be killed simply on account of me alone—my heart, my body. You must all flee from the west gate of the castle tonight under cover of darkness. I will bring my life to an end here, bitter though it be to me: I will set fire to the castle, then quickly stab my wife and child before dying myself. Jirotarō, you too must run. Here is how you shall do it," he said, laying before them in clear detail his intentions.

His men would not hear him out, though, but answered him as one: "Your Lordship's word is our command, but having nourished our wives and children on your stipends, to seek to evade hardship when once confronted with it would hardly serve. Let us, while breath remains in these locust-husk bodies, strike by night at the enemy's encampment, that we may each trade swordthrusts with an opponent worth the name and then go down to the Yellow Springs, there to proclaim our gratitude to Your Lordship. We desire nothing, not a whit, more than this." Yoshizane sought in earnest to convince them of his demands, but none showed signs of willingness to undertake them.

---

1. A warrior who fought heroically by Liu Bang's side during the latter's rise to power as the founder of the Han dynasty.

At this time, Yoshizane's son, Jirotarō Yoshinari, had entered his sixteenth year. Listening to his father's expressions of benevolence and love, and his officers' and men's evidence of loyalty and faith, he felt they would never end, and so, gauging his father's mood, he said:

"Far be it from me, a puny youth, to speak in opposition to you, sir, but 'Celestial timing is no match for geographical advantage, and geographical advantage is no match for harmony between persons.'[2] The castle is empty of provisions and Your Lordship's officers and men are besieged by hunger and thirst, but not a man of them considers fleeing your side; rather, their desire to remember their debt to you in virtue even unto death unites them in perfect harmony. Man's nature is good: even the enemy's soldiers know good from evil, perfidy from rectitude. And although our provisions have run out, day by day we send up smoke, so our foe cannot suspect that we have come to such a pass. That they do not attack forthwith is due to their dread of your martial valor, Father. Let us weigh these two factors. Choose you someone who can produce a great noise and send him up to the top of the tower, there to denounce Kagetsura's immoral behavior: the crimes he has committed by breaking his oaths, returning enmity for charity, and starting an unrighteous war. Instantly overcome by shame, his officers and men will lose the will to attack. Then if we strike from the castle we shall scatter them with a single stroke. We cannot fail to triumph. What think you of this counsel?"

So bracing was his speech that his listeners all found themselves moved by it. "Hear, hear," they said, and so Yoshizane tried the experiment. He sent forth a loud-voiced man to enumerate Kagetsura's unrighteous acts and denounce his crimes, but even he whose voice would have carried on a normal day found that hunger shortened his breath, and the tower was high and the moat wide. He worked his jaw until his face grew red and he got a stitch in his side, but his curses went no farther than his mind. His voice failed to reach the enemy's encampment, and the effort ended in tears and a parched cough—fruitless labor.

All the while, Yoshizane was racking his brain for a means of saving his officers and men, who had so rashly elected not to desert him, but he could find no easy plan for driving off the enemy. Feeling that he was getting nowhere, he took up his walking stick and went out to wander the garden. The dog Yatsufusa, beloved these many years, saw his master and came to him, wagging his tail. Long starvation, though, had given him an

---

2. A quotation from the second part of the second chapter of *Mengzi*.

unsteady gait, and so wasted his flesh that his bones protruded; his eyes were sunken and his nose dry.

Yoshizane turned his gaze on the dog, reached out his right hand to stroke his head, and said, "Alas—you, too, must be hungry, and in my constant worry about my soldiers' privations, I forgot all about you! Men may differ from one another in intelligence, but as they are all what may be termed the spirit of all things,[3] they all have a certain degree of wisdom. If they follow teachings, obey laws, and know deference and gratitude, they can banish their desires and resist their passions; if they come to consider death by starvation Heaven's decree, fate choosing its time, then they can resign themselves to it. Beasts, though, have not that wisdom. Receiving no teaching, knowing no laws, unable to discern deference and gratitude, they have no way of banishing their desires. They simply pass their days in their masters' care—if they starve they cannot know why, so they frisk and fawn all the more in hopes of food. Ah, the pity of it! And yet, though beasts may indeed be fools, ignorant of shame, in some things they excel men. Dogs, for example, never forget their masters, and their noses lead them aright—in neither of which things are men their equals, much less superior by nature. Then there is the old poem by, I believe, the Reverend Jichin:[4] 'Few indeed/are those whose hearts/are scrupulously kind/and yet a dog—how moving!—/ his master knows.' I shall try you: how well do you know your ten years' debt of gratitude? If you know it, then make your way by stealth into the enemy camp and bite the enemy general Anzai Kagetsura to death— you will be saving everyone in my castle from certain doom. You shall be counted as having earned the greatest merit. How about it? Will you do it?"

Yoshizane wore a broad smile as he made this request; Yatsufusa looked up intently at his master's face, as if understanding just what he meant. Yoshizane pitied him even more, and patted his pate and stroked his back. "Go do your best now. Earn some merit. We will feed you fish until you can eat no more." The dog turned his back in what appeared to be refusal.

Yoshizane in jest asked again: "Shall I give you a position, then? Or shall I reward you with lands? If you do not desire rank or property, shall I make you my son-in-law—marry you to Princess Fuse?"

At this Yatsufusa wagged his tail and raised his head, staring unblinking at his master's face and barking sharply.

---

3. A phrase from chapter 27 of *Shu jing*.

4. More commonly known as Jien (1155–1225). The poem in the original runs: *omoiguma no/hito wa nakanaka/naki mono o/aware ni inu no/nushi o shirinuru*. The poem is found in *Fuboku wakashū*, book 27.

"Aha!" Yoshizane laughed. "Indeed, Princess Fuse loves you as much as I do—no wonder you want her. When you have accomplished this, then, you shall marry her." Yatsufusa bent his forelegs as if in obeisance and keened. The dog's voice struck Yoshizane as sad, and his merriment left him. "Stuff and nonsense, and worse. This is no time for idle jests," he said to himself, and went back inside.

The great general and all his officers and men had made up their minds that that night would be their farewell to this world, so Yoshizane spent the evening in his inner chambers with his wife Isarago, daughter Princess Fuse, and son Yoshinari gathered by his side, then summoned Ujimoto and his other senior vassals to him, that he might present them with a cup. And yet the long-handled vessel was dry, and there was not a drop of sake to fill it with, so they made do with water; and instead of fish set out some little fruit on the branch, so worm-eaten, for the most part, that normally even the humblest of servants would have refused it, but at this time it was welcomed with gratitude. The assemblage was particularly drear, its members making desultory conversation upon this topic or that, or discussing what had occurred, but never breathing a word about what would befall them: master and men had plumbed death's depths, and their courage was strong. Nor did they stint, these military men, in fond farewells for as long as their long black hair, to wives and children, drawing apart their robes, their sleeves still wet with unreproaching tears, with hardly a sound, as, when the seaweed-dwelling creatures slough their carapaces off; maids, guessing what was in their mistresses' hearts, gushed tears as from undammable springs, and all sank into the very same laments.

"Indeed, 'tis as it should be," said Ujimoto and the others, involuntarily sighing as one and exchanging looks with eyes sunken, like their cheeks, from seven days without a morsel of food—so discolored were their complexions, so attenuated, that they could have looked no worse were they already dead and turned to dust. Footsoldiers, having already received the command to "move out and strike at the setting of the moon on this, its tenth night," gathered in knots here and there as their inclinations moved them, exchanging cups of water flattered with the name of sake, reflecting starlight that, like th'frost upon their armor, soon would fade, as—alas!—would they themselves.

Now came the third quarter of the hour of the ox.[5] "The time is right," said Yoshizane, and he and his son quickly threw on their armor and took up the longswords and glaives proffered by Isarago and Princess Fuse and

5. The hour following the midnight hour.

Caption: Yatsufusa, believing words spoken in jest, presents the head of the enemy general.
Figures: Sugikura Ujimoto [*far right, kneeling*]. Satomi Yoshizane [*right, standing*]. Satomi Yoshinari [*center, kneeling*]. Yatsufusa [*dog*]. Princess Fuse [*seen through window*].

the elderly women waiting on them; the sound of distant temple bells came sharp on wind as keen as blades to sound to them the evanescence of all earthly acts.[6]

Just then, from without came the bark of a dog. Yoshizane pricked up his ears, then said, "That must be Yatsufusa. And yet does not his bark sound strange to all of you? Somebody, go out and have a look."

Two or three men stood up immediately, saying, "Yes, sir," and went out to the veranda, lamps held high. "Yatsufusa, Yatsufusa," they called, and when they looked around they saw an awful sight: a freshly severed head sitting on the veranda, and Yatsufusa, forelegs on the stone step, standing careful guard over it. "What is this?" The men panicked and ran back inside, where they baldly reported what they had seen.

Master and followers, men and women, all were astonished and amazed. Alone among them Ujimoto spoke, turning to the men and saying, "It is the way of dogs to feed on human corpses when they are starving. No doubt he brought the head here to show it off, but it is bound to be someone we knew, is it not? Their Ladyships [MEANING ISARAGO AND PRINCESS FUSE] are here—chase him off at once."

But as the men stood again to go, Yoshizane stopped them, saying, "Wait—there is no reason why the dog should not be there. If in the throes of hunger he has desecrated the corpse of one of our men, though, it is something we cannot let stand. I will go and see for myself."

As he spoke he stood to go, and before Ujimoto could say anything the menservants and maidservants had, though quaking, taken up candles and assumed places either in front of or behind their lord. Out to the veranda, small as it was, they all together went, and there they saw the head.

Yoshizane knit his brow and said, "Kisonosuke, who does that look like to you? The blood makes it difficult to tell, but does it not resemble Kagetsura? Wash it off so we can see." Ujimoto, wondering, took the head to the basin in the garden and ladled water over it until the smeared blood washed away. Then master and men looked again, and saw that it was beyond any doubt the head of the enemy general, Kagetsura, taken as a trophy. "What happened seems clear," said Yoshizane. And indeed, while they had no way of knowing the cause, the onlookers' wonderment was dispelled, even as they all as one envied the merit with which the dog had battled, beyond what any man had been able to achieve.

---

6. Reminiscent of the opening lines of *Heike monogatari*, in which the Jetavana Monastery (J. Gion Shōja) bells sound a similar message.

Yoshizane, then, sighed, and said, "We see before us a weird prodigy, but not one entirely unprefigured. Only now, though, do I comprehend it. I was pondering how to spare my men who had made up their minds to throw away their mayfly lives for my sake, but was unable to think of anything. Disconsolate, I went out into the garden alone, where I saw that Yatsufusa was most painfully hungry. This I could not bear to see, and out of compassion I said to him, 'If you will make your way by stealth into the enemy's camp and bite Kagetsura to death, thereby saving the hundreds of soldiers and officers in the castle, I will surfeit you with fish every day.' This did not appear to please him. 'Then shall I give you title to property, or high position?' I asked, but this, too, failed to please him. 'Shall I give you Princess Fuse, who has loved you so unceasingly?' I said, at which Yatsufusa broke into an expression of joy, barking and wagging his tail in a way unusual for him—quite startling. ''Tis idle of me to say things I do not mean, even in jest'—so saying to myself, I came inside and summoned people to the final council of war, which so took up my thoughts that I forgot all about the incident, but the dog seems not to have forgotten a bit of what I said to him. Sharp as a blade, or indeed as a hound's tooth, he took my hollow words for sincerity, and stole into the camp of our attackers where he easily killed Kagetsura, leader of some two or three thousand mounted men, and brought back his head as a trophy—to call it mystifying hardly does it justice. A prodigy, this is."

Saying which he called Yatsufusa closer and praised him unstintingly, while Ujimoto and the rest, with tongues tied in astonishment, managed to say by way of accolade, "That this beast was able to exceed men in his merit is all due to Your Lordship's benevolence and virtue—and yet even so, there must have been darkling help from the gods and buddhas."

At this moment, a man-at-arms on reconnoissance came running in by the garden gate. "Something strange is happening with the enemy—they have suddenly broken into chaos and confusion! If we strike now, milord, there can be no doubt of victory," he said, but before he had finished, Yoshizane spoke.

"As well it might be! Let us lose no more time—strike now!" He hastened to make known his command to all his companies, and was about to lead the attack on the enemy camp himself when the youth Yoshinari stepped forward and said, "With Kagetsura already dead, it will be easy enough to chase away our attackers, great in number though they be. It is not fitting that Your Eminence should so lightly go out in person. It will suffice for you to send me, Yoshinari, with Ujimoto by my side. Forgive me, Your Eminence."

With this petition, he rushed out by the garden gate and sprang into the saddle of an emaciated horse that had been brought out for him. Ujimoto, meanwhile, called out encouragement to the officers and men, saying that since such and such had happened, "Kagetsura has been cut down—any who lag behind now will come in second to a dog! On, now! Charge!"

Three hundred mounted men they had, and they split them into two companies: one Yoshinari led out through the front gate, and one Ujimoto led out through the rear, throwing open the castle gates and plunging their men straight into the enemy's roiling confusion. The castle's forces displayed a hundred times their usual vigor, and there was no standing against them. The enemy was thrown back on their heels—not over half of them fled, and the rest surrendered immediately. The darkness in the men's hearts lifted with the night.

Yoshinari and Ujimoto took all of the enemy's mountainous hoard of provisions and brought it into the castle, and then reported the state of affairs to Yoshizane, who loosed the bonds of each man who had surrendered, entrusting them to Ujimoto; this morning an honest smoke rose from the castle as they allotted a bowl of rice gruel to each man-at-arms who had been besieged in the castle. Only a single bowl, however, as to suddenly eat to satiation after long starvation would have killed them immediately. Nor was this all, for they dispersed half of the provisions among the folk living outside the castle, to relieve their hunger and thirst: the people received this worshipfully, divided it among themselves, and ate until their bellies were tight as drums. Thus were their lives spared. They were like the fish trapped in a wheel-rut when he regains the open water.

Meanwhile, Anzai Kagetsura's senior vassal Kabuto Toppei had gone to attack Tōjō Castle. He and his men surrounded it in ten ranks, twenty ranks, and assailed it without regard for day or night, but that castle had a half-month's stores more than had Takita. From the start, Sadayuki's only thought was to scatter the enemy and come to Takita's relief, and with this in mind he sallied forth on rainy nights and windy evenings, two and three times a night; but the enemy's forces were far greater than his own, and though he might win skirmishes, it was like sweeping in a gale: the enemy always brought in fresh troops, and showed no signs of weakening.

Then one day rumor reached Tōjō, from no particular source, that Kagetsura had been cut down, his transient life ended; that the ranks surrounding Takita had been instantly dissolved; and that the Satomi scion, Yoshinari, accompanied by Sugikura Ujimoto, was coming to Tōjō's relief with a great army. Hearing this, the castle's soldiers' courage swelled a hundredfold, while the attacking men-at-arms were thrown into an uncommon confusion.

At first Toppei pretended not to have heard this, and cursed his officers and men to drive them on, but day by day the rumor became more persistent.

"This may indeed be no idle report," he thought, and at last began to fear. Careful not to reveal himself to the army at large, Toppei took two or three intimates and fled under cover of darkness. Morning broke, and the enemy army at length discovered that its general had absconded. Everyone was left all but speechless, grumbling at "that damnably sorry excuse for a general," and otherwise without recourse. The entire army held a council, after which they sent an emissary to the castle to truckle and surrender.

Sadayuki summoned a mounted messenger and sent him off to "tell His Lordship at Takita about this." On the way, this messenger met men-at-arms from Takita, coming to give news of the victory there. These emissaries, upon their arrival at Tōjō, explained how Kagetsura had lost his life, and how an army, commanded by the Satomi scion [YOSHINARI] and seconded by Sugikura Ujimoto, was to move out before long for the purpose of scattering the enemy here and attacking him at his two Tate castles.[7] Sadayuki received his lord's decree in humility, and then sent another messenger to offer congratulations on the victory.

While Sadayuki waited in impatient anticipation for the Satomi scion's army, the people of Awa and Asahina, both samurai and commoner, goodly and mean, having already come to hold Yoshizane's virtue dear, heard of Kagetsura's demise and betook themselves to his castles at Hiratate and Tateyama where they attacked and defeated the commanders keeping them: Kabuto Toppei's head and others they took as trophies, entrusting them to a few dozen men of respectably elderly mien who came to Tōjō on the very day that Yoshinari and Ujimoto arrived to make camp. Together with Sadayuki, these two wrote out a description of the affair and submitted it to Takita Castle along with the heads; Yoshizane summoned the men of Awa and Asahina and showered gifts upon their heads, while unto his scion and Ujimoto he granted a rescript placing the two castles in their keeping.

Thus did Yoshizane come to oversee the four districts as one land. His power and moral authority rose as the morning sun, and blessings showered down upon him as rain; devious folk fled, and the day belonged to the good. From this time forward, nobody locked their doors at night, or found and kept what another had lost. The wind and waves were calm at Shirahama, all turbulence gone none knew where, and not only did the warriors in neighboring lands take notice of it, but even the youngest son of Mochiuji, Minister of the Court Nariuji (who, having reached an appropriate age, had returned to Kamakura), vouchsafed a letter to Takita at this time praising Yoshizane's meritorious deeds in uniting that country. The Shogun at Muromachi heard

---

7. I.e., the castles at Hiratate and Tateyama.

of it, and proclaimed Satomi Yoshizane Lord of the Province of Awa, in addition naming him Lesser Assistant in the Governance Ministry, upon hearing which Yoshizane danced for joy. He dispatched messengers to the Capital and Kamakura to present them with all manner of produce from his lands. [MOCHIUJI'S YOUNGEST SON WAS NAMED NARIUJI. SOME TEN YEARS PREVIOUSLY, IN KAKI-TSU 3,[8] HE HAD, THROUGH THE OFFICES OF NAGAO MASAKATA, BEEN WELCOMED BACK TO KAMAKURA AND GIVEN THE POST OF OVERSEER, BUT CIRCUMSTANCES DID NOT ALLOW NARI-UJI TO STAY IN KAMAKURA, AND IN THE KŌEI[9] PERIOD HE RELOCATED TO KOGA, IN SHIMŌSA. TOTALLING UP THE YEARS SUGGESTS THAT IT WAS IN FACT DURING THIS PERIOD THAT THESE EVENTS TOOK PLACE. NARIUJI IS DISCUSSED IN THE RECORD OF NINE GENERATIONS;[10] NO TALE WILL BE TOLD OF HIM HEREAFTER.]

The only thing that weighed on Yoshizane's heart amidst this unbroken succession of joyous and blessed events was the fate of him whom he had, at the very beginning, sent to beg provisions of Anzai—Kanamari Daisuke. "He is still young, but he is hardly one to truckle to the enemy, to allow himself to be taken captive and shackled. Was he perhaps tricked and then cut down? Or did he lose his life in vain, rashly seeking to hold back the attackers by himself, without assessing their numbers? Were it otherwise, he could not have failed to return by now. It is due to his father's help that this land opened up to me, who had no special tie to it, and that I here found wealth and status: for this reason, as his father was dying I said that I would make his son the district official over Nagasa and lord of Tōjō Castle, which things I have not yet done. Not only that, I had something in mind for him, so that never to see him again, not even his corpse, would leave me nothing but regret. Cut down every tree, uproot every blade of grass if you must, but tell me if he yet lives!" This he said, and dispatched men in eight directions, each to make a careful search and send word back to him; but he did not learn where Daisuke had gone.

---

8. 1443.

9. The Kōei period lasted from 1342–1345, well before Nariuji's birth. Bakin means the Kōshō era, 1455–1457. Nariuji (most modern sources read his name as Shigeuji) was the son of Ashikaga Mochiuji, the Kamakura overlord (kubō) whose rebellion against the shogunate led to the Battle of Yūki, as depicted in Chapter I, where forces still loyal to the by-then-dead Mochiuji were defeated by forces loyal to the Kantō overseers (kanrei), who still followed the shogun. Nagao Masakata was a retainer of Overseer Uesugi Norizane, and through his intervention Nariuji was allowed to assume the post of Kamakura overlord. However, Nariuji was never reconciled to Uesugi power, and was expelled from Kamakura in 1455. Thereafter he set up a power base in Koga, and spent decades vying with the Uesugi for power over the Kantō. Despite Bakin's disclaimer here, this rivalry will become a significant backdrop to the rest of the book.

10. Most likely the Kamakura kanryō kudaiki, a record of the Kamakura kanryō or kanrei compiled in 1672.

Meanwhile, Yoshizane distributed to each of his senior vassals, officers, and men, increases in land and promotions in rank, rewards of uncommon generosity given in careful consideration of their valiant and meritorious service; and to begin with he decreed that the dog Yatsufusa's merit was the greatest. Yoshizane caused the utmost care to be taken to ensure that the food Yatsufusa was fed day and night and the bedding he was given to sleep on were the finest, and for Yatsufusa's care he established the post of Dog-keeper, attaching numerous servants thereto, that they might clear the way for Yatsufusa when he went out and watch over him when he was within.

Yoshizane treated him with such favors as to astound the eyes and ears, and yet Yatsufusa's head hung low and his tail drooped—he would neither eat nor sleep, but stayed ever close to the spot on the veranda to which he had brought the head of the enemy general Kagetsura on that fateful night. When his lord and master came out, the dog would place his forepaws on the veranda, wag his tail, and snuffle, almost as if he were begging for something, but Yoshizane knew not what. He personally brought Yatsufusa fish and rice cakes on a charger, but the dog would not look at them, but only stared at Yoshizane, seeking something.

After this had happened several times, Yoshizane began to make a rough guess as to what was on the dog's mind. "Could it be so?" he wondered, immediately losing all love for the dog, and thenceforth avoiding that corner of the house. The dogkeeper and others tried to lead Yatsufusa away, but the dog growled with mad ferocity and would not heel.

In the end he ripped apart his chain, attacked and bit those who would stop him, and bounded up onto the veranda and thence into the house, where he ran back and forth through the inner chambers. The dogkeeper and his assistants stood, their way barred by hesitation as if by a shut gate: all they could do was raise their hands and call out, "See there, see there!" The women of the house collapsed in a heap of panic and fear of this mad dog that would not obey even a man's command—if he ran here, they would flee there, if he chased them there, they would run here. Not only was the dog mad, but the people of the house, too, were losing their minds, breaking down sliding doors and ramie-fiber screens, yelling and shouting, until finally, without intending to, they reached Princess Fuse's room in the innermost hall.

At this time the Princess was alone, with no companions; she sat, elbows on her writing-desk, perusing *The Pillow Book*—she was reading the passage where a dog named Okinamaro, having incurred imperial disfavor, is abandoned, but then forgiven and brought back.[11] So charmingly was the scene

---

11. See Chapter VIII, note 22.

described that it filled Fuse with envy for Sei Shōnagon's talent; she read the passage over and over, muttering to herself that "such things happened in olden times."

Just then she heard women screaming, and something ran up behind her at the speed of flight, knocking down a Tsukushi koto[12] that had been standing in the alcove, and prostrated itself on her hems. "Oh!" she exclaimed, and upon looking around she saw that it was Yatsufusa. His spirit, as reflected in his countenance, was in a state of unusual agitation. "You must be ill, poor thing," Fuse said, pushing aside her writing desk and trying to stand up—but when the dog had lain down he had buried his forepaws in her long skirts, and now she could hardly move either forward or backward. With that strong old dog, big as a draught-ox from ten years of keeping, as a weight upon her, the Princess found herself pinned, pull back though she might. She called out again and again, and her maids, ladies, and girls came running before they had even had a chance to reply: but when they saw the scene they were too amazed to come any closer. They merely beat on the floor-mats with the brooms they were carrying, saying "Shoo, shoo!" They tried to chase the dog off, but were so fearful themselves that when Yatsufusa bared his fangs and glared and growled at them, all the women dropped their brooms and fell back in the face of his ferocity.

Just then Yoshizane, having been notified of the situation, arrived bearing a hand-spear. He scolded and scattered the girls who stood cowering in the doorway, and then hurried into the room. "Now then, you beast! Get out, at once! Get out!" Thus saying, he thrust the butt of the spear at the dog, trying to chase him away, but Yatsufusa would not budge, and only stared up with bared fangs, his growling growing fiercer and fiercer as if he were ready to bite at any moment.

All of a sudden, Yoshizane could contain his anger no longer. "Little can it profit to speak to a beast who cannot tell reason from unreason, but surely you know your beloved master! Otherwise, I shall teach you to know him!" he bellowed, and, renewing his grip on his spear, he made as if to run the dog through.

But Princess Fuse shielded the dog with her body, saying, "Stay your hand, Your Eminence, head of this house! What has come over you, that you raise your hand against a beast for its wrongs, like a child poking an ox—is this not

---

12. A koto is a stringed instrument of a type similar to the zither, with a long sounding board across which strings are stretched. The Tsukushi koto was a koto meant for the performance of pieces arranged by the late-Muromachi monk Kenjun, who hailed from Tsukushi (northern Kyūshū).

inappropriate to your person and your station? I have something in mind—please, I beg you, forgive him." She wiped at her eyes as she spoke.

Yoshizane lowered the spear in mid-thrust and tucked it under his arm. "A curious remonstration for a princess to make. If you have something to say, say it quickly," he said.

At her father's urging, she refused to shed the tears that were brimming over in her eyes; bringing her expression under control, she said, "It is with the greatest hesitation that I would point out that in olden days as today, in the Han empire as well as in Yamato,[13] the wise prince conducts his government so that where there is merit, it is rewarded unfailingly, and where there is crime, it is unfailingly punished.[14] Where merit goes unrewarded, and crime unpunished, the state will fall. Take, for example, this dog—his conduct was meritorious, but he was not rewarded, and now punishment is being visited on him in the absence of any crime. Do you not think him pitiful?"

Yoshizane spoke before she had finished. "Your admonishment is exceedingly wide of the mark. Since the swift downfall of our mighty enemy, I have created a position especially for that dog, and given him rare delicacies to dine on and brocaded gauzes and twills to sleep on. And yet you say he goes unrewarded?"

Thus pointedly did he speak, but she raised her head and replied, "A lord's words are like sweat, it is said: they cannot be retracted.[15] Again, holy writ says that even a team of four horses cannot keep pace with a single word from a prince[16]—or so it is quoted in storybooks I have read. It is sad but true—is it not?—that you, Father, promised me to Yatsufusa here—made him Your Lordship's prospective son-in-law—in order to destroy Kagetsura and save your men from starvation. Perhaps this was a jest—let us say conditionally that it was—but even so, Your Lordship's promise, once made, cannot be taken back—not even a team of horses can accomplish this. Thus, the reward for which the dog begs is that which Your Lordship originally allowed him. He displayed great merit, yet you immediately reneged on your promise, substituting instead delicacies from the mountains and the sea, and bedding of twill and brocade, thinking that they would suffice. Were he a man, he would deem it a rotten thing to have done, and think of Your Lordship with resentment. Make up your mind, Father, that for this

13. An ancient name for Japan.
14. A dictum contained in chapter 193 of the Song-era chronicle *Zizhi tongjian* (J. *Shiji tsukan*).
15. From *Han shu*, chapter 36.
16. From *Lunyu*, chapter 12.

里見よしさね
得已以女妻槃瓠。槃瓠得女。
負而走入南山石室中。險絶
人跡不至。經三年。生六男六
女。槃瓠因自決妻。好色衣服。
製裁皆有尾。其母後以狀白
帝。於是迎諸子。衣裳斕斑。言
語侏㒧。好入山壑。不樂平曠。
帝順其意。賜以名山廣澤。其
後滋蔓。號曰蠻夷。今長沙武
陵蠻是也。又北狗國人身狗
首。長毛不衣。其妻皆人。生男
為狗。生女為人云。見五代史。

Upper register:

Caption: Yoshizane in his wrath chases Yatsufusa.

Figures: Princess Fuse [*right*]. Yatsufusa [*dog*]. Satomi Yoshizane [*left*].

Lower register:

Text: Factual basis: Long ago, in the time of Gao Xin, there was a Prince of the Quan Rong who caused the Emperor great suffering with his depredations. Attempts to subjugate him were unsuccessful. And so he searched everywhere under Heaven, seeking one who could take their general, General Wu. To such a one would he give eight hundred pounds of gold and a territory of ten thousand households, and also his daughter's hand in marriage. He had a dog whose coat boasted five colors, and his name was Panhu. After the Emperor issued this command, Panhu suddenly came before him with a man's head in his mouth. The assembled ministers examined it in apprehension and found that it was the head of General Wu. The Emperor was overjoyed. However, he considered it inappropriate to give his daughter's hand to Panhu, nor could he enfeoff him. In his counsel, he desired to reward Panhu, but knew not what sort of proclamation to issue. His daughter, hearing this, thought that the Emperor, having issued a command, must not be unfaithful to it, and thus she begged to be allowed to go. The Emperor had no choice, and gave his daughter's hand to Panhu

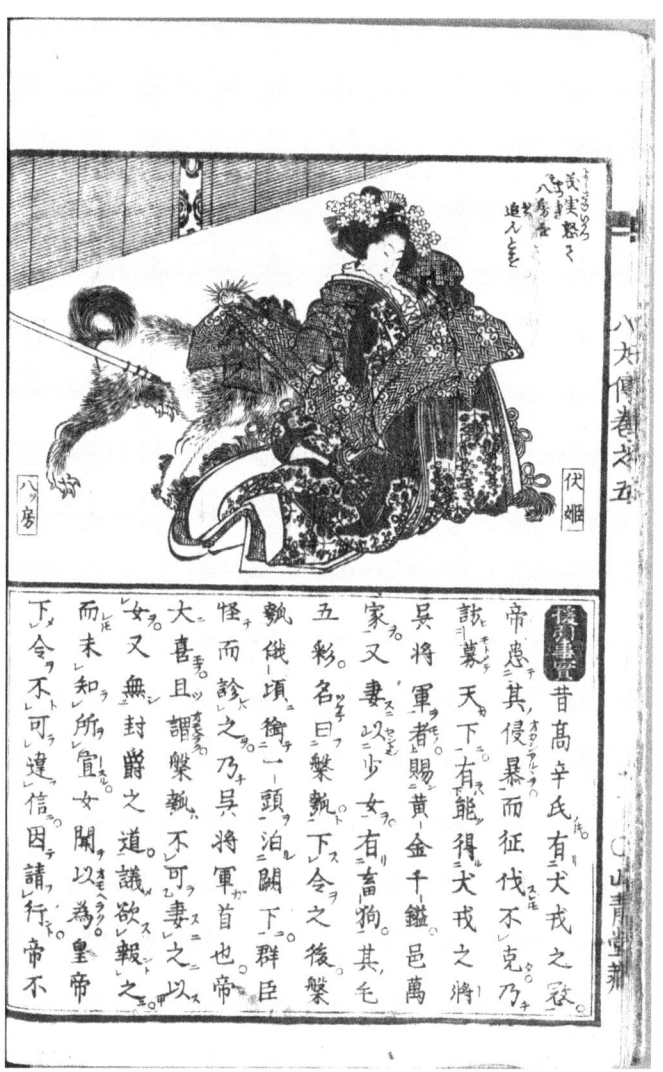

高辛氏 有犬戎 之寇。
帝 患其 侵暴 而征伐不克。乃
募天下 有能 得 犬戎之將
誅墓。天下 有能 得 犬戎 之將
吳將軍者。賜 黃金千鎰 邑萬
家。又妻以少女。有畜狗。其毛
五彩。名曰槃瓠。下令之後槃
瓠而詣 之乃 吳將軍首也。帝
怪而診之乃 吳將軍首也。群臣
大喜且 謂槃瓠 不可 妻之以
女又無封爵之道。議欲 報之。
而未知所宜 女聞 以為皇帝
下令不可 違 信。因請行。帝不

in marriage. Panhu bore the girl on his back and ran until he came to a cave in the rock on South Mountain, in a place so steep no man could reach it. Three years passed, and she bore six boys and six girls. Then Panhu was parted from his wife. [Their offspring] liked colorful clothing, and all they made had tails. Their mother later communicated with the Emperor by letter, asking him to welcome all her children back. Their clothing was garish, their speech gibberish. They preferred mountainous terrain and did not like wide open spaces. The Emperor deferred to their wishes and gave unto them famous mountains and broad fens, in which their descendants thrived. They were named the Man barbarians: these are the barbarians of Changsha and Wuling. (Furthermore, in the north, the inhabitants of the Country of Dogs have the bodies of men but the heads of dogs. Their hair is long and they wear no clothing. Their wives are all human. It is said that their male offspring are born as dogs, while female offspring are born as humans. This may be seen in the History of Five Dynasties.)

Note: Although it closely resembles the relevant passage from *Soushenji*, this version of the Panhu story in fact comes from the version of the legend given in vol. 86 of *Hou Han shu*, with the only differences being a few characters missing or changed. The parenthetical observation at the end of the passage comes from chapter 73 of *Wudaishi* (J. *Godaishi*) by Ouyang Xiu (1007–1072).

beast to have displayed greater merit than any man, and for Your Lordship to have promised him me as a reward, are karmic retributions for previous lives, and that Your Lordship must, for the sake of your country and future generations, abandon your child while yet alive to the way of the beasts, in order to prove to your people that there is no falsehood in Your Lordship's rule, in order to rule peacefully and bountifully, lest by breaking your oaths and forgetting your promises you give the people reason to say that you, Your Lordship, are no different from Kagetsura. Though shallow is the sea of wisdom that stretches out before a girl's eyes, unmuddied it remains, and that is why my heart so clearly sees whereon my deepest sighs are founded, why from this day forth the ties of gratitude and love that bind us we must sever—let me go today. Search all the billion worlds and nowhere will you find another child who begs her parent to abandon her, another maiden willing to follow the way of another species." And as she attempted to persuade him, upon her sleeves fell jewels of dew, to course and flow as if there alone had autumn arrived.

Yoshizane listened, silent except for his sighs, and then cast aside the spear he carried with a clatter. "Ah, but I have erred, I have erred! Those above make rules, but if they first break them, then those below will also break them, and chaos will result. I never truly meant to give you to Yatsufusa, Princess. I never meant to, and yet I said it: the words came out of my mouth and entered his ears. Had I the courage of Lin Xiangru, that I could recover the Night-Shining Gem,[17] yet could I not take back a slip of the tongue; now become my enemy is this dog that lies in the gate of calamity.

"And yet, pondering now on what has happened, this was not unprefigured. When this child of mine was very small, I sent her in secret to a cave in Susaki to send up prayers, and on the way the party encountered an old man who, upon seeing Princess Fuse, beckoned them closer and said: 'This infant's frequent illnesses, her colic night and day, all come from a spirit's curse. I fear that were I to elucidate every particular, I should risk revealing the workings of Heaven. Understand what you will, what you can, from her name: Fuse. Return and tell your lord and master of this.' And so they did. Now, the Princess was born in the second year of Kakitsu, in the summer, on a Concealment Day, and for this reason did I name her Princess Fuse, after

---

17. Lin Xiangru was a minister in the state of Zhao whose biography is included in chapter 81 of *Shi ji*. Zhao possessed a priceless jade (Yoshizane refers to it as the Night-Shining Gem), which the king of Qin offered to buy with fifteen cities. Lin Xiangru was sent to Qin with the jade, but after delivering it he realized that Qin had no intention of giving Zhao the cities. Through cunning and bravado (including threatening to smash the jade and kill himself), Xiangru regained the gem and smuggled it back to Zhao.

the Three Concealments. Bidden thus to judge by her name, I racked my brain but hit upon nothing. Had I a man as talented as Yang Yongxiu, who scoffed at the Duke of Cao for an understanding that came thirty leagues too late,[18] I should have asked him what it meant, but I had none. Only today, after these long years of waiting, have I chanced upon the interpretation. The character for concealment that I used to write 'Fuse' consists of the character for human followed by that for dog. She was fated to this catastrophe since she was in swaddling clothes. Well might it be said that the name names the thing.

"I know not who the spirit might be that enacted such an obsessive curse—but were I to venture a guess, might I not think it was perhaps Tamazusa, that was Sadakane's wife? That seductress was rumored to have conspired to bring harm to her master and eliminate the loyal and good from his realm. In spite of that, I said I would spare her life—but then I did not, and as she could not bring destruction upon me, she seeks, I fear, to visit her unreasoning wrath upon my child by showing her the furthest reaches of misery.

"Now, again, this dog's mother disappeared, and he was raised by a tanuki, or so I have heard. The tanuki is also known by the alternate names of yabyō, or wild cat, and gyokumen, or jewel-face. The characters for gyokumen, when given their domestic reading, are pronounced 'tamazura.' Tamazura and Tamazusa are alarmingly close in sound. I never noticed it, but thought I was clever for noting that the character for tanuki comprises that for village accompanied by that for dog, signifying, I thought, the dog of the Satomi—and so I kept him and showed him such favor. Oh, how I regret it now! Verily do the gods in Heaven see to it that that which waxes must also wane. The old man's intuition was on the mark, and regret it a hundredfold—nay a thousandfold—though I might, no good will it do me now. If I abandon my daughter to a beast, only my shame will be left to me—though many countries accrue to me, so that my descendants prosper for a hundred generations, what pleasure can I take in it? I cannot show my face again!"

Thus upon his mortifying shame, as far as broken heart and reason quick allowed him to, did Yoshizane speak; no comfort could the women standing

18. As Tokuda notes (p. 193), the name here should be Yang Xiu, an advisor to Cao Cao. The incident (found in the Liu Song—era miscellany *Shishuo xinyu* [J. *Sesetsu shingo*]) concerns a stele inscription that the two passed on the road. Yang was able to decipher it immediately, while the Duke only managed to figure it out after they had gone thirty *li*. Tokuda, *Hakkenden zenchūshaku*, 193.

by him offer as the tears that had begun in fear soon swelled to cataracts of grief and overcame them, and all sobbed together.

Princess Fuse, seeing herself thus wept over, forced down the lump in her throat and spoke. "When even those who serve him sink beneath unbearable lament, then all the more do I my father's feelings comprehend, e'en as I feel the weight of sin I bear from filial disloyalty that I commit, though never do I will it. And yet it seems he has decided that, once that he has committed me unto the demon-beast and finally made his word no lie, his life, so precious as to be engraved on jewels, shall be o'er. 'Tis no easy thing to achieve birth as a human—shall I allow this body into which I was born, into which I have grown, this heirloom of my parents, to be before their eyes defiled by a beast? Please, set your heart at ease." Shame so overcame her that she could speak no more; she covered her face and sank to the floor.

Yoshizane nodded vigorously. "That was well said, to my sorrow. I think of strange and distant lands, and of how much the affair of King Gaoxin and his dog Panhu resembles my present troubles.[19] Also, Gan Bao's *Inquiries into the Divine* says that in ancient times there lived a great man who went to war in a faraway place and did not return for a long time. His wife died, leaving behind their only child, a daughter who was, it is said, sixteen. Now, in that house there was a horse, a stallion, and as the girl spent every day and night yearning for her father, one day she turned to this horse and said, 'If you bring my father back to me, I will give myself to you to do with as you please.' The horse seemed to take her at her word, for one day he broke his tether and was gone. The days passed, and then the horse returned, bearing her father. Then it began to whinny and neigh, as if it wanted something. The girl's father, alarmed, asked her about it, whereupon she told him what had transpired. Her father, thinking that things could not be left as they were, slaughtered the horse in secret, skinned it, and hung its hide from the eaves of the house. The girl saw the horse's hide and cursed it, saying, 'Beast, this is your reward, and none too soon, for seeking a human in marriage. Now that you are nothing but a hide, do you still want me?' Then the hide crashed to the ground, and wrapped itself around the girl; a wind arose, and sent both hide and girl sailing up into the sky. The following day her dead body was

---

19. Gaoxin was one of the mythical Five Emperors of ancient China, the immediate predecessor of the sage-king Yao. Chapter 14 of *Soushenji* tells how Gaoxin promised his daughter to anyone who could bring him the head of his enemy. When his dog Panhu brought the head, Gaoxin balked at fulfilling his promise, but his daughter insisted that he keep his word (this story is also related in *Hou Han shu*, chapter 86). See note 10 of the *kanbun* preface to this Volume. The story that Yoshizane proceeds to relate, concerning the horse, is also found in chapter 14 of *Soushenji*.

found hanging in a mulberry tree in the yard. The worms that grew in her corpse were silkworms, it is said.

"As difficult as it may be to accept, this story has been handed down in China since olden times—at least since the days of Wei and Jin. The meanness of these people consisted not only in turning their backs on a promise they had made, but in killing the one to whom they had made it—in their hearts they were lower than animals. Had I succumbed to my moment of rage and killed Yatsufusa, I should have been no better than this man of antiquity written of in *Inquiries into the Divine*.

"That said, as luck would have it, I have sent Yoshinari and Ujimoto to Hiratate and Tateyama with orders to secure those castles, while Sadayuki is in Nagasa, in Tōjō Castle, and besides them there is no one with whom I can discuss such internal matters. For better or for worse, it is my heart alone that has led me to the decision I have reached. Well, then, Yatsufusa, you have accomplished that which in jest I bade you do: in recognition of your distinguished deed, I give you Princess Fuse. Leave us now a little while and wait for her. Go now, go!"

Yoshizane urged the dog on. Yatsufusa studied his master's expression closely, then at long last stood up and, with a shake, went silently out of the room.

Chapter X
Ignoring a ban, Takanori loses a woman;
Slitting her belly, Princess Fuse looses
eight dog children[1]

Yoshizane's wife Isarago was astonished to hear about Yatsufusa, and she came running, hems in hand, to the children's chambers where Princess Fuse was. She had arrived to see, all in those close quarters, the women in the doorway, along with His Lordship of the Governance Ministry [YOSHIZANE], and the Princess unharmed, father and daughter engaged in a dialogue over the dog within the room. There Isarago stood, silently shedding tears, and listened, waiting for them to run out of words. The women, when the dog left, fearfully gave way, drawing back on either side of the doorway. As they did so they unwittingly opened a passage for Isarago, who, unable to remain hidden, rushed in and collapsed heavily at Princess Fuse's side, weeping now with no effort to keep quiet, while Yoshizane, ashamed, just looked at her, saying nothing. Princess Fuse patted and petted her mother on the back, as if to calm her, saying, "You have heard the news, then? What must you be feeling?"

At this comfort her mother lifted up her head and wiped away her tears and said, "Would I be thus lamenting had I not heard? Ah, Princess Fuse, so fine is your mind that you have kept His Lordship's decrees consistent, and made right his administration of rewards and punishments—and yet you

---

1. The original here is *hakkenshi*, written with characters that mean "eight dog children," but homophonous with the characters used throughout the book to refer to the "Eight Dog Warriors."

have stained your own name, thrown yourself away. This may be a fine display of filial duty to your father, but it runs counter to every feeling, every custom of the world—who is there that would praise you for this? Every living thing has two parents—how can you fail to consider the laments of your mother? And yet I will be strong in my heart. Now that you have finally so far outgrown your sickly childhood as to make your mother's travails but a tale of the past, you are fair to behold, more beautiful than moon or flower, and what do you do with this body of yours? You elect to offer it up, with no thought of regret. This must be the work of a spirit possessing you, moving you with its obsession. I bid you awake, awake! Oh, what has become of the protection of the gods, the efficacy of the buddhas, on whom my thoughts have centered these many years?"

Fuse listened to her mother's rehearsal, her arguments and sobs intermingled, until her mother's charity was too much for the Princess to bear. Burying her tear-streaked cheeks in her sleeves, she said, "Your words weigh heavy upon my heart, already burdened with my crime of filial impiety. I am not unaffected by a parent's lamentation, nor am I without sorrow for the stain I shall leave on my name after I am gone, but I am resigned to this as the workings of fate, of ineluctable karma. Look at this."

From her left hand hung suspended a string of prayer beads—now she took them lightly in her right hand, saying, "These were given me, I am told, by a mysterious old man, a manifestation of En the Ascetic, when I was very small, and I have always kept them on my person. Among these crystal prayer beads there are eight for counting, on which could be read the characters for Benevolence, Righteousness, Propriety, Wisdom, Loyalty, Fidelity, Filiality, and Fraternity. These characters were not graven in the beads, nor were they written upon them with lacquer, but appeared naturally, as it were; and though I handled the beads daily, the writing never grew faint or rubbed away. And yet, when I happened to look at them after the death of Kagetsura, the eight characters inscribing the virtues had disappeared without a trace, and in their stead appeared different characters. It was from this time, I learned, that Yatsufusa's thoughts turned to me. This was a singular and mysterious thing. Not only for yesterday's sake and today's do I lament this karmic reward decreed for lives past, and many times have I thought to die without waiting for it to come to pass—yet whenever I take blade in hand, I think of how, unless this evil karma I deplete in this life, never shall I rise in life to come, but like the flower shall I be, whose petals scatter on a storm-swept mountainside, ne'er to come to fruition, but to an end instead, in which I would defer to parents and gods—and then am I cast into the lusterless autumn of this floating world. If, my lady, in your wisdom you understand these things, then let them straightaway your grudge disperse, that it might no more occupy your thoughts. And yet, if you feel that the child who would turn ten-and-seven years of merciful love to enmity is no child at all but a former life's wrathful foe, then cut me off this very day from your favor, disown me where I stand, and I will consider that the shame I shall bear alone will be for the sake of the life into which I shall yet be born, and though I lay my body down in Amitābha's regions in the West, beneath the threads of silvergrass the Buddha holds, I shall die easy if at last I can exhaust this evil karma. But I would ask this: that you look at this, and forgive me."

With this she proffered her prayer beads, a bead-like tear on each, one for each of the fivescore and eight passions that torment us, in whose tormenting maze her mother struggled still. Her mother, dubious, turned her gaze on them, and said, "Why, if there was so much more to this, did you not tell your parents of it from the beginning? And just what characters are they that appeared on the beads?"

"Here," said Yoshizane, taking the beads in response to her query. He turned them over and over, examining them closely, then groaned. "Isarago, put an end to your hopes. Benevolence, Righteousness, Propriety, Wisdom, and the other characters for the virtues are gone: the eight characters here now read, 'Even thus can a beast conceive a heart to know truth.'[2] It occurs to me, reading this, that the eight virtuous acts, the five eternal virtues,[3] are things pertaining to humanity, while the heart to know truth is common to all sentient beings, with no distinction between man and beast. This must mean that even with her karma, if the Princess allows herself to be guided by a beast into the way of the Buddha's truth, she can rest easy with regard to the lives to come. Truly, we all reap the fruits of our own karma, be it poverty, ignominy, glory, or shame. Ever since the spring of her fifteenth year, lords great and petty from hither and yon, not to mention warriors from all the countries round about, have come to me seeking the Princess's hand in marriage, either for themselves or for their sons—suitors so many I have lost count of them, but I have refused them all. My intention was to this year make Kanamari Daisuke lord of Tōjō Castle and give him Princess Fuse in marriage, by way of recompense to Takayoshi, who refused

---

2. From *Taiheiki*, chapter 9, section 9, where the phrase is used as an example of the power of the Buddha's mercy—if even animals can learn to understand the law, then how much more so is there a chance for humans, as bestial as they may be, to reach enlightenment?

3. The eight virtuous acts (*hakkō*) are those virtues originally found on Princess Fuse's beads. The five eternal virtues (*gojō*) are benevolence, righteousness, propriety, wisdom, and fidelity. All are virtues defined in the Confucian tradition, which concentrates on ethical behavior in society, while the "heart to know truth" is a specifically Buddhist concept.

his much-deserved reward and took his own life, but I misspoke and gave my beloved daughter to a beast: this, too, had karma as its cause. Think not of me with anger only, Isarago, but see the characters on these beads, and understand it for yourself." He delivered himself of this explanation in an earnest attempt to comfort her, but nothing would disperse the rain that drenched her sleeves nor chase away the hov'ring clouds that covered o'er her voice as she yet wept.

It was a thing that should not be, but Princess Fuse hurried about her preparations to leave that evening. "I do not expect I shall return alive—and so I will simply go." So saying, she removed her jeweled bodkins and discarded them, put on a white tight-sleeved robe over what she was wearing, and hung the prayer beads around her neck; she took with her nothing but a sheaf of blank paper and a copy of the Lotus Sutra, and firmly refused any escort or companion. "I will go where Yatsufusa goes, though I know not where that be, and there I will stay; there, most likely, I shall die. If he does not leave here, he will not last the night." Thus resigned, she went to leave. Twilight was fast approaching. Her mother Isarago, loath to be parted from her, clung to her daughter's hem as she tried to go, choking on her sobs; the women who had served her these many years, too, sank to the floor under the weight of their tears, huddling here and there, of no use to anyone.

Princess Fuse rallied her strength with all her heart, that she might not dampen her sleeves with the dew and frost with which she was to disappear; she comforted Her Ladyship her mother, and bade her farewell; and then, seen off by her women, she went outside, where the day had darkened and the bright moonlight spilled through the trees into the inner garden. Yatsufusa was below the veranda, where he seemed to have been waiting all this time for the Princess to emerge.

Then the Princess walked up next to the dog, faced him, and said: "Now hear this, Yatsufusa. Among people there is a distinction between noble and mean. In marriage we observe this division—we each take one of our own kind as a companion. I have never heard of anyone taking a beast to husband or being taken to wife by one, not even among the lowest of the low, the defiled butchers and beggars. Meanwhile, I am the daughter of the lord of this land—it is unfit for me to marry a commoner, and yet I am now to abandon my body and give over my life to a beast. Perhaps it is a karmic reward for a past life. However, my father's decree weighs heavy, and that is why I do this. If you fail to understand these things, and seek to satisfy your passions upon me, then I have here my dagger. I will kill you and then myself. If, on the other hand, you maintain yourself in all righteousness, staying unwaveringly by my side, and observe the boundaries between human and beast, casting off all desire for love, then to me you shall be a guide to the Buddha's truth. Then I will go with you wherever you wish. Which will it be?"

As she posed this question she took out her dagger, clutching it in a reverse grip; the dog seemed to have grasped her meaning, as his face assumed an expression of exceeding mournfulness. But he immediately raised his head to look at the Princess and gave a long howl, then gazed up at the sky, as if swearing an oath. Princess Fuse put away her blade, uttering the words, "Well, then, let us go."

Yatsufusa led the way out through the garden gate, then the inner gate, and finally the western gate of the castle, and as they passed each, one by one, the Princess was right behind him, walking silently; behind her she could hear her mother and her women weeping and wailing, while from afar Yoshizane watched her go. His resentment was even greater than that of the Han emperor as he watched Zhaojun depart as a bride for the country of the Huns;[4] to call his feelings sad, on the occasion of this most dubious of separations, would be foolish understatement.

Princess Fuse had firmly refused the company of an escort but both Yoshizane's and Isarago's hearts were uneasy for her safety on the road, and so in secret they sent Amasaki Jūrō Terutake, with several mighty warriors, "to watch her and then report, hiding as necessary." Now, this Amasaki Terutake had originally been a country warrior in Tōjō. He had first attached himself to Sugikura Ujimoto, and then been rewarded for his military service in taking and presenting Nobutoki of the Maro's head: he was called up to Takita, where he served close beside Yoshizane. He having reached a ripe age, Yoshizane chose him from among his men and sent him along with the Princess. And so Terutake, riding, led his troops out after the Princess, staying at least a hundred yards behind her.

Once Yatsufusa had gone some distance from Takita Castle, he allowed the Princess to ride on his back, and then struck out at a run in the direction of Fuchū, faster than a bird on the wing. Terutake whipped his horse on so as not be left behind, while his troops, panting and dripping with sweat, chased him, until, many roads later, as Terutake reached the village of Inukake, he had so far outdistanced his men that only one or two were left with him. But

---

4. Zhaojun, one of the concubines of Emperor Yuan (r. 48–33 BCE), was given as a political bride to the leader of one of the Xiongnu, a nation on the outskirts of the Han empire. Only after the Emperor had promised Zhaojun did he realize that she was the most beautiful of his concubines. The story is told in chapter 89 of *Hou Han shu*.

this horse was a singular creature, bearing an accomplished rider, and they raced on through the night, unwilling to lose their quarry, until dawn, taking them unaware, found them far up the side of Mount To.

Now, Mount To is the highest mountain in the province of Awa, along with its brother, Iyo Peak. It is said that if one clambers to the top, one can see the waves rolling in at Nako, Susaki, and the Seven Inlets. The mountain's slopes are empty of human habitation, and dark from the huge-boled trees that tower and boughs that droop over it. The woodcutters' tracks are choked with briars and the moss is slippery, while the mists are ever thick. Straight on rode Jūrō Terutake, up the mountain paths; he and the two troopers who remained to him clambered up the mountain without a pause for breath, and as the clouds subsided from peak after peak, they looked up and saw Princess Fuse in the distance, the sutra on her back and the writing paper and inkstone on her knees, seated on Yatsufusa as he bounded across a river in a ravine and yet deeper into the mountain. Terutake managed to reach the riverbank, but the water was deep and the current swift, and there was no way for him to cross it.

"Have I come all this way for nothing? Shall I be thwarted by a river from seeing where she has gone to? Am I to simply turn back? Let us wade across," he said, hurriedly dismounting. And so, leaning on a staff, he strode into the water, but no sooner had he done so than he was swept off his feet—he had time to raise a single cry before his head smashed into a rock and his body was swept away by the rushing, falling waters, wherever they would take it.

When his troops saw Amasaki Terutake—who had grown up by the shore, an accomplished swimmer—washed away so easily to a watery grave, they were greatly alarmed. Their tongues trembled in their apprehension, and at length they returned to the skirts of the mountain, where they rejoined those who had lagged behind. Together they traveled day and night until they had returned to Takita Castle, where they reported the state of affairs to Yoshizane. Having listened closely to their detailed account, he elected not to send any more men, but instead circulated a strict proclamation throughout the province, laying down a strict prohibition that "no one, not even old woodcutters or charcoal-makers, is to climb Mount To. Anyone entering its precincts shall be put to death."

Yoshizane was deeply pained by the violent death of Amasaki Terutake, and he summoned the man's child to serve him in the same capacity as his father. Isarago, however, found it more difficult to forget about Princess Fuse with every passing day, and every month she would pretend to send her old women on a visit in her stead to the Cave of the Ascetic, sending them

Caption: Remaining true to a word, Princess Fuse goes deep into the mountains in the company of a beast.
Figures: Kanamari Daisuke [*top right corner*]. Princess Fuse [*center*]. Yatsufusa [*dog*].

いちごんまさ
一言信を守て
ちくしやうあんさえ
伏姫深山か
もいたに
畜生に
とりひ
伴の海

Note: In the first edition of Volume I, published by Sanseidō, this illustration was printed from two blocks, the first rendering the illustration itself and the second adding a wash of grey ink (*usuzumi*) over Yatsufusa and the river, suggesting mist. The later Bunkeidō edition of Volume I does not use the grey ink, losing the mist effect but better allowing the reader to see what lurks in the water below Princess Fuse: a reflection of her with a dog's head. The Bunkeidō version of the illustration appears on the following pages.

一言信を守て
伏姫深山ふ
畜生に
伴居

青堂梓

instead in secret to Mount To in search of her daughter's whereabouts—she wanted so to know if Fuse was safe—but none possessed the courage to go beyond that mountain torrent that had carried Amasaki Terutake away. That side of the river had always been shrouded in clouds of mist, and as their vision could not penetrate it, it was in vain that the old women ventured there, and in vain that they returned, through the months' ebb and flow, until all too soon a year had passed.

We now turn our attention to Kanamari Daisuke Takanori, who, having had a march stolen on him by Anzai Kagetsura and not knowing that the enemy had already surrounded Takita, fled at a run when he began to have an inkling of what was happening; but on the way he was overtaken by Toppei and his men, so that he fought a bloody battle against a numerous foe. All his escort were cut down, and he alone escaped the tiger's maw, finally returning to Takita only to find that Anzai's great army had already arrived in force to surround the castle and that their assault was at its height, and that therefore he would be unable to enter. Thence he hurried to Tōjō, thinking to join what strength he could offer to Horiuchi Sadayuki's, only to find that place, too, caged like a bird, surrounded by a great army led by Kabuto Toppei and his men; there was no easy way for him to enter that castle, either. "Had I only known, I would have ridden alone against the enemy, making the castle's bridge my deathbed when I was cut down—but such regrets are useless now. Not only have I failed in my weighty charge as a messenger, but now I cannot even join my lord in the hour of his greatest trial. Yea, though both castles' sieges be broken and my lord escape unscathed, how could I show my face in audience before him? I shall rush into Kabuto's encampment and die fighting."

Thus decided he in haste—but then he forcibly calmed himself, and reconsidered. "For me to go up alone against an enemy army of many hundred mounted men would be akin to using an egg to push a boulder. I should be throwing away my life without bringing either loss to my opponent or gain to my allies. Would not that be disloyalty? Both castles were low on provisions to begin with. What better way for me to ameliorate my mistake than by going up to Kamakura to report our distress to the Minister of the Court Nariuji and beg him to muster troops for our relief, thereby scattering our enemy and averting catastrophe? Shall I not make straightaway for Kamakura?"

Having posed this query to himself, he boarded a boat at Shirahama and before many days had passed was presenting himself at the palace of the Overseer as Yoshizane's emissary. He explained his reason for coming, reported their distress, and begged mightily for salvation; but as he bore no letter from Yoshizane, they were skittish of him and would not cooperate, and again he spent several days in idleness. When, convinced of the futility of this endeavor, he left and returned to Awa, he found that Kagetsura had already been destroyed, and that the whole province was united and at peace.

"A joyful thing," he thought to himself, but there was no opportunity to present himself as having returned: and yet he could not slit his belly at this late date. "I will await a suitable moment to offer up an apology for my negligence in this affair, and until then I will take myself to a hiding place," he decided. He hied himself to the village of Amaha Barrier in Kazusa, for it was his home village, and there he ensconced himself in the house of a certain peasant, a relative of his grandfather Issaku.

He stayed there for over a year, and then heard vague tidings of Princess Fuse's fate—he was told that "no one is sure if she is safe or not, or even if she still lives, since she went into the furthest reaches of Mount To with Yatsufusa the dog. Her mother has long since gone down to her sickbed from worrying about her daughter day after day."

Daisuke was greatly astonished to hear this, and thought, "Even if His Lordship did misspeak himself, 'tis a rank and regrettable thing that the daughter of such a true nobleman as he should have a beast as her companion, to be spoken of thus by the people hereabouts and elsewhere. Even if that dog has been possessed by a spirit, unto the gaining of godlike powers, can it be a matter of any great difficulty to shoot him down? I will climb that mountain, kill the dog Yatsufusa, and return to Takita with Her Ladyship the Princess. If I do this, can there be any doubt that my former wrongs will be forgiven me, even without an apology?"

These thoughts he kept to himself, telling the master of the house with all evident sincerity only that "I have a heart's vow to make, so I go to visit a shrine." Then he departed and returned in secret to Awa, a fowling piece at his side. With this he made his way into the furthest reaches of Mount To, searching everywhere for Princess Fuse's whereabouts; he greeted the night on those mountain roads even as he greeted the dawn, and after five or six days, it seemed to him that there was a person on the opposite side of a river in a mist-filled ravine. "Could it be?" he thought, trying to calm his heart as it leapt within his breast. He crouched at the water's edge and listened intently until he heard, ever so faintly, a female voice, reciting a sutra.

Author's note: It was my intention, in this section, to tell all about the origin of the Eight Dog Warriors, of how they came to be—I had already decided that I would end Book V of this Inaugural Volume that way when I included the subject of each of the ten Chapters in the initial Book—but the story became much longer than I had expected it to, and the pages of this Book filled up without my having concluded this section. The number of Books is set, and there is a limit to the number of pages each can have within it. I am told that when I exceed these limits in a given installment, it poses inconveniences for the vendors; it is a hard thing to ignore booksellers' wishes. Therefore I shall put what remains of my draft into a new Book, and add it without fail to next year's installment. All in all, what I am writing here is but the very beginning of this novel. Hereafter we shall see the Eight Dog Warriors take their first steps out into the world. Thenceforth will follow, as the years go by, the serial accounts, long and short, of the lives of those eight, as eight children born in eight different places, as warriors sometimes together and sometimes asunder, and finally, as a result of a certain promise, as retainers of the house of Satomi. I have not thought it all out completely yet. As the years pass and the volumes pile up, I expect that the whole book will be comparable to my previous opus, The Bow-Crescent Moon.[5] O Reader, read and enjoy. Thus do I lay down my brush in the bird house[6] on this autumn day, the seventeenth of the ninth month of the wood-dog year of Bunka.[7]

End of Book V of the Lives of the Eight Dogs of the Satomi of Southern Fusa

---

5. *Chinsetsu yumiharizuki* (The bow-crescent moon: An outlandish tale), 1807–1811.
6. Tokuda (p. 210) notes that Bakin had recently begun keeping birds.
7. Bunka 11, or 1814.

AUTHOR   KYOKUTEI BAKIN

Copyist   Chigata Nakamichi

ILLUSTRATOR   YANAGAWA SHIGENOBU[1]

Xylographer   Asakura Ihachirō

- An abbreviated list of new illustrated novels by Kyokutei in the domestic script, published by Sanseidō

The Lady Kesa's Seventh Avenue Sermon.[2]

> IT WAS PREVIOUSLY ANNOUNCED THAT THIS BOOK WOULD BE PUBLISHED THIS YEAR, BUT AS THE AUTHOR WAS WRITING *EIGHT DOGS* HE WAS UNABLE TO GET TO IT. WE DO, HOWEVER, HOPE TO PRINT IT SOON. THEREFORE WE LIST IT HERE AGAIN.

Old Silks from Mino: An Outlandish Tale Woven from Hachijō Twill.[3] Illustrated by Hokusū Shigenobu.[4] Complete in five fascicles.

- Fans illustrated and inscribed by Bakin, along with:

  WATER OF THE DIVINE LADY—A FAMILY TRADITION * MIRACULOUS BOLUS, EXACTINGLY PREPARED * A CURE FOR THE MONTHYBUGS ETC., ARE WITH KAWACHIYA TAISUKE, BOOKSELLER, JUST INSIDE KARAMONO-CHŌ, TO THE SOUTH, SHINSAIBASHI-SUJI, OSAKA. FANS ARE ALSO WITH KASHIWAYA HANZŌ, NABE-CHŌ, KANDA, EDO.

A Record of Asahina's Travels through the Isles.[5] Volume I, in V chapters. Illustrated by Utagawa Toyohiro.[6]

---

1. 1787–1833. Disciple, son-in-law, and adopted son of Katsushika Hokusai (1760–1849).

2. *Kesa gozen Shichijō hōgo.* Never published.

3. *Mino no furukinu Hachijō kidan.*

4. Better known as Katsushika Hokusū (n.d.). A disciple of Katsushika Hokusai, like Yanagawa Shigenobu.

5. *Asahina shimameguri no ki.* The first volume appeared the following year (1815).

6. 1774–1830. An influential print designer and book illustrator; among his disciples was Utagawa Hiroshige (1797–1858).

THE TITLE OF THIS BOOK HAS BEEN LISTED FOR SOME TIME, BUT THIS YEAR
THE MANUSCRIPT WAS FINALLY COMPLETED AND THE BLOCKS HAVE BEEN
CARVED. BOTH THE FIRST VOLUME AND THE SECOND VOLUME WILL BE PUB-
LISHED WITHOUT DELAY.

The Lives of the Eight Dog Warriors of the Satomi of Southern Fusa. Volume
II, in V Books.

TO BE ISSUED WITHOUT DELAY IN THE WINTER OF THE COMING YEAR OF
THE BOAR.

Bunka 11[7] (sign of the wood-dog)
Publishers

Morimoto Taisuke (just inside Karamono-chō, to the south,
   Shinsaibashi-suji, Osaka)
Wakabayashi Seibei (Bakurō-chō 3, Edo)
Hirabayashi Shōgorō (Matsuzaka-chō 2, Honjo)
Yamazaki Heihachi (Hiranaga-chō, Kanda, just outside the Sujigai-
   bashi gate)

On sale beginning on an auspicious day in winter, in the eleventh month

---

7. 1814.

VOLUME II

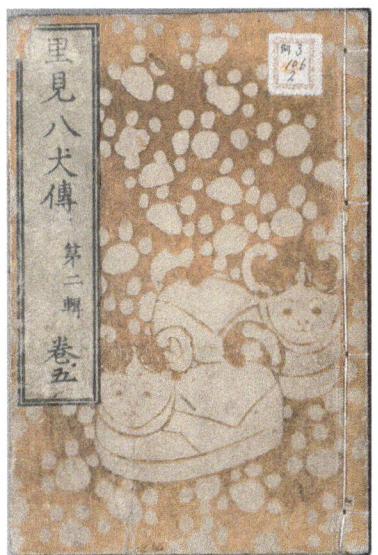

Like Volume I, Volume II of *Hakkenden* was originally published by Sanseidō, proprietor Yamazaki Heihachi. Volume II was reprinted a number of times while Sanseidō owned the blocks, but with little variation in the covers, most of which bore this illustration of papier-mâché dogs against a background of pawprint-like snow.

When Bunkeidō, proprietor Chōjiya Heibei, reprinted Volume II, it received this new cover design showing toy dogs among falling cherry blossoms.

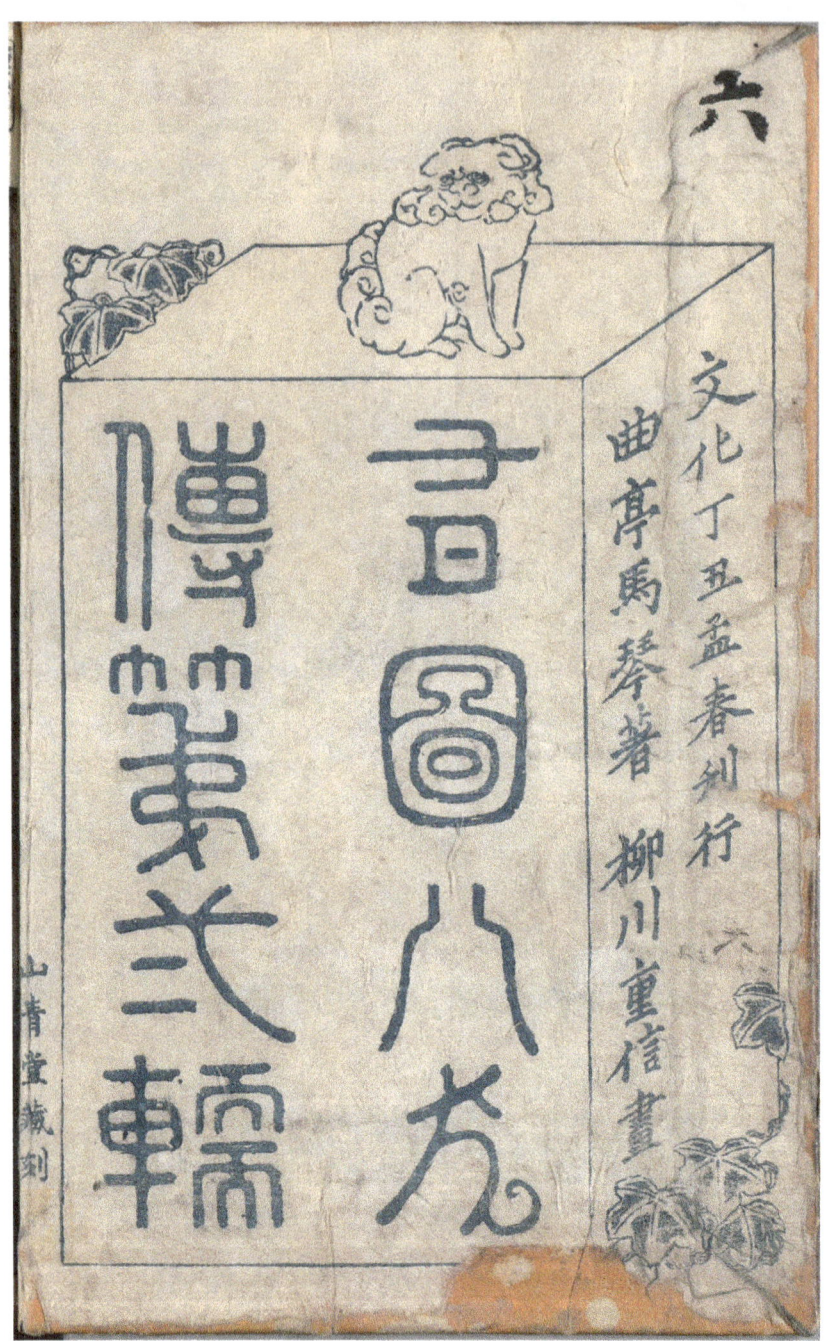

Center: The Lives of the Eight Dogs, Text and Pictures, Volume II.
On the right face of the pedestal: Published in the fire-ox year of Bunka at the inception of spring [the first month of Bunka 14, or 1817]; written by Kyokutei Bakin; pictures by Yanagawa Shige-nobu. [Volume II was actually published in the last month of 1816.]
To the left of the pedestal: Blocks owned by Sanseidō.
Top right corner: 6 [hand-written].

Preface to the Lives of
the Eight Dog Warriors,
Volume II

The author stores up in his breast the novel tales of the collectors of petty histories. At first he considers all manner of karmic causes and effects, and when he is unable to grasp one, he is left nonplussed, directionless in his heart, like a tiny boat tossed on the vast green ocean. When he gets the intent, however, he sails like a leaf on the wind, rejoicing within himself. He sees things no one has seen, and knows things no one knows. In this way there is nothing he dares not write concerning peace and war, gain and loss, nothing he dares not record concerning the ways of the world; and, after spending some length of time compiling his materials, he finally puts them into a book. He is like a sailor who drifts for thousands of leagues before reaching an isle in the sea, where he chances to meet an immortal who teaches him the secrets of wizardry and then allows him to return and proclaim them to his fellow men. However, it is as in the old story of the raft-rider who visited Peach Blossom Spring[1]—the multitudes refused to believe him. His contemporaries took him for someone swept away on the current of his words; only the curious and the hobbyists

---

This preface is written in *kanbun* (with minimal glosses).

1. From *Taohua yuan ji* (J. *Tōkagen ki*), written by Six Dynasties–era poet Tao Yuanming. A boatman follows a river upstream to its source in a forest of blossoming peach trees, beyond which he finds an undiscovered utopian village. After he leaves, no one is ever able to find it again.

were pleased, and they chose not to look into the truth or falsehood of his claims. Centuries later, literati poets wrote odes on the subject; later generations sang them again and again and never doubted them. Alas, one cannot put one's faith in a book. Yet there is faith and there is faithlessness. Once the writing of national histories ceased, novels and civilian histories emerged, enough to fill five carts, as superfluous as building a roof under one's roof—now is the great day for these things. They speak in jest, in words sweeter than candy, and at the end of the day they leave readers unfulfilled, lighting their lamps amidst dissatisfaction; only rarely do they profit those who love them. They are like tobacco, which, though it intoxicates its users, provides neither sustenance nor medicinal effect. Alas, one cannot put one's faith in a book. Yet there is faith and there is faithlessness. Faithful words are not beautiful, and thus they guard themselves against further study. Beautiful words are not faithful, and thus they entertain women and children. Evaluating petty histories by the standards of true histories is like placing a round vessel on a square base. Even a vulgarian recognizes that as a mismatch. Yet no one will believe that which is not matched with history. To read such, never for a moment believing them: what fault lies in liking this? The novels I write year after year are all made with that in mind. Now I have continued the *Lives of the Eight Dog Warriors*, and as it is being committed to blocks, the bookseller again asked me for an introduction. Therefore have I written these things, hoping thereby to forestall any and all accusations.

At the full of the moon in the intercalary month in mid-autumn of Bunka 13[2] (a fire-rat year), I took up my brush in the shade of the osmanthus blossoms in the southern window of Opus Hall.

Selected and Interpreted by Saritsu the Old-Fashioned

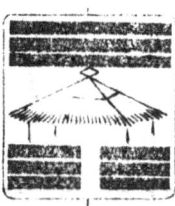 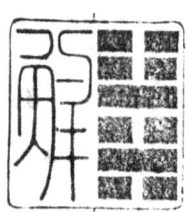

---

2. 1816.

Character for Toku (Bakin's personal name) in seal script (*left*); Daoist hexagram named for the same character (*right*). This seal contains the character for Toku (Bakin's personal name) in seal script, along with the Daoist hexagram named for the same character. For more on Bakin's personal name, and an explanation of the seal found to the right, see note 14 in the *kanbun* "Preface to the Lives of the Eight Dog Warriors" in Volume I.

The Lives of the Eight Dogs of the Satomi of Southern Fusa

Volume II

Table of Contents

---

1. As with Volume I, the chapter names in the Table of Contents are written in *kanbun*, with complete pronunciation glosses to enable them to be read as Japanese. When the chapter names reappear at the beginning of each chapter, they are written out as Japanese. When written as *kanbun*, the chapter names take the form of couplets, each line having the same number of characters (six characters per line for Chapter XI, nine characters per line for Chapter XII, and so on). Grammatically and syntactically, too, they suggest poetic couplets through their use of Chinese-style parallelism.

Book III, Chapter XV:[2]
Bansaku exacts vengeance at Kinren Temple;
Tatsuka detains a traveler at Nenge Hermitage

Same Book, Chapter XVI:
Under bare blade, phoenix and luan[3] bind their fates together;
In the chapel of the heavenly maiden, a couple prays for a child

Book IV, Chapter XVII:
Girding himself with jealous hatred, Hikiroku takes in a stray;
Steeling himself with filial piety, Shino performs ablutions under a waterfall

Same Book, Chapter XVIII:
Kijirō lays down his life on the banks of the River Hi;
Yoshirō suffers a wound in the house of the village headman

Book V, Chapter XIX:
Kamezasa coaxes Nukasuke with a nefarious scheme;
Bansaku entrusts his orphan to a far-sighted plan

Same Book, Chapter XX:
A pair of gem-children make a pact with righteousness;
A youth only three feet high speaks of his aspirations

XX Chapters total, of which Chapters I through X have been collected in the Inaugural Volume, beginning with its Ist Book.

---

2. As explained in the Introduction, *Eight Dogs: Part One* only includes Chapters I—XIV of the original, i.e., only part of Volume II. For the sake of completeness, however, the entire original Table of Contents is included.

3. The luan (J. *ran*), like the phoenix (Ch. *Feng*; J. *hō*) is a bird of Chinese mythology, and they are often paired, as here. Unlike the phoenix, no English equivalent has become standard (although some scholars use "simurgh," from the Persian mythical bird).

Frontispieces

Caption: The spring breeze/nurtured/the blossoms into bloom;/why does the spring breeze/also scatter them?

Figures: Inuzuka Bansaku [*standing*]. Tatsuka [*kneeling*].

Notes: Inuzuka Bansaku and Tatsuka are characters first appearing in Chapter XV. The poem is in Japanese, in *waka* form, and like its counterpart on the facing page, ties in with cherry-blossom viewing.

Caption: Unintoxicated/I could hardly be called in spring/with flowers in full bloom/as cherry blossoms, too, rest on/my shoulders as I go along.

Figures: Nurude Gobaiji [*standing*]. Kamezasa [*beneath Gobaiji's feet*].

Text on barrel: Fire-Ox No. 188.

Notes: Nurude Gobaiji and Kamezasa are characters first appearing in Chapters XXIII and XVI, respectively. The poem is in Japanese, in *waka* form, and ties in with the cherry-blossom viewing party seen in the background of this and the neighboring illustration. The inscription on the bucket contains a reference to the year of publication and what may be a stock number for a bucket that was meant to be returned to the vendor who sold the sake.

Caption: Ride not/the lonely abalone's/pearly palanquin/shouldered though it be/by Ise diving girls.

Figure: Inuzuka Shino.

Text on box next to caption: Ten Thousand Times Hemp.

Notes: The poem is in Japanese, in *waka* form. The reference to Ise, as well as the ladle on which Shino is leaning, suggest a pilgrimage to Ise (the ladle was often carried by pilgrims). Ten Thousand Times Hemp was a type of charm obtainable at Ise Shrine, a box containing a used hemp ceremonial wand.

Caption: A distant spring cannot save a traveler from present thirst/a single post cannot support a great hall when it leans.

Figure: Gakuzō, a manservant.

Notes: The poem is a *kanshi* couplet. The second line references a question posed in the seventh-century *Wen Zhongzi zhongshuo* (the same phrase was used in Chapter IV). The toad and turtle at the bottom left of the panel no doubt represent Hikiroku and Kamezasa, whose names contain the words for "toad" and "turtle" respectively. Gakuzō (the future Inuyama Sōsuke) first appears in Chapter XVIII. The caption is written on a spool of string, as might be used for a kite, while Gakuzō is dressed in the kabuki-style costume used for manservants on the popular *yakko-dako* (manservant-kite).

Caption: The rain drips in/noisily, incessantly,/but even so/I wish it would leak more/moonlight from the eaves.

Figure: Hamaji.

Notes: The poem is in Japanese, in *waka* form. Hamaji first appears in Chapter XVII. Although this illustration and the one on the facing page (spilling over onto this page) are divided by clear frames, the light from Hamaji's lantern crosses the frames and illuminates Samojirō's struggle. In the later Bunkeidō version of this illustration (shown on the following pages), shading is added to emphasize this connection.

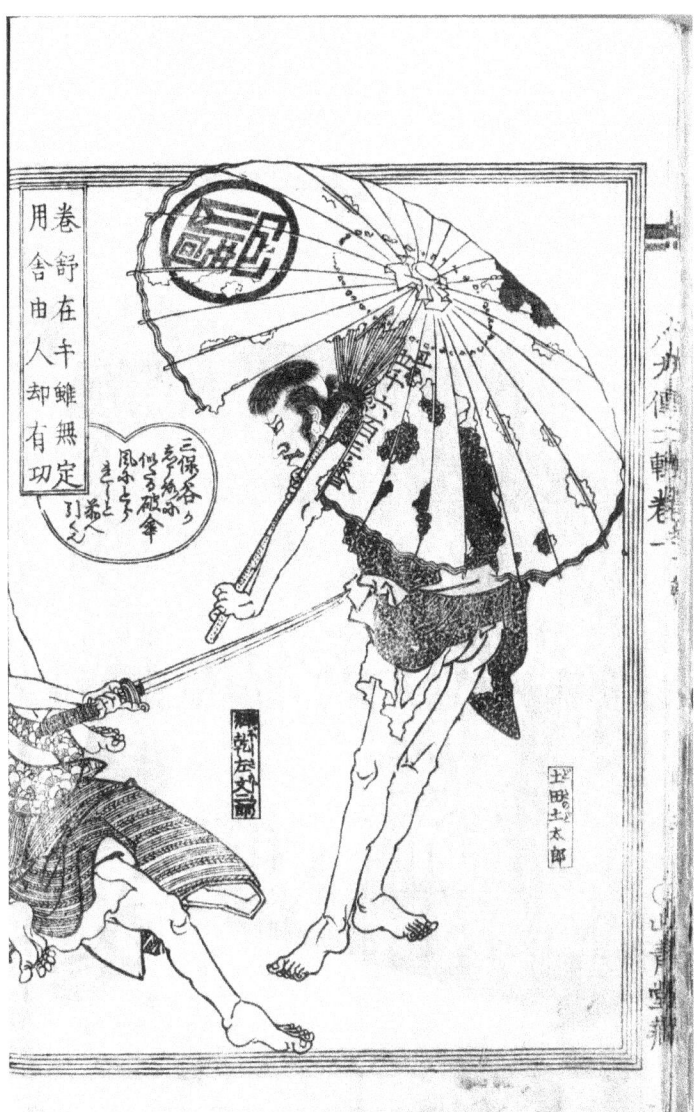

Captions:

In rectangular panel: To hide or to show—either is possible, neither is certain/to employ or reject—the merit in this depends on the person.

In fan-shaped panel: He pulls/his tattered umbrella/forward/against the wind's grasp/like Mihogatani's neckguard.

Figures: Dotarō of Dota [*with umbrella*]. Aboshi Samojirō [*holding sword*]. Katano Katarō [*standing over Samojirō*]. Itano Itarō [*held down by Samojirō*].

Text on umbrella: No. 5603.

Notes: The poem in the rectangular panel is a *kanshi* couplet; the one in the fan-shaped panel is in Japanese, in *waka* form. In book 11 of *Heike monogatari*, Mihogatani Jūrō is a warrior trying to flee the battlefield, when an enemy grabs his helmet's neckguard and a tug-of-war ensues. The logo on the umbrella says Yamazaki, probably a nod to one of Hakkenden's publishers (although in the picture probably meant to suggest the logo of the inn that owned this umbrella), as well as to the Yamazaki Highway scene in the play *Chūshingura* (A Treasury of Loyal Retainers, 1748, by Takeda Izumo II, Miyoshi Shōraku, and Namiki Senryū), which featured a bedraggled outlaw with an umbrella at night, an image this depiction of Dotarō would have conjured up to readers. Samojirō first appears in Chapter XXIII, Dotarō in XXIV, and Itarō and Katarō in XXVII.

The first two Books of this edition will be devoted to Princess Fuse's story. This being so, the heading for Chapter X in the Inaugural Volume [*"IGNORING A BAN, TAKANORI LOSES A WOMAN; SLITTING HER BELLY, PRINCESS FUSE LOOSES EIGHT DOG CHILDREN"*] properly belongs to Chapter XIII. The reason this was given too soon was in order to make known the outlines of the story, publication having been hastened before its beginning had been finished—even the illustrations revealed early that which is to come later. It had been my desire that the first seven Books (fourteen Chapters) be made into the first installment, but the booksellers would not be gainsaid in their preferences, which are that the work be released annually in editions of five Books each.

Then, too, in some of the preceding illustrations that began this Volume, characters appear who are not explained until the Books that will comprise Volume III, such as Nurude Gobaiji, Aboshi Samojirō, Dotarō of Dota, Katano Katarō, and Itano Itarō. What has come thus far is but the beginning, and I am not yet certain as to our Eight Warriors; however, to forestall assaults from the booksellers, I have blindly gone ahead and prepared pictures for sections my manuscript has not yet reached—sections whose plotlines I have not even invented yet. Later we shall find the story written in an attempt to match these pictures, although I doubt they will differ greatly. This is something I myself can reckon with; what I have no leisure to correct very well are the many mistakes in the work of the copyists and xylographers. I pray thee, O Reader, to be wary of them, as this is the usual thing.

Recopied by Bakin

This preface is written in Japanese.

The Lives of the Eight Dogs of the Satomi of Southern Fusa

Volume II, Book I

Assembled by the Master of the Crooked Pavilion in the Eastern Capital

Chapter XI
In a dream, a hermit marks the way to Mount To;
In darkness, Sadayuki is entrusted with a spirit missive

Satomi Yoshizane, Lesser Assistant in the Governance Ministry and Minister of the Court, had vanquished his great enemies Yamashita, Maro, and Anzai, thereby establishing his rule in the four districts of Awa, where affairs had formerly been as tangled as hemp thread, and there was now no warrior in any corner of Kazusa who did not bend before the wind of his authority. Yea, the two Overseers in Kamakura, Yamanouchi Akisada and Ōgigayatsu Sadamasa[1] [IN THE FIRST YEAR OF KŌSEI,[2] AFTER NARIUJI'S WITHDRAWAL TO KOGA, THE TWO OVERSEERS WERE AKISADA AND SADAMASA] seem to have deemed it imprudent to hold Yoshizane in disdain, for they appealed repeatedly to the Capital for a higher position for him, and so he was made Major Assistant in the Governance Ministry.

---

1. Better known to historians as Uesugi Akisada (1454–1510) and Uesugi Sadamasa (1443–1494). The Yamanouchi and Ōgigayatsu were two branches of the larger Uesugi family, and Bakin uses these names for Akisada and Sadamasa. The historical Sadamasa does not seem to have held the post of Kantō *kanrei*, but in the novel he does.

2. 1455. What Bakin glosses as Kōsei is now usually read Kōshō.

Each year saw a succession of such happy events, and yet Yoshizane had known only vexation and sorrow since the previous year when, suffering the privations of besiegement under Anzai Kagetsura's assault and thinking only of saving his officers and men from starvation, he had, because of an ill-considered word, delivered his beloved daughter Princess Fuse to the dog Yatsufusa, with whom she had gone quickly into Mount To: thereafter Yoshizane had heard nothing of her and knew not whether she was secure or imperilled, while the rumors and censure of the world at large left him never a moment's forgetfulness.

He refused to allow this to color his expression, however. "Those trackless river gorges may prevent me, her father, not to mention any of my men, from meeting her, but if she should happen to be seen by a woodsman or a hunter, it would surely be to her a shame eight times greater than that of meeting her kin," he thought. Straightaway he issued a proclamation throughout the country that all who sought their livings in the mountains, be they gentle folk or base, warrior or commoner, were forbidden to climb that peak—"Any who disobeys forfeits his head."

Decreeing thus did nothing, however, to lighten the burden of worry he bore in his heart for Kanamari Daisuke Takanori. "I have heard nothing of him since he departed in an endeavor to borrow provisions of Anzai Kagetsura: I know not if he yet lives. If he fell prey to a plot and was taken captive, may he not have lost his life? And if not there, then must not he have died in combat? If so, then brought to nothing are my plans for him, by which I would have given him a castle to rule and my daughter to wife in fulfillment of the oath I took to his dying father, Takayoshi, whose hand I could not stay when he refused his well-earned rewards and slit open his belly. The fate of men is what we cannot trust—the moon, that wanes and waxes, stays unchanged from last year unto this, while lives have all decisive alterations undergone. What has become of him?" But this was not something he could inquire of to another, and so he was left alone in his thoughts, unable to conjure anything to illuminate the enduring darkness of the paths a parent's heart must wander for his child.

When even a general who, possessing the triple virtues of wisdom, benevolence, and courage, could look on an enemy of a million riders and deem it dross was thus helplessly cast down in his thoughts, little wonder that his consort Isarago wept as each evening passed away, and wept as each day dawned, day after day, month after month, the image of Princess Fuse at their parting ever before her eyes. "Let her be safe from harm—let the day come when she may return home!" Thus she prayed oft to the gods and buddhas, pressing together the palms of hands that seemed to be wasting away—thin were the fingers that morosely took up her chopsticks at meal-times, only to lay them down again unused.

The housemaids and attendants who served at her elbow, with no words of comfort to offer her, were reduced to saying, "As you wish, milady." In secret they said, "If we each steel ourselves and go up into Mount To, shall we not eventually discover our lady the Princess's whereabouts?" Therefore they would often set out for that peak under the excuse that "we would make a pilgrimage to the Ascetic's Cave on Your Ladyship's behalf," only to wander in search of Princess Fuse. Some, despite their aspirations, were too cowed by the terrible-ness of those alpine tracks to climb, and turned back at the foothills; some, with dispositions made mannish by years of service to a military house, forced themselves to enter the mountain, allowing their guides to precede them. But those guides were too afraid to cross the mountain river down which Amasaki Jūrō Terutake had been swept, and as the mists ever roiled on the far side of that thundering river, nothing could the women make out, and so they merely stood there among the flowering briars on the bank, each woman feeling like one who sits on a bed of needles, every hair on their bodies standing on end, until finally they were forced to retreat, having failed to gain their aim.

They then told these things to Isarago, whose looks had lost their luster from her long and hopeless struggle with the barrier of mist enshrouding her, a mist that now was manifested as a cry that seemed to emanate from every part of her: "The very mention of her name I crave, but how the Princess must be suffering! And I—the wall of birth that separates beasts from humans in this world keeps me apart from her and any news of her, and I, like summer's moth in lantern-light, burn—as who would not?—from thoughts of her. I would rather die." Hardly had she uttered this when coughs and weeping overcame her, and she took to her bed with an illness that had been long in coming.

Physicians were desired to use all their arts of potted fire and bottled ice to turn back death, but their effects would not have earned them Dong Feng's apricot grove;[3] spiritual practitioners were desired to use their amulets of the Syncretic Realms[4] to dispel bale, but their Law was not wondrous enough to make dead trees bloom. Danger presented itself in her aspect day after day, month upon month; each night Yoshizane would visit her bedside and inquire personally about her suffering. "His Lordship is here," her attending women would say, at which Isarago, with the girls' assistance, would barely manage

---

3. *Shenxian zhuan* (J. *Shinsenden*), a Jin-era collection of stories about gods and immortals attrib-uted to Ge Hong, tells of Dong Feng, a physician who refused payment for his services, instead asking his patients to plant an apricot tree in his garden.

4. Tantric Buddhist ritual often involves the dual invocation of the Diamond and Womb Realms.

to raise herself and turn her wordless, importunate gaze on Yoshizane, who returned it in kind, sighing often as he noted how her eyelids drooped at the corners, how her cheekbones stood out in stark relief, how the tears coursed down them like dewdrops in gem'd threads—her countenance said she could not be counted on to be long in this world. "How are you feeling today? The physicians say that in four or five days, the worst will finally be past. Please, my lady, be patient and, above all, strong in your heart, as you convalesce."

He said this to comfort her, but she placed her hands on her knees and shook her head, replying, "The physicians may say what they will, but wasting away like this, I fear that I, like water that flows not backwards, am on a journey, and not a long one, from which there will be no return. And whose fault is it that I suffer so in sickness? I need not say—I am sure Your Lordship can guess. What to me are ageless medicines, th'immortalizing arts of Mount Penglai?[5] For after all, this body, in this life, is but a sad and empty locust husk—if I thought I might, as a last memory of my time in it, see Princess Fuse once again, that to me would be a Wizard's Pill, a prodigious formulation, than which there could be no more effective medicine. No doubt Your Lordship will take what I say as merely a woman's warped, shallow grumblings, but if you abandon the Princess, who made herself a sacrifice by accompanying your pet dog into foot-dragging mountain ways— if you consign her in your thoughts to what Your Lordship considers her unique design and singular karmic fate—then I call you a lord benevolent and righteous toward his people, but a father lacking in compassion toward his child. It may not be my place to say so, but is not Mount To, on which you have discarded your daughter that you might not break faith with your country, within the four districts over which you hold sway? If you would not be seen going there yourself month after month, year after year, to seek after her welfare, then why have you forbidden it to the wood-cutters, the charcoal-makers, the cowherds, and others who might in your stead have provided that which could comfort us in our desolation? A terrible, devilish place it may be—but the truth must be faced that you are her father and she is your daughter. If you would deign to decide that, by virtue of your authority as Lord Protector of the country, you would know how the Princess now fares and if she yet be on yonder mountain, how can it be any great feat for you to find it out? Will you not make up your mind to it, Your Lordship? This is all I would ask of you now. Be not hard of heart."

Yoshizane heard her reproofs, her apologies, her breathless and urgent importunings, in silence, and then raised his head to speak. "What you say is

---

5. Penglai (J. Hōrai) was a mountainous island of Daoist legend, the domain of those who had attained immortality through magical practices, elixirs, and the like.

true and reasonable. If we pursue the matter to its root, it is all because of a mistaken word on my part that we have been forced to abandon a child while retaining the shame of it; how much more must it gall me than you? I am not made of wood or stone: the tether of love is hard for me to sever, the bonds of attachment not easy to dissolve. It is because I fear that letting my heart have its head like a rampaging steed to chase the dog of passions would lead me to shirk or even spurn my public duties, throwing this land once again into chaos, that I have thrust away from me my feelings and forbidden myself my desires, and not looked back. I have forbidden that mountain even to the mountain-folk for the Princess's own sake, to hide her shame, as well as to let the people know that even foundering in my love for her I do not bend the law or overstep the statutes. However, your laments move me to pity. I will withdraw and turn the matter over in my head—I will let you know how the Princess fares. Set your heart at ease, I pray you."

Hearing his assent, Isarago said, "Then Your Lordship's heart has melted? And yet only illness and suffering finally procured this statement from you. The waiting will be hard—when shall I hear from you?"

He considered for a time, and then said, "It will be no easy feat, but for your sake I will hasten it: I shall have tidings for you, for good or ill, before long. For your heart's sake, I pray you, take tender care of yourself, and await my word." With these earnest words, Yoshizane went to leave; noticing this, the girls attending on Isarago accompanied him in front and behind for a considerable distance, to see him off.

At this time Yoshizane's son, Jirō Yoshinari of Awa, was in Mano Castle, where he had been stationed since the previous year mopping up the stragglers among Anzai Kagetsura's vassals and establishing the peace thereabout. But when he heard that his mother's illness had placed her in a dangerous state, he left the protection of the castle to the senior retainer Sugikura Kisonosuke Ujimoto and went to Takita, where he watched attentively over his mother, never stinting in filial piety. Yoshizane, impressed, secretly summoned Yoshinari before him and explained to him what had happened, omitting nothing. "I made a show of undertaking this charge that I might set Isarago's heart at least somewhat at ease, but whom can I send to look for the Princess when the example of Terutake has made everyone afraid of that mountain? And even if I had someone indomitable to send, it might mean destruction for him, as well as a weakening of my authority, if he failed to carry out the mission. In every respect, it is a vexing matter. What are your thoughts on the subject, sir?"

In response, Yoshinari inched forward on his knees and said, "Sir, I had already heard these things from the whisperings of the women, and while I too would find unsurpassed joy and happiness in learning how fares my elder

Captions:
Top right, in frame: Sadayuki gallops for Takita.
Bottom right: The reason for this picture is to be found on the reverse of sheet XVI.
Figure label: Horiuchi Sadayuki.
Note: "The reverse of sheet XVI" corresponds roughly to page 236 of the translation (where Sadayuki describes riding for Takita Castle).

駒を砥
そくり貞さ
ひき意さ
多瀧田
かむ
ふ赴
く

この画の解
第十六張の
背みえ

sister from whom I have been so long separated, these considerations Your Lordship mentions are not unfounded. You cannot simply choose someone from among your retainers and bid him do this. The right of it is that she is my only sister: I, Yoshinari, will undertake to do this thing, and I shall not fail to seek her out if I have to climb to the furthest reaches of Mount To. That dog may be possessed of a spirit that can raise clouds and call forth winds to confuse the minds of men, but we are told that the monstrous can never triumph over the virtuous.[6] With my mother's charity as my shield and my father's martial virtue as my armor, with bow and arrows passed down through our family for generations, I will go forth, and nothing shall stay me. Only command me, Your Lordship."

As he made this request in hurried words, he rubbed his fist in his palm, looking all in all like a man who wished to set forth as soon as ever he might, but Yoshizane raised a hand and shook his head as if to restrain him. "Your kind of courage comes only from the blood. Is it not said that the wise man approaches matters fearfully, and prefers strategy?[7] Stay close while your father and mother are alive, and above all eschew danger. I have not many children, after all, and you are the base on which the pillar of our house now rests: it would be exceedingly unfilial of you to rush recklessly into error. Then, too, my reluctance to go is not owing to my fear of a curse. Only two years have passed since the lid was shut on the Princess's jeweled comb-box— since she parted from us, vowing never again in this life to see us—and for us now to seek her out, as if we could not bear it, well, we could hardly hold up our heads were we to do such a thing, and it would only pain her further. This is not a matter for this night only: I will consider it further, and doubt-less we shall find some means of which we may avail ourselves. Make sure the women, too, know that this is not to pass beyond these walls." His father having vouchsafed him this explanation, Yoshinari could find nothing more to say; he made his obeisance and withdrew.

Yoshizane retired to his bedchamber straightaway, but he could not sleep for worry, feeling hemmed in on every side. When the dawn had come— and quickly did it come—he found himself standing alone on the near edge of the river gorge far up Mount To, not knowing how he had come to be there. Then a lone old man, in age surely closer to a hundred than eighty, approached Yoshizane from behind and spoke to him, saying, "Allow me to be Your Lordship's guide, now that it has pleased you to come so deep into the mountains. However, this river is difficult of crossing. On your right

---

6. A maxim from chapter 3 of *Shi ji*, previously quoted in Chapter VIII.
7. From *Lunyu*, chapter 7.

you will find a track that the wood-cutters used. Since all such work on this mountain was forbidden last year, the track has become so overgrown with thornbushes that the path could hardly be distinguished, and so your servant has broken branches and made wreaths of grass to mark it, that Your Lordship might not become lost on it even without my company. Carry out your purpose, Lordship, I pray you. Go around in that direction." He pointed with a finger as he explained the way. Yoshizane thought this mysterious, but when he went to ask the old man's name, he abruptly awoke.

"Have I been dreaming of the land of Huaxu,[8] as the story goes? A dream about what has been weighing on one's mind can hardly be trusted," he thought, refusing to let his mind dwell on it. Instead, he busied himself that morning with hearing and deciding the people's various petitions, so that by the time he retired to his inner chambers, it was nearly the hour of the ram.[9]

One of his close retainers came to him there through the corridor from the outer rooms, and, touching his forehead respectfully to the floor, said, "Horiuchi Kurando has arrived from Tōjō in response to Your Lordship's summons."

Yoshizane knitted his brow, cocked his head to one side, and said, "I never summoned Sadayuki. No doubt he came of his own accord, hearing that Isarago has been struck ill. Be that as it may, he comes at a good hour: I have something about which I would inquire of him. Bring him to me, and be quick about it." With that urging, Yoshizane sent away his attendants and settled down in eager anticipation of Sadayuki's arrival.

Now, Kurando Sadayuki had been at Tōjō for a long while, for so great was his dedication to cultivating the people with kindness that even after peace had been established in that district he observed the sage's teaching that one should reflect on one's deeds thrice daily,[10] and refused even the briefest of complacent rests from his many labors, with the result that he had not visited Takita since the previous year. Chance now having brought him here for an audience, Yoshizane invited him to take a seat close by his side, saying, "Have you been safe from harm, Kurando? I have not heard the slightest word of blame spoken about you since I sent you to Tōjō. There can be no greater joy than that which the workings of your loyal heart bring me. I take it that your present visit is rooted in your concern for Isarago's welfare—that you have heard how dangerously sick she is?"

---

8. Chapter 2 of *Liezi* tells how the Yellow Emperor visited the idyllic land of Huaxu in a dream; the name then became a by-word for dreaming.

9. Mid-afternoon.

10. Found in the first chapter of *Xunzi*.

To this query Sadayuki slowly raised his head and said: "It pleases my liege to say so, but it has been my office, since the day I received Your Lordship's command, to defend that castle; how could I have come here without your permission, as much as I might desire it privately in my heart? Now I have laid everything by and come to wait on Your Lordship in answer to your urgent summons—I trust that Your Lordship is but jesting when you say that you did not summon me."

Yoshizane replied before the other had finished speaking. "Hold, Kurando—what amusement should I find in summoning you all the way here in mere jest, as weighed down with sorrows as I am? But first, who delivered unto you my command—who enticed you here? Have you a witness? Let us be clear about this."

Sadayuki could not understand his lord's words, spoken in such wrath, but he answered without a shadow of perturbation. "I fear to contradict that which it pleases Your Lordship to say, and yet, if I may, I will recount the sequence of events that has brought me here. Yesterday an aged menial came to Tōjō, proclaiming himself a messenger from Your Lordship, but upon stepping out to see him, I failed to recognize him. Suspicious, I yet thought humbly to accept my liege's command, and the messenger spoke unto me thus:

"'My master having decided at his consort's request to go himself to Mount To in search of Her Ladyship Princess Fuse, preparations are proceeding apace—preparations that must needs be extraordinary, as this peak is well known as a high and treacherous one, notwithstanding that he may not undertake this expedition in grand style, but must make it rather a secret hunt, rendering it inconvenient for him to take along a numerous escort. Therefore it has pleased my master to settle upon you, milord, as his escort on this journey, and thus he has caused me to hasten here to summon you to him. As for myself, I am but a nameless servant who has lived near the caves at Susaki these many years: my master heard that I know that mountain well and saw fit to summon me into his service as a guide, and even as a bearer of this message, and so I rushed here on aged legs. Here is His Lordship's rescript.'

"It hung around his collar by a cord, which he then undid in order to hand it to me; I perused it, and saw that it agreed with what the old man had just said to me. Therefore I doubted him not a whit, but sent him back and then saddled my horse and rode for this place, not waiting for my attendants to follow—all through the night I kept to the road, but now that I have arrived at the manor and Your Lordship has received me, I find that nothing is as he said it would be. Well then, it would seem that the old man was a villain entire—and yet, here is Your Lordship's rescript, plain as day. May it please my liege to look at it."

Sadayuki took the letter from his bosom and returned it to his lord. Yoshizane opened it gingerly, then turned it and showed it to Sadayuki, saying, "What have you to say about this?"

Sadayuki was again astonished. "Indeed, the words I saw there yesterday are gone—they have changed to these eight characters in two lines: 'Even thus can a beast conceive a heart to know truth.' A prodigy, my lord, a prodigy!" Wonder rendered them speechless for what seemed like an age.

Then, abruptly, Yoshizane understood the meaning of the phrase; he rolled up the document and said, "Kurando, there is no lie in what you have spoken, and that is the mystery of it. The old man who gave you this letter yesterday, who claimed to be my messenger—what did he look like? How old did he appear to be? Tell me everything."

Sadayuki replied shamefacedly, "The old man looked to have lived over eighty years—perhaps even a hundred. His eyebrows were long, and resembled cotton flowers layered on his brow; his teeth were white, like a row of calabash seeds. In body he was thin, but sturdy—one look told that he was aged, yet in spite of that he seemed young. His eyes had a light that could pierce a man—authority without ferocity. He had, as the phrase goes, the Way in his countenance, wizardry in his bones."

Upon hearing this, Yoshizane clapped his hands once in a paroxysm of surprise and said: "Here is a prodigious tale, and what a resemblance it bears! It cannot be doubted that this was a vision of En the Ascetic, whose traces are left to us in the grotto at Susaki. I shall tell you all, from the beginning." And he told of how he had undertaken, for his consort's sake, to inquire after the welfare of Princess Fuse; of Yoshinari's courage and filiality; and of how, his mind occupied with these things, he had dreamed of an excursion to the farthest reaches of Mount To, where on a riverbank he had met an old man—he related the dream in every particular, and then added, "I had considered dreams things proceeding from the fatigue of the five organs,[11] not to be relied upon—but this old man you tell me of is strikingly similar in appearance to the one I saw in my dream.

"And these eight characters that seem to speak of past and future, 'even thus can a beast' and so forth—when Princess Fuse was an infant she was sickly and cried constantly, but through the efficacious intervention of En the Ascetic, he of the grotto at Susaki, she grew up in health. At that time she acquired a string of crystal prayer beads bearing the eight characters

---

11. The heart, liver, spleen, lungs, and kidneys.

for Benevolence, Righteousness, Propriety, Wisdom, Loyalty, Fidelity, Filial-ity, and Fraternity. Later, when, as we were suffering under siege, I spoke a word in error and yielded the Princess to Yatsufusa, those eight characters vanished, replaced by the phrase 'Even thus can a beast conceive a heart to know truth.' That led me to reflect thus: I named my daughter Princess Fuse because she was born during the season of the Three Concealments, near the end of the summer of the second year of Kakitsu; and yet subsequently she, a human, ended by following a dog—the name names the thing, and her fate was the inescapable effect of a karmic cause. But the reason she was thus fated, the reason she abandoned herself for her father's sake and her country's, was in order that the eight virtuous acts might not be lost from the world of men, and may it not be that her perseverance and faithfulness in the face of her suffering, guided by the principle that 'even thus can a beast,' will bear the fruit of good karma in the form of allowing her to enter into the highest level of true enlightenment? Cognizant of this, I dared not stay the Princess, but allowed her to do as she wished.

"Two years have passed, and quickly, since that day, during which time I neither made nor allowed to be made inquiry into her welfare—I even for-bade the wood-cutters and hunters to set foot on that mountain. But now, with Isarago's illness at a critical pass, it is hard to ignore her fervent requests, and I am unable to suppress a desire to know whether the Princess be safe—and the old man I saw in my dream differs not a whit from him who you say gave you this letter. These encounters that you and I were vouchsafed were transfigurations divine and unfathomable: visions of the Ascetic, beyond any doubt, meant to dispel my reservations and guide me into the depths of Mount To. The time has come for me to overturn my rule and bend my will, that I may be reunited with Princess Fuse: I will go, relying on the vision of the Ascetic, and you shall follow.

"Let this not be spoken of. People are simply fascinated by prodigies—if I am not mistaken in these visions and spiritual correspondences and I succeed in finding the Princess, then folk will chatter of prodigies and their virtuous circumspection toward gods and demons will be thrown into disarray, while if I go into that mountain and fail to find Princess Fuse, then folk will know that I foolishly believed a dream and chased a shadow, saw a counterfeit and fell captive to a whim—I shall become the whole world's laughing-stock. Now then, for our companions I will take, besides you, fourteen or fifteen beaters—we should choose men of few words, men of proven diligence. I make ready to leave on the morrow—I charge you prepare yourself."

His master laid these explanations and commands out before Sadayuki in such stirring fashion that Sadayuki offered no further debate, but quickly answered, "I knew, in a general way, of En the Ascetic's mystical intervention on behalf of milady the Princess when she was very small, and of the crystal prayer beads, but only Your Lordship, by virtue of your perspicacity, was able to connect those events with the present marvel. Leaving that aside, how great milady the Princess's perseverance in the cause of good, how advanced she is in the attainments of righteousness, to make such a marvel possible! The hammer's blow may fall amiss, but Your Lordship's judgment in this matter cannot be mistaken. It is well that you should go to the mountain—I pray you, make haste." With this, he repaired to the guard-house.

Yoshizane kept his intentions secret: he spoke to his consort of none of this. To his son and heir Yoshinari he whispered them, and Yoshinari's only reply was incessant noises of exclamation. He should have liked to travel to the mountain in his father's stead, but it was impossible, as the avatar's guidance was not given to him. Meanwhile, on this day his mother Isarago's illness seemed to strike deeper than before; Yoshinari was powerless to do anything but stay by her side and watch her in her time of danger. Yoshizane waited impatiently for the dawn, anxious that he might accomplish his task while Isarago yet lived. He put it forth that he was going to worship at the Ōyama Temple on the skirts of Mount To in Nagasa, and departed before it was yet light. As his train was to proceed in stealth, his escort consisted only of Horiuchi Kurando Sadayuki and some men beneath him, no more than twenty.

Yoshizane and Sadayuki rode abreast, and both so quickened their mounts' pace with brandished riding crops that at the end of a day's journey they were already on the slopes of Mount To. Coming to the side of the river gorge, Yoshizane found everything—the shapes of the rocks, the appearance of the trees—to be precisely as he had seen it that night in his dream. As an experiment he began searching among the thornbushes for a track, and some hundred yards away to the right he found it, leading into the brush, marked here and there by broken branches and wreaths of grass.

As master and man beheld these markings they were moved to exchange a glance that communicated the faith that in their hearts was growing into courage. Looking behind them they saw their companions far off in the distance—aside from Sadayuki, the escort was on foot, and none had yet overtaken them. After a time, a lone groom had climbed, panting, to where they were. Yoshizane saw him and said, "We have already received mystical intervention, and need no more companions. Have that man lead our horses back to the others, and then have everyone go back down to the foot of the mountain and await us there. Quickly, now!" Acknowledging his lord's command, Sadayuki called the man closer and, pointing to their steeds, which

Caption: Master and man have their doubts dispelled by a spirit missive.
Text on paper held by Sadayuki: Even thus can a beast conceive a heart to know truth.
Figure labels: Yoshizane [*right*]. Sadayuki [*center*]. Yoshinari [*left*].

如是畜生
發菩提心

had been tethered to a mountain arborvitae, relayed his liege's command and sent the man back to the mountain's base.

From that point the two of them, master and man, made their way forward along the path as it was marked, cocking their sedge hats against the mountain leeches, exchanging loud cries to warn each other against the vines that would rob them of their footing—they forced their way along that mountain track, tangled as a sheep's innards, now climbing, now descending, hardly knowing that they did so, and must have circled around by the head of the stream, for when they finally emerged from the darkness beneath the trees, they had come out on the far side of the river.

Chapter XII
In a grotto on Mount To, a beast conceives a
   heart to know truth;
Climbing upstream, a divine child speaks
   of future fate

In this impure world, this realm of lusts
and tormenting passions, who can escape the burning house of the five
dusts?[1] The Jetavana Monastery's bells resound with the impermanence of
all things, but those who prefer to glut themselves on lascivity hear them
with hatred and enmity, as they signal a parting at morning like shared silks
separating. The hue of the blossoms of the dual sal trees manifests the principle that the mighty must weaken, but those who idly prize perfumes resent
the passing gale and rain, and vow eternal spring.[2] Seen, the world is but a
dream; unseen, it is yet but a dream: either way an illusion. Though their
hearts may be set on earning a place in one of Maitreya's three gatherings
under the dragon-flower tree,[3] the average know not the straight road to

---

1. In Buddhist discourse, the five kinds of dust are the five fleshly diversions that work against
us: the temptations of sight, sound, smell, taste, and touch. The "burning house" image is drawn
from a famous parable in the third chapter of the Lotus Sutra, in which the world of temptation and
delusion is compared to a house on fire from which sentient beings must flee.

2. The Jetavana Monastery (J. Gion Shōja) and sal-tree imagery here echoes that found in the
famous opening passage of *Heike monogatari* (see also Chapter IX, note 6). The monastery was where
the Buddha delivered many of his teachings, while he entered nirvana beneath paired sal trees, the
blossoms of which turned white when he passed away.

3. Maitreya is a bodhisattva who, according to tradition, will appear in the world in the future.
It is said that he will achieve enlightenment beneath something called the Dragon Flower, and will
then propound his teachings in three assemblies.

detachment. But the enlightened, though they be in the tiger's cave or the dragon's pool, are filled with the pleasures of yogic realization. Even to such a degree had she forsaken the world, spending two springs and two autumns in the furthest reaches of Mount To.

Princess Fuse, daughter of Satomi Yoshizane, Major Assistant in the Governance Ministry, had, for the sake of her father and her country, that their people might not lose their faith in words, sacrificed herself and gone, companion to the dog Yatsufusa, along those mountain paths, and once that she like setting sun had hid herself, no more did anyone inquire after her. Between the torrent and the cliffs of clay there was a cave, and this she lined with sedge and made of it her sleeping chamber—there she passed the winters, and when spring had come, when birds at morning their companions call through eightfold mists she gazed at alpine blooms and thought of springtimes past, at home with dolls and mop-topped maidens[4] all paired off like ducks and drakes and plucking, this fine morning—ah! how dear its name!—mother-and-child grass;[5] the stone on which she sat, a diamond shape like rice-cakes on the third[6] (but made by whom?), on summer nights was faintly warm to touch in mossy robes it could not shed, but cool against her hems the wind that through the pines like comb through tangled hair did pass, and brought the evening show'rs to wash them—then, beneath those dripping, drying tresses insects sang of autumn's coming, and the brocade bed of many colors woven by the leaves of all the trees on all the valley-sides; this blanket now so brightly dyed would fade—this temporary state the hinds knew not who cried for mates in rain that never ceased until one unknown day it turned to snow that softened, as it fell, the corners sharp of stones she used for pillows: thus she had a view for ev'ry season of the trees, the spindle-trees and podocarps, in bloom but she was wretched as she knelt, beast-like, upon her mats, refused to go outside, but only thought about the life to come, the merit of her sutra-copying and chanting. Day by day she sadly grew accustomed to her sadness, felt it not as sadness. Calls of birds and cries of beasts, who nothing knew of th'floating world, she heard as long-sought boon companions' voices: thus exalted was she in her heart and mind.

---

4. The word used here suggests both the generic image of girls who wear their hair loose, and a specific reference (although written with different characters) to the Unai Maiden, who, pressed by two competing suitors between whom she could not decide, drowned herself in a river. This story forms the basis of the fourteenth-century noh play *Motomezuka*, attributed to Kan'ami.

5. *Gnaphalium affine*, one of the seven herbs traditionally gathered in spring.

6. In the Heian period, rice cakes were traditionally eaten by newlyweds on the third night after their nuptials.

When Yatsufusa, bearing Princess Fuse on his back, had first come onto this mountain, it was to a cave, located in a cramped space amidst the steep slopes and girded about by a broad river. The mouth of the cave looked as if it had been hewn out of the rock by hammer and chisel; to the northwest towered pines and oaks, forming, as it were, a hedgerow. The cave opened to the south, and its interior was not at all dark. Here the dog stopped, bending his forepaws and lowering himself to the ground; it dawning upon the Princess what he meant by this, she gently dismounted and looked about her.

It seemed as if someone had anciently lived there: there was a tattered old straw cushion in the cave, and a small pile of ashes, as from a fire that had been abandoned. "It would seem I am not the first to take refuge on this mountain, abandoning the world and by it abandoned." So saying to herself, she walked into the cave and sat down. The dog came to be beside her.

Upon leaving the manor at Takita she had taken the eight scrolls of the Lotus Sutra, some paper, and an inkstone, and these she had with her yet; she spent that night reading the sutra by the light of the moon, and before she knew it, the sky had grown light again. The crystal prayer beads vouchsafed her she had hung round her neck, and they hung there still. All she could rely on now was the protection of the gods and buddhas.

"I believe he understands human speech uncommonly well. If this beast snared me into accompanying him here into the depths of the mountains— or if, even, there should occur anything reckless, of a passionate nature— then I will finally forget my original vow: if he approaches my body with lascivious intent, he will be guilty of disobeying his mistress—and I will run him through with my sword." Calming her racing breast with this resolution, she stealthily loosed the the cord of the pouch in which she kept her blade, the sword she carried for self-defense; drawing the blade with her right hand, she continued her sutra-reading.

Perhaps Yatsufusa understood the look on her face, for he came no closer, but merely gazed at the Princess adoringly as he now lay down, now stood, with lolling tongue and dripping spittle—licked now his fur, now his nose, panting all the while. He spent the night watching her in this manner. In the morning, he abruptly arose and went down into the gully. When he returned, it was with berries and bracken root that he had gathered, that he now offered to Her Ladyship the Princess.

They brought every day to a close in this manner, and opened each new day likewise, without fail, until by the time a hundred days had passed, Yatsufusa had begun to cock an ear to the sound of the sutra as it was read, like one whose heart has been cleansed, and he ceased gazing at her. The Princess pondered this. "The 'Moon on the Peak' chapter of the *Tale of Flowering*

Fortunes[7] speaks of a cow-buddha at the Seki Temple, and do not old books make frequent mention of dogs rejoicing at the voice of scripture? The Buddha, in his compassion, hates neither defilement nor pollution. The birds that soar through the heavens, the beasts that run on the earth, the insects that crawl through the grass, even the scaly, shelly denizens of the waters—all alike shall achieve buddhahood. That this dog should forget his lusts and come to find pleasure in listening to the reading of the sutra, that he should thus become a companion in my return to essential Buddhahood, is entirely due to the power and authority of the sutra. Nevertheless there is no doubt that some darkling assistance from En the Ascetic, he who foretold my fate when I was very small, is also at work."

Touched with gratitude, she redoubled her dedication to her sutra-reading, never shirking, while in the mornings she rubbed together the prayer beads, praying to far Susaki; sometimes she copied out passages of praise from the sutra for her father and mother and sent them floating down the mountain current that flowed by the cave; in the springtime she picked flowers as offerings to the Buddha, while in the autumn she gazed at the setting moon, yearning aimlessly after the western heavens. She made her meals on the fruits of the mountain that fell at her knees, she took refuge from the autumn gales in the warmth of a brushwood fire, she staved off the cold at night with her thin robes. Steep the slopes of the mountain on which she walked, but she did not have to suffer resentment over picking bracken on Mount Shouyang;[8] the plum bloomed late by the stony portal of the cave, but she did not have to suffer learning the Hun language as a bride.[9] The Princess was not yet twenty, and her countenance, which had always been such as to put jewels to shame, still retained the beauty of the dream in which the goddess of Wu Mountain transformed herself into a cloud, the elegance that Komachi of the Ono in song had likened unto flowers.[10] Raised beneath metal roofs and behind blinds, such had indeed been proper for her in the past; but

---

7. *Eiga monogatari*, an eleventh-twelfth century account of the life of Fujiwara no Michinaga. Chapter 25 tells of how the temple of Sekidera on Mount Ōsaka had a black cow that was used as a beast of burden until one day a local resident learned in a dream that the cow was a manifestation of the Buddha. Thereafter the animal was treated with reverence, and people came from far and wide to see it.

8. Brothers Bo Yi and Shu Qi went to serve the state of Zhou, but when the new ruler of Zhou proved to be bent on conquest, they went into voluntary exile on Mount Shouyang. They lived on bracken until it was pointed out to them that even the bracken belonged to Zhou, after which point they starved themselves to death. The story is related in chapter 61 of *Shi ji*.

9. A reference to Zhaojun, concubine of Emperor Yuan (see Chapter X, note 4).

10. Legend has it that the goddess of Wu Mountain transformed herself into a cloud to visit King Huai of Chu in dreams. Ono no Komachi (ca. 825–ca. 900) was a famous *waka* poet, one of whose most famous poems compares her fading beauty to that of a flower: *hana no iro wa / utsurinikeri na /*

even now, after so long living alone in the mountains, her skin, though clad in raiment stained and torn, was whiter than any lingering snow, and her black locks, though untouched by comb, were more lustrous and fragrant than any flower in spring. Her already slender waist grew thinner, until she resembled a willow unable to stand against the wind; her jewel-like fingers grew thinner, until they resembled bamboo shoots struggling through thorns. Her lineage was that of a daughter in the main line of the Satomi clan, lords of Awa; in the quality of her heart she could hold her head up in the company of Princess Chūjō, daughter of Yokohagi.[11] She had inherited her honored father's skill in handwriting and reading books, and was of herself a quick student of righteous principles; she had learned needlework and music from her mother, and she could blow a wondrous air. Was it because this maiden's happy endowments had aroused the marriage god's jealousy that he had given her to Yatsufusa, so utterly different from her, that she might end her days in wretchedness? It pains me to write in any more detail of this—my brush drags—and I leave you, O Reader, to imagine her situation.

The year drew to a close, and then one day, when the short grasses on the riverbank had begun to send forth shoots and the trees in the valley had begun to display buds of green, Princess Fuse went out to rinse her inkstone at a little spring in the rocks. She bent to scoop up some water at a pool fed by the spring, and as she did so she happened to see her reflection on the water. Her body, in the reflection, was that of a human, but lo, her head was that of a dog. This was unexpected—she could not bear it—with a cry she fell back at a run. Then, when she stepped up and looked at the water again, the image she saw there was her own, unchanged in any aspect.

"It must have been but the confusion of my heart. And yet—what a shock!" Turning the incident over in her mind as she recited the name of the Buddha in her heart, she set about her day's sutra-copying; and yet there was raging disorder in her breast, and her mood was no better the following day. From about this time her menses ceased, and as the days and months piled up, her belly began to swell unbearably. "Might this be what they call bloating? Ah, that I might die!"

She thought thus, but to no avail: spring ended, summer passed away, and melancholy autumn came. "Now that I think of it, 'twas a year ago this

itazura ni/waga mi yo ni furu/nagameseshi ma ni (The flower's hue/has faded;/vainly/I have gazed too long/at rain falling on the world).

11. Princess Chūjō was a legendary figure, daughter of Fujiwara Toyonari (also known as the Yokohagi Minister). Toyonari and his wife were childless until they prayed at the Hase Temple. Chūjō's mother subsequently died, and Chūjō suffered at the hands of her stepmother, until ultimately she became a nun at the temple of Taima and wove a mandala from lotus fibers.

month that I left Takita Manor. What truly pains me, beyond any comparison with my bodily illness, is my mother's condition—the look on her face as she tearfully watched me leave is with me ever, something I cannot forget no matter how I try. Perhaps it is the same with her. Perhaps she ails, she suffers, she wastes away, thinking continually of me, who shall not return. And my lord sire, my brother Yoshinari—oh, how I miss them! We are not mountain pheasants, cock and hen, to spend our nights divided by a peak;[12] yet just like them, my parents and brother and I, while in the selfsame land and district, live in distant, sundered places, out of sight each of the other, knowing bitter pangs of parting, separation's sufferings, the cruelty of this short mayfly life." With thoughts like these her breast did overflow, and speak them hundredfold she would; instead she pressed her forehead 'gainst the rock and wept, a single helpless whimper all she voiced.

After a time, she wiped her eyes and said, "Ah, but I have erred in my foolish complaints. The Buddha taught that 'to forget one's debt of gratitude and enter into a state of transcendance is to truly repay one's debt of gratitude,'[13] and shall not the pain of parting from loved ones be changed to the joy of entering into the one true and necessary gate? All of this is for my parents' sake; to think of them longingly is deeply sinful. O forgive me, all ye buddhas of the three worlds!"

Then, "Yatsufusa went out a while ago, and has not returned—has he been unable to forage anything? When he goes out to find food for me, he never returns until he has something. Have I been lax in my service to the Buddha? 'Tis the time when the dew will dampen me, but wildflowers are scarce this deep in the mountains—I will go look for some to offer up." Thus muttering to herself, she hoisted herself up—her body was quite heavy now—and made her way along the stream to where chrysanthemums among the tangle grew—she picked them—several hundred yards ahead she pressed, as dewdrops drenched her garment's hem.

Then faintly she heard, off to the northwest among the roots of the mountains in their serried ranks, the sound of a flute. Princess Fuse pricked up her ears. "Strange—no wood-cutters come here, no mountain folk live here. In all the time since I came to this mountain, I have never met another person—and yet now, all unexpected, the sound of a flute reaches me. Has some herbreaper wandered here lost? Or is this the glamor of some mountain demonspirit, set as obstacle to test my heart's dedication to the Way? Either way,

---

12. Poetic tradition held that male and female *yamadori* (mountain pheasant) slept on different sides of mountaintops.

13. A slightly abridged version (lacuna supplied in the translation) of a phrase found in the seventh-century Buddhist text *Fayuan zhulin* (J. *Hōon jurin*).

I have already abandoned hope for myself—why then should I fear this, flee, or hide? I will have a look," she said, and set off toward the sound.

The music rang ever clearer as she drew closer, until a look revealed a reaper-boy of twelve or thirteen, sickle and digging-spike thrust through his belt, a pair of baskets slung from his saddle, and a flute in his hands, sitting astride a black ox that was plodding through the forest—the boy looked at Princess Fuse from the corner of his eye, but never paused in his sylvan melody as he drove the ox into the stream as if to cross it. Princess Fuse hastily called to him—"Hallo there!"—and then asked, "What village do you come from, child? You seem to know your way, although I cannot understand how you have come alone to these deep mountain paths, from which all sign of human passage has long since disappeared. Know you me?"

The boy flashed her a broad grin and tucked the flute away gently into his collar. "How could I not recognize you? 'Tis you who do not know me. Is there anything that will dispel your doubts save telling you all about myself and the others? Nay. This mountain was never traversed by any but the wood-cutters and hunters and the rare traveler, but His Lordship your father, the Minister of the Court Yoshizane, has not allowed anyone onto this mountain since last year, reckoning that the shame should be bright were you to be seen by another. This is why all sign of human passage has long since disappeared. Notwithstanding this, Her Ladyship your mother misses you greatly, Princess, and has several times sent her housemaids and nurses on secret missions to inquire after your well-being. However: Amasaki Jūrō, at his liege's command, escorted you here in secret, at which time he drowned to death in this very mountain stream. Because of this, none have since dared to cross it and every mission has been in vain, turned back at the far shore there, never learning how you fare. This is all a matter of Heaven's will and timing.

"Now I will tell you of myself. I am no simple scyther of grasses for cattle. I have a teacher who lives sometimes at the foot of this mountain, and sometimes at Susaki. How many hundreds of years old he is I know not. He is always treating people's illnesses, or telling fortunes for money—by this he makes his living. If he gives you medicine, you shall be spared death, preserved in life, and healed of all that ails you. When he takes up the yarrow stalks he can guess that which has not yet come to pass, and know everything about that which has already been. If he predicts a hundred things, not a one of them will fail to come true. I have come here today at my teacher's behest, to gather medicinal herbs. Truly, while human traffic is presently forbidden on this mountain, before very long those who made their livings on it will be allowed to do so again, as of old. My teacher knows this, which is why he has sent me for the medicine."

Caption: Seeking flowers and grasses, Princess Fuse meets a divine child.
Figure: Princess Fuse.

伏姫

Princess Fuse sighed upon hearing this. "Truly my parents' charity shines on me like the moon and sun, leaving nothing touched by shadow: they have effected these things not knowing how I thrive here, keeping myself pure. And yet how deep am I in sin, if for my sake Amasaki Terutake drowned, and the wood-cutters have lost their means of livelihood, and the travelers have been detained. O, forgive me!" she started, then began to weep.

After a time, she turned back to the boy and said, "You say you serve a great physician—then is it not likely that you, too, have an eye for people's maladies, beyond your years? I have a matter about which I would inquire of you. I have not had my menses since the spring, and I feel a terrible pain in my breast, while month by month my body grows heavier. Tell me, I pray you, what sickness this be."

In response, the boy smiled at her and said, "A woman's menstruation lapses, then a month or two later she feels discomfort in the chest, often accompanied by a liking for tart things: this is what is commonly known as morning sickness. At three or four months, the belly has already grown big, and at five months the child has begun making slight movements. Women know all these things: there is no need to ask a physician about them. Milady, you are pregnant, and have been for some five or six months. What doubt can there be?"

Princess Fuse hardly heard him out before saying, "How mature your words! However, I have no mate, and since coming to this mountain a year ago this month, I have seen no other person. I spend all my energies intoning the Buddha's name and reading the sutras, and have done nothing else, so how could I be with child? Truly, you jest." She could not restrain herself—a little laugh escaped her.

The boy returned her gaze, and her laugh, with scorn: "How can you say you have no husband? What of the one your parents gave you—Yatsufusa?"

A change came over the Princess's countenance at this rebuke. "You know only the beginning—you know nothing of what came after. It is true that, for a certain reason, I came—my parents could not stay me—into this mountain fastness, wretched, with our pet dog, and here I have spent the days and months since. But due to the protection of the sutras, I have, happily, remained unsullied—and he, too, has taken joy only in the hearing of the sutras. Though there be no proof, I am pure and chaste in body, as the gods themselves will show—why should I have become gravid by Yatsufusa, who belongs to another species? Even to hear of such a thing is abhorrent, filthy! And to have it said to me by a child, for no reason—how appalling!"

She wept for anger, but the boy merely laughed the harder. "I have made careful observations, and have grounds for detailed knowledge. It is you, Your Ladyship, who know the first thing but have not yet understood the second that follows. Allow me, then, to solve your puzzlement. The dark wonder of the mutual affinities between disparate classes of things is that which cannot be compassed by ordinary wisdom. Take fire: it is produced by stone and metal. And yet a stick of cypress or the like, brought together with another of its kind, will also produce a flame. Moreover, the excrement of pigeons, if much is accumulated over the course of many years, will also produce fire. Are these not truly examples of reason beyond reason? Unless there be mutual affinity of yin and yang between things, they cannot produce offspring. And yet vegetation is without passions—we speak of male and female pine and bamboo, but they propagate quite without copulation. To them we might add the crane, who lives a thousand years without engaging in intercourse, even though it is often observed to be pregnant. The gentleman Autumn takes no wife, but engages in spiritual exchange; the lady Spring is not taken to wife, but bears child. Have you not heard of the consort of the King of Chu in China, whom it pleased to be ever leaning against an iron pillar, and who at length gave birth to a ball of iron, from which were made two swords, male and female?[14] Then in our land there was the peasant woman of Ōmi, who took delight in having pressure applied to areas that bothered her, and who in the end gave birth to an arm. The incident has left its traces in the name of her village: Teharami—Great-with-Arm.[15]

"All of these are the effects of mutual affinity between disparate classes of things, although none can be deduced by reasoning upon what appears to the eye. What doubt can there be that it is the same thing that has caused Your Ladyship's womb to be filled? Indeed, Your Ladyship's body has not been violated, nor does Yatsufusa now have lusts. And yet you did yield yourself to him, when you accompanied him here to the mountain—and when he thus took you, he thought of you in his heart as his wife. It is because of the love he bears for you that he found joy in listening to you read the sutras—and when Your Ladyship saw him thus submit, you had compassion for him, as your equal. Your feelings were already in mutual affinity. Yea, though you knew not one another, how could you not become great with child?

"Reading the signs carefully, I say that you carry octuplets. And yet this is a feeling, not reality—your children grow from the intermingling of nothingness, and so they have no form. They will be born here without taking form, and after they are born they will be born again. This is the working of a karmic cause, but also the effect of good works.

---

14. This story is found in chapter 13 of *Taiheiki*, where it is given as the origin story of the legendary swords Gan Jiang and Mo Ye (named after the husband and wife swordsmiths who forged them).

15. This legend is recorded in the collection *Kōeki zokusetsu ben* (1717–1727), by Izawa Banryō.

"What cause? Take Yatsufusa—in his previous incarnation he was a woman of perverse nature. Her resentment toward your father, the Minister of the Court Yoshizane, was such that her vengeful spirit became a dog in order to bring shame to Your Ladyship and your father: this is the karmic cause. What of effects? Yatsufusa, while taking possession of you, never violated you; instead, through the merit you acquired by chanting the Lotus Sutra, the resentment was dispersed and he grew a heart to know truth, like yours, and because of this, he has left you these eight children. Their number comes, in other words, from Yatsufusa's name, and also from the number of volumes in the Lotus Sutra.

"Ten thousand soldiers are easily come by; a single general is not. Should these children each prove to excel in wisdom and courage, in loyalty, fidelity, and integrity, should they aid the Satomi and cause their authority to shine over the eight provinces, it shall all be as a gift for you, for who shall say that the mother of such was not great in her own right? This, then, is the effect of good works. Yea, good fortune and ill are like a rope intertwined. Who can look at present ill fortune and know to what future good it will turn? The world's scorn comes from its likes and dislikes; pollution comes from purity. Such slander is not worth the hating of it; shame must simply be endured. Nothing is more visible than that which is hidden;[16] what is concealed must surely emerge. This is only natural.

"Dogs spend sixty days in the womb, while humans spend ten months—a difference between humans and beasts. Combining the two in evaluating the present case, I say that Your Ladyship, who has been pregnant for six months, will give birth this month. I know not when it will be, but at that time you will see your father and another man, your husband. Of what is beyond that, what has yet to come to pass, yet to be ordained, I cannot speak in any greater detail, for fear of revealing the workings of Heaven. Another man will come after me, and he shall know of the children. I leave you now. It was foolish of me to speak for so long on a short autumn day. Sooth, my master awaits me, and I must to him."

With that, the boy the ox's nose pulled round, directing him into the mountain stream to cross it—when the Princess looked again by th'light of th'jewelled katsura tree of the moon, a close mist had risen in his wake, obscuring from her sight where he had gone.

End of Book I of Volume II of the Lives of the Eight Dog Warriors of the Satomi

---

16. From the Confucian classic *Zhongyong* (J. *Chūyō*), commonly known as *The Doctrine of the Mean*.

The Lives of the Eight Dogs of the Satomi of Southern Fusa

Volume II, Book II

Assembled by the Master of the Crooked Pavilion in the Eastern Capital

Chapter XIII
The Princess leaves a letter, expounding her karmic causes and effects;
Clouds and mists are cleared, and the mysterious first gives way

When Princess Fuse had received this quite unlooked-for explanation and discourse from that so wondrous child, she wakened from a lightless sleep—his words, which seemed as dreams to her, no longer had she room to doubt—the tears rained from her eyes and damped the robes she used as pillow—would that she could wring them out, as sorrow wrung her innards now. She sank in grief. And yet the Princess's heart stood stronger, as it ever did, than most—was, as it were, a manly heart, and so with force she quieted her raging breast, she brushed aside the ebon hair that hid her face, she wiped her streaming eyes and said:

"Alas, I have no way to know the weight of sin I bear from former lives, how light it be or heavy, but upon me now it all at last has come as my reward—but O! th'obsessive hate of her who has thus brought me low, to know such horrid thoughts! Notwithstanding that, now that I hear of my father shouldering such a curse, I would sink to the depths of Hell for lives to come and more lives after them, and would not hold it something to regret, if I could help him. What shames me, though, what brings me suffering—for my parents, and for others—is that, despite this spotless heart of mine, I should have somehow taken this beast's seed, his spirit, as I bear eight children—his!—within my body—how can such thing be?—when ever since the day I came unto this place, parting the thickets of the crane's woods and gazing at the eagle's peaks above,[1] to sutra-chanting have I given my whole heart and mind in effort unstinting, while Buddhas condescend to save me not and gods their honorable aid withhold—if it be true that I am now with child then even if we never shared bed-chamber, where is the proof by which to clear my name? This shame, not mine alone but parents' too, shall not for generations nine[2] be wiped away—as pure as snow I nevermore shall be, but always as a beast's wife shall be known. Living shame and dying resentment: to what may they be likened or compared? I only wish that I, in Takita, while knowing less of this than a drop of dew that rests on th'tip of a hare's hair, had killed that dog, and that I had died along with him. I had a chance to die and I died not—shall this, too, find its cause in karma? Too great a chain of karmic cause is this to be found in any of the writings the Buddha deigned expound as his expert expedient means. Yea, though the birth of these children redound unto my family's happiness, increase the glory of our house, can that replace the shame unparalleled I bear? The anguish!" Thus cried she in upraised voice as if speaking to one beside her, unable from her thoughts to drive this shame, her clever mind, wise heart, in disarray, in tangles, like the silvergrass and brush bamboo at foot of which she now collapsed, unable any longer to endure.

When the autumn sunlight in peace had passed its peak and the heat of midday was but a lingering memory, when the mountain ravens soared crying past the peak on their way to the bank to bathe in the stream, Princess Fuse raised her head with a start and, looking up at them, said:

"Lo, there is no one here but me. I have truly entered the Way of Beasts—I have been chased up a road through mountains of swords piercing me through into the Avīci Hell[3] I have been consigned to the world to come. That child, though—mysterious was he. He knew all about the way

---

1. Both of these images have Buddhist overtones. "Crane's woods" refers to the sal trees beneath which the Buddha died, conventionally described as being white as cranes, while "eagle's peaks" suggests Holy Eagle Peak (also known as Vulture Peak), a spot where the Buddha delivered many teachings.

2. Possibly a nod to the historical Satomi of Awa, who lasted for nine generations before the final Satomi lord, Tadayoshi, died without an heir in 1622, leading the Tokugawa shogunate to confiscate their lands.

3. The eighth and lowest of the Buddhist hells. A mountain of swords is a common feature of descriptions of hell.

I have trodden, and that which I am to tread, as if he had seen them with the eyes of Heaven. Furthermore, how he spoke—'twas as fresh and free from hesitation as this mountain torrent as it rushes between the rocks; and he talked of ill fortune and good, blessing and catastrophe, as if indicating something in the palm of his hand. Even the 'pointing priests'[4] and bent-backed crones of yore would have been hard pressed to say as much. Who, if it be not a god, could have done it? I have heard of no centuries-old physician in Awa, and can therefore conceive of no way a divine child could be in the service of one. No, it was simply a ruse, telling me that he was a physician's pupil out gathering medicines. He has no fixed abode, he said, being sometimes at the foot of this mountain, and other times in Susaki, which makes me wonder: Was this, then, perhaps a vision of En the Ascetic? Such benefice have I received before. Scant memory have I of it, as I was very small, but proof of it I have—have never let it leave my side—the beads of prayer he gave me then—nor have I yet ever neglected my orisons. But though he show me marvels here again, oh, what can gods and buddhas do against these karmic causes inescapable? And yet, the sadness of the common herd makes it hard to be enlightened, and easy to become lost. What can it mean that these eight children I bear are to be born here without taking form, and that after they are born they shall be born again? Or that when I give birth I will see my father and another man, my husband—this, too, I cannot understand. Even tentatively, I have never been betrothed to any man. But even should that not come to pass, if yet my father should come here in search of me, chagrin alone would be my lot. O, rather than have my family see me with child, my shame burning bright, I would commend my body to this river, let its current bear my bones away, that water thus in death might hide my shame. Yes, let it be so!" She asked herself and answered herself back, and finally, making up her mind, there on the flattened grass she raised herself to kneel, and then she stood.

She went to the water's edge. "And yet," she said, "to now make flotsam of myself would be to gravely sin, as if to disregard Her Ladyship my mother's care for me in daily sending housemaids, messengers, unto this river's farther bank. If I but leave for her a note, then perhaps, somehow, she will find it possible to leave me to my karma. And if, with no one here to see it writ, my letter rot, then let it rot: I shall at least extend my brush to write and thus

---

4. The "pointing priests" (*sasu no miko*) were occultists mentioned in the *Genpei jōsuiki*, a medieval variant text of *Heike monogatari*.

extend my life a little while. Now to it," she muttered to herself, and stooped, her broken, fallen blossoms 'gain to gather, petals on the edge of scattering, fragile as her equilibrium of heart and foot as gingerly she walked back to her cave.

Yatsufusa was there waiting for her with wild yams and fruits on the branch, which he had plucked with his mouth and brought back for her. Now, seeing that she had returned, he scampered up to greet her, playing in her trailing hems, now leaping backwards, now standing in her path, his tail a-wag, his nose all sniffs and snuffles, all as if to welcome Princess Fuse to her home, to bid her take refreshment and to rest.

The Princess found it abhorrent, an ordeal, even to look at him, and refused to favor him with a word, but took her seat at the stone chamber's edge. Then, on her inkstone grinding out some ink, she took what little paper yet remained, smoothed out the wrinkles, and began to write of her condition and her vision of the Ascetic's avatar, in phrases clipped and dutiful and sad.

At that time of times the water thundered in its rocky bed such as to stir up even the Grandee of the Three Lineages' resentment and sympathy,[5] while the wind sang in the pines on the peak such as to show Prince Arima's transience.[6] "From times of yore down to the present day, how many of the clever and the foolish, the straight and the crooked, have ended miserable lives and left exposed their corpses in just such hollows, along just such wilderness tracks, as this? And how innumerable the mates, the children, they left behind? And yet, be that as it may, when my mother is told that I am lost, my body unrecovered, taken by a fate the like of which has seldom been heard of, I fear that she will perish as she hears of it. If it be not so already, certainly then she will have cause for weeping without end—and I, who shall have given it to her, shall have committed against filial duty a sin that can never be atoned for. How oft I think to put a stop to this—but love and duty's tethers make it hard. Forgive me!" were the words she wished to say, but deep into her heart they sank, like roots of pine along which runs the dew like tears in droplets running down her sleeves to end as finally a mighty river deep and unstemmed as her sorrows or the brush by which they were committed to her note.

---

5. Qu Yuan (ca. 343–277 BCE) was a poet who held this position in the Chu court until he was exiled due to slander. Utimately he drowned himself in protest. His life is recounted in chapter 84 of *Shi ji*. His poem *Li sao* (J. *Risō*), expressing his bitterness in exile, is one of the most famous ancient Chinese poems.

6. An imperial prince (640–658) executed for treason. *Man'yōshū* #141, attributed to him on his journey to his place of execution, mentions pines.

She read it over, rolled it up, and sighed. "How uselessly I let my thoughts run on. How can I cut through the bonds of tormenting passions without recourse to the sword of Amitābha in the West? The only thing to do upon departing for the Yellow Springs, that darkling land, is to invoke his Name."

At once she turned her mind to it. She picked up the chrysanthemums she had gathered and brought back with her, wetted them with pure water, and with great ceremony placed them as offerings to the Buddha. Then she took in hand the prayer beads that ever hung around her neck and began to rub them together—but they did not make the sound they always made. "'Tis strange," she thought, and held them up this way and that to examine them. When she did so she saw that the eight characters that read, "Even thus can a beast conceive a heart to know truth," that had appeared upon the counting-beads[7] had disappeared without a trace, and had been replaced, unbenownst to her, with the eight characters for Benevolence, Righteousness, Propriety, Wisdom, Loyalty, Fidelity, Filiality, and Fraternity; they could be read quite distinctly.

Seeing this marvel, Princess Fuse, far from having her doubts dispelled, found herself deep in wonder. "In the beginning these beads bore the characters for Benevolence, Righteousness, Propriety, Wisdom, and the rest. Then when I came to the mountains accompanied by Yatsufusa, they were transformed to the eight characters in the saying, 'Even thus can a beast.' In the event, Yatsufusa did indeed, in this place, conceive a heart to know truth, to desire enlightenment, in accordance with the phrase. For this reason, the writing pertaining to beasts and all that walk on four legs has disappeared, restored to that which shews the eight virtuous acts of the Way of Humanity—but how unfathomable the expedient means of the avatar! How can it be told with a woman's shallow wisdom? Were I to judge by appearances, I should say that in receiving the dog's spirit and entering my present special condition, I have in store for me an unnatural death, and one that resembles in no small measure the torments of the Way of the Beasts. Meanwhile, through the potency of the Law, even Yatsufusa—a dog—has entered into the way of enlightenment.

---

7. Curiously, given the importance of this string of beads, the reader does not get a full description of it until this chapter. Upon the string's introduction in Chapter VIII, only the eight beads bearing the characters for the eight virtues are mentioned, so the reader might naturally assume that it is a string of only eight beads. Here, we learn that those eight beads are "counting beads" (*kazutori no tama*), place markers in a longer string of beads to help the devotee keep track of how many prayers or recitations have been performed. Buddhist prayer bead strings can come in a variety of sizes, but the standard contains one hundred and eight beads, one for each of the defilements to which people are subject. Later in this chapter we learn that Princess Fuse's string does indeed contain one hundred and eight beads. One hundred and eight is also, of course, the number of heroes in *The Water Margin* (*Shuihu zhuan;* J. *Suikoden*), the Ming vernacular novel that was Bakin's great model for *Eight Dogs*.

Is this a sign, then, that in the life to come he shall be reborn into the Way of Humanity, with its eight virtuous acts available to him? In which case, should I kill Yatsufusa, too, with my own hand, to deliver him from the sufferings of beasthood? No—no—there would be no benevolence in that. He defeated his lord's arch-enemy: he has shown himself the possessor of unsurpassed loyalty. Yea, and for the past year on this mountain he has staved off starvation for me—I owe him a deep debt for his nurturing. I could not bear to hasten with my blade his death—'twould be too pitiless an act, yea, even though in the life to come he be born a human, child of some house of wealth and nobility. Rather, I shall proclaim these things to him without adornment, and leave it to him whether to live or to die.

"Well then," she said, draping the prayer beads over her left hand and facing the dog, who sat gazing at her, forelegs propped against her. "Now then, Yatsufusa, listen well to what I say. There are in this world two who are unhappy above all others; there are in this world two who are happy above all others, as well. They are me and thee. I, the daughter of the lord of the country, placed great weight on righteousness, and because of it have become a beast's companion: this is my unhappiness. Nevertheless, I have been neither defiled nor violated, but rather, as chance would have it, have escaped the world and entered in by the gate of self-realization, craving that the Three Treasures[8] might be vouchsafed me, and my yearning has been fulfilled, so that this day I pass from this life as I have long desired to: this is my happiness. You, though but a beast, have accrued great merit in the service of your country, even unto the obtaining of the daughter of the lord of the land. The Ways of beasts and humans being different, you were unable to satisfy your lusts, but by hearing the marvelous Law in all its majesty, you were able to conceive a heart to know truth: this is your happiness. And yet, without changing the form of your life, you will be unable to escape the sufferings of the four-footed; alive, you will not increase in wisdom, and dead, you will simply be skinned: this is your unhappiness.

"You are seven or eight years old—hardly what one would call young for a dog or a horse. If you now vainly cling to life, if you watch me die and then go back to your home with the Satomi, you will be bitten and lashed—punishments will be laid immediately upon you. And even if you stay on this mountain, who, after today, shall read for you the sutra? With the voice of scripture no longer resounding in your ears, you will eventually lose your truth-knowing heart. If, though, you simply quit this life and take your joy in death, placing your hopes for the Way of Humanity in the karma you have

---

8. The Buddha, his teachings, and his priesthood; here used as a metonym for enlightenment.

earned, shall you not in the life to come be reborn as a human? Thus, if you understand this principle, O let us cast our bodies into that same current, reach together the far shore. Still, the time is not yet ripe. I find that I, too, yet harbor regret to think that I might leave this floating world, and so I shall the sutra chant awhile, and thus restore my heart to its former quietude. You should listen, and, when my reading draws unto its end, should rise and go out to the water's edge—or else, if recklessly you still stint at abandoning your life, grow old and die in wilderness or town. If you do so, however, you shall never achieve rebirth as a human. Use all your discrimination."

Thus in all earnestness did the Princess strive to awaken Yatsufusa to his situation. Yatsufusa, for his part, now hung his head as if in sorrow, now wagged his tail as if in joy, now seemed as if moved to tears. Princess Fuse watched his manner closely, and thought to herself, "Truly has this dog attained salvation. The second coming of a vengeful spirit he may be, but now that he has achieved Buddhahood, that spirit shall no longer be an obstacle to us—to my younger brother Yoshinari or to any of his descendants, even unto the seventh generation, so distant as to have hardly heard of him. I can rest at ease." She picked up the note she was to leave, and the scroll containing the Devadatta chapter,[9] and took a few steps outside the cave. Her intent was to chant the sutra, and when she had finished, to roll her testament up in the scroll and place it in the grotto. To this end she seated herself in front of a flat-topped rock suitable for use as a desk, pressed the scroll to her forehead in prayerful meditation, and then quickly began to read. Yatsufusa pricked up his ears and listened even more attentively than usual.

Now, the Devadatta chapter is in the fifth volume of the Sutra of the Lotus of the Wondrous Law.[10] It is a text that expounds upon how the daughter of Sagara the Dragon King, possessing great wisdom at the age of eight, meditated deeply and attained comprehension of the Law in its entirety and thus obtained the Buddha's truth. Women are unclean and defiled: by nature they are not fit vessels for the Law: and they are subject to the Five Obstacles.[11] Therefore, for them, Buddhahood is extremely difficult to attain—and yet the eight-year-old dragon-girl had already obtained the Buddha's supreme

9. The twelfth chapter of the Lotus Sutra, named for the Buddha's assurance therein that even such an evildoer as Devadatta (an erstwhile disciple turned foe) can be enlightened.

10. The full name of the Lotus Sutra is *Myōhō renge kyō* (Ch. *Miaofa lianhua jing*; Skt. *Saddharmapuṇḍarīka Sūtra*).

11. As enumerated in the Lotus Sutra itself, these are the inability to be reborn as a Buddha or any of four other categories of sagely being. The translation here and in the next paragraph borrows freely but inconsistently from Burton Watson's translation in *The Lotus Sutra* (New York: Columbia University Press, 1993), 187–89.

Caption: The efficacious virtue of the wondrous sutra parts the clouds of tormenting passions.
Figures: Kanamari Daisuke [*right*]. Tamazusa [*center*]. Great Bodhisattva Divine Transfiguration [*left*].
Note: The spirit of Tamazusa, next to the transfigured En the Ascetic, is surrounded by what are usually taken to be lotus petals. These petals are seen more clearly in the later Bunkeidō version of the illustration. The gray shading in the Sanseidō version (seen here) was created using a second block, and Tamazusa and the lotus petals, along with the rays emanating from En, were depicted as negative space on this second block. The Bunkeidō version (seen on the following pages) clearly uses a new second block, resulting in several obvious differences from the original version of the illustration. It should be noted that the text does not describe Daisuke experiencing a vision of this nature.

妙経乃
くわげぎ
切く煩ぎ
の徳を
悩んん
の雲を
霧を披ひ
をむ

金はり大をけ

truth. She was the first of womankind to attain Buddhahood. It was for this reason that Princess Fuse, nearing the end of her life, read the Devadatta chapter for her own sake and the dog's. This was, she thought, her time of times, and so she lifted up her voice—it carried, clear, never flagging, like lotus-thread[12] unreeling or a rushing spring. The wind in the pines on the peak harmonized with her, the echoes in the valley responded to her calls. For audience she had the gathered stones. It must have been like this in days of yore. How happy, she, to have a heart for the Way!

When she came to the end of her sutra-reading—when she read the passage that says, "Three thousands of living beings conceived a heart to know truth and were vouchsafed signs of enlightenment—the bodhisattva Wisdom Accumulated, and Shariputra, and all the living beings there, believed and received these things in silence"—Yatsufusa suddenly stood up and, looking back again and again at Princess Fuse, made his way toward the water's edge.

Just then the farther bank resounded with report of musket shot. Two balls, a double charge, flew swiftly, piercing Yatsufusa's throat—he thudded to the ground 'midst clouds of smoke—and the extra ball found Princess Fuse, too. Shot beneath the right breast, she collapsed sideways with hardly a cry, the sutra scroll still clutched tight in her hands.

Ah, the timing! The haze that had obscured the far side of the river ever since the previous year—and which had never for a moment cleared—now, at the sound of the musket, dispersed all 'round as if wiped clean away, and left a lone, young hunter. He wore gaiters of paper-mulberry cloth dyed with persimmon-lees, with spats of the same color, and a mat-woven headkerchief whose cord had been loosened so that it hung down around his neck; he held in his right hand a fowling piece. He stood, revealed now, on the facing bank, and though he gazed upon the rushing river, he seemed to know where the shoals might lurk, for after a time, he scrambled down the bank and began to cross, musket on his shoulder. Swift was the current, but shallower than it looked, and the water hardly reached his upper thighs. This stirred up the youth's courage even more, and with the vigor of a mad tiger chasing its child, or a drunken elephant chasing its mate, he advanced with mighty strides; and though the river was thirty yards or more in width, he sliced his way through its current in the blink of an eye, and when he reached the near bank, up he ran. Immediately he flourished his fowling piece, and into fallen Yatsufusa he shot some fifty or sixty more balls, breaking his bones and ripping his flesh, that never could he come again to life.

---

12. Fibers from the lotus plant, said to bind one to rebirth in the Pure Land.

Then with a grin the hunter tossed aside his musket and went to the edge of the grotto, crying, "Now to find the Princess!"

Yet when he looked, he saw the Princess fall'n, robbed of breath. "What is this?" he said in astonishment, and hastened to take her in his arms and raise her up. He exposed her wound to view and saw that, happily, it was not deep. Flustered, he quickly took some medicine from the bosom of his robe and poured it into her mouth, but though he sought again and again to call her back to life, his fingers at her wrist could find no pulse, and the Princess's body began to feel like ice. As it came to seem to the youth that even the skills of a Yuan Hua[13] could not save her, he raised his eyes to Heaven and amidst his sighs cried:

"Oh, what have I done? All my purposes have come to naught, as crossed amongst themselves as a crossbill's beak—the mist that months on end had never cleared now clears, and I shoot Yatsufusa down, but now I come and see that a further, needless shot the Princess has felled, and severed now at last her life's thread. Not fearing any dog, no matter how strange his goings-out and comings-in, and knowing that this mountain was forbidden, still I put aside all thoughts of myself and was prepared to lay down my life if only I might save Her Ladyship the Princess—but my loyalty in thinking thus has been turned to disloyalty, has fermented into sin ten thousand times over. Regret it I may—a hundred, a thousandfold—but now there is no going back. I would apologize, whole-heartedly—I will cut open my belly and accompany the Princess on her way to that darkling land. Wait for me, I pray you!"

He grasped his garment at the collar and pulled it open, then drew the sword at his waist and wrapped the blade in a handkerchief. Chanting "Hail Amitābha Buddha," the youth was about to thrust the blade's point into his side when a hunting arrow, shot with an echoing twang from a thicket of pine and oak by he knew not whom, grazed his upper arm. "What is this?" he cried, and, in spite of himself, dropped his blade—he looked around in wonder.

Then came a loud voice, its owner still hidden in the wood, singing out an old lyric poem:[14] "Flying squirrel seeks/tenderest ends of branches/but the huntsman/in the foot-dragging mountains/lo, he has found him!" The youth had barely time to call out, "Who goes there?" before he was greeted with a shout: "Kanamari Daisuke, be not hasty! Stay your hand a while!"

---

13. A legendary Later Han–era physician, better known as Hua Tuo.
14. *Man'yōshū* #267.

Then Satomi Yoshizane, Minister of the Court and Major Assistant in the Governance Ministry, clad in bearskin leggings and bamboo-grass vambraces,[15] with a panther-skin scabbard-cover and carrying a bow and arrows, stepped slowly out of the shade of the trees. He had no attendants behind him; only Horiuchi Kurando Sadayuki, equally imposing in appearance, followed at his lord's left hand.

Yoshizane's expression was pained. He saw Princess Fuse's dead body from the corner of his eyes, but as yet said nothing, though it was the end for her. He gazed at the prayer beads and last testament that she had dropped so abruptly and that now lay beside her. "Kurando, pick those up," he said, and Sadayuki, acknowledging his lord's command, hastened to collect them and bring them to him. The Minister of the Court Yoshizane discarded his bow and arrows and draped the prayer beads o'er the hilt of his sword, examining first of all the testament, each phrase, each line of which elicited a sigh. After reading it he showed it to Sadayuki. All this time, Kanamari Daisuke Takanori, mortified with shame, a cold sweat bathing his forehead, was prostrating himself, his blade laid out by his knees.

Then Yoshizane sat himself on a nearby stone and addressed Takanori: "A rare thing this is, Kanamari Daisuke. Not only have you recklessly disregarded my rule in coming to this mountain, but also it would appear you have shot and killed Princess Fuse and Yatsufusa. Put away your blade, come closer, and tell me about these things. What happened?"

Takanori, however, could neither face nor answer him—could not even raise his head for a time. Seeing this, Sadayuki went to his side and reiterated the command. "Daisuke, His Lordship has spoken. Will you not put away your blade? Will you not answer him this instant?"

Finally, Takanori raised his head. He slid his sword into its sheath and then presented it, along with the other that he carried, to Horiuchi Sadayuki. After handing them over, he retreated some little way, turned to Sadayuki, and said:

"I did not die quickly enough, and thus it is that I am able to behold my lord's face once more, as I had never expected to do—and yet there is no joy in this for me, only regret for my repeated failings. There are a thousand, ten thousand, things I would say to him, and I shall tell my story, though at this pass it may appear an attempt to adorn my useless actions, the wrongs I have laid upon myself.

"Last year I fell prey to Anzai Kagetsura's plotting and was unable to carry out my mission and alleviate the crisis. I escaped, but as I fled I was overtaken

---

15. These are vambraces reinforced with metal strips that resembled bamboo grass.

by enemy soldiers, with whom I fought a bloody battle. When I managed to reach Takita, I found it already surrounded by Kagetsura's great army, which filled the field like stalks of rice or hemp. They were in the midst of attacking the castle, and thus I was unable to make my way into it. I thought at the very least to join my strength to His Lordship's, to flex my arm in the cause of loyalty, and so I hastened at last to Tōjō. This too was in vain, however, as that castle had been surrounded by Kabuto Toppei's great army, which never backed down an inch from the tiger's maw, but lit up the night with their watch-fires and kept their guards on continual alert—there was no way for me to enter that castle short of sprouting wings. I then made up my mind to charge alone into the enemy camp and thus meet my death, but upon retreating and considering the matter further, this, too, seemed futile to me. Rather than flick my fingers individually in irritation, better to unite them in a fist. Both castles had been short on provisions to begin with—this autumn was to prove the crisis, whether our soldiers lived or died. It occurred to me that I could do my lord no greater service than to go up to Kamakura, there to proclaim our needs to them of the Overseers' house, to beg the mustering of a relief force, and with them to smash the armies that surrounded our two castles. Accordingly, I took ship at Shirahama, and once I had arrived in Kamakura I explained the reason I had come, proclaimed our needs, and begged for troops to relieve us, but as I bore no letter from my lord, I was not believed, and accomplished nothing. After many days spent in this fruitless hope, I returned, empty-handed, to Awa, only to find that Kagetsura had already been destroyed, and that the whole country now belonged to my lord.

"How I rejoiced at this—and yet, I could not bring myself cravenly to appear before him, having earned not a smidgen of merit. Nor could I at that time slit my belly—and so I waited, hoping for the day when I might perform some meritorious deed and then present myself to my lord. I required a hiding place until then, and so I hied myself to the village of Amaha Barrier in Kazusa, it being my home, and stayed at the house of a certain peasant, a connection of my grandfather Issaku's. There I remained, with nothing to do, through the end of last year, until this year, too, assumed the hues of autumn, deep beneath which I hid myself. At the beginning of this month, I began to hear dim intimations about Her Ladyship the Princess, and then someone told me definitely that she had gone into the furthest reaches of Mount To, accompanied by Yatsufusa the dog.

"This was an unexampled prodigy of a story, and of itself formed a flaw in His Lordship's gemlike honor. As for that dog, even if he were so old as to have a spirit to fascinate humans,[16] as long as he presents a form on which the eye may alight, he can be shot with little difficulty. So thought I, and so it seemed to me that by secretly making my way up this mountain, killing the dog, and saving Her Ladyship the Princess, I should be able to atone for my previous wrongs and gain the means of presenting myself before my lord once again.

"And so I stole back into this country and, carrying a fowling piece that I had prepared for the purpose, I entered the mountain's precincts. I spent some five or six days in searching for the Princess's whereabouts, and found this place where mists swathed the opposite bank, never clearing for a single day, where the water, of a width incompassable, thundered in depths unfathomable. Having heard of Amasaki Terutake's death by drowning, I presumed that this was the place, and resolved not to attempt a crossing lightly. And so it appeared to me that, my way blocked by a river beyond which I could not see, I was to end this day, too, in frustration; tired, I sat myself on a pine at the water's edge to gaze across, and as I gazed, though I could not see anything on the other side of the ravine, I began, ever so faintly, to hear a distant voice chanting sutras.

"What was this? My heart leapt within my breast, and as I struggled to calm it, I walked to the very edge of the water and pricked up my ears: I listened hard, and made out that it was a woman's voice. There could be no doubt that this was the Princess. And yet, though I could hear her, I could not catch even a glimpse of her. It seemed that I must be hard pressed to accomplish my aim without the darkling aid of the gods and buddhas. I prayed with all the sincerity I could muster to the Great Bright God of Susaki in this country, and to the Bodhisattva Avalokiteśvara in Nako, that if Takanori's loyalty be not in vain, then let the mists be overruled, that I might be able easily to cross this river; and after a while, when I opened my eyes, lo! the mystery! river mists which had until this moment never parted, ne'er allowed me black and white to tell apart, now cleared, as if they had been wiped away.

"And as I gazed across, afar I saw, beside what seemed to me to be a grotto, Her Ladyship the Princess. And the rapids—they were shallower than I had thought, so how could I not take courage? I had already started to cross when Yatsufusa—had he seen me?—ran toward the water's edge. It would not do, I felt, to let him close with me: I must shoot him down and then go to him, I thought. The range was perfect, and so I adjusted my hold on the fowling piece I carried, took careful aim and snapped open the pan-cover: two

---

16. Folklore held that animals (and objects) of sufficient age could develop sentience and magic powers.

balls flew unerringly and dropped the dog at water's edge—I had my prey. I crossed, more swiftly than the water ran.

"But when I looked I saw the Princess, too, had fallen, wounded by a straying, needless shot: his death-pillow she shared. And yet, her wound was shallow, and I thought she might be saved—I did all that heart and hand could do—but she had reached her end, and could not be helped. The snapping of an already attenuated thread of fate—I might call it thus, but my regret told me it was due to my overzeal, what the ancients called 'searching for a wound, even unto the parting of hairs,'[17] and I could not stand; I thought at least to accompany her on the road to that darkling land, and I had made my preparations when to my surprise His Lordship called to me to stop.

"That I thus failed to die is in itself a punishment from Heaven. Not only in breaking His Lordship's code and surreptitiously climbing this mountain, but also in harming Her Ladyship the Princess, I am guilty of the Eight Treasons.[18] My only wish is that His Lordship punish me as he sees fit. Master Horiuchi, milord Kurando, bind me," he said, kneeling and waiting with his hands held behind his back.

Sadayuki, while knowing Takanori's loyal heart, could only nod at every new thing he heard; he consulted his master's expression. Yoshizane heaved a great sigh, and after a time said, "Yea, verily, ill fortune and good, gain and loss, are things that cannot be improved by human effort, nor truly understood by what passes for wisdom among us. My word, Daisuke, you truly are guilty of crimes and will find punishment hard to escape, but Princess Fuse's death was ordained by Heaven. Had she not fallen by your shot, she should have become flotsam upon the river. Kurando, read us the letter she left behind."

"Yes, my liege," replied Sadayuki, who came to kneel beside Daisuke. Then he read the letter in a loud voice, from its first line to its last. Takanori grew more and more ashamed in the face of Princess Fuse's intellect and integrity—he was moved to tears that defeated any efforts to wipe them away, and he bewailed his recklessness.

When Sadayuki had finished reading, Yoshizane addressed himself to Takanori, saying, "Daisuke, what must you be feeling? For myself, it was not in order to prevent the Princess's death that I came here in secret. Isarago is ill, and the burden of fatigue from ever missing her beloved Princess Fuse has brought her sickness to a crisis. Although it was Isarago's wish, I had

---

17. An expression from *Han shu*, chapter 53.

18. Eight crimes under ancient Japanese law for which punishment was particularly heavy, encompassing disloyalty, brutality, and various kinds of conspiracy and insurrection, all defined as actions detrimental to the tranquility of the state.

misgivings as to whether I might safely come into the depths of these mountains to see the Princess. As I was turning the matter over in my mind, I—and
not only I but Kurando as well—saw a vision in which . . .," and he described
the vision. "Therefore I had my escort stay at the foot of the mountain while
I and Sadayuki alone climbed. Trusting to the vision, we did not cross the
river, but rather circled far around upstream, until we came out behind this
grotto. But just as we, master and man, were about to approach this spot, we
were astonished to hear the report of a musket. When we came to see, we
found that both Princess Fuse and Yatsufusa had been shot, and lay where
they had fallen. It was apparent to us that whoever should come across
that river was the Princess's enemy—this we should know without further
inquiry. And so we hid ourselves a while in the shadow of the trees to watch
the course of events. But how could we have foreseen that the villain would
be Kanamari Daisuke, whose fate had weighed so heavy on our hearts these
many days and months? In a state of much agitation, you did all you could
to recall the Princess to life, and when your treatments availed you not, you
made preparations to kill yourself; seeing this, we came to think that it was
not out of any wildness of heart that you killed the Princess, and so we called
to you to stay your hand.

"Now, I would have you consider this: If it had simply been a matter of
killing the dog and rescuing the Princess, would I, Yoshizane, have endured
unsurpassed shame, abandoned my most beloved daughter, and waited this
long for you to take action? Rewards and punishments are the very mecha-
nism of government. When once a word has left my mouth—well, a team
of horses is no match for the tongue. Though it was but a jest, I did give
Princess Fuse to Yatsufusa. As a result of this word a mighty enemy was
destroyed and the four districts were placed in the palm of my hand, and as it
was all due to Yatsufusa's meritorious conduct—and neither could I alter my
bargain, nor would Princess Fuse allow me to do so—she went with the dog,
intending to stay deep in the mountains for the remainder of her life. Happily, she escaped defilement: her single-minded devotion to reading the sutra
proved potent, and even Yatsufusa entered into the Buddha's truth. That he
was free of all lascivity the Princess saw, and she pitied him. So deeply did
she pity him that soon, all unbeknownst to her, she was touched by his spirit
and became with child.

"A prodigy! I see these now, these sufferings, as things conceived by karma's principle of causes and effects, because I have read these lines traced
by her brush. When I raised my righteous army and struck down Yamashita
Sadakane, I captured his wife Tamazusa alive. Her explanations and apologies
seemed reasonable to me, and so I spoke the word that she might be forgiven,

at which point, Daisuke, your father Hachirō Takayoshi remonstrated with me strenuously—and so I had her head lopped off. I first noticed that her vengeful spirit had begun to curse myself and my men when, at Kanamari Takayoshi's suicide, the form of a woman, indistinct though it was, presented itself to my eyes. Tamazusa's resentment was not slaked then, however, but took the form of the dog Yatsufusa, who led Princess Fuse into this remote mountain fastness, hiding her from her parents that they might ponder it; and then, what none could have expected, Princess Fuse was shot by Hachirō's son. What is more, you, Daisuke, found yourself first exiled without having committed a crime, and then committing a crime out of loyalty. All of this depended on karmic cause and effect, and were one to guess at the cause of it all, it would be the error of one man, me, Yoshizane, that gave rise to everything. That I was moved to speak to Yatsufusa in such a way as to allow him Princess Fuse was due to my wrongful speech in sparing Tamazusa, who should never have been allowed to live—speech whose results have fall'n, like dew from leaftips, into this steep river gorge, insufferable mountain peaks, there to live and die in rebirth's sea, which thing I cannot bear to see for grief. But there is no use in wailing now. Among divine spirits there are those that are true and those that are baleful. A god's wrath we call punishment, while demoniacal wrath we call a curse. Tamazusa is an evil spirit: Princess Fuse's death was the result of a curse. You yourself, Daisuke, were unable to escape this curse, and so happened to incur guilt. Truly, there is a cause to all of this, so do not resent it."

In speaking thus, Yoshizane so plainly accused himself, by way of earnest explanation to Takanori, that the latter was moved by the former's perspicacity, and without thinking he advanced on his knees and said, "My lord, you have spoken, and that is sufficient for me to understand both my father's suicide and my own tenuous claim to life. However, doubt still lingers in my breast. If Yatsufusa had indeed already entered into the Buddha's truth, then the evil spirit should not have been able to effect its curse. If Your Lordship saw an avatar in a vision that caused you to come visit the Princess, then even were her fate decreed by karma, should not the gods and buddhas have exercised their power to keep her safe here for a day, lest you climb this mountain in vain? How can this be?"

In response to this query Sadayuki slapped his knee and, from his position beside Takanori, said, "Spoken with exquisite subtlety, Daisuke! And what you say applies not to my lord alone. That these river-mists, which never for a day dispersed, should so instantly clear away bespeaks some darkling aid from gods and buddhas on your behalf, even while what issued was all wrong. I myself find it difficult to accept these things."

At his suddenly serious look, the Minister of the Court Yoshizane nodded, saying, "I myself, not being a god, cannot distinguish these matters with any certainty, but ill fortune and good are like a rope intertwined. Our lives are dependent on the will of Heaven. Had Princess Fuse passed away and I not come unto this mountain, she would have been spoken of simply as the wife of a dog. That is to say, perhaps the avatar I saw, its guidance, was in order that the Princess's parents and the world at large might know of her integrity and virtue, and that Yatsufusa had indeed entered into the Buddha's truth—and if such be the case, then though I failed to see her before the brief flash of her mayfly life faded, still it cannot be said that my coming here was in vain. Then, too, had it not been for the clearing of the river-mists, both Princess Fuse and Yatsufusa, rather than being shot by Daisuke would have alike become flotsam on the water, and despite the note she left behind, the ignorant would have said that theirs was a lovers' suicide. Would she not have hated that?

"I am sure I need not remind you, Daisuke, but your father Hachirō, while the possessor of great merit, refused reward for it and instead took his own life, a thing most pitiful. I often wondered how I might elevate his son—I had thought to make you lord of Tōjō Castle, and to marry you to Princess Fuse, but then I sent you on that mission and you never returned, while the Princess went with Yatsufusa into the depths of the mountains. Now is my long-harbored desire become as unavailing as a picture of a rice cake is to assuage real hunger, while great and numerous are become my shames. This marriage is not one that can be celebrated openly, and yet it is one that the girl's parents countenance. Then there are the words of the divine child to Princess Fuse, that she should meet her father and another man, her husband—this must have meant you. Might this be why both the Princess and the dog were shot by your hand, Daisuke? Would it not be smartest to label this one of the wondrous aspects of the great expedient means adopted by the avatar we saw? Karmic connections being thus, whom should we blame, and whom should we hate? The strongest bowstring must someday slacken; anything taken to its furthest limit must there rest. From this time forward, I expect there will be no more obstacles set before us— those of my house—by spirits. My descendants, I believe, will prosper even more than have I. Think you not so?" As he elucidated the matter to Sadayuki and Takanori, their doubts like snow in spring did melt away, and tears fell from their eyes.

After a while Takanori closed and straightened his collar, and himself assumed a more formal posture. "I owe more of a debt of gratitude to my lord than to any darkling aid, not least for this marriage that Your Lordship secretly contemplated—but it would be wasted on me. Though I never knew of it, had I succeeded in saving the Princess, people would later say that I had only done it out of the feelings of my heart for her. I pray you rather, my lord, to let my head be speedily cut off."

He spoke with singleness of purpose, but Yoshizane would hardly hear him out. "That goes without saying. And yet, look carefully, with a discerning mind, at how shallow Princess Fuse's wound is. If she were to revive, then I should have been hasty in killing you, should I not? Looking closely at her prayer beads, I see that the phrase 'Even thus can a beast' and so on has returned to what it was at the beginning: the beads once again show forth 'Benevolence, Righteousness,' and the rest of the eight virtuous acts. By this I know that they have not lost their mystic power. However, when the Princess collapsed, these beads were separated from her; thus was it that though her wound is slight, it felled her. Ever since she was an infant, she has carried these beads, and through them she has known security from all threat; even though her allotted days be spent, if we but pray upon these beads, how can there not be benefice? If it accomplishes nothing, then we will let the matter rest—nothing more can we do."

He took up the prayer beads, which hung from the pommel of his sword, and, pressing them to his forehead, concentrated a while; then he hung them about Princess Fuse's neck. From either side, Sadayuki and Takanori lifted her lifeless body while intoning the name of En the Ascetic in earnest orison, whereupon Princess Fuse immediately opened wide her eyes, and parted her lips in sudden breath.

Sadayuki and Takanori could not contain their elation. "My lady, Princess, do you know us? Kurando is here, and Daisuke. His Lordship your father has come, too. How farest thee, lady?"

Questioned thus, she looked from side to side, then shook loose the hands that held hers and pressed both sleeves to her face; tears streamed from her eyes. "As well she might," said Yoshizane, coming closer and pulling her sleeves away.

"Princess Fuse, be not ashamed. Only myself and these two of my men are here. My escort is all at the foot of the mountain. I have come myself, at your mother's request—and not from a short morning's counsel, but because of the avatar that appeared to me in a vision. I have seen your letter; I know of you, and of Yatsufusa. Kanamari Daisuke, who has been in Kazusa since last year, heard of your state, and with the single-mindedness of youth that pauses for no inquiry into causes or consequences, decided on a course to save your life; and thus, before me, surreptitiously, unto this mount he came. He shot, he felled Yatsufusa, and a ball escaped and thus you bear this slight wound. Yatsufusa's death is to be pitied, and yet his shooting at the hands of Daisuke attests a karmic connection, for Daisuke and Daisuke alone had I intended to make my son-in-law. Was it not for this reason that the divine child, of whom you wrote in your letter, spoke of you meeting your father and another man, your husband? Bend your will to mine, daughter—return to Takita and comfort your mother, who wastes away in illness. Princess Fuse?"

After he had thus pressed her with reason in his explanation of matters, Sadayuki and Daisuke spoke together, joining their arguments to his. "As a matter of course, Your Ladyship, you should come home. On a righteous principle you came onto this mountain in the company of Yatsufusa and spent over a year concealed here, but that is now over. Yea, though you may yet aspire to turn your back on the world, how can that desire displace filial piety? Return, we pray thee."

In response to their well-meaning wheedling, Princess Fuse wiped vigorously at the tears that still welled from her eyes and said, "If only I were still my former self, I never should ignore my father's word, which he himself has traveled far to speak. But such a karmic weight from former lives has dragged me down that I am, like a beast in foot-dragging mountains, shot with musket-ball such as to end my life. And with such sin upon me, sin so far removed from what is common among men, sin that else could not be, and indeed was not, expiated—and with such shame upon me, now exposed to Father and to others—how could I now truckle and return, and to what home? The proverb tells of how the parent bird her one-winged nest-bound hungry child yet loves the more, with an eightfold love—this must be true, as must, I feel too well, my parents' love be true, my father's favor, mother's care, and thus their cries, like (if they be compared) the crane's at night, missing its child. And mine are like the pheasant's lonely cries in spring's scorched fields, though 'tis not a mate I miss.[19] A rain of tears welled up and overflowed my heart to make a sea of sorrows that today I would escape, and thus my brush, my life's nib, I took up and wrote it all, in hopes that someday you might read it, sire. I leave the burning house,[20] companion to a dog of passion's torments, now a friend in Buddha's truth. I never was defiled, was never violated, yet I bear within me others—nor are they the

---

19. The crane crying on a cold night for a chick that has left the nest, and the pheasant crying for its mate when its nest has been burned by farmers scorching fields in springtime, are both classic poetic images of longing. They are paired in the noh play *Tango monogurui* (ca. fourteenth century, attributed to Iami), for example, which deals with the separation of parent and child.

20. See Chapter XII, note 1.

seed of mountain sedge—and I was bound, nor could I choose myself 'tween nothingness and being, and here I am.

"And, Father, you who say that in your heart my husband you had chos'n: I doubt not you have your reasons, but by only now, at this pass, telling them, do you not compound your errors, which men can never fully understand? Even if Kanamari Daisuke and I shared no lovers' ties, was it not unrighteousness unsurpassed for me, as a woman, to go with Yatsufusa and thus turn my back on the husband to whom my father in his heart had given me? What matter that I never knew I was betrothed? I knew not, and he knew not: only you, my lord, knew of it, and that is as useless as leaving a sword on a tomb.[21] Furthermore, if Yatsufusa was my husband, then now is Daisuke become mine enemy above all others. Yatsufusa is not my husband, but neither is Daisuke my mate. Alone I was born, alone I shall depart, returning 'cross death's mountain, and although to stop me may seem merciful, it goes too far—unfeeling, rather, is it to me. I think upon my debt to you, my sire—the lofty mountain axemen you forbade from coming here—a duty I repaid with filial impiety beyond impiety; and if, though I have longed for all these days to see my parents' faces, I go not, although I see you now and know you now, it is because I bear a weight of sin, of guilt's impedimenta, I cannot evade—this know, and think of me no more. I pray you, tell this to Her Ladyship my mother, and apologize for me, and say I wish for her a hundred years of happiness, and nothing more. Oh, to be seen in this wretched state! What profit for me now to hide my corpse? They say that pregnant women's new-made ghosts all sink into the Lake of Blood[22]—if such is to be my karma inescapable, then shunning it cannot avail me. And yet, unless I open to the world this seed that somehow, fatherless, has lodged within me, never shall the world's doubts or my confusion be dispelled. Watch me now."

Close by her elbow lay the dagger that was meant to protect her; she drew it now, and plunged it straight into her belly, drawing it across herself in a line absolutely straight. Then, wonder of wonders, out from the wound came flashing a cloud of white vapor. It enveloped the crystal prayer beads that hung from her neck, and then was seen to climb into the air. The string

---

21. A reference to a story from chapter 31 of *Shi ji*. While on a state visit, Ji Zha of Wu was treated hospitably by Xu Jun (king of Xu); he also noticed that Xu Jun admired a sword he carried. As Ji Zha was on official business, he refrained from giving Xu Jun the sword until after his mission was completed, by which time Xu Jun had died. Ji Zha laid the sword on Xu Jun's tomb in order to remain true to his word.

22. Bakin here writes "blood bowl" and glosses it "lake of blood." The apocryphal Blood Bowl Sutra (*Xuepenjing*, J. *Ketsubonkyō*) characterizes the Blood Bowl Hell as Princess Fuse does here.

Caption: Princess Fuse slits her belly and lets eight dog warriors run free
Figures: Horiuchi Sadayuki [*far right, behind Yoshizane*]. Satomi Yoshizane [*right, holding sword*].
Kanamari Daisuke Takanori [*right, kneeling*]. Princess Fuse [*left, slitting her belly*]. Housemaid
[*behind Princess Fuse*]. Maidservant [*behind housemaid, bowing*].
Note: As with the first illustration in this chapter, a second block was used to apply gray shading,
and negative space on that block was used to depict otherworldly figures. In this case it is the
spirits of the soon-to-be-born Eight Dog Warriors, appearing in the "white vapor" that emerges

from Princess Fuse's belly. Also, as with Daisuke's vision in the first illustration, the text does not describe these eight figures, which appear to have both human and canine characteristics. A third similarity to the first illustration is that the later Bunkeidō edition (on the following pages) uses a different second block from that used in the original Sanseidō edition (seen here). Several differences may be observed, the most important of which is that the eight figures are more clearly visible.

of beads snapped, and the hundred, still threaded together, fell with a clatter to the ground, while the eight beads that remained in the sky flew about in tangled paths, emitting all the while a polished white light, in brilliance not unlike shooting stars. The three, master and men, who had been unable to prevent the Princess's suicide, forgot themselves in staring at the sky azure, the lights that dazzled all their eyes. And as they looked—now here!—now there!—the eight lights scattered in eight directions, blown on a gale that came rushing down the mountainside, and in their wake the only thing they left was th'evening moon, rising o'er the peaks in the east. Truly was this a harbinger of the appearance, years later, of the Eight Dog Warriors who would ultimately gather under the Satomi roof.

All this time the Princess did not succumb to her deep wound, but watched the lights as they soared off. "What joy! My womb harbored nothing of import! The god-tied belly band[23] is now relaxed, as are my doubts— no cloud upon my heart! I hurry now toward the western heavens,[24] with no last look at the moon of th'floating world! O, lead me on, Amitābha Buddha!" She hardly had intoned the name when she with bloodied hand the bloodied hilt did grasp, extracting and abandoning the blade, and then the Princess finally collapsed. So stout her heart and words, nearly unbecoming a girl—how moving was her end!

---

23. Traditionally worn by pregnant women.

24. Bakin here writes the character for "heaven" (which has Confucian overtones in an early modern Japanese context), but glosses it "sky," as the same character was often used simply to denote the firmament. Early modern readers would likely have also understood "western heaven" as a phrase denoting the Western Pure Land or Western Paradise of Buddhist belief.

Chapter XIV
Serving women hurry their conveyance across the ravine;
Chudai jingles his staff in search of the prayer beads

Sadayuki and the others by the Princess's side were not in time to stop her suicide: like flowers that, once placed as ornaments in a woman's hair, now scatter their petals, she died: the men were filled with impotent regret. Among them only Takanori acted. His courage stirred by Her Ladyship the Princess's final verse, superior to any man's, he could not stay still, but quickly took up the bloody sword that lay beside her body and made again as if to slit his own belly.

Then Yoshizane raised his voice: "My word, Daisuke, have you taken leave of your senses? You are guilty of a great crime: it is a fearsome prodigy for you to take your life without awaiting your lord's command. Princess Fuse came back to life, for a time—this lessens your crime by a degree, but nevertheless, in coming onto this mountain you have broken a law that I decreed punishable by beheading. I will not hear of you slitting your belly just as you please. Say your prayers!" With this Yoshizane drew near until he stood beside him, bearing his blade.

"'Tis my only wish," replied Takanori, rearranging his posture, pressing his palms together, and stretching out his neck. No sooner had he done so than the blade flashed overhead like lightning and descended upon him like a gale, severing, to Takanori's surprise, his topknot, which fell with a thud to the ground.

The guilty man looked up and said, "What is this?" while Sadayuki, too, who could not sway his master, looked with wonder at his lord's benevolence, with astonishment and fear at his display of unbidd'n righteousness.

Yoshizane put away his icy blade in its scabbard, wiped away the tears that had begun to glisten in his eyes, and said, "See here, Kurando, I have by mine own hand punished this criminal. True and golden are the words of the ancients, that while the lord makes the laws, he can also break them. Had I ascended this mountain with the people today, then Daisuke would have incurred no reproach. I cut off his topknot rather than his head as a small token of what I think of his late father. From childhood this boy has been called 'Daisuke' in celebration of his future, of the fact that one day he would be a retainer to assist in the ruling of a great country;[1] but at length I was advanced to the office of Major Assistant in the Governance Ministry, due to which it so happened that we came to share the same name, for while the pronunciations are different, the characters are the same.[2] Perhaps that is why you, unfortunate youth, took upon yourself a curse meant for your lord—why you were destined to remain buried and forgotten like wood that petrifies. I pity you deeply. Your father Hachirō was a man of great merit, and you, Daisuke, are not without loyalty. That the valor and merit of both father and son should go unrewarded—that at the hour of their deaths they should each have fallen into such guilt that even their lord is helpless to save them—grieves me more than if you were my own son. I cannot keep back my tears. Now then, Daisuke, Takanori. If you understand what I am feeling in my heart, then for your late father's sake, for the Princess's sake, preserve your own life—love yourself, serve the Buddha with austerities, and make yourself known as a great and learned monk. Will you not accept this charge?"

When Yoshizane had in earnestness expounded and explained these things to him, then Takanori did prostrate himself, did nearly choke on tears of gratitude that mingled with embarrassment to squelch whatever answer he would make his lord, as well he might. Sadayuki then advanced a step, sniffling back tears, and said, "This is not the first time His Lordship has displayed the benevolence of his heart; but nevertheless, for him to speak of his retainer thus, without a hint of reprehension about the way Her Ladyship the Princess met her end, must be unto you, Daisuke, a satisfaction greater

---

1. Daisuke is written with characters that can be taken to mean "great assistant."

2. The characters used for the *daiyū* in *jibu no daiyū* (Major Assistant in the Governance Ministry) are the same as those used for Daisuke.

than if he had given you one entire district's protectorate, and a stipend of ten thousand strings of cash."

Finally, hearing these words, Daisuke lifted up his head and spoke. "I am truly unworthy, but we have thus seen how even a beast can enter into the Buddha's truth. From this day forward, I shall travel the length and breadth of Japan, making pilgrimages to holy mountains and shrines, performing rites for Her Ladyship Princess Fuse, who has now passed on to another life, and praying for success at arms for my lord and his children. And since both Her Ladyship the Princess's passing and my celebration of the tonsure are owing to the dog Yatsufusa, I shall take 'Chudai' as my name in the Law, splitting the character for 'dog' in two while retaining the 'Dai' of Daisuke,[3] that was not equal to a dog's greatness."

When he had spoken, the Minister of the Court Yoshizane said, "Ah, how beautifully spoken, that! We named him Yatsufusa for his coat—the dog was black and white with eight great spots upon his body. But now that I think of it, the two characters in the name 'Yatsufusa' can be taken to mean 'one body in eight directions,'[4] and lo, from Princess Fuse's fatal, suicidal wound we saw a single streamer of white vapor issue forth, lifting the string of a hundred and eight prayer beads bearing the characters for the eight virtues—the beads flashed, and those with no writing upon them fell to the earth, while the remaining eight, shining brightly, were scattered in the eight directions, until at length they disappeared; and this did not occur, I say, without a cause. There will come a time, perhaps far in the future, when it will make sense to us. Now, there can be no better parting gift for you as you depart on your journey to the Buddha's truth than these prayer beads. I bid you keep them secret, Initiate."

With this explanation he at length presented the beads to Takanori, who took them in his hands and raised them to his forehead twice, thrice, saying, with great determination, "'Tis with gratitude, my lord, that I accept this gift. Henceforth I shall make a pilgrim's progress through every land, seeking the place where each of the eight beads that flew has fallen, and I shall not return to this country and enter into audience with Your Lordship until I have strung those eight back with these, until the full tale of one hundred and eight is complete. If years pass and you hear not from me, then may it please Your Lordship to think that I have died on my journey, and that my

---

3. The character for dog consists of the character for "large" or "great" (*dai*) with one extra short stroke, which may also be treated as a separate character in its own right, read *chu*.

4. The character for *fusa* may be broken down into elements that individually mean "one," "body (or corpse)," and "direction."

remains lie in a field somewhere, nourishing starving dogs. Indeed, this is truly a parting for life."

Already by this time the sun had set and early evening had made its descent: a half-moon, brighter in the cloudless sky than mid-day sun, revealed every tree on the mountain. The beating of the water on the rocks, the whispering of the wind in the pines, were gut-wrenching go-betweens for the deer who cried on the peaks;[5] mourning the pearly dew as it turned to frost, the monkeys screeched in the dark-shrouded valleys, chilling the solitary traveler under his bedclothes. Only these men, master and followers, had hearts stout enough to brave the deep mountain paths, too lonely to be but seldom trod—only they had come this far, and they thought only of Princess Fuse as they sighed.

Then did Horiuchi Sadayuki take counsel with Takanori. "Long have we tarried here, due to the Princess's suicide: the night is dark and the way steep, and I have misgivings about the descent. If, therefore, we stay here to greet the dawn, what shall we do about her body? We cannot pronounce this place safe from poisonous serpents and ravenous beasts. Either way presents grave dangers. What think you, my lord?" said the one.

After a little thought, the other replied, "There is reason in what you say. For His Lordship to await the dawn here would seem to lack foresight. Let us then carry the Princess's body, you and I, while His Lordship himself carries a torch, and we can hurry down the mountain. I understand that you left companions at the foot of the mountain—surely they will come to meet us. Well might they refuse to cross this ravine, this stream, taking fright at what they have heard, but they can hardly fail to come meet us on the opposite bank, or beyond. What say you?"

Hardly had they finished speaking when Yoshizane said, "Princess Fuse lived here all alone ever since last year, and yet you would have the three of us, warriors and armed, hurry to the foot of the mountain rather than guard her body for a night, out of fear of poisonous serpents and ravening beasts? All things considered, Princess Fuse had a heart that I would fain see in a boy—as her father, it puts me to shame. Isarago did weep and wail until in the weakness of my heart I came myself to see the Princess—now I cannot bear the redoubled shame of it. This is why, now that she is dead, I will not let a single tear be seen in my eye. As long as her soul has not departed this place, she laughs at your womanish debate. Break branches and build a fire, and I will open up our food basket. Why should we hurry?" His words moved

---

5. In poetry, the cries of deer were traditionally taken to be expressions of yearning for their mates.

Sadayuki and Takanori. Thenceforth they carried Princess Fuse's corpse into the cave, and then they joined their lord, seating themselves beneath the trees around the mouth of the grotto, where they quietly awaited the brightening of the skies.

Into the midst of this scene, there came from the opposite bank the flick'ring light of many torches, and the sound of human voices, dimly heard. Sadayuki gazed into the distance and said, "It would seem that somebody has come to meet us. Le me help them cross the rapids." No sooner had he said this than he stood—he ran until he reached the water's edge, and shouted with all his might: "Those torches I see yonder must be His Lordship's escort—ho, there, your lord is here with me, I say! We have crossed the river! Regardless of what you have heard, the shoals are shallow and the current slow! Cross, now, I bid you!"

At this time it so happened that the wind was at his back, and it seemed that his voice must have been clearly audible, for he saw the torches flaring here and there descend the slope until it seemed to him they stood upon the opposite bank. Some came ahead, some lagged behind, leading horses, talking together, and a great number of people began to cross to him, and as they approached the near shore he saw, to his surprise, a woman's palanquin, clamped to a carrying-pallet of sorts and shouldered by seven or eight strapping, bare-naked men. As for the rest, they were the escort that had been left at the foot of the mountain, as well as some who had come from Takita.

Sadayuki quickly spied all this and called out, "Who goes there?" And then the men lowered the palanquin, and everyone knelt at the water's edge and said, "When the sun began to set and the master of the house had not returned, we set out to meet him, having already taken counsel among ourselves to do so, whereupon a messenger reached us from the mistress of the house with the speed of flame. Therefore together did we hasten on, although ere long the sun put out its light, so that when we had come to yonder shore and heard you calling us we could not cross alone. We clamped the messenger's palanquin to the pallet on which we had piled our raingear and torches, and with great effort we made it across."

Sadayuki nodded. "How very well managed. Now quickly, bring the messenger here." Five or six men stood up to do the job. With nimble fingers they untied the slender hempen ropes and pulled open the door of the palanquin.

A look revealed the messenger to be a housemaid, some forty years or more in age, by the name of Kaeta. It was she who had, in times past, undertaken secret missions to learn how Princess Fuse fared, she who had come as far as the far shore. Today it appeared that she had been sent on an urgent mission, one that had caused her bearers to carry her along the road at great speed, for inside the palanquin was hung a white cloth some three feet in length, while the woman herself, beneath her overrobe, wore a length of white glossed silk wrapped around her torso at a point above her sash and below her solar plexus, and a headband of the same stuff. She resembled those messengers vulgarly known as "beaters," and was quite imposing in appearance, so that when she emerged from the palanquin, dizzy and unable to stand from the jostling she had endured on the long journey here, everyone nearby stepped forward to help her out. Sadayuki preceded her in going to Yoshizane's side and reporting all that had occurred, and Kaeta followed him in audience with her lord.

"I have misgivings about this messenger," said Yoshizane, but he asked her business, and Kaeta, without a shade of cowardice, quickly answered, raising her head and saying, "After you left the manor this dawn, my lord, the mistress of the house sank even deeper into illness and began to ask after you constantly, saying, 'Has His Lordship not returned yet?' At times, in her delirium, she would even speak as if Her Ladyship the Princess were standing there before her, and then break into tears. In my humble opinion, she has reached the limit of what she can suffer. We women, not to mention the Scion [MEANING YOSHINARI], gave her what comfort we could, but it was not enough, until finally he ventured to say unto her, 'In truth, my sire has gone to Mount To, to inquire personally after my sister. Wait, my lady, this one day—tomorrow, without fail, he will return, leading my sister.' Upon hearing this, she replied with amazement: 'Mount To is haunted, 'tis well known—if His Lordship has gone there, he will not return without incident. Call him back at once, I pray you!' So great a fuss did she make that in the end the Scion was left with nothing to do. 'Kaeta,' he said to me, 'I have heard that you know your way around that mountain. It cannot have been two hours since the master of the house departed; if you hurry, you should be able to overtake him on the way. Go and tell him of this.' I hastened to leave the manor, and hurried along at such a pace that my bearers tired, so that I had to enlist a new set of shoulders at each hamlet we passed, until, after many hardships, I have come to be here."

As she finished speaking, the members of the escort that stood around her began to clamor, saying, "There were lights flickering on the opposite shore—now they have come down to the water's edge. It looks to be another palanquin—is it or is it not?" Their voices rose in raucous excitement.

Sadayuki and Takanori immediately rushed down, saying, as they gazed across the water, "Another beater? This cannot be good news. We shall help them from our side, that they may cross sooner." They commanded, and the escort said, "Yes, sirs." Ten or so strong servants shouldered the pallet again and stepped into the stream, treading carefully between stones, until they reached the opposite bank, where they clamped the palanquin to the pallet as before. Then, together with its escort, they crossed back to the near side and lowered the palanquin.

The door was opened, and from within emerged another maid, this one not yet twenty years of age, by the name of Saori. Dressed in imposing fashion with a glossed silk headband around her fair brow and bangs, she presented an even more impressive appearance than Kaeta. Saori stepped out of the palanquin, which proved to be the limit of her strength: she immediately collapsed. Sadayuki and Takanori, shocked, did trickle fresh spring water on her face—with medicines they plied her variously until she repaid their desperate efforts by regaining consciousness—and then she made her greetings to them all. She had, after all, been chosen for this mission, and so she made nothing of her fatigue from the long journey, but allowed Sadayuki and Takanori to lead her before Yoshizane, who addressed her at once: "Not one messenger, but two—my misgivings increase. How is it with Isarago?"

She could not wipe away all her tears, so thickly did they flow. "This morning, at the hour of the snake,[6] the mistress of the house . . .," she began, but could not finish; she slumped to the ground, and Kaeta, who had preceded her, did join her in her sobbing and her tears.

Yoshizane was wracked with sighs. "So it is over?" he asked, and Saori raised her head slightly and said, "To speak of how Her Ladyship faced her end is beyond me. She died shortly after Kaeta left on her errand. The Scion said unto me, 'It would be easy enough for me to send a rider with this news, but as my father has gone to the mountain in secret, I scruple to do so. I hear that you undertook secret missions to Mount To with Kaeta—go now and inform the master of the house of what has happened. Do it before the night has passed!' And so I had myself borne straight here."

Takanori met Sadayuki's gaze, then bowed his head and sighed. Yoshizane listened to every detail, then spoke. "I am here at Isarago's fervent request, but was unable to do what she asked me to do. I regret it mightily. Perhaps it was better that I was unable to see her at the last. Had she clung to life one more morning to see me return, I do not know what I should have said to her. Look there, you two," he said, turning to the cave and showing them the body that lay therein.

---

6. Late morning.

Caption: A serving-woman sent as a "beater" crosses the river at night.
Figure: Horiuchi Sadayuki.

使女の
急ぎ松を
水を渉る夜

堀内貞利

Kaeta and Saori, with racing hearts, followed after him and gazed into the grotto by the scant illumination of the moonrays that slanted into it. When they saw what was there they both exclaimed as one, "Why, 'tis Her Ladyship the Princess! Has she been rent by fearsome beast, or was it blade that caused her end? Oh, what is to be done? What a wretched, painful thing!" They threw themselves down at her pillow, at her feet, and sobbed.

Yoshizane did not watch this, but addressed himself to Sadayuki and the others. "No doubt Yoshinari is anxiously awaiting us. So many have joined us here. I will spend the dawn descending the mountain. Daisuke, you shall remain behind with a dozen or so of these servants, and on the morrow you shall inter Princess Fuse's body here. Give Yatsufusa a proper burial, too. Kaeta and Saori having come unbidden to spy on the Princess, I leave them, too, here for the night as her companions. Let the messengers observe her wake; let them be an offering unto her spirit from her mother. Now, about the burial," he said, speaking earnestly; he gave them thus and such directions, making the women understand his intentions even as he thanked them for their labors. He also praised the members of his escort, after which he mounted the horse they had led to him and rode toward the opposite bank of the river. Those who with Takanori were to stay, stayed crouched at water's edge along with him, while Sadayuki and the others who were to follow their lord by torchlight gingerly did tread the shoals.

The next day, sometime after noon, the headmen of the villages at the foot of Mount To did come to the grotto along with a priest and several peasants, breathing raggedly and carrying a coffin. This had been arranged by Yoshizane at dawn that morning when, on his way back to his manor at Takita, he charged Sadayuki with going to the village headmen and priest and explaining to them his will, bidding them make ready at once a coffin and other items for a burial, and sending them up into the mountain to "deliver them to Kanamari Daisuke." In addition, from this day forward he allowed wood-cutters and charcoal-makers, and all others who made their living in the mountains, once again to traverse the slopes of Mount To.

Now Takanori the initiate did take possession of the proffered coffin and placed within it Princess Fuse's body. He enlarged the grotto, that it might serve as her tomb: but there was no stone on which to carve an epitaph, only the pines and oaks, standing side by side as natural markers of her grave. The tale of this was told, until the place came to be known as the Grave of the Valiant Virgin. He buried Yatsufusa, too; he did not use a coffin, but simply placed the dog in a hole. He was buried to the northwest (the direction of the dog) of Princess Fuse's grave, some ten yards away, at the base of an old cypress tree. People came to call this the Dog Barrow. The burials were plain and simple in each particular, in accordance with what Yoshizane bade Takanori do, and with due attention to what the Princess herself would have wished.

When all was done, Kaeta and Saori departed at the head of their dozen or so servants, weeping, for Takita, while the village headmen, the priest, and the others returned each to his own hamlet. Kanamari Daisuke Takanori, now transformed into a bald-pated, black-robed bonze whose name in the Law was Chudai, alone remained a while on the mountain, where day and night without surcease he read aloud from the Lotus Sutra that Princess Fuse had left behind, until some forty days had passed.

Meanwhile, Lady Isarago's funeral was held at Takita. Then, on behalf of those who had departed, much rice was distributed as offerings, which caused great excitement among the poorer folk; also, Horiuchi Sadayuki was despatched to the Ascetic's Grotto at Susaki, where he made many a donation, and caused a road and a bridge to be built for the sake of others who would worship there. Everyone pronounced these acts meritorious and full of virtue.

In all this activity, the forty-nine days since Isarago's and Princess Fuse's deaths were fulfilled. Therefore it was decided that a great memorial service should be held for them at the Satomi family cloister in Takita, with the heir Yoshinari, Minister of the Court, as sponsor. When he heard of this, Yoshinari said, "Let us summon the bonze Chudai to take part in the ceremonies," and so a messenger was despatched to Mount To, only to find that Chudai was no longer on the mountain. Upon inquiring in the vicinity, the messenger was told by some wood-cutters that "that priest seems to have been expecting something like this, and to have prepared himself, for this morning, when he shouldered his traveling-chest and went down the mountain, jingling the rings on the end of his staff, he looked back at us and said, 'Should the lord of Takita inquire after me, tell him of this,' after which he left, we know not whither. Your Worship can wait, but he will not be returning."

Helpless to do otherwise, the messenger returned to Takita, where he reported the incident. Yoshizane exclaimed in admiration, then spoke as if to himself. "He made a vow, saying, 'I shall make a pilgrimage through all the sixty-odd provinces, and shall never so long as I live return to Awa until I have gathered the eight beads that flew away and have strung them together with their fellows.' I doubt we will see him again, though it pains me to say it." Yoshizane caused no more inquiries to be made after Chudai, and yet the priest was never far from his mind; ever did Yoshizane wonder if Chudai was safe from harm. To provide solace for him should he return, on the anniversary of Princess Fuse's death Yoshizane erected on Mount To a hall dedicated to Avalokiteśvara. Within it he placed a small shrine, in which was kept the Princess's testament, along with a record that told of her virtue, and of Yatsufusa. A hall to Avalokiteśvara stands on Mount To to this day.

In this way many years elapsed with no word from the bonze Chudai. What became of him in the end? The answer to this will be given in later Books.

> *Author's note: In this tome, everything from the Ist Book of the Inaugural Volume through to the end of the present Book constitutes but the opening stage of the whole, the beginning of the appearance of the Eight Warriors. The Books that follow, and those to be written over the next months and years, will cover events of many years later. There is no story to be told of the intervening years, even as in that tale of* The Water Margin, *where dozens of years elapse untold-of between when Hong Xin removes the tablet on Dragon and Tiger Mountain and the first appearance of Lin Chong.*[7]
>
> *The author would add that among the illustrations in this book, some, such as that of Kanamari Daisuke Takanori crossing the river, illustrate that which is not in the text, or, rather, contain text within the illustration. Without reference to this illustration, one would be at a loss as to why the clouds of mist so suddenly cleared. As for the depictions of Kaeta and Saori, the serving-women sent as "beaters," one notices that their presence is shown, and then their arrival. This may make it seem as if we have confused the order of things, but it is not so. In compiling my brief account of these people, I have relied somewhat on what they said afterwards, and placed the event before the telling of it; the pictures simply do the same. That being said, the illustrator merely makes pictures as pictures, and cannot always make them mean what they mean; this can cause gaps between them and the author's intent. There are such instances in these chapters. Please, O Reader, be wary of them.*
>
> *End of Book II of Volume II of the Lives of the Eight Dog*
> *Warriors of the Satomi*

---

7. Hong Xin is an imperial official sent to consult the Daoist sage Zhang on Dragon and Tiger Mountain. Hong climbs the mountain, and after many hardships meets a boy riding on an ox and playing a flute. The boy mysteriously knows Hong's errand without being told, and sends him back down the mountain, turning out to have been Zhang himself. The following day, Hong discovers a sealed temple building called the Suppression of Demons Hall. Despite warnings, Hong insists on opening the doors and removing the stone slabs embedded in the building's floor. This reveals a great pit, out of which bursts a black cloud, which splits into a hundred and eight golden rays that go shooting off in all directions. They are later embodied as the Outlaws of the Marsh, the heroes of the story. All of this happens in the first chapter of the novel. Lin Chong, one of first outlaws to be introduced, first appears in chapter 7.

APPENDIX

CHARACTERS IN *Eight Dogs,* CHAPTERS I–XIV

This is a list of characters appearing in *Eight Dogs, Part One.* The list is confined to named characters and thus omits various unnamed soldiers, attendants, and the like. It also omits various political figures mentioned by the narrator who do not appear in the story, even if (like Ashikaga Nariuji, for example) they do appear in the story in future chapters.

In parentheses after each name is given the number of the chapter in which that character first appears. This is followed by a very brief note as to the character's place in the story. Formal titles are omitted from this list, though particularly significant ones are included in the explanation of the character's place in the story. Names appear as they are given in the translation; the translator has elected to translate the *no* element of medieval samurai names, which means that, for example, the character known in the original as Amatsu no Hyōnai is called Hyōnai of the Amatsu in the translation, and is listed that way here.

Amasaki Jūrō Terutake (VI) Local samurai from Tōjō who joins Sugi-kura Ujimoto and eventually serves Satomi Yoshizane directly.

Anzai Saburōdayū Kagetsura (II) Ruler of the Awa district of Awa province and lord of Tateyama Castle when Satomi Yoshizane arrives in Awa.

Azana Wazahei (VIII) Farmer and original owner of Yatsufusa.

Bokuhei of Somaki (II) Farmer and former Kanamari follower.

Chudai *See* Kanamari Daisuke Takanori.

Fuse (VIII) Satomi Yoshizane's daughter, and the spiritual mother of the Eight Dog Warriors. Called Fusehime in the original; the *-hime* element means "princess," and is sometimes used alone as a title, so in the translation she is known as Princess Fuse.

Horiuchi Kurando Sadayuki (I) Hereditary retainer and companion of Satomi Suemoto. Sent with Sugikura Ujimoto to escort Yoshizane away from the Battle of Yūki. He and Ujimoto become Yoshizane's right-hand men.

Hyōnai of the Amatsu (II) Retainer of Jin'yo Mitsuhiro.

Isarago (VIII) Satomi Yoshizane's wife and mother of Fuse and Yoshinari. Isarago is the daughter of Jōren, lord of Shiitsu Castle in Kazusa (who is mentioned but does not appear in the story).

Issaku of Kazusa (VII) Peasant who sheltered Kanamari Takayoshi while he was in hiding. Maternal grandfather of Kanamari Daisuke Takanori.

Iwakuma Donpei (V) Retainer of Yamashita Sadakane.

Jin'yo Nagasanosuke Mitsuhiro (II) Ruler of the Nagasa and Heguri districts of Awa and lord of Takita Castle when Satomi Yoshizane arrives in Awa.

Kabuto Toppei (VII) Retainer of Anzai Kagetsura.

Kaeta (XIV) Housemaid to the Satomi family. She is not identified by name until Chapter XIV, where it is revealed that she was one of the women who had been sent to search for the Princess Fuse in earlier chapters.

Kanamari Daisuke Takanori (VII) Kanamari Hachirō Takayoshi's son by Issaku's daughter Kohagi (who is mentioned but does not appear in the story). When he first appears, he is called Katami. In Chapter XIV he assumes the priestly name Chudai, by which he will be known for the rest of the story.

Kanamari Hachirō Takayoshi (IV) Former Jin'yo retainer who went into hiding after his lord's death. Father of Kanamari Daisuke Takanori.

Kogorōbei Nobutoki of the Maro (II) Ruler of the Asahina district of Awa and lord of Hiratate Castle when Satomi Yoshizane arrives in Awa. On first mention, his middle name is given as Kogorōbei; subsequently it is given as Kogorō.

Mukuzō of Susaki (II) Farmer and former Kanamari follower.

Nisō (IV) Farmer in Kominato.

Nobutoki of the Maro *See* Kogorōbei Nobutoki of the Maro.

Sabitsuka Ikunai (V) Retainer of Yamashita Sadakane.

Sanpei (IV) Farmer in Kominato.

Saori (XIV) Housemaid to the Satomi family. She is not identified by name until Chapter XIV, where it is revealed that she was one of the women who had been sent to search for Princess Fuse in earlier chapters.

Satomi Suemoto (I) Satomi Yoshizane's father, loyal to Ashikaga Mochiuji.

Satomi Yoshinari (VIII) Satomi Yoshizane's son and heir. He is called Jirotarō as a child, and often referred to as the Scion (*onzōshi*, a term applied to the young sons of noble or samurai houses, particularly of the Genji line; the term is also applied to Yoshizane in the early chapters).

Satomi Yoshizane (I) Son of Satomi Suemoto, and founder of the Satomi line in Awa. Father of Fuse and Yoshinari.

Shichirō of the Nako (II) Retainer of Jin'yo Mitsuhiro. In Chapter XXXII it is revealed that his full name was Shichirō Yoshitake of the Nako.

Shietage Kokuroku Motoyori (IV) Yamashita Sadakane's retainer, in charge of Tōjō Castle when Yoshizane arrives in Awa. On his second mention, his middle name is given as Kokurokurō.

Shijirō (IV) Farmer in Kominato.

Sugikura Kisonosuke Ujimoto (I) Hereditary retainer and companion of Satomi Suemoto. Sent with Horiuchi Sadayuki to escort Yoshizane away from the Battle of Yūki. He and Sadayuki become Yoshizane's right-hand men.

Tamazusa (II) Concubine of Jin'yo Mitsuhiro and later of Yamashita Sadakane. Much of the story involves her dying curse playing itself out.

Tsumatate Togorō (V) Retainer of Yamashita Sadakane.

Yamashita Sakuzaemon Sadakane (II) Retainer of Jin'yo Mitsuhiro, who, as Yoshizane arrives in Awa, has usurped his master's domain. In Chapter V, he is called Sakuzaemon-no-jō.

Yatsufusa (VIII) Dog originally owned by Azana Wazahei, then by Satomi Yoshizane. Spiritual father of the Eight Dog Warriors.